CRASHING THE NET

CHEYENNE MEADOWS

Dedication

For Edward, who is always encouraging, helpful, and insightful. Without you I'd still be stuck at the beginning of most stories.
For my parents and my sister, who are my biggest fans. I hope you enjoy this one as much as I did writing it.

Books by Cheyenne Meadows

Wind Warriors

Tiger's Lily
Loco
Summer's Night
Sky's Lark
Silver Spoon
Blue Blood's Trifecta
Ghost's Treasure

Sexy Snax

Triad
Broken Bridges

Single Titles

Turbulent Rain
Worth Fighting For
Cowgirl Up
Cowgirl Strong
Crashing The Net

Crashing The Net

ISBN # 978-1-78686-102-3

©Copyright Cheyenne Meadows 2016

Cover Art by Posh Gosh ©Copyright 2016

Interior text design by Claire Siemaszkiewicz

Totally Bound Publishing

Published in 2016 by Totally Bound Publishing, Newland House, The Point, Weaver Road, Lincoln, LN6 3QN, United Kingdom.

Prologue

"Piper. Hold up a second."

Piper Darrow swung around to find the team's owner, Rob Stearns, approaching from down the hall. She'd just finished the championship game, cleaned up and left the locker room on her way to meet the other ladies at their favorite watering hole to celebrate.

She watched him come near with leeriness, unsure what he could want with her. After all, he'd received the prize trophy not an hour earlier, surrounded by the whole team.

Rob came to a stop, his arms hanging loosely at his sides. "I have a proposition for you."

Heard that before. Men are jerks sometimes. Still, the idea that Rob might hit on her fell flat. The man wore a nice wedding ring. He also held a high status and powerful reputation in the hockey world. The last thing she'd expect would be for him to throw all that away. "Such as?"

He stuck his hands in the pockets of his black slacks. "As you've probably heard, Gunderson blew out his knee and is done for the season."

Piper nodded.

The news had flown through the hockey world. One of the best goalies in the sport had torn some knee ligaments and had been scheduled for surgery. His recovery would take months. The resulting absence would hamstring the rest of the team, the Denver Wolfpack. Their season had proved lackluster thus far. This last blow could sink them deeper into the loss category. Rumors already abounded that the players were frustrated and discouraged. The head coach, Tommy Smith, seemed to be at a loss on how to fix the mess and waiting for the ax to drop. Not a good state of mind for a team to be in, especially near the end of the season.

Rob studied her for a long moment. "Your season with the Bobcats is over. There isn't any conflict of interest."

"I'm not following." Piper frowned, completely bumfuzzled at where Rob might be going with this.

"To make this short, I need a goalie."

The picture began to clear in Piper's head. "You have Rayovic."

Rob shook his head. "He's a rookie. Just had a few starts. He's not ready to assume the starter role."

"Trade?"

"In February? For a top-level goalie? Keep wishing." Rob sighed. "Look, I know this is a bit unconventional, but I'd like you to take Gunderson's spot."

Piper blinked at the man. "You want me to play with a men's hockey team as a lead goalie? For the rest of the season?"

"Yes."

As the owner of both teams, Rob had the power to hire anyone he wanted. Including a woman to play on the men's team. A definite rarity, too. Most owners focused on a single team. As far as she knew, Rob was the only owner who'd ventured into the women's game and picked up another team. Same city. The teams just differed in names and the gender of the players. Either way, he held her contract in his keeping and was her boss, season over or not.

She blinked at him. "Is that even legal?"

"There's no rules against women playing in the men's league. I already checked. Had the legal rep run over things. He gave me a thumbs up. No, it's not been done before, but that's not to say it won't work out. Just think of the splash you can make." He offered up a lopsided grin.

Well, that's something. Piper ran through possible chinks in the plan, coming up with a blank slate. It just couldn't be that easy. *Or could it?*

Rob glanced away then turned his focus back to her. "You're the best in the women's league. Men's hockey isn't that much different."

Piper snorted. "Just that they're bigger, faster, love to slam bodies together on hard checks and actually are allowed to fight it out when tempers flare." The sport, unlike many others, did have some differences. Most notably, the hard checking, sending opposing players crashing into the boards. As a rule, goalies were protected from this. That didn't mean goalies didn't receive their fair share of stick whapping, shoving and being knocked down in the crease when the puck rebounded.

"You've been there before. Nothing new."

"Yeah, but that was in college. This is the pros." Piper chewed her bottom lip uncertainly. The fact that he was asking fluffed her ego. Not to mention the lure of being the first woman to play professional men's hockey compelled her to agree.

"I'm not expecting miracles. We're in a slump. A big one. Times are hard and the men need a shake-up to spark the team. I'm betting on you."

Piper frowned. "You do know some of the guys will resent me, right?" She'd played with enough men over her entire life to understand some of them believed women had no place on the ice. She bristled at their attitudes and worked that much harder to prove them wrong.

Rob shrugged. "They don't have a say in the matter. We need a goalie. Now. You're available and one hell of a player." He paused a second. "You're just what we need to save our season. What do you say?"

Piper peered down at her shoes and considered the options. Go to the party, celebrate a brief moment in time, then return to work the next day. Or she could take a leap of faith, jump in with both feet, and be the first girl to play with the big boys. Her heart sped at the challenge.

First things first. "Are you going to make it worth my time?"

"Of course." He grinned as if in victory.

"I want equal pay, equal benefits. Hell, I want the same everything as you gave Gunderson."

Rob narrowed his eyes. "You don't have his experience or his reputation."

"No, I don't. I have more." She grinned wolfishly and waved her hand. "That's the deal. Take it or leave it." She adjusted the strap of her duffel bag on her shoulder, pivoted and started toward the exit.

"Show up tomorrow morning with your lawyer. We'll iron out the details."

Piper bit back a proud grin. "Will do." She waved at Rob and walked off, still concealing the surge of excitement that made her want to jump up and down. Tomorrow would be soon enough to let that out. As soon as the ink dried.

By mid-week, I'll be on the ice with the best of the best. They won't know what's coming.

With a happy chuckle, she left the building.

Chapter One

"What the hell are you talking about?" Ranger Deacon, the captain of the Denver Wolfpack, voiced the question probably every man in the room had on their mind.

"Piper Darrow is taking Gunderson's place. She'll be the number one goalie for the rest of the year."

"Holy shit," one of the guys in the corner muttered.

"We must be pretty damn awful to have to invite women to play with us," Adam Lancaster, seated behind Ranger, hollered out.

"Who came up with that fucking awful idea?" another asked.

A chorus followed, voices filled with exasperation.

Tommy Smith, the head coach, held up his hands. "It's a done deal. No use in getting all pissed off when we have to fill that crucial position. Besides, she's one hell of a goaltender."

"Let Rayovic play," Des Croft, one of the second line players, tossed out.

Smith pinned the guy with a firm stare. "I am letting Rayovic play. But he can't be expected to play every minute of every game for the next thirty games." His voice rose and turned hard as steel. "You know as well as I do one goalie can't do it all."

Ranger glanced across the room, noting the confusion and frustration painted on the guys' faces. They'd had a tough year thus far. The loss of their goalie had nearly proved to be the final nail in the coffin containing the men's morale. He knew many of them had voiced concerns, even whispering about finding a new home for the next season.

As much as he hated to break up a team who'd previously gotten along so well, Ranger understood their sentiment. He couldn't claim to be happy right now either.

But a woman?

He pulled up what he knew about Piper Darrow. Certainly, the last name rang clear as a bell. Her Canadian father had been one of the game's best scorers in the almost twenty years that he'd played. Big, fierce, he had a talent for attacking the goal, combined with stamina, durability and a hell of a backhand shot. The name alone invoked reverence and legendary awe. At least to Ranger.

He'd seen Piper play a couple of times. Quick of hand. Fearless. She defended her goal like a momma grizzly defended her cubs.

Still, she wasn't big or bulky. The nature of the women's game protected her smaller frame from hard collisions commonly found with men. She'd have to be one tough woman to hold up physically for the rest of the season. As a goalie, she had a shot. As a forward, like her father, she'd be likely be out before the week was done from teeth-jarring checks meant to crush her against the boards.

Uncertainly flared. Again.

"She just won the women's league championship and was named MVP," Tommy added.

"Whoopee." Anthony Hillman twirled his finger in the air.

"Big fucking deal," Riley Dickenson snarled.

Ranger swung around to glare at Dickenson for that comment. "I don't care what sport or what gender plays that sport, being the best there is demands respect."

"The decision is final. So if anyone still has an issue, there's the door." Tommy bit out every word and pointed toward the exit. He would have made a drill sergeant proud.

Murmurs answered.

Sometimes being captain sucks.

Ranger stood up and moved to the front of the meeting room. "It boils down to this. We have to have a goalie. As

10

hard as Rayovic tries, he can't do it all." Ranger nodded toward the young rookie, who dipped his head in acknowledgement.

Time to think outside the box and get this motley crew on board. "Think of it this way, you all know who her father is, right?"

A chorus of "yeah" followed.

"Well, who do you think she faced all those years in practice?"

A few laughed. Others began to smile.

"If nothing else, it should prove to be an interesting rest of the season." Tommy grinned encouragingly.

The men agreed. Ranger eyed each one, saw the various reactions, and knew Piper faced a formidable challenge before even meeting their first opponent. She had to earn these men's trust and belief. Hard enough for any new player. Let alone for one who started with predisposed attitudes against them. He had no doubt most men would consider her gender a handicap.

"Get geared up. Practice starts in fifteen." Tommy waved them toward the door. "No cheap shots. The first man who lays a hand on our new goalie will answer to me."

The stern tone told Ranger all he needed to know. The head coach already saw Piper as a daughter figure. To cross him would earn his wrath.

Good. That just might keep Piper standing after today's practice.

Heaven knew she needed all the help she could get.

A few minutes later, Ranger ambled up to the ice, his eyes drawn to the woman with the long blonde hair streaming behind her as she zipped from end to end, chasing a puck with decent skill. She ducked, dodged and finally flipped the puck on edge, pulled back her stick, and let loose. The wobbly shot hit the upper right corner of the net.

"She's the goalie?" Rocky, the left winger on Ranger's line, asked.

"Looks like more of a forward to me," Sven, his linemate and the right winger, pointed out.

Ranger watched the gliding motions, the power contained

in a small body. As he stared at her, she stopped on a dime, lifted her chin and turned to face the lot of them. He caught a glimpse of narrowed deep blue eyes, a short sigh and a furrowing of her forehead. Defensive mechanisms if ever he'd seen any. She stood up straight, then rested her hands on the stick before looking back at the guys. Her body language spoke of irritation from having her playtime interrupted along with bracing herself for the impact of dealing with twenty men, all new to the idea of playing with a woman. On the ice. Ranger had no doubt the guys had spent many hours playing with a woman in bed. Including himself.

She checked them all out, sizing them up. As a group or individually, he didn't know. The second her focus landed on him, his breath caught as an electric zing carried through his body. Intelligence showed in her features, along with classic beauty tempered by fitness and strength.

Interest piqued, he skated out on the ice toward her. "You must be Piper."

"Yep." She tilted her head and raked him from top to bottom and back again. Cautious appreciation flared in her eyes. "You must be Ranger." She pointed at the big C on his jersey.

"That's me." He noted the others closing around them.

"She's not dressed for practice," Hillman, another forward pointed out.

Piper cut him a glare. "First of all, I was told practice started at three. It's only two-fifteen now. Plenty of time to put the pads on. Secondly, since I don't have a Wolfpack jersey, the best you're gonna get is my Bobcats one until someone provides me with a uniform." She shifted her gaze to Tommy.

"The order's in already." He offered up a small smile. "Since that's taken care of, do you think you can get into gear so we can get to work?"

Piper grinned at him and saluted. "Yes, sir." She kicked the puck at her feet into motion. In a flash, she flew to the other net, spun and fired.

Another strike.

"Damn." Ranger couldn't take his eyes off her. Beauty. Talent. All with a fiery attitude. Impressed, he found himself staring at his new teammate with avid interest and more than a hint of desire.

"Shit, she's good," Adam remarked.

"Don't start handing out line places yet, Adam." Anthony rubbed his forehead. "Scoring is easy when there's no one in your way."

Ranger had played hockey most of his life, starting on the frozen ponds of Minnesota as a small child. He'd seen a girl occasionally play with the boys during pickup games, but never one in organized play. He didn't doubt Piper had plenty of skills. What he did question was whether she could be the answer they needed and hold up under the pressure of the big leagues.

Time will tell.

* * * *

Piper watched one of the forwards approach, pass the puck off to another guy, then swing his stick as it sailed back to him on the ice. Instinctively, she did the splits, preventing it from sliding under her and across the goal line. Her glove came down fast, covering the puck before anyone could smack at it on a rebound try.

The whistle blew. None too soon, as the two huge men crowded her space just in front of the net.

Tommy skated over. "Nice save."

"Thanks." Piper regained her feet and tossed the puck back out and into play. She'd spent the past hour fending off pucks sailing her direction. None of them had gotten by. A pretty snazzy showing, if she said so herself. Of course, she'd carry a few marks tomorrow morning for her efforts. She'd thought some of the women had powerful line drives. The men had them beat easily. One puck to her chest had stolen her breath and nearly put her down for a good couple of minutes. Sheer pride and determination had forced her back to her feet as if nothing had happened. Good thing she had years of practice with that particular move. Her father had taught her toughness above all else.

Gunther Darrow, her father, could be considered a hockey legend. He'd taken her to the rink with him one day while her mother was away. Piper had been six at the time. He'd strapped hockey skates to her feet as well as those of her brother, Darius, and let them loose. Piper had never once looked back. The ice offered her more than a chance at playtime and exercise. It gave her an outlet.

"Change lines." Tommy waited a beat before tossing the puck toward the middle of the ice.

Piper resumed her butterfly position, her focus completely on the small piece of black rubber zipping across the ice. As the other team brought it over the blue line, a tall, solidly built man took up position three inches from her crease, the blue area directly in front of the net. She craned her neck, shifted back and forth, and struggled to keep her eye on the puck with such a big man right in her way. Tempted to give him a shove, she maintained her composure instead, knowing she'd face this situation over and over again in the near future. Screens weren't limited to the men's game. Women had also developed the practice. Although none were built like the moose presently blocking her view. She'd seen enough of that from peewee games all through college. With no women's leagues at that time except for the professional level, she'd had no choice but to play with the boys. Hadn't bothered her. She had still kicked their butts at every given opportunity.

"Hey, Moose. You might have one fine ass, but I really don't need a bird's-eye view, all the same. So move it."

Ranger turned around and flashed a quirky grin.

She poked him with her stick while keeping a close eye on the puck. A player took it down the middle, then cut across near the face-off circle. He pulled back, then lined up for a shot.

The slash of a hockey stick caught her across the shoulder, the force spinning her around. She maintained her balance, found the puck in her peripheral vision, and grabbed it with her glove at the last second.

After a moment to suck in air, she dropped it in front of her and stared back at the men gaping in her direction.

Aha. There it is. The look of amazement and shock she'd been waiting to see since the rest of the team had stepped on the ice that afternoon.

Hiding a smile, she used her stick to nudge the puck back toward the tall man with black hair and green eyes. Ranger. Ranger Deacon. The team's captain and one of the best power forwards in the league. Built like a true position guy, Ranger towered over her and could easily outweigh her twice. Just now in his prime, he'd played with the team for a couple of years after doing his time in the minors. Skill, talent and plain old hard work had carried him to the pros and landed him a spot on the team. Attitude, people skills and leadership had netted him the captain position as well.

Rumor had it he didn't take crap off anyone. Normally laid-back, he was slow to rile, but once there, he made sure his opponent never trod down the same path again. Big and strong, the guy could generate speed as well as send another player flying when checked.

Piper liked that in a man.

Too bad most of the guys carried a chip on their shoulder and attitudes that belonged in the caveman days. Just another reason she didn't date hockey players. Hell, lately she hadn't dated anyone, athlete or not. She'd lost interest after finding too many toads and none that turned into a prince with a mere kiss.

The couple of men that she had dated hadn't ended up working out, either. Mostly, they'd had sex on their minds. Typical for guys that age, she figured, especially athletes who lacked shyness and had primed bodies to show off. The difference between men and women. Intimacy ranked low on her totem pole behind companionship, friendship and romance. A traumatic childhood had made trust difficult, pushing that level of closeness way down the line. Only time, familiarity and love could motivate her to sleep with a man. Her beaus, on the other hand, had made it known that getting hot and heavy in the sack hovered around the top of their list of goals. At an impasse, they had each gone their separate ways. Since she refused to be a trophy put on display, she'd turned her interests to other, more meaningful activities. Until a man wanted her for her, she wouldn't bother to give them more than a fleeting look.

When and if that happened, she'd reconsider her take on men. In the meantime, she focused on making a place in the world for herself and trying to do a bit of good along the way.

"Penalty shots, then we'll call it a day," Tommy hollered from the nearest blue line. He moved to the edge of the rink and watched them all with a critical eye.

Piper perked up. *Time to shine.*

She banged her stick on the side bars and resumed her stance. The past couple of days she'd spent hours watching video on these guys, in preparation for this very moment. She'd learned their preferences, their tendencies. All that studying would pay off. It always did.

Skater after skater approached her with speed, snaking their way toward her before taking their shot. She rejected each one in turn. Until Rocky flew past her, caught her going low, and shot a nice top-shelf laser that streaked by her before she could do more than blink.

He waved his stick in celebration.

She flipped up her goalie mask and smiled at the team's leading scorer. Since creating masks took time and precision, she'd kept her old one. While the bobcat painted on the side might not match up well with a wolf for a mascot, she didn't really care. As long as it fit well and worked, she would hang onto it. "Good shot. Guess that's why you're the sniper on the team."

"Yeah. You could say that." He grinned at her before tipping his head. "You're not so bad yourself."

She accepted the compliment with a quick grin.

"Nice job." Rayovic skated to a stop in front of her. "You've sure got the fast glove."

"Thanks. You've got some guts standing there with the whole team crashing the net."

Rayovic smiled proudly. "That happened a lot on the ice when I was a kid." His Czech accent came through well, though his words weren't hard to understand, testament to his time and practice speaking English.

"You've got a bright future." She sobered. "I'm sorry it had to happen like this. I feel like you've been given the stick."

Surprisingly, Rayovic offered up a sly grin. "It is okay. I'm not one of those men who have a problem with women playing the game. You play great and the team needs someone like you."

"Thank you." Piper smiled softly. "How do you say thank you in Czech?"

"Děkuju."

"Děkuju." She stumbled over the word the first time, earning a chuckle from the other goalie. "Děkuju." Her second try earned her a nod of approval.

"With your size you have to focus more. If the other team realizes this weakness, they'll take advantage big time."

Piper's grin faded with the heavily accented words. "Stanza. I was wondering when you'd appear." The old Swede had written the record books on goaltending back in his day. He'd turned coach a couple of decades ago and passed his nuggets of advice to his players. *More like beat it into their heads.* Stanza believed in a hardline approach and in-your-face challenges rather than praise and uplifting inspiration.

He snorted and skated closer. "You want to play men's game, you have to think like a man."

Piper rolled her eyes. "That might be a problem. I'm not

one to ogle boobs and think with a dick that I don't happen to have. Guess that leaves out scratching the balls as well."

Rayovic laughed openly.

Stanza stared at her for a long moment before his lips twitched. "You're going to be difficult."

"Who? Me? Difficult?" She shrugged. "I'm not the one trying to turn me into a man."

Stanza's lips curled up into a reluctant grin. "Point taken. Now, we still have some work to do."

Piper caught a glimpse of the rest of the team leaving the ice for the day. She had a momentary longing before shaking it off. The ice had become her home away from home years before. With a non-existent social life and the decided lack of hobbies, she had nothing waiting for her at the house anyway.

"When you see the shooter coming…" Stanza rattled on.

She tuned into him completely, needing to get her head on straight before the first game, when she faced opposition in the form of a rival team. Filled with men. Who probably didn't want a woman invading their territory.

The story of my life.

Chapter Two

Piper took to the ice. Ranger had led the rest of the team out first. She followed at the back of the pack, a little hesitant and unsure of what her reception might be. A chorus of cheers mixed with catcalls and wolf whistles answered her question. A mixed bag. Better than she'd feared. Worse than she'd hoped. Despite being at the home rink, she obviously had several naysayers to silence.

Ignoring the crowd, she made her way to the net, securing her water bottle in the holder at the top. Task complete, she started her normal stretching routine by sitting on the ice and spreading her legs wide. Satisfied, she lifted up marginally before dropping into a side-to-side split, which lowered her pelvis all the way to the ice.

"Damn," Sven, one of the forwards, said with a Swedish accent.

"Holy shit," Keith, the third line winger, uttered loudly enough for her to hear.

"Guess that takes the five hole away today." The five hole was a slang term for the space between a goalie's legs where many pucks slid past and scored.

Piper had heard all the same comments before, although not from her own team, and not for several years. In college, when she'd last officially played with men, she'd been the recipient of accolades and boos, hate and awe. The price a lady paid for daring to enter a man's domain.

"She's too small. How in the hell is she going to see past a screen?" Sven asked.

"Same way I did when we played the Soviets in the Olympics," she answered. "Those ladies were stout," she added with a bit of humor.

Sven Karlsson, the right winger, shook his head, spouted something off in a language she didn't recognize and skated away.

Keith stared at her for another second before following.

Not taking offense, Piper finished her stretching and returned to her feet as the official called the two teams over to center ice.

Piper puffed out air, focused on the puck and centered herself.

It's now or never.

The small bout of nerves she suffered quickly disappeared at the first face-off. The Wolfpack took the puck to the far end, only for it to be stolen. On a quick break, the Silks dashed toward her, passing from the middle to the edges as they came.

She slid back and forth, staying deep in the net to keep the puck in focus. A large guy set up right in front of her, forcing her to alter her stance and edge to the right. Out of the corner of her eye, she saw the guy take a shot. Managing to lift her stick in time, she blocked it, sending the puck flying to the far corner. A Silks team member collected it and sent it back into the zone. His buddy swung to meet it. Piper snared the puck in her glove, then held on tight as a player slid in, knocking her down and into the side bar of the net.

The whistle blew. She sat up and handed over the puck.

"You okay?" the referee asked.

"Yep. Just another day at the office."

The guy smiled before skating away with the player who'd tried to run her over. He'd earned two minutes in the penalty box, giving her team a one-man advantage for that same time period.

Over and over again, the Silks attacked. Piper turned them away each time. More than once she hit the ice, being bowled over for one reason or another. Hot, sweaty and tired, she ignored the discomfort of her muscles as she fought to get to the end of the period without giving up a goal.

With a minute to go Cushing, the best scorer on the Silks team, made a breakaway. He sped her direction, setting up the puck as he came.

She focused on the man and the puck, actively moving her feet in order to prevent getting caught flat-footed.

He zipped by, hitting a sharp-angled backhand hard in her direction.

Piper dropped down into the splits, felt the puck bounce off her thigh pad, and immediately covered it lest someone snare a rebound and catch her unprepared. A strong knee smacked her in the jaw for her efforts.

She grunted, but held on.

Men started yelling, then pushing. She heard another whistle blow, got to her feet and opened her glove so the nearest ref could take control of the puck. Turning, she saw one of the Wolfpack wrapped up with a Silks player.

"You okay?" Ranger shielded her from the fight with his big body.

She rolled her eyes. "I'm fine. Really. It would be awfully nice if you guys could knock off the boxing match so we can get this period finished, though."

Ranger laughed. "It's all part of the game."

"Uh-huh." She took advantage of the break to get a much-needed drink of water. After replacing her water bottle on top of the net, she caught her breath and prepared for the next onslaught.

The opponents kept coming. She'd give them credit for aggressiveness and hits on goal. Over and over again she faced pucks hurled her direction with speed. Each time, she managed to stop the puck, despite the shooters aiming for all parts of the net. The crossbar helped her out now and again, too. She'd thank it later, as she had more than enough to handle with the constant defensiveness they forced her into.

Come on, Wolfpack. Do something. Anything.

As if he'd heard her, Ranger took control of the puck and sent it down to Rocky, who angled across the area in front of the net. Ranger set the screen. Rocky played catch with Tomas before finding his spot and smacking the puck. The red buzzer sounded loudly in the arena, setting the spectators off into small celebrations for the score.

The play started quickly again. The Silks took possession and sprinted for her end. They hung to the perimeter before banging another shot. She got in front of it just in time. The rebound had her sliding to the left side of the net. Out of the corner of her eye she saw a guy shoot. Instinctively she lunged the opposite way, catching the puck in her glove as she skidded down on her side.

The whistle sounded again.

"Shit. What do I have to do?"

Piper ignored the disgruntled player as she handed over the puck again.

"Great save." Riley Dickenson skated by.

"Thanks." She lifted her mask, wiped at the dripping sweat, and took another drink of water.

All too soon, play resumed. She panted as she tried to keep up, facing endless pressure as the Silks kept the puck at her end of the ice most of the time.

Ranger checked a guy right in front of the net, stole the puck and started a pile-up. Piper kept her focus until Rocky slammed her into the side bar, knocking the net off its moorings.

He hurriedly got to his feet and reached down to help her up.

Piper glared at him. "What did you eat for breakfast? A whole buffalo?"

He snorted. "Not quite."

"You're damn heavy," Piper complained as she regained her footing.

Ranger skated over and nudged him with an elbow. "Nice penalty. Maybe next time you can trip the other direction and spare our goalie?"

"Yeah, right." Rocky skated toward the bench.

Ranger's gaze cut through the mask and straight to Piper's soul. She couldn't tear herself away from those green eyes. Her heart picked up speed at the intense look.

A nearby whistle broke through the moment, putting Ranger back on the move.

Piper watched him go with interest.

* * * *

"She can't take much more of this." Ranger watched as yet another Silks player slammed into Piper, sending her sprawling on the ice.

The official blew his whistle and led the man responsible to the penalty box for interference.

Ranger had lost count of how many penalties the Silks had committed, mostly for going after Piper. He stood up and slapped at the wall in front of him. Anger and annoyance threatened to spill over. "This is one hell of a Gong Show." The hockey term was used to describe a game with lots of penalties and fights. Normally it meant lots of scoring too, but Piper had blanked the Silks so far.

"She's playing like she has something to prove."

Ranger spared Axel, one of the defensemen, a glance. "She does. She's showing that women have a place, even in the pros."

"Still not sure I believe it." Axel took in some water.

"Square up, Piper."

The man's voice came from behind the bench. Ranger turned to find Gunther hollering at his daughter.

"Stand your ground," the woman beside Gunther yelled. "Make them earn it."

Her mother. Had to be.

Ranger took a second to study the couple. Both had dark hair and strong frames. Gunther had always been huge, but Piper's mother didn't appear to be a petite woman, either. Not anywhere near fat, the woman reminded him of a professional sprinter—muscular and strong. Oddly enough, Piper didn't resemble either parent.

Before Ranger could consider the fact further, the buzzer honked, signifying the end of the second period. Men stepped away from their bench and back to the locker room. Piper brought up the rear, having just skated in off the ice.

He took a second to look her over, finding her sound and seemingly unfazed by the lowball tactics used by the other team. "Way to hang in out there." He would have tapped her rear, but convention told him she might slap his face for doing so.

She removed her mask and spared him a small smile. "Thanks."

Sweat poured from her forehead, causing strands of her hair to stick to her face. Her eyes twinkled and her steps appeared sure.

"You're loving this." The words slipped out before he could bite them back.

"Oh, yeah. Every time one of those goons thinks he's going to look like a real man by showing me why women don't play in this league, you guys get another power play to hurt them where it counts the most." She smiled as she gestured toward the scoreboard.

Ranger shook his head. He'd give her credit for bravery and steadfastness.

The shock came when he realized that she enjoyed the roughness of the game. All those hits seemed to have wound her up rather than beat her down. Still, she'd carry her fair share of aches, pains and bruises by the next day. Probably more so than one of the hotshot forwards who had no problems sacrificing their bodies for the good of the team.

Water bottles were passed around, as well as cups of Gatorade and juice, as the guys filed in and took seats in front of the lockers.

Tommy stood at the front of the room, a serious expression on his face. Ranger noted the older man studying Piper with professional intensity. He was sizing her up. Seeing how much more she could take.

From his recent experience, Ranger would say a hell of a lot more.

She grabbed a towel and wiped the perspiration off her face.

Ranger did the same, slugged some juice and plopped down in order to listen to directions Tommy was sure to put out.

"We've got to be more aggressive. Stop playing in our own end. Piper is getting it done, but she needs some help." Tommy drew on the dry-erase board. "We're getting knocked off the puck at this point. If we attack here, and keep the puck on the move, we limit some of the losses."

"And increase the hits."

Ranger glanced over at Tomas. As big as the guy was, he could handle a few checks.

"We have to take the hits to them. We're being too passive. Too hesitant. Quit sitting back and passing when a shot opportunity arises."

Tommy went on. Ranger returned his gaze to Piper.

She drank thirstily, used the towel again, then blew out a breath. He wondered how this game compared to her experiences, either playing with the guys in her earlier years or with the women's professional league. Certainly she'd seen some tough competition, especially in the Olympics.

His gut told him she'd endured more hits in the first two periods than she'd received in two whole games playing against women. Bravely, she battled on. Even her male counterparts rarely received as much jostling and as many bumps as she had. Obviously she knew they were out to prove a point to her. Yet she stood her ground.

Respect for her grew.

Idly, he scanned the room, finding several of the players checking out their newest goalie. Curiosity and admiration prevailed in some of their expressions. A nice change from the animosity of the meeting where they'd learned about her joining the team. A handful remained stoic or critical. Ranger knew they'd come around, once they saw Piper was the real deal.

Piper turned to face the other direction. He noted a slowly forming bruise on her cheek. Probably the result of that bastard kneeing her in the head.

Anger rose. Ranger shoved it down, knowing it did nothing for his play except cause an unneeded distraction. Cool heads prevailed.

Oddly enough, protective instincts rushed to the fore. While he'd feel the same way if one of the guys had suffered the same bullying, he felt doubly so since Piper was a woman. Considering the fact that women weren't on his good list right now, that said something.

To borrow Piper's words, the way to hurt them most was on the scoreboard.

He emptied another cup, tossed it into the trash and absorbed Tommy's advice for the third period. Ranger couldn't protect Piper from more vicious hits, but he could keep the opponent off her by maintaining the puck in the Silks' end of the rink.

With a plan in place, he listened in, preparing to have a bit of a chat with the guys after Tommy finished. Piper was busting her ass to keep them in the lead. He wasn't about to let her down on his end.

Nineteen minutes into the period, Ranger watched as the Silks pulled their goalie. The extra man skated hurriedly out onto the ice, taking the pass as he did so.

Ranger stood up, focusing on the game as the Wolfpack formed a protective ring around the goal. "Hold on. Just a little bit longer."

A player shot, missed, and a scramble for the rebound caused a traffic jam in the far corner.

Seconds ticked by.

Another shot. Another rejection.

He held his breath as the Silks drove to the net for a final shot. *Ping.* He heard the puck bounce off the crossbar and into the corner a second before the buzzer sounded.

"Yes." Smiling wide, he took to the ice in order to celebrate. They all lined up then made their way to Piper, congratulating her on the shutout with words and gentle taps to the shoulder.

She returned the favor, pointing out good things each of the men did and praising them for their hard work. Something most of them didn't hear much from other players. It was a nice touch provided by Piper, paying the compliments back to the men instead of taking the credit all for herself.

His turn to compliment her came. "Nice game. I never doubted you'd pull through."

Since she'd removed her mask right after the buzzer sounded, he could see the victorious smile that brightened up her face. "I had some help." She wiped at the perspiration trickling down her cheek. "You've got one hell of a slapshot."

"Thanks." Ranger glanced around the stands. "I think you made an impression."

"Good or bad?" She tilted her head.

He shrugged. "Depends on what team you're rooting for."

She met his eyes. "Think we set a precedent?"

"Oh, yeah. The other teams are going to be watching this game and taking notes. We've not seen anything yet."

"Bring it on." Her smile turned wolfish.

Ranger shook his head. "A chip off the old block."

"Yep." She gathered up her water bottle and skated for the bench.

He followed, pretty damn happy with their new goalie and the outcome of their first game. They still had a long row to hoe, but getting a few wins would improve morale in the locker room. Add in a bit of hard work and adjustment and maybe, just maybe, they could make something of the lackluster season.

It was a start. A really good one.

Chapter Three

On the way off the ice, one of the national sports reporters shoved a microphone in her face. "Piper. Great game out there."

She decided to play nice. No sense in beaning the guy with his own microphone for simply doing his job. "Thanks."

"I gotta ask. What differences have you noticed going from the women's league to playing with the men?"

She shrugged. "The men."

He snickered. "Besides that."

"Well, I have to say the locker room doesn't reek of flowery perfume after practice."

People close by laughed.

She waved and continued on her way. A few unflattering comments followed, but certainly fewer than before. She tried to ignore them.

Fatigued, Piper sat on the far bench to unstrap her protective gear. Normally she'd shed her stuff in the women's locker room. However, since the coach would be in shortly for an after-game speech, she had opted to hang out with the men, secretly hoping none of them decided to get naked right before her eyes. That would definitely be uncomfortable. Not that she didn't appreciate a fine physique, but she had to skate with these guys for a couple more months. Seeing one without clothes ranked right up there with catching her brother coming out of the shower. Not a moment she chose to dwell on.

Hot and worn out after the long game, she reveled in the small victory. Sloppy play had allowed for a single goal for their team. Luckily, that was all they'd needed to count the win. She'd held the other team to a shutout, for which she'd received a few pats on the back and some love from the crowd. Nothing like she was accustomed to. Then again, she'd invaded the men's domain. She couldn't expect them to embrace her with open arms after a mere two days.

Clint, the equipment manager, took her skates from her. "How did they feel?"

She smiled at the middle-aged man who busted ass all over the place trying to keep skates perfectly sharpened, gloves dry, sticks in working order, and any other piece of equipment shiny and in good shape before, during and after games. "Great. I like the three-quarter cut best, I think." She handed him her glove as well. "Thank you for all that you do. I know you work your rear off. I'll try not to add to your workload."

He flashed a contagious grin. "You're easy to get along with. I spoke with Frank about what you liked." Frank held the same position, only for the Bobcats hockey team. "He told me everything I needed to know. Said you were pretty laid-back about it all."

"I try."

Clint placed the skates at her feet and hurried off while Piper started removing her padding. As much as she'd have loved to have disappeared for some privacy, to do so would leave a bad taste in the coach's mouth as well as irritate the rest of the team. If they had to stick around, so did she.

"What the fuck was that all about?"

Piper glimpsed rage building on Hagan's face. The hot-headed defenseman had been primed for a fight all game. She'd seen the anger in his face before they'd taken the ice and throughout the game. What had gotten his dander up, she didn't have a clue. Unfortunately, he'd picked a rotten time to unload. Against his teammates, in the locker room, no less.

She started making her way toward the commotion.

"What? You think you can do fucking better? I didn't see

you scoring any goals," Keith fired back, nearly nose to nose with the bigger man.

"I'm a fucking enforcer. You're supposed to score, prick. Not me."

Piper saw Hagan clench his fist, noted the tension in his body, the reddening of his face. She hurried to the center of the action. "Stop it. Both of you! We're teammates, for God's sake."

"I could score if you would get off your lazy ass and—"

Piper jumped in between them just in time for Hagan's fist to connect with her jaw, sending her tumbling backward. She would have hit the floor had one of the guys not caught her.

Belatedly, she realized that Hagan had pulled the punch before he could unleash all his power. That didn't matter. Nothing did except her gut reaction due to the locked doors flying open on her carefully buried past. Tremors shook her body as she regained her feet. Emotions boiled over and self-defense instincts launched into full gear. She lashed out, catching Hagan in the balls with a precisely aimed kick.

He went down as strong arms wrapped around her, yanking her away and refusing to budge even as she struggled.

Flashbacks raced through her mind. The beatings, the screams, the eerie silence that followed.

"Calm down, wildcat." Ranger's smooth voice broke through the red haze.

Piper drew in air, still unable to quell the shaking.

Get a hold of yourself, Piper. You can't fall apart now.

She closed her eyes, forced the terrible images away and grappled for cool control.

"That's enough!" Tommy's yell carried through the entire room. He turned his angry gaze on her. "You, young lady."

She swallowed and met his eyes.

"That's a major penalty."

"You're sending her to the box?" one of the guys asked in amusement.

"No. Suicide sprints."

A few of the men groaned. Others remained mute.

Piper's shoulders fell. She hated those most of all. Proudly, she lifted her chin, slipped her skates back on, left her goalie gear on the bench and headed back to the ice.

The crowd had left, leaving only a few stragglers. Quiet had ensued where loud cheering had rung from the rafters only minutes earlier. The tranquility soothed her senses and assisted her in collecting her temper and recklessness.

She skated to the closest red line to use as a starting position and waited.

Tommy ambled back out onto the ice, minus his skates. He walked over and stared down at her, displeasure evident in every feature.

"I'm sorry. I shouldn't have retaliated." Piper offered up the sincere apology, knowing it did nothing for her punishment. She'd just reacted. Hadn't thought. The combination made for a bad mix.

"You shouldn't have been in the middle of that punching fest to begin with."

"I couldn't help it. I thought I could defuse the situation. With the Bobcats—"

Tommy cut her off. "You're playing with the Wolfpack now. Men fight. I suggest you take this as a learning experience to stay out of it next time." He stepped back a few feet and blew his whistle.

Piper darted off. *First blue line. Stop completely. Turn. Back. Middle red line. Back. Second blue line. Back. End red line and back.* She fed her emotions into the dreaded drill, letting them flow out with each strike of the blades on the ice.

Once she finished, she stood up, already breathing hard. *Damn, I need to get in better shape.* It would have helped if she'd had her forward skates instead of the heavier goalies' ones, too. Since she only had the one pair with her, they'd just have to do.

Tommy blew the whistle again. Off she went. More tired, she forced her legs to keep moving.

Another sprint. And another. By the seventh one, her legs felt like spaghetti noodles and about as strong.

The sound of skaters snared her attention. She glanced up to find Ranger approaching. The others trailed behind.

Curious, she could only stare at him, too out of breath to speak for the moment.

One by one, the entire team lined up on either side of her. Ranger took the spot to her left.

"Mind if we join you?"

She blinked numbly at him. Everyone hated suicide sprints. *Everyone.* Yet the entire team voluntarily came out there to join in her punishment session. The fact amazed her and endeared them to her all the more.

She offered up a small smile. "You don't have to."

"We took a vote. Seems we're a team so we stick together no matter what," Ranger said.

A few of the other players frowned in obvious disagreement.

Way to go, Piper. Not the way she wanted to get on their good sides.

Hagan pulled up on her right.

She cleared her throat and took the opportunity given to apologize. "I'm sorry, Hagan. Really. It was just a knee-jerk reaction."

He nudged her gently in the shoulder. "I deserved it for what I did. Let's call it even."

"Deal."

He lowered his center of gravity and took off at the sound of the whistle. Piper tried to keep up, but ended up lagging behind. Fresh legs put her to shame, the previous sets of sprints having zapped her energy. Still, she gave it everything she had.

After three more rounds, Coach raised his hand. "Hit the showers."

Thankful, Piper bent over, resting her arms on her thighs. She would have sat down if she didn't think her butt would freeze solid before she had the strength to get back up. Standing might risk jostling her stomach contents too much, ending with them projecting onto the ice. Much better to huddle there a moment and focus on keeping her lunch down.

"You all right?" Ranger asked.

"Swell. Thanks for asking." *Please, just go away and let me suffer in private.*

He eyed her for a minute before chuckling, his breathing a bit harsh after the run. "Try to make it to a trash can at least. Less mess for the poor Zamboni guy to clean up." He skated ahead, hitting the exit with fluid precision.

"Gee, thanks." She sucked in much-needed oxygen, stepped off the ice and plopped down on the first seat available.

At least something came of today besides the painful workout. The guys seemed to have come together. Whether in support of her or because they just wanted to show her up, she didn't know. Nor did it really matter. Never before had she seen a whole team take on the punishment of one.

The fact the Wolfpack did said something. Namely that, like it or not, she was one of them. For the time being.

The thought cheered her.

* * * *

Not ready to go home, yet, Piper stopped by the local watering hole where all the Bobcats tended to gather after a game. Deep down, she hoped one or two of the girls might be in attendance. She needed good friends and someone to shoot the bull with who didn't possess balls.

Her luck ran out. She scoured the area, finding no sign of any familiar face, except one — Keith, the third line right winger.

He sat at the bar nursing a drink, looking downtrodden and depressed.

Piper found herself heading his direction, unable to just let him be. "Hey, Keith. Fancy meeting you here."

He lifted his head and met her eyes.

The initially slack face, the frown and furrowed eyebrows told the story. That, along with the heavy scent of alcohol, proclaimed him well on his way to drunk.

He lifted his glass and took another swing before lightly banging the empty cup against the bar. "Another."

Oh, boy. Piper bit her lip and cautioned herself not to argue with the big guy. She'd been punched once already today. "What's up, Keith?"

He turned on his stool and sized her up, listing a bit to the side. "My girlfriend dumped me. Can you believe that?"

"That sucks, buddy. I'm sorry."

"Hockey. She says hockey or her." His words slurred as he took another swallow.

She saw no one else around who seemed to be a friend, meaning Keith had most likely driven himself to the bar. No way could she let him drive himself home. "Want to come home with me?"

His eyes widened before a goofy smile appeared across his face. "Bow-chicka-wow-wow."

Piper sighed. "No. No. None of that. Just come home with me and I'll let you sleep on the couch." She took another gander at his build and changed her mind. "Scratch that. You can sleep in my bed. I'll take the couch."

"Ohhhh. I like that. Me and you in the bed."

"Ummm. How about we just get you to my place first?" She offered up her best tantalizing grin.

"Okay." He stood up a bit unsteadily.

Piper wrapped an arm around him, latched on to his and drew it over her shoulder. "Bartender? Does he owe you anything?"

"Nope. All paid up."

"Good." Piper tugged on Keith. "Come on, big guy. Let's go."

Together they meandered to her car a bit less than gracefully. He grabbed onto her rear halfway across the parking lot. She clenched her teeth and kept moving, knowing arguing would prove futile. Besides, if the lug decided to lie down on the asphalt, she'd be out of ideas for how to get him up and moving again.

Piper sighed heavily as soon as she had him settled in the passenger seat of her car, buckled in and all. So far Keith appeared to be a happy, if handsy, drunk. Much better than the alternative.

As soon as she shoved the key in the ignition, she paused for a second to think. His size and the close proximity in the car rattled her nerves. Not to mention the stench of alcohol permeated the air, reminding her of the volatile nature of some intoxicated people.

I don't think I thought this all the way through. What am I going to do with him?

She turned to appraise him. Keith plucked at the seat belt with a perplexed expression written clearly on his face. He could probably tell her his address. Most likely he carried his keys to his front door as well. However, in his present state and his emotional upset which led to this situation, she couldn't be sure he wouldn't drag out the liquor at home or even try to go out to another bar. If something tragic happened because she left him alone, she would never forgive herself. Yet, he was a grown man who made his own decisions, either good or bad. This fell into the not so bright category, definitely.

Sometimes people needed a helping hand. Keith did tonight.

I could take him to my apartment.

Or not. Just the idea of bringing a man home with her set loose a myriad worries. Keith seemed like a good guy, but she'd known him for a week. That wasn't near long enough to invite him over, especially drunk, and let him crash. What if he became belligerent? She'd be one on one with a large, powerful guy filled with anger and diminished reservations. Not a smart move at all.

Which leaves me where?

She wracked her brain for a second before cranking the

engine, pulling out of the lot and onto the street headed south. To her parents' house. They'd be home. She could take Keith over for the night. Her father could deal with just about any man on the planet, plastered or not. So if Keith got out of hand, her father would settle him right down. Or her mother would take her goalie hockey stick and smack him over the head.

Piper grinned at the image. Yeah, her mother would do just that if she didn't smother him with sweetness first. Darla Darrow didn't get riled often, but when she did, look out. Even Piper's father dodged his wife when her feathers had been ruffled.

Since Piper's old bedroom had remained unchanged since she'd moved out, she could easily crash there as well. To top matters off, she knew where her mother stashed the chocolate.

A win-win for all.

Piper clicked the button on her steering wheel which connected her with her cell phone. "Call Mom."

Her mother answered on the second ring. "Hello?"

"Hi, Mom. I have a favor to ask."

"Sure, honey."

"One of the guys on the team is wasted. I found him at the sports bar drinking away his sorrows. Do you mind if I bring him there so he can sleep it off without killing himself or others?" Piper glanced over to find Keith staring out of the window as if enthralled with the streetlights. Obviously he was easily entertained in this state.

"Of course not. Wouldn't be the first time we've had teammates sleeping over."

More than once Piper had woken up to find hockey players sacked out in the spare bedrooms or on the couch. Both men and women. Teammates of her parents over the years. "Thanks, Mom. I'll be there soon."

"I'll have the spare bedroom ready for you."

"Perfect. See ya in a few." She hung up and peered over at Keith. "Okay, buddy. We're almost there."

"There?" The word came out slurred.

"Yep. Home for the night."

A few minutes later, Darla met Piper at the door. "You didn't tell me you were bringing home one of the goons." Enforcers or the big guys on the ice that dealt out the punishment to the opposite team were loosely termed goons. While Keith might not be a defenseman, he still had the look of one.

Piper chuckled, keeping a steadying arm around Keith to ensure he didn't crumple on the front porch. "I know. He's dang heavy too." She navigated them through the house and straight to the bedroom. After lining him up, she sat him down on the bed, then dropped to her knees in order to take off his shoes. "Damn, Keith. You have big feet." She held up one of the sneakers and shook her head.

"Big feet. Big cock." He smiled crookedly at her.

"I'll take your word for that, buddy." She finished her task, hurried into the kitchen, filled a glass with water then returned to his side. "Drink this."

He took the container and stared inside, closing one eye in an effort to get a better view. "What's this?"

"A drink. You'll like it."

"Okay." He guzzled down the whole glass. "Tastes like water." His face scrunched up.

Piper stole the glass before he could drop it on the floor. After setting it aside, she lifted his feet onto the bed, encouraged him to stretch out, then covered him with the blankets, tucking him in soundly. "Now, go to sleep."

"Hmmm."

"Just don't pee in the bed." She whispered the last, watching as Keith curled up into an oversized ball and relaxed.

Deciding he'd stay put for the night, she pulled the door not quite shut and returned to the living room, where her mother waited.

"All tucked in?"

"Yep. Hopefully he'll stay that way." Piper plopped down

on the couch. "Dad's not home?"

"He ran to the store. Should be back soon."

No sooner than the words left her mouth than the back door opened and her father's voice rang through the area. "I'm home."

Piper hurried to the kitchen to meet him. "Let me help you." She took a couple of grocery bags from his hands and placed them on the counter. Darla started unloading them.

"What brings you by?" Gunther, her father, asked.

"One of my teammates decided to go on a binge because his girlfriend broke up with him. Hit him hard, I guess. I found him at the sports bar the girls and I visit after games. With him three sheets to the wind, I couldn't just leave him to his own devices. So I brought him here to spend the night. I hope you don't mind." She blinked up at him.

"It's fine. You know that." Gunther frowned. "I might have to talk to that kid in the morning. Point out a few things about his poor decision making."

Piper smiled to herself. Her father would make a great coach if he ever accepted one of the many offers placed before him. He didn't just worry about people on the ice, he tried to lend support and assistance to keep others in line away from the rink. Just another special feature about the man who had adopted her years before.

Gunther gathered up an armful of shampoo. Piper took the rest of the hygiene products and followed her father to the guest bathroom.

She handed him each item while he placed them on the shelf. Darla remained in the kitchen, sorting the rest of the stuff.

Finished with the task, Piper started to turn, only for her father to stop her. "What happened here?" Gunther cupped her chin and turned her head slowly to the side.

That man doesn't miss a thing. The slight darkening of a bruise on her jawline hardly showed, especially after she'd covered the mark with makeup. Leave it to her father to pick up on it. "Two of the guys got into it. I tried to break it up just as the fists started flying." She met her father's eyes. "That's after I took a knee to the chin from a Silks player."

His lips pinched. "You know better than that."

Fighting had been a part of men's hockey for as long as she could remember. She'd never cared for it, though. "Yeah. I'll remember next time."

"Uh-huh." He stared at her for a long moment. "Are you okay?"

"Of course. I get banged up worse during even the easiest games."

His gaze hardened.

She'd known her redirect wouldn't dissuade him. A long sigh followed. "I went off for a second. Tried to kick the guy's balls into his chest cavity." Peeking up, she found a ghost of a grin on her father's lips. "Coach stepped in, sent me to skating suicide sprints. The rest of the team joined in toward the end. That guy that accidentally hit me apologized. I did as well. We called it a truce."

"Then you bring one of them home because you're worried about him." Gunther shook his head. "You're just like your mother. Babying these guys and watching out for them even if they're a hell of a lot bigger than you."

What else is new? She'd always been a sucker when it came to teammates. They were a loosely joined family in her opinion and she treated them as such. "Is that so bad?"

Gunther pulled her into a hug. "No. Either they'll protect you with everything they've got or be introducing you to their mothers."

Piper returned the affection before stepping back with a rueful grin. "So, which will it be?"

"Six of one. Half a dozen of the other." His expression sobered. "I'll slap them on the back for protecting you, sure. But remember I have no qualms punching them in the mouth, otherwise."

Piper adored her father all the more. He'd always been her protector, even as he'd encouraged her to spread her wings and fly. Considering her rotten first impression of men, Gunther, even with his large frame and physical mass, had never frightened her after the initial meeting. She thought of him as a grizzly bear with a heart of gold. He could rip people apart and be one heck of a force, but he preferred to watch over his family, laugh and see the goodness in life instead.

Her kind of man.

She squeezed him again. "Thank you, Daddy. I don't know what I'd do without you."

He held her close. "I'm proud of you, angel. Always have been, always will be."

She kissed his cheek. "I'm living up to your good name?"

He released her with a chuckle. "Absolutely. Now, let's go check on your friend, then get to the kitchen before your mother wonders where we've wandered off to."

Chapter Four

Ranger hit the remote button, held it, then stopped the play again. He'd programmed his television to record the game and store it until he was home and could go over it once more. Just like football players spent hours studying film, so did he. All part of the effort to stay at the top of his game and understand the opponents they played. Many times he'd find weaknesses in their lines or even errors in his own. By pointing them out, the guys could learn from them and move forward to become an elite team and one to be feared by others.

At least that had been the plan until this year crumbled. High hopes had taken a nosedive with frequent losses. Gunderson going down had topped it off. Having Piper join didn't sit well with many people and pretty much had proven to be the last straw for many of the men.

He hit Play and watched the Silks players as they flew down the ice then took aim at Piper. Only the knowledge that she was indeed all right after the game kept his anger leashed. Bastards thought it their lot in life to prove a woman couldn't play the sport.

At least Piper had proved them wrong and ended up placing a check in the win column for the Wolfpack in the process.

He took a moment to analyze Piper at work. He'd never been a goalie, always a forward for as long as he could recall, but he'd faced enough goalies to know a good one when he saw them. Piper fit the bill. Despite her much smaller size, she moved well, quickly, and seemed to have a knack for anticipating the shots. He could easily see why she'd earned the MVP in the women's league. She was that good.

After the announcement of her joining the team, he couldn't help but be intrigued. While a bit skeptical about her ability to play in the men's league, he wasn't nearly as harsh as some of the other guys, who wanted nothing to do with a woman invading their ranks. He'd been raised with more of an open mind and judged people for their actions. That game had showed him plenty about Piper. Namely, that she had earned her spot on the team.

Hard work had been a constant companion of his over the years. A person didn't reach the level of play that he had without it. Small details clued him in that Piper not only put in the time and energy, but she studied the game and learned from the best. Her movements were natural, efficient and automatic. That only came from years of devotion and dedication. If she'd slacked, she'd have never developed such skill.

Her play impressed him, as did her pep and personality. Not to mention the pretty package she presented. Never before had he considered a teammate in the realm of dating. Especially since he'd only played against men since junior high. Even if he'd had ladies on his teams once he hit the age of dating, he'd still not want to break a general policy of not dating teammates. Too many complications if the relationship failed. Yet something about Piper made him want to change that policy.

She didn't flaunt herself, didn't hold a grudge as he'd seen with Hagan. Instead she seemed content to take her knocks, get up and go at it again. Determined. Likeable. She'd made an impression on people. Definitely on him.

The team needed a fresh start. Piper, with her bubbliness, optimism and skill could just fit the bill.

Ironically, those same qualities clicked when it came to what he sought in a woman.

His phone rang, breaking into his thoughts. Without paying attention, he answered. "Hello?"

"Ranger."

"Hi, Dad." He clicked Stop again on the remote. "What's up?"

"Just checking in. Saw your game. A good one. Strong play. Looks like the team is starting to come back around."

"Yeah. Pretty physical, but at least we're back in the win column."

"That female goalie is something."

Ranger heard the admiration in his father's voice. As a kid, Ranger had spent almost every available free hour on the ice. His father had gone with him after work, always there to encourage him while watching the ice on the ponds, ensuring their safety. While his father had never played hockey above a college level, he'd instilled a love of the sport in his only child. Ranger had grown up wanting to be just like his father — the man he idolized. "She's tough."

"Yeah. Those bastards were hitting her every chance they got. Damn refs waited too long to step in. Set a precedent." A hint of exasperation carried through.

Ranger heard it and agreed readily. "Piper expected it to be that kind of game. She's carrying marks, I'm sure, but wasn't about to throw in the towel. Not her style."

"So she's pretty formidable, huh?"

Ranger rolled his eyes at his father's sense of humor. "She's a tigress at times. Kind of like Mom when she goes on the warpath."

His father groaned. "That bad, huh?"

"Nah." Ranger chuckled. "Actually, Piper is pretty cool. Nice too. No ego that I've seen. Just seems to be thrilled with her opportunity and determined to prove that she belongs."

A long pause followed. "Sounds like you've been hanging out with her."

And here we go. Ranger's mother wasn't the only one nosy enough to delve into his personal life. His father had been the one way back when to have the sex talk. He'd warned Ranger of the pitfalls of being a popular athlete and his stern reminders had laid a solid groundwork. That had proved to be the saving grace when the paternity suit had reared its ugly head.

At least his parents were supportive all the way. That meant something. They hadn't doubted him for a moment, or hadn't seemed to, anyway. Without them, he would have had a hell of a lot more stress during the whole proceedings. As it was, they'd stood by him without censure.

Which I didn't really deserve as a jock with a chip on my shoulder and an attitude of 'too many women, so little time'. I got cocky. Too cocky for my own good.

Sure, his father had understood. That had been the basis of one long lecture when Ranger had gone off to college as a highly recruited hockey player. His father had been there, done that and passed some of his acquired knowledge down to his son. Including the side effects of popularity and the abundance of girls wanting a piece of him.

He'd played. Found out the consequences the hard way, and come out smelling like a rose. However, that lesson had stuck with him and would continue to do so. Just another reason he saw Piper in a totally different light.

"Not all the guys are on board with her. I'm trying to make her feel less isolated and a maybe a bit welcome on the team. She has enough on her plate with the opposing teams without having to deal with the same crap from the guys."

"I'm proud of you, son. It takes a strong man to accept such a huge change and try to watch over a new player. Especially the first woman to enter the men's league."

Ranger smiled slightly. While other boys had gruff fathers who refrained from hugging or praising much, his father proved the opposite. Open-minded, Preston Deacon believed in optimism, reward and being a damn good human being. Ranger still tried to follow in his father's footsteps in that regard. "I've been the new guy before. It sucks. Piper feels it twice as bad, I'm sure."

"Probably more than that," his father added.

"Well, I'm trying to ease the transition on both sides. It's getting there at the speed of molasses."

"She keeps playing like she did the last game, she'll earn fans fast. If she's as laid-back as you claim, the rest of the team will come around."

"She is." There wasn't an arrogant bone in Piper's body. Ranger would lay bets. Her personality aided her in making friends and influencing others. Sweetness toward the guys and in the locker room would sway the team almost as quickly as her high level of play. He'd bet in the next few games she'd find herself as part of the Wolfpack clan in more than just sharing a matching jersey.

"You mother has been singing her praises. Thinks she's pretty too."

Ranger stared at the paused picture on the television. "Meaning?"

"Meaning that she'd like to meet the girl."

"That can be arranged. You guys always come to the final game of the season. I'm sure I can line up an introduction."

His father snorted. "I don't think that's what your mother is going for."

Ranger read between the lines easily enough. "Look, Dad. I barely know the girl. Things are difficult enough with our piss-poor record without jumping feet first into the dating game again."

"I get it, Ranger. I do. But don't let that one witch sour you on the rest of the female population."

Ranger blew out a breath. "I'm not. Trust me. I've had my eyes opened. I was arrogant and pompous. Too full of myself. That whole situation was like a hard check into the boards. I've gotten my bell rung and learned from my mistake."

"There's some nice ladies out there. You'll find one and regain your footing, fast. Just like I did with your mother."

"How did you know she was the one?" Ranger asked the question for the first time in his life. Before, he'd been too excited about the prospect of sex to give commitment much thought. Now he'd changed his expectations and needed a bit of guidance from someone who'd been in those very shoes.

"Not to be poetic, but the world is brighter and happier when she's around."

Ranger could almost see his father grinning on the other end of the line.

"You crave her presence. That's the closest I can get to explaining."

Thinking about Piper, Ranger applied his father's words of wisdom and wasn't able to discard them immediately. So far, Piper had started to turn things around and made hockey fun again.

Not just for him, but for the other guys as well. He saw it after their decisive and hard-fought win.

If she could tip the scales for the rest of the season, he'd sing her praises.

Anything more would be a matter of wait and see.

* * * *

Piper entered through the kitchen door, finding her mother tossing together ingredients into a large pan despite the still early hour of nine. "What are you making?"

Darla smiled over the large pot. "Chicken vegetable soup." She cut up a celery stalk and added it to the mix.

"Sounds good."

Piper slipped off her shoes before wandering toward her bedroom to drop off her ice skates and the two-foot-tall get well card she'd picked up for Gunderson at the store on the way home. She'd gotten up before dawn, headed to the rink for some private practice time, and had only now finished. On her way, she stuck her head in the spare bedroom to find it empty. "Mom? Where's Keith?" She backtracked so she wouldn't have to yell through the house.

"He woke up earlier. Your father took him back to pick up his car. Something about going to have a chat with your teammate along the way."

Piper groaned. Her father had more than talent on the ice. He could lecture a person into submission. She'd been on the receiving end more than once. After he pointed out a person's folly in fifteen different ways, he switched gears, came up with better solutions, and added a tidbit of encouragement for good measure. "Well, crap. I was hoping Keith might start to like me. Setting him up for an hour-long torture session probably won't endear me to him anytime soon."

Darla waved her hand dismissively. "I think you're wrong. Your father is a legend to many of those kids. They admire him. If he takes time to give them life lessons, they'll be all ears." Darla tilted her head and pursed her lips. "Probably."

"Uh-huh." Piper turned around and started toward her bedroom once more. "I'm going to gather up my stuff then head out. The team is leaving this evening for a two-week road trip."

"You're staying for lunch?" Darla hollered from the kitchen.

"Yeah." Piper yelled back. Might as well. Packing wouldn't take too long, especially since she didn't have tons of clothing to worry about. Despite being raised in an affluent household, she'd never needed much. Shopping didn't appeal in the least. Whether that was a carryover from her early childhood or just a side effect of her tomboy nature, she couldn't say. Sure, she had the basics, but the idea of seventy pairs of shoes in a closet that some people had astounded her. A definite waste of money, in her opinion. She preferred a simpler life. Less stuff. No clutter. More down to earth.

After gathering her shower essentials, she headed into the bathroom to clean up after her intense workout that morning.

Thirty minutes later, she stepped out of her room dressed in yoga pants and an oversized sweatshirt advertising one of her father's old teams. Her damp ponytail dripped now and again onto her back. She ignored it as she went in search of her mother. She found Darla in the living room chatting with Gunther, who'd obviously returned while Piper was showering.

"Hi, Dad."

He glanced up at her with a soft smile. "Have a good practice this morning?"

He knows me too well. Unless she had a game, Piper spent most early mornings at the rink, sharpening her skills and stamina. "Yep. How did it go with Keith? Is he seeing straight yet?"

Gunther chuckled. "He's not bright-eyed and bushy-tailed, no. But he's getting there. Should be good to go this evening when you guys leave."

"That's a relief. I'd hate for him to still be hungover when having to face the coach today. I have a feeling Tommy would lower the hammer for that."

"If he's smart, he would." Gunther nodded. "Got to keep the men focused on the game. Things happen off the ice all the time. They have to put that aside, play, then pull themselves together for the next one. It's never easy. There's more to being a professional than how many goals one scores or saves are made." He leveled his gaze at her.

She got the hint and held up her hands. "I know. I get it. Don't be sticking my nose in the middle of senseless fights between Neanderthals who think the only way to work things out is by throwing punches."

"What might work in the women's league doesn't do a thing in the men's."

"Different brains," her mother added. "A bit more on the primitive side, too." She laughed when Gunther reached over to tickle her. "It's true." She squirmed and giggled as she half-heartedly tried to escape Gunther's hands.

Piper grinned. For as long as she could recall, Darla and Gunther had had that kind of relationship. They played. They laughed. They loved. They were best friends as well as marriage partners.

Which was one of the reasons Piper didn't have a boyfriend and rarely dated. She wanted what they had. Nothing else would do. Great in theory, a challenge in the real world. The men she went out with seemed to fall into one of two categories. They either wanted the prestige of going out with a professional athlete, a prodigy at that. Or they wanted to drop her into their bed and prove their prowess as a tough man who favored himself a gift to the ladies. Neither attitude gave her warm fuzzies.

Add in her traumatic past and her social life quickly dropped off.

She shoved those memories back into a closet in her mind and locked the door. They colored enough of her life without dwelling on them. She couldn't change them, could only move forward. Maybe a special man existed who could give her the happiness and contentment her parents seemed to share. Maybe not. Piper didn't really care either way. Long ago, she'd learned to avoid getting her hopes up as they were bashed time and again. Lessons learned the hard way.

"Piper?"

She blinked and pulled her focus back to the present, only to find both her parents staring at her with a bit of concern marking their faces. "Sorry. My mind was elsewhere. What were you saying?"

Darla gestured to a nearby chair. "Have a seat."

Here we go. Piper didn't dare argue, though. She sat and waited to hear what Darla had to say.

"Are you worried about this road trip with the guys?"

Piper shook her head. "Not really. I know I'm not going to be welcomed by everyone. They did stand up with me during wind sprints. That told me a lot."

"What about the opposing team?" Gunther's jaw ticked. "I'd like to think otherwise, but you know some of those idiots are going to be lining you up in the crosshairs."

Goalies were afforded more protection than the rest of

the players on the ice. No taking out the goalie, no cheap hits, no checking. That didn't mean the goalie never ended up flat on his or her back. Aggressiveness and sneakiness were part of the game. Piper had no doubt some of the other players would take offense at her playing with the men. Those would be a threat. One that she intended to face head-on. "I know. Part of them will be respectful, I'm sure. There's always a bad apple in the bunch, though." Piper shrugged. "I can't do much about it. Just go on the ice and do my job."

Gunther sighed. "If you were just bigger…"

Piper rolled her eyes. She'd heard that statement often over the years. "Sorry to break this to you, Dad. I really don't think I'll be growing any more at this late date."

Darla patted Gunther's thigh. "She'll be okay. You know as well as I do goalies are protected. If she were a winger, you'd be a nervous wreck and rightfully so. But the refs, the league and her teammates are going to have a big blowout if someone decides to get nasty."

"I'm up to it, Dad. Promise." Piper flashed a confident smile.

"I know." He stood up, strode over and kissed her on top of the head. "You're a great player. The best. It's just a father's prerogative to worry."

She hugged him. "I wouldn't have it any other way."

* * * *

"Coach?" Piper knocked on the doorjamb of Tommy's office.

He glanced up. "Piper. What is it?"

She walked in and laid a huge card on his desk. "I was thinking that Gunderson might be feeling a bit left out right now. I thought maybe the team might sign this. Then, on the way to Calgary, we'll be really close to his home. Maybe someone can make a side trip to drop it by?"

Tommy picked up the get well card, stared at the front,

then opened it up. The theme from *Rocky* started playing. He chuckled, closed it, and peered up at her. "I think he'll love it." He stared at her for a long moment. "Have a seat."

She sidestepped over to an old wooden chair and sat down.

He folded his hands together and held her gaze. "How are things going with the team?"

"Fine." She'd expected him to question how the guys treated her. While, in truth, she'd had little interaction with them thus far, she wasn't about to complain to Tommy. Even if they treated her like sloppy joe leftovers, she wouldn't say a word. Respect was earned. She hadn't been there long enough for them to widely accept her.

He steepled his fingers and tapped his chin. "You know it's going to be rough. Not just the crowds who may or may not appreciate a woman in the mix, but the other teams might have their own agenda about proving that women have no place in their league."

"You're not telling me anything I don't already know." She met Tommy's eyes. "I'm here to do my job. Don't think of me as a weak, insipid princess needing to be saved by her knight in shining armor. There's nothing further from the truth. I can handle what they dish out. Promise."

He bobbed his head once. "I can see that. Okay. We'll take it one game at a time. If the opponents get too rough, I won't hesitate to pull you."

"Coach." Piper frowned. "That's not fair."

"Show me you can stand in the paint and handle it, Piper. I think you can. But it's not worth a career-ending injury because some bastard has a superiority complex."

"Yes, sir." She nodded slightly, unable to argue with his reasoning. Hopefully it wouldn't come down to that.

"Good. Now get going. We leave soon."

Fifteen minutes later, Piper climbed up the steps onto the bus. After depositing her suitcase and stuffed duffel bag in the storage area, she made sure to keep her carry-on bag close. It held everything from her purse, money and identification to her computer and iPod.

She glanced around, discovered several members of the team already on board, and slowly made her way to the back. Each stared at her as if sizing her up or wondering how their season had slumped to the point of having to use a female goalie. She smiled wanly and kept moving.

In all honesty, she would have preferred to curl up somewhere out of the way, put on her headphones and zen for the duration of the four-hour-long trip. If that option didn't exist, she'd pull out her laptop and do some work. While most of her male counterparts didn't have to worry about a second job, the lady professional hockey players did. After all, they enjoyed a much shorter season. Their paychecks reflected that and then some. The average salary hovered around fifteen thousand. A handful more thousand for the best players. While Piper sat on top of the pay scale, she didn't feel comfortable calling that her sole income. Too many variables existed that could topple her from her throne, leaving her scraping by. Nope. She believed in preparedness in life. That meant she worked two jobs for a part of the year in order to keep a safety net under her at all times. Times were hard and, as a rule, hockey didn't pay. Not for the ladies.

After finding an empty seat, she settled in.

Keith paused in the aisle, grinning somewhat sheepishly at her. "Thanks."

She smiled back. "You're welcome." At least he'd said something. She hadn't been sure if he would speak to her or not.

He kept moving farther back.

Piper pulled out her laptop, connected to the bus's Wi-Fi and pulled up an unfinished spreadsheet. Intent on completing it so she could send it back to the small business, she ignored everything around her. The motor starting and the bus rolling out of the parking lot barely registered as she made additional columns, added numbers and tallied them. How long she sat there pecking away on the keyboard and using her mouse to make adjustments, she didn't know. Time flew when she got into a project.

"What are you doing?"

She glanced over to find Ranger sitting across from her, now leaning over to stare at her screen.

"My job."

He tilted his head. "What job?"

"I do accounting for small businesses on a contractual basis."

"Why?"

She turned her attention to him. "Because none of the women make millions of dollars for playing hockey. Most don't earn enough to sustain them for a year. So unless they're depending on a spouse to help out, we have to have another job lined up."

He blinked in obvious surprise as his lips parted. "You mean they don't make enough to live as they'd like."

"No. I mean that some make less than ten or fifteen thousand per year. Hard to raise a family and pay the bills after paying taxes on that."

He shook his head. "I always thought they were paid better than that. A hell of a lot better."

Piper nodded. "So does the rest of the world. The hard truth is much different than the perception."

"Seems so." He rubbed his chin. "So you do the books for different companies?"

"Yep. It's something I can do online, don't have to punch a clock, and works well with my accounting major in college. The pay is decent. The downside is there's no benefits, not that I'm complaining. It's better than some of the other alternatives."

"Sounds like it." Ranger straightened back up. He drummed his fingers on his knee for a few beats before speaking again. "Ready to take on the Eagles?"

She paused in her work in order to flash him a confident grin. "Absolutely."

He shook his head and smiled almost reluctantly. "You

have your father's fighting spirit, I see."

"Yep."

"You'll need it."

His declaration wasn't really news to Piper. "I can handle it."

Ranger's pretty green eyes caught her gaze. "I know you can."

She tipped her head at his support. When he said nothing more, she returned to her work, determined to be done today in order to buy herself some down time once the games started falling into line, one right after the other.

"Hey, Piper."

She glanced up to find Riley Dickenson staring down at her. The big enforcer smiled a little shyly. "Hi, Riley."

He squatted down beside her. "I was hoping you might help me with a small problem."

"If I can." She scooted over so he could sit down in the aisle seat next to her.

"It's my wife. She's fit to be tied."

Piper peered over at him. "What happened?"

"She called me yesterday. Ranting about her day, the problems she faced. I told her how to fix them. Even said I would do it for her. She about took my head off." He scrubbed his face. "I don't get it."

She considered the information for a minute and tried to formulate a rational answer. After mentally placing herself in the woman's shoes, she worked the angles. "Well, I'm no expert, but I think I can offer up some advice. Some women don't expect or want you to try to fix things for them. They're upset, but not looking for a solution. Instead, they just want someone to listen and be supportive. Telling her how to 'fix it'"—she did the finger quotations in the air—"only made her feel like she was incapable of coming up with answers and that she needed a man to set things straight." Piper patted Riley's arm. "Sometimes women just need an understanding ear rather than a problem solver."

He stared at the seat directly in front of him. "Could it be that simple?"

Piper grinned. "Yep. Women are pretty easy when you get right down to it."

"Said no man ever." Riley snorted. He turned back to her and smiled. "I should call her."

"Good idea."

He stood up and strode back to his seat.

Piper adjusted her laptop, glimpsing a small smile on Ranger's face. She glanced over, shrugged, then returned to her work.

Maybe, just maybe, she could fit in after all.

"Thanks."

She glanced up to meet Ranger's gaze. "For what?"

"For watching Keith's back and helping out Riley."

"That's what you do when you're on a team. Look out for one another. Put out a helping hand now and again." She smiled slightly.

Ranger gave a brief nod, yet his eyes spoke the truth. She'd made a dent in his wall. She'd bet on it.

Feeling more upbeat, she returned to her task, eager to finish the job so she could once more focus entirely on hockey.

Chapter Five

Ranger stepped out into the hallway of the hotel, immediately finding himself surrounded by women. He grumbled under his breath and pushed through the small mob, hurrying well away before one of the overeager women started to tug at his clothes.

Puck bunnies. Roadies. Groupies. Whatever anyone wanted to call them, they were a downright nuisance. Always dressed in tight clothing, short dresses and heels. Their attire wasn't the problem. Their determination to get into his bed and into his pocketbook was.

Years ago, when he'd first entered the league, he'd appreciated the rapt attention. Nothing like a beautiful woman throwing herself at him to bolster his already large ego. He'd spent many a night sampling the wares, although always being careful to use precautions. He might have been horny, but he wasn't stupid. If they were willing to screw a virtual stranger, they'd been around the block a time or three. Not to mention their ulterior motives. At least some of them would have happily gotten pregnant if he hadn't insisted on condoms. They thought the way to a marriage ceremony revolved around having his child. They were wrong.

His attention to detail had paid off a couple of years back when one of those women had tried to slap a paternity suit on him. DNA didn't lie. She'd lost. He'd walked free, though a changed man. No longer did he see the masses of women as anything more than a gaggle of troublesome geese. They didn't care about him, his wishes, or his feelings. All they wanted was a piece of his pie. Too bad he didn't share. Not anymore.

He sighed heavily.

When did I get so cynical? When that bitch tried to slap me with a paternity suit.

"Ranger. Ranger!"

He kept walking, having learned to mute the calls of the all-too-eager women long ago.

After figuring out a few things along the way, he abhorred dealing with the numbers of ladies who seemed to plague him. He wanted peace and rarely found it, especially on road trips. More than once he'd had to have a trespasser escorted off his property at home — insistent women who refused to take no for an answer. The endless roadies turned him off. Sure, they'd been fun and stoked his ego way back then, but now he tired of meaningless sex. Maybe he'd simply grown up. Maybe he wanted what some of the other guys had — a happy wife and family waiting for him at home, ready to welcome him back with open arms when he returned from a trip. Whatever the reason, the bimbos in miniskirts and heels patrolling the hotel and the games turned his head — away.

He stepped into the elevator, hit the down button and watched the door close as a couple of the more outgoing women reached it a few seconds too late. Making a mental note to speak to the main desk on his way to dinner, he rubbed at his chin and let his thoughts take him away for a few seconds.

What seemed like eons ago, he'd been a normal guy who'd dated girls starting in high school. Though he'd always been an athlete and earned more than his fair share of attention from the opposite sex, he could now see that had been a much more innocent time. Girls had wanted to be with him for a variety of reasons, most didn't revolve around sex. Sure, he'd lost his virginity at the ripe old age of seventeen. Perhaps a late start if the boasts of other guys proved correct. Yet that hadn't been his reason for going out with girls. Not entirely anyway.

Now he had the additional complication of his salary added into the convoluted mix of dating. More than anything he wanted a lady who could stand up for herself, be independent, fun and sweet all while seeing the man he was inside. One who could overlook his finances and see the true him. Was that possible? Maybe. The question still remained how he would know.

Life had been both better and worse before entering the professional ranks. Money drew attention and caused him and many other guys to question the motivation of women wanting to spend a night in a player's bed.

Hell, I lived it up as a sex god for the past few years. Singled out one of the lovely ladies and lined up a night of erotic delights. No harm, no foul.

I was so fucking stupid.

He'd turned over a new leaf and left the easy one-night stands in the past. Taken notice of how the married guys lived and saw many relationships in the process. Some worked well, others were rocky. Still, the guys were solid in their belief in family and love. Something he desperately wanted to try on for himself. A wife. A family. A lady who could see beyond his checkbook to the real Ranger underneath.

If only I knew where to start looking.

The road seemed endless during the season. Rarely were they in the same city two nights in a row. Down days were hit and miss. Not to mention long-distance relationships were always built on trust and determination. He might have the determination, but lately his trust in the opposite sex had waned.

Not like I have to find Mrs. Right this very moment, anyway. He had a few years before arriving at his dotage and had the luxury of taking his sweet time in singling out a woman who met all his criteria.

With that optimistic thought, he rotated his shoulders and turned his thoughts back to the present. And to the newest member of the team.

The trip had been long, but uneventful. Most of the guys had watched movies, played around on their phones or listened on their headphones. Some had curled up and napped for the duration. Piper had been the exception. She'd worked on her laptop for a time before packing it away.

They'd arrived at the hotel in the evening. Just in time to go out for dinner, then come back and crash in their rooms for the night. Ranger had been to San Jose many times before, knew the best place to eat, and had parked there for a while. A couple of the other guys had tagged along, too. Where Piper had opted to eat, he didn't know. She seemed to have disappeared into her hotel room and not emerged since.

He would check on her if she didn't turn up soon. After all, someone needed to look after the smallest Wolfpack player.

He'd been amazed to learn of such low-end salaries for even the top women in the league. To think they had to juggle home, work and hockey bumfuzzled him as well as increased his level of respect. Talk about being pulled in a dozen different directions at once. Not for the faint of heart, for sure. Still, he couldn't help but grin when Piper had pulled out a pillow, curled up in the pair of seats in her section, then dozed off. Pretty cute. She exuded a softness in her sleep that promised sweet dreams and gentle warmth.

Something he craved.

Her caring nature struck a chord as well. She'd helped out the guys without asking anything in return, from what he'd heard. After the cold reception she'd received, she had no reason to lift a finger for them. Yet she had done just that.

Like a mother hen, he could easily see her babying the guys if they allowed it. Oddly enough, the idea of her turning her sweet expression and smile on him caused his spirit to buoy. Her heart was in the right spot, that he could attest to.

The women he'd been with in the past had been looking

for a hookup. A couple for something more permanent. None of them held a candle to what he'd seen out of Piper thus far.

Maybe, just maybe, she could be more than just the exception in the men's league. She might just be able to be the exception in his social life as well.

He'd spoken the truth when he'd said he believed she could handle the roughness of the men's game. Maybe if she played another position, not so much. But as a goalie, she should be able to sustain. Hell, she'd make one fine forward if she cared to try out for that position. He'd give her credit for speed, puck control and a wicked backhand. The problem would be the other players would make a point of slamming her into the boards as hard and often as possible. Her smaller stature would take a beating only for so long. Eventually, she'd be unable to withstand any further punishment after months of playing a seemingly endless schedule most nights of the week. It was hard enough for the strongest man, let alone a woman half his size. Deep down, he worried about her longevity. No matter her skill or talent, Piper was still a woman playing a hard-impact men's sport.

Time will tell.

The ding of the doors opening jolted him from his thoughts. He stepped out and breathed a sigh of relief when no masses of women met him. With only a couple of the other guys standing around bullshitting in the hallway, Ranger relaxed and strode into the hotel dining room. The scents of hot breakfast foods made his stomach growl. He'd have time to eat, catch a nap, then rouse in time to prepare for the afternoon game.

He headed toward the buffet, catching sight of Piper as he went. She sat alone at one of the corner tables, trying to dig out a hunk of grapefruit. Ranger shook his head. The guys loaded up on protein and carbs for breakfast before games. Fruit was an important part of their diet, except grapefruit. He'd never known another hockey player to bother with it.

After picking up a plate, Ranger filled it with scrambled eggs, sausage, a piece of French toast and all the fixings. As an afterthought, he added three slices of cantaloupe to the growing pile. He snagged a couple of containers of milk from the end of the bar and sauntered over to the corner. Since the team picked up the tab for all meals, he didn't have to bother with paying. "Hi."

Piper glanced up. "Hi." She returned to her battle with the grapefruit half.

He pulled out the chair and plopped down. A few seconds to organize and he began to eat earnestly. The large meal would have to get him through until around noon, when he'd put together a sandwich and some yogurt to help maximize his energy for the upcoming game. Granola bars were a staple in the locker room as well.

Ranger watched her work with a sense of amusement. Personally, he didn't think grapefruit tasted good enough to spend fifteen minutes trying to pry small chunks out of each section, getting sticky in the process. "Are you winning or losing?"

Her head snapped up. She blinked at him before his meaning obviously sank in. A reluctant smile followed. "Losing, I think."

"Here." He forked a slice of cantaloupe and dropped it on her plate. "Have some melon. It's good for you. Not to mention a hell of a lot easier to eat." He stared at the grapefruit once more. "At least you don't have to butcher it first."

"Thanks." She picked up her knife and cut the fruit into small sections before popping one in her mouth.

He noticed her shirt for the first time. The white material carried a red representation of a devil on the front. Despite the jersey being probably three sizes too big, she wore it proudly. "Your father's away game jersey when he played with the Sun Devils?"

"Yep." She smiled. "It's my lucky charm."

He understood the role of superstitions in sports. Almost

every player had a lucky something or other they depended on. The irony in her choice of items amused him. "Not sure I'd be wearing that around when we actually play them. The guys might forget which side you're on."

Piper shrugged. "I've never had anyone protest before, but it's a new day. So we'll see." She finished the fruit.

He put away his eggs and started on the meat. Her blonde locks snared his attention. The lightness without a hint of brunette or dark roots spoke of a natural color instead of a dye job. He remembered her family cheering for her at the game. Once again, he thought about the physical differences. Betting that he was right, he tossed out the pressing question. "I noticed your parents both have dark hair. You don't." He left the question hanging between them, hoping she'd take the bait and offer up an explanation.

She gripped her fork tight enough for her knuckles to show white. The muscles in her face grew taut as well.

Shit. I hit a nerve.

Just as he started to apologize, she answered. "They adopted me when I was six."

Why did you need adopting? What kind of home did you come from that adoption became necessary? Under what circumstances did that have to happen? The questions hung on the tip of his tongue. As much curiosity as her answer prompted, he didn't want to pressure her. They'd just met not too long ago. Her willingness to open up would be iffy at this point. Most importantly, he didn't want to alienate her because he'd stuck his nose where it didn't belong. Carefully, he chose his response. "They sound like great parents to have."

Piper beamed. "They are. Tough, but caring. I never got away with anything. On the good side, neither did my brother."

"Your brother Darius?"

"Yep. We'll play against him in a couple of weeks when we take on the Devils."

Ranger arched an eyebrow. "How do you feel about that?"

Her smile turned absolutely wolfish. "I can't wait. He's been bragging about being a superstar. I've been playing against him my whole life and just happen to have his number."

Ranger chuckled. "You don't have a fearful bone in your body."

"Nah." She took another bite then swallowed. "Fear traps a person in the corner. Been there, done that. Never again."

He read the flash of pain in her eyes. His gut told him she'd faced hell in her past. Concern spread through him. Protective instincts leaped to the fore. Never before had he reacted in such a way. A bit unsettled, he finished one of his milks before trying to detour the topic of conversation to something less tension-filled. "What do you know of the Eagles' scoring attack?"

"Some, but probably not as much as I should. Stanza gave me pages of information to absorb already. It's all a blur at the moment."

He started filling her in, enjoying her rapt attention and intelligent questions. She leaned forward, took in every word and seemed to be right in her element.

Never before had he met a woman who loved hockey as much as he did. Now he sat at a restaurant table, discussing strategy with a lady who'd grown up under the guidance of one of the game's legends. She'd picked up nuances of the game that even some of the men didn't get.

Oddly enough, he could see them sitting on a couch, near a roaring fire, watching hockey on television and having the debate of his life.

He could handle a verbal battle even if it ended up in a stalemate or loss, for making up had always been his strong suit. He'd live to fight another day.

And have the time of my life in the meantime.

Whoa. Slow down, buddy. She's a teammate. A woman. While she might not have been in the same group as puck bunnies, that didn't mean she was filled with all the inner goodness he casually looked for these days. Putting the cart before the horse would only land him in horseshit. He'd already made some mistakes and refused to chance it again. Until he knew for certain a lady possessed the qualities he demanded, he wasn't about to do more than speak to them.

Still, his gut told him Piper would stand hands and feet above the rest.

We'll see. Until then, he'd cool his jets and focus on being her friend.

* * * *

"So, what's on the agenda until game-time?" Piper asked as she walked along beside him.

"Down time until an early lunch. We load up at noon." Ranger quoted the schedule everyone received yesterday.

She shook her head. "I meant your agenda."

He shrugged. "Nap time. It's my hobby, after all."

"Napping is a hobby?" She grinned. "Somehow I pegged you for an adrenaline guy. You know, working out, playing a pick-up game, conquering the bad guys in the latest computer game."

"Now and again. Game days are different. I'd rather save my energy for later. 'Cause we're all going to need it." He glanced over at her. "Are you nervous?"

"Nah. Not really. Yeah, it's a bigger stage and there's probably a few guys out there that would like nothing better than to pound me into the ice for daring to invade their male-dominated world. It's part of the game and the consequences of being the first person to cross a hard line in sports."

He admired her for her tenacity, bravery and realistic attitude. Still, he hated the thought she'd face such potential violence due to her gender. Stereotypes existed and were damn hard to eradicate. "You held up well in the last game. I don't think they gave you enough credit."

"Thanks. It's my job. No room for slackers."

They stepped on the elevator. He hit the button to his

floor. "Keep up the excellent work and the door might open for another woman or two to join the league."

She smiled. "That would be nice, but I'm not holding my breath. This is a special situation. As long as there's plenty of huge men with some goalie skills, they'll be preferred over smaller women. Size is half the battle in front of the net."

"But not everything. You've shown that."

"In one game. There's harder ones yet to come." Her words carried a hint of worry.

He considered what she faced each time she took to the ice. Fans who either loved or hated her, some quite vocal about their opinions. Opponents who wanted to take her down, even if they respected her for being there. Her own teammates. While most were on board now, a few hung back, still not thrilled with her presence. He knew if they continued to win, the guys would fall in line. While much of the responsibility rested on Piper's shoulders, she couldn't provide the offense. Thus, the rest of them had to step up as well.

The elevator stopped and dinged before the doors opened. He walked off first, quickly followed by Piper. "Where are you staying?"

She gestured down the long hall. "Last room on the right. Next to the fire escape. It's well away from the rest of you guys. Like an afterthought. But hey, I have a room to myself."

"You don't always?" The thought boggled his mind.

"When traveling, the girls have to share. It's always been that way."

Ranger shook his head. "That sucks, especially if you get a roommate like Riley. He snores like a hibernating bear."

She giggled. "Does he know that?"

"Uh-huh. The whole team tells him often enough. Hell, I think one of the guys got him those nose Band-Aids for Christmas. They didn't work." Ranger grinned in remembrance. "We stopped sharing hotel rooms a couple years back. Thank God."

He slowed as they approached his wing. A group of scantily clad women surrounded his door.

"Friends of yours?" she asked.

"Shit, no. Puck bunnies. They're relentless, I swear. They always find a way back in. At least until they lock the doors for the night."

"The price of being famous and single?"

He grumbled under his breath. "It's too fucking high if you ask me. A man can't have any privacy with them around."

"Have a chat with management yet?"

"Yeah. As you can see, it's not done much."

Piper pursed her lips. "Maybe if you told them that you're off the market, they'd go bother someone else?"

"I have my doubts. They pursue all the guys, even the married ones." Those, in particular, irritated him. He couldn't say that all married men stayed true on the road, but the greatest majority did. Cheating, in his book, hovered around the bottom of the barrel. Games kept them on the road. Trust became key on both sides due to the frequent separation. If he could find a woman of his dreams, no way would he jeopardize their relationship by selecting one of the women hovering outside his hotel hoping for a quick fuck. The sentiment had to run both ways. He had to have absolute belief that his girlfriend would remain faithful at the same time.

One glance at Piper told him that she'd most likely be one of those who would stick by his side through thick and thin. Nothing he'd seen thus far spoke of men parading through her hotel room or a habit of picking up strays from the bars. Unless he missed his guess, the innocence she portrayed rang true.

She scratched at her sleeve. "Okay. How about if you just show them that your interest lies elsewhere?"

"How?"

"Couple of options. Change rooms with me or we can go

into yours together. That will give them something to talk about as well as dampen their expectations."

He pondered the various reactions and slowly smiled. "I like it. Let's go to your room and gather up your stuff. You can hang out with me until lunch."

She grinned back. "Tell me you have a spare bed in your room."

"Oh, yeah. Two beds and a couch."

"Damn. You're living it up in the presidential suite."

"I'm not complaining." He followed her to the back wall of rooms, around a curve, and way down a never-ending hall. She stopped at the last door, shoved her key card in the lock, and opened the door. He stepped inside and scanned the room. Like she'd said, it covered basic needs. Barely. "Why do you get the economy room?"

She collected her bags and pocketed the key. "Isn't it obvious? Either they thought I needed plenty of space away from the team or they didn't have much else left when someone in the front office called to request another room."

Ranger snorted in exasperation. "I'll have a talk with Coach. You're part of the team and should be treated as such."

"It's okay. Really." She placed her hand on his upper arm. "I don't want to make any waves. Being the new kid is tough enough. The last thing I want to do is get a reputation as a complainer."

He read the truth in her eyes and sighed. "Okay."

"Thanks. Besides, it's not so bad. I don't have a group of lust-filled women giggling outside my door." She grinned mischievously up at him.

His stomach somersaulted at the playful expression that snared his attention and prodded his sleepy libido into wakefulness. "There's something to be said for peace and quiet."

"Yep." She tossed the strap of her laptop bag over one shoulder, the duffel over the other, then reached for her suitcase.

He beat her to the handle, lifting with ease. "Let me get this. And the bag, too."

"I can get it. Do it all the time."

"True. But I happen to have a chivalrous side that comes out now and again."

Piper tilted her head and smiled. "So let you play the knight for now?"

Maybe for a hell of a lot longer than that.

Here we go again. He chastised himself. *Teammate. End of story.*

"Yeah."

"Deal." She handed over her duffel without argument. "Besides, we have to make a good impression on those ladies." Piper batted her eyelashes at him.

He chuckled. "You're enjoying this."

"I've never had groupies. So chasing them off should be an adventure."

Her energetic optimism proved contagious as he walked beside her back to his room. As they approached the group of women, he took Piper's hand in his and pulled her close to his side. "Coming through." He added command to his voice.

The women looked at him, then to Piper. More than one mouth fell open in shock.

He bit back his amusement, shoved the card into the door, pushed it open, then nudged Piper to enter first. He followed and slammed the door in the face of an overly aggressive girl who thought she'd invite herself before he quickly turned the lock. After striding over to the phone, he set his load on the floor and rang the front desk. "There's a crowd in the hallway right outside my room, number two-oh-one. I've asked repeatedly for them to be escorted out. Do I have to make a call to my lawyer or will you actually provide some decent security today?"

"I'm so sorry, sir. We'll be right on it."

"You have ten minutes. I'll be sure to report this to team management so they can find another hotel to use for future games. If you can't keep the public out then I can't see any reason in staying here and paying these exorbitant prices."

"You have my word, sir. I have staff on their way as we speak."

Ranger hung up. He turned to find Piper lightly bouncing on the bed closest to him. She did so for a few seconds before doing the same to the other. "Find what you're searching for?"

She tossed him a grin. "Yep. Lumpiness." A bright laugh followed. "Actually, they're not too bad. Which one do you want?"

The one you'll be sleeping in. He buttoned that response up immediately. *Stop acting like a horny teen.* She might be the toughest, most pleasant and brightest woman that he'd run across in a while, but that didn't mean she was in the market for a sizzling-hot fling. Best to shelve that idea. At least until the end of the season. Not to mention he'd been burned before. Badly. With his luck lately, women were dicey. Where Piper landed on the list, he still wasn't sure.

"It's not rocket science." She patted the mattress. "You're thinking way too hard about this. You're getting frown lines."

He grinned. "Frown lines? Is that supposed to be frightening?"

"Oh, yeah." She nodded.

He shook his head at her silliness even as he found her refreshing. "You take that one. I'll take this one."

"Okay." She slipped off her shoes, pulled the covers down and slid in.

Ranger did the same, resting on his side to face her. *I feel like a kid again, attending a slumber party.*

She flipped over toward him. "Thanks, Ranger."

"For what?"

"For accepting me when others wouldn't have. For getting the rest of the guys on board. For being one hell of a nice guy."

Her words soaked in, warming him. "You're one of us

now. We take care of our own."

She smiled, snuggled down into her pillow, then closed her eyes.

Ranger fell asleep with visions of holding her close, snuggling the night away — with a treasure wrapped securely in his embrace.

Chapter Six

Piper tugged her gear off, tossed her jersey onto a chair, and started packing her stuff into the oversized pink duffel with the Bobcats logo on the side. She'd been annoyed to learn that the arena had no women's locker room. Since the city had no women's hockey team, they simply hadn't put one in. No basketball. Nothing that would indicate a duplicate set of locker rooms were needed. Granted, if it were simply two female teams playing, they could use the regular facilities and do just fine. The problem revolved around needing a spare for times like these. Since there probably had never been a time like this, she really couldn't expect them to have lush accommodations ready to go. Thus, she'd been relegated to using the public ladies room and shown to a small storeroom in order to change.

It could be worse. She could be in the locker room with the men, listening to them pee and shower after the game. "Not really my cup of tea." She smiled to herself.

Despite the less than perfect accommodations, she really didn't have a gripe about the Eagles, their fans, or their way of play. No dirty shots. No booing. Much better than she'd feared, definitely. Other teams should take a lesson. Well, not in the lack-of-a-separate-locker-room department.

A couple of the players had even skated over at the end of the game to congratulate her on the win. She'd let only one puck by, a knuckle puck deflected by a stick. Not much that anyone could have done in the blink of an eye that it had sailed past her right shoulder. Still, she hated to miss even one.

She brushed at the dripping sweat with a towel and

lamented the lack of a shower facility for her. The guys were cleaning up now as the team bus would take them to a nice restaurant for dinner. She, alone, would still be sweaty, stinky and less than presentable. The guys would walk into the restaurant looking like a million bucks. She'd be the street urchin in tow.

If only…

No use crying over spilled milk or an absent shower.

A knock pulled her from her thoughts. "Piper. Get your rear in gear." Stanza's accented voice carried through the wooden door.

"What's the hurry? The guys are probably still getting dressed."

"They are dressed already and waiting for you."

"Well, crap." She had no mirror. Nothing to evaluate her unkempt appearance. With no help for the situation, she grabbed her dirty shirt and opened the door, still wearing her T-shirt and sweatpants.

Stanza gestured with his head. "Come on." He led her back toward the locker room.

Piper noted most of the guys stood outside, chatting and leaning against the wall. Sure enough, they'd cleaned up and looked as fresh as ever. Dressed in nice casual, they appeared to be a bunch of well-off friends out for a night on the town. Truth in advertising, as it were.

Stanza stopped so suddenly Piper nearly barreled into him. As it was, her duffel smacked him in the back. He turned back to her and pointed to the entrance to the men's locker room. "Go shower."

She blinked at him. "With the other guys? Thanks but no thanks."

"No others." Stanza insisted.

Keith stepped forward. "I'll check again, just in case." He disappeared only to return a couple of minutes later. "It's empty."

Piper's mouth fell open. "You…?"

"We'll make sure you're not disturbed," Marek Rayovic

promised.

"There's no time to go back to the hotel and still make our reservation, so the guys decided to hotfoot it through their showers so you could take one, too." Tommy gave her a slight nudge. "Go on before we're late."

Piper beamed. "Thank you. All of you." She scanned their faces then hurried inside. A laundry basket filled with game jerseys caught her eye. She dropped hers on top of the pile. Not about to waste time, she stripped down in record fashion, gathered up her shower items, tossed her flip-flops on the ground and stepped into them. No way would she take a chance on athlete's foot. A lesson drummed into her from the peewee leagues. She turned on the hot water, entered the huge stall and let the warmth wash over her. *Heaven*.

She scrubbed down before tackling her hair. As soon as she'd rinsed, she shut off the water, grabbed the towel and dried off. In a hurry, she did the best she could with the long locks, leaving them damp and hanging down straight. She returned to her bag and dug out a cozy light blue sweater and matching slacks. After slipping them on, she pulled on socks and flats. Comfortable yet classy. Piper brushed her teeth, applied a light coating of makeup, then checked herself in the mirror one last time. Satisfied, she gathered up her stuff and left the locker room.

The guys stood around just where she'd left them.

"Wow. Ten minutes. I wouldn't believe it if I hadn't seen it with my own eyes." Riley checked his watch then tapped it as if to make sure it hadn't stopped.

Piper rolled her eyes. "Hey, you guys did me a favor. I wasn't about to make you late for dinner after that."

"You clean up nice," Ranger said.

Several pairs of eyes flicked her direction. She blushed at their rapt attention. Especially Ranger's. The flash in his gaze spoke of appreciation and admiration. Her breath caught in response. "Thanks."

Stanza waved his hands. "You are ready now. We go to

eat."

"Thanks, Stanza." She shot him a sincere smile.

"Ehh." He strode toward the exit with the rest of the guys.

Piper pulled up the rear, pretty pleased with the events of the night. They'd won the game. More importantly, her team had rallied around her. While letting her share their showers might not seem like a big thing to most, it meant the world to her. It represented their acceptance of her into the fold. Something she hadn't been sure would be possible.

They walked out into the night.

"Puck bunny heaven." Axel whistled.

"Look at that rocket in red." Rocky stared so hard Piper could have sworn he drooled a little.

She glanced at the gathering of women and shook her head. *Men experiencing flaring testosterone levels after a battle with lust on their minds. Wonderful.* "Where's the tomcats?"

"The what?" Adam, one of the forwards, asked.

"The tomcats. After every Bobcats game a legion of men would hang around the back door hoping to entice us to their lairs." She waggled her eyebrows.

"An entire legion? Really?" Riley asked over his shoulder.

Piper hemmed and hawed. "Well, three or four."

The guys chuckled. "Three or four, huh?"

Recognizing her captive audience found her amusing, she layered it on. "Oh, yeah. But they were top-of-the-line tomcats. Pretty, too."

"Uh-huh."

Speaking of pretty…

Piper automatically searched for and locked on Ranger. He headed up the team, his perfectly shaped rear covered in dark slacks that molded to his assets quite well. Her heart sped at the sight of one of the most handsome men in the game dressed for a night out on the town. His black hair tickled the collar of his deep blue button-down shirt. The color brought out his bright green eyes. She knew because she couldn't quite get the picture of him standing next to the locker room out of her mind.

Yummy. Lickable. And way out of my league.

She needed a distraction and fast. "What's a rocket? Is that anything like a crotch rocket?"

The guys around her burst out laughing. Axel guffawed so hard, he had to stop for a second.

She blinked innocently up at them. "Well?"

"Care to share the joke?" Rocky asked.

Ranger and Rocky stood near the bus with curiosity covering both of their faces.

"She wants to know if a rocket has anything to do with crotch rockets." Adam went off on further peals.

The rest of the team snickered.

Piper crossed her arms over her chest and stopped near the bus. She tapped her toe impatiently on the asphalt. "Well? Does it or not?"

Ranger shared knowing looks with a couple of the other guys. "You don't want to know."

Piper punched him lightly in the gut. "Yes, I do."

He grabbed her hand. "I have a feeling if we told you, you'd blush scarlet to your toes."

"Try me."

Axel leaned over and whispered in her ear. "Rockets are sexy women. We like to think of them as pretty ladies that will do just about anything in bed. *Anything.*"

"Anything?"

"Oh, yeah." Axel grinned wickedly.

Piper's face heated. She barely resisted the urge to fan herself. *Why did I bother asking? Because I'm an idiot, that's why.* While she'd always heard of crotch rockets in reference to motorcycles, she could finally see where the guys found her comparison humorous.

"Told you." Ranger looked smug.

"Yes, you did." She placed her stuff in the storage area of the bus, then started for the steps only to pause and turn. "Dare I ask what anything entails?" She grinned ruefully and hurried onto the bus, not stopping until she found her previous seat and plopped down.

Ranger soon took his. "You're a little spitfire. I'll say that."

"All part of the package that is me." She lifted her chin proudly.

"So, about this legion of men…"

Piper leaned toward him, noting several of the other guys gathering around to listen in. "Yes?"

"Did you take them up on their offers?" Ranger asked.

Piper sat up straight and arched an eyebrow at him. "Playing truth or dare, huh?"

"Just asking a question." He shrugged as if inquiring about the weather.

"Fine. If you must know…" She watched as the others leaned in closer to hear her answer. "It'll cost you."

His lips parted. "What's your price?"

She tapped her chin. "Show me how you do that spin-o-rama into a slap shot."

Ranger's lips twitched as a slow smile appeared on his face. "Deal."

The expression sent a sweet bolt straight to her heart. Unwilling to pause and analyze the reaction at the moment, she turned and winked at Axel instead. "No, I've never given those men much thought. No wild sex stories. No escapades. I'm a bit picky, you see."

"Well, shit. I thought we were getting to hear one hell of a story." Riley huffed dramatically.

"Sorry to disappoint." She picked at her sweater. "I guess in this one area, women are a little different than men."

"Not all women," Axel informed.

"Touché." Piper lowered her chin in acknowledgement.

She thought of the women surrounding the exit, wondering how many of the guys actually took them up on their forthright suggestions. Probably most of them at one time or another. Since approximately half of the team was married, she considered them past that stage. Yeah, men were definitely different from most of her Bobcats teammates. The ladies might go out and have a drink. Maybe a couple would hook up with guys and take them home. However, she'd say the vast majority weren't that loose.

The bus pulled into the parking lot of a restaurant. Everyone filed out and through the front doors.

Peter, the team conditioning coach and nutritionist, met them. "You guys are in for a treat. Organic foods from around the world. You have to try this to believe it." He opened the door and waved the team in.

Piper blinked at Peter. She remembered him from a couple of lectures he'd presented to the Bobcats a while back. Since the women's league drew in less money and had a much shorter season, they lacked as abundant a staff as the Wolfpack enjoyed. Whether that ended up being good or bad, she hadn't decided yet. Most of the time the team went their own ways, finding their own meals at nearby restaurants. That seemed to be the norm. Except for tonight, when the whole group ended up at fancy place bragging of natural goodness.

The other guys seemed to want to get far away from the nutrition guy, leaving her the seat right between Tommy and Peter. *Just great.*

She sat down with as much dignity as she could manage, picked up the menu, and nearly choked on the prices. *Holy crap.*

Tommy edged over to whisper in her ear. "Close your mouth. The team is paying for this one so order whatever you want."

She blinked up at him.

He gave her a small nudge. "Welcome to the big leagues, kid."

"Uh-huh." She peeked at the menu items again, trying unsuccessfully to block out the prices. In the end, she settled on a grilled chicken salad with a side of fruit. Something healthy, but fairly light. She knew many of the players pigged out on pizza or junk food after games. She'd never been one of those. Perhaps it revolved around being a lady and the constant attention to diet and exercise. Maybe it came from the homemade meals her mother always served. Either way, Piper preferred to stick with the program that had worked thus far.

"If you're going to play like a man, you have to eat like one, too," Peter pointed out.

Piper scanned the table, finding a handful of her teammates rolling up pizza slices and eating them half a piece at a time. She shuddered. *Talk about heartburn city. No thank you.*

"Try the lamb," Peter recommended.

Piper crinkled her nose. "No thanks. I don't like lamb. I'll stick with the salad." She waited for the waitress to address her before rattling off her order.

Peter tsked at her. "You don't know what you're missing."

"Yeah, I do." She recalled the one time her mother had tried to feed her lamb. Nasty stuff. Piper shuddered in remembrance.

Tommy tapped his fork on his water glass, bringing everyone's attention to him. He stood and held up the card Piper had purchased. "If I can have your attention. Someone came up with a great idea. We're all going to sign this get well card for Gunderson. Anyone who wants to tag along after dinner to drop it off at his house is more than welcome." He opened the card.

The theme from *Rocky* carried loud and clear.

All of the guys smiled. Some of them laughed. In the end, all of them signed and several volunteered for the ride to deliver the gift.

When the food was delivered, Piper dug in, slowly eating as she watched the entourage. They laughed, they teased. They ribbed one another for one transgression or another. She couldn't help but grin at the comradery she witnessed.

"Maybe Rob knew what he was doing."

Piper twisted to peer at Tommy. "Why do you say that?"

He gestured down the table. "Look at them. Not long ago, they would have been up in arms and all surly if even asked to go out for a team meal. Would have used the table as a line drawn in the sand. Today we have a couple of wins under our belt. They're happy. Upbeat." He met her gaze. "Rob said you'd be a breath of fresh air. I honestly didn't believe it myself. Now I'm beginning to see the difference."

Piper stabbed a piece of lettuce. "It's not me, Coach. It's because things are starting to click on the ice. That's all."

He shook his head. "No, Darrow. You're the spark we've been needing."

Humbled and honored, Piper reluctantly accepted his compliment. "I only hope that continues to be the case. We have a long road ahead and a short time to get there."

"We'll get there." He picked up his glass of soda and took a long drink.

I hope so. I really do. For their sake.

Chapter Seven

"Gunderson said you had good taste," Ranger said as he paused at the steps to the team's private plane. Two days had passed since they'd ridden the bus back home, only to turn right around and pack for another road trip. This one much farther away. Thus the jet instead of the much less comfortable charter bus.

Piper smiled tiredly. "He liked his card?" She handed her gear over to a loading person then thanked him earnestly.

Ranger nodded. "Oh, yeah. He got a kick out of it." He recalled Gunderson's grin when he'd opened the giant card.

Ranger and a handful of others had made the trip after the game to Gunderson's home to deliver the present in person. The guy had seemed to appreciate the gesture, had invited them in and prodded them about how things were going with his replacement. Ranger had told him the truth. She wasn't a Gunderson, but she held her own. Morale had increased, as had the looseness around the locker room. Their injured goalie seemed happy with the situation, if not frustrated that he couldn't be there to finish out the season.

After easily navigating the stairs, Ranger found a spot and stowed his carry-on above his head.

Piper boarded next. She stopped at the entrance and stared, her mouth falling open. "Oh, my God."

Ranger grinned, having expected such a reaction from her. "I take it the Bobcats haven't flown in luxury yet?"

"Are you kidding?" She ran her hands over the nearest seat. All leather, oversized, filled with padding, and able to recline into a halfway decent bed.

"Welcome to the big leagues." Stanza snuck past her. "We

travel well."

"So unfair. We're stuck on a team bus for hours at a time." She glared toward the cockpit, only to find Tommy in her path.

He held up his hands. "I don't make the rules. Take that up with Rob."

"I just might." Piper readjusted the strap on her bag before making her way down the wide center aisle. "I'm still in shock. This is amazing."

Ranger grinned. "We're spoiled. I admit it."

"Absolutely." Piper found a seat to her liking and plopped down. Her eyes widened immediately. "This is better than my bed at home. I'll be rocked to sleep in no time."

"That's an option. Some of the guys play cards. Others tune in to music." Ranger took a seat and stretched out his long legs, thankful for the extra room not found on most airplanes. "We even have a flight attendant to take care of everything you might need."

Piper shook her head. "I'm waiting for the wicked witch to fly by on her broom."

Ranger laughed. "If you see her, let the pilot know. We probably should try to avoid that flying house if at all possible."

She giggled, a contagious sound that rang easy on his ears.

The flight attendant cruised over to them. "Hello, Ranger. Nice to see you again."

"Clara."

Clara turned to Piper. "I don't think we've met, although I've been hearing quite a bit about you. I'm Clara. Stewardess for the Wolfpack team plane."

"Hi, Clara." Piper offered up a nice smile.

"If there's anything you need, just let me know."

"A blanket?"

Clara opened a compartment above Ranger's head, pulled out a white, fluffy blanket and handed it to Piper. "Here you go."

"Thank you." Piper felt the material before brushing it across her cheek. "So soft. I might have to swipe this to take home with me."

Clara chuckled. "I won't tell anyone if you do. My lips are sealed."

Piper grinned before snuggling down in her seat, reclining back, then spreading the blanket over herself.

Ranger watched as she flipped over and became a lump in the oversized seat. He shook his head, pulled a sports magazine out of his bag, and started reading. The three-hour flight would zip by at this rate.

An hour and a half later, Ranger rubbed at his blurry eyes. He'd gone through half a dozen articles, trying to learn more about the top players in the game. Opponents that he would soon face. While they never listed weaknesses, sometimes he could find players' preferences, which allowed him to predict their moves on the ice.

Rambunctious laughter drew his attention. He lifted his head to see Axel and Ivan jump up from playing cards, each with a bottle in hand, squirting water at one another. Not the first time those two got carried away on a flight. Probably not the last.

He tried to tune them out until they headed his direction at a fast clip. Ivan flung water at Axel, who jumped to the side, caught the edge of a seat and fell on top of Piper.

Piper screamed.

Not a scream of surprise, but one of terror. How he knew the difference Ranger couldn't say. Still, the bone-chilling sound brought him to his feet.

Axel scrambled to get up, dodging Piper's hands as she fought him. Her wide, frightened eyes and panicked response spoke of previous terrors buried in her past.

"I'm sorry, Piper. Shit. I'm sorry." Axel regained his feet and backed off to give her plenty of room.

Ranger glanced as the men gathered around, concern apparent on their faces at this latest development. He turned his focus to Piper and spoke softly to her. "Piper?

It's okay. The guys were just messing around."

Her chest heaved as if she'd just finished a dozen suicide sprints. Her hands trembled as she clutched her blanket to her chest.

A couple of beats went by before she closed her eyes and opened them once more. No longer did she appear in the midst of a nightmare. Instead, shame and embarrassment flashed across her pale face.

She wiped at her forehead and sprang out of her seat. "Excuse me." She bolted to the bathroom at the rear of the plane.

"What the hell was that about?" Axel stared in the direction Piper had gone. "A bad dream?"

"That was more than a bad dream. That was gut reaction." Adam leaned against one of the unoccupied seats.

"She acted like you were an ax murderer," Axel said. "Or a guy with a baseball bat about to beat her brains in."

Ranger listened to the conversation, trying to make sense of Piper's extreme reaction. His gut still clenched as a cold chill ran down his spine. Something in her past held the answer. That was for sure.

"Think her father hit her?" Adam asked.

"No way," Keith defended. "I've spent some time with her father. That man would sooner cut off his arm than hit his daughter."

"Not Gunther Darrow," Ranger agreed. "But maybe another man in her life. Or something else entirely. A collapsed structure trapping her underneath perhaps?" He ran a hand through his hair. "Something traumatic, that's for sure."

"Definitely some bad shit in her past. So bad that it stuck with her," Adam added quietly.

"How do you know?" Hagan asked.

"I was a psychology major. Spent some time at a homeless kids' shelter as part of a class project and helped out with some community outreach programs. I saw the same reactions there."

Silence reigned.

"Damn." Hagan ran one hand through his blond hair. "And I punched her when she got between me and Keith."

"Yeah, and she just about kicked your balls into your gut, too." Keith grinned then sobered quickly.

The door clicked. Piper exited the bathroom, her face lightly pink as if she'd washed it. Her eyes remained downcast as she slowly made her way back to her seat. "I'm sorry. I didn't mean to cause such a commotion." She lifted her gaze to look at the men almost sheepishly. "Please forgive me."

"Nothing to forgive," Keith reassured her before returning to his seat.

"My fault." Axel offered up an apology. "Promise. It won't happen again."

"It's okay. Really." Piper plopped back down in her seat. "Great. Now I upset the whole crew."

Ranger watched the other guys gradually return to what they were doing. He studied Piper closely, finding her still a bit unsettled. Wracking his brain, he searched for a way to put a smile back on her face. "Nah. They were just worried that Axel flattened you. Coach would have to list you as on injured reserve due to being pancaked by one hoss of a defensive man. Talk about a media storm to follow."

She peeked up at him from under her lashes. "That might be a bit complicated to explain, why he was on top of me, huh?"

"Oh, yeah. You know people. Their minds would drop into the gutter and come up with all kinds of ridiculousness."

"Well, we can't have that." Her voice sounded stronger. More confident.

"Nope. Because I'm sure your father would waste no time in catching a flight here and pummeling Axel for not only squishing you, but for trying to get all handsy in the first place."

She grinned slightly at that. "Oh, he would, too."

"That's what fathers do when it comes to their baby girls."

He paused and shrugged. "Or so I hear."

"Not speaking from experience?"

"Who? Me? No way. I might have been around the block a couple of times, but I guarantee I don't have any kids out there." He heard the bite in his tone and cringed. Now wasn't the time to get all wound up.

She blinked over at him. "Those puck bunnies, huh?"

"Yeah." He left it at that, picked up his magazine, and tried to find where he'd left off.

"I'm sorry." Her quiet words soothed him.

He glanced up. "Thanks."

Piper inclined her head, scrunched down in her seat and shut her eyes. He doubted she'd manage to fall asleep again before the plane reached its location.

Too bad. They had back-to-back games starting tonight. She'd need as much rest as she could get. Especially since their opponents were known for hard hits and physical play. Penalties were a given.

For the first time in forever, he wanted to soothe a woman. Hold her. Share a moment of time and quiet humanity while erasing the last of her fears. Keep her safe, warm and free of any more return trips to her traumatic past. The thought of her suffering in the slightest left a sour taste in his mouth. She deserved better and he'd do his damnedest to see that she would be treated with respect and a bit of pampering as long as the season lasted.

Her kindness extended to everyone she met. Even those she hadn't, as evidenced by her get well card to Gunderson. The gesture showed her caring side once again. And drew him closer, needing to bask in the light she exuded.

If they were alone, he'd pull her onto his lap, cuddle her against his chest and let her soak up his calmness. Hell, he'd snuggle with her for a short nap. The thought of spooning up behind her and enfolding her in his arms clicked in all the right places.

His libido sat up and took notice, too. He ignored it. For now.

Women were off his list. After being dragged down by deviousness, he wasn't keen on playing with fire again. Yet, Piper proved the exception to his rule. Given the opportunity, he'd gladly take a chance. Not just for a good time. No. Piper deserved more than a fling. She would be a commitment kind of woman.

Oddly enough, that word didn't send a wave of anxiety through him like it had before. Maybe, just maybe, the difference revolved around the little blonde sitting across from him. She could be the one.

If only he could find a way to get up close and personal without setting her off in a panic attack and a fight for her life. If she could return his interest and want to actually date a hockey player. If he could wave aside his newfound distrust of women and give her a fair shake. There were hurdles to jump. Some big ones along the way.

The question of how rang through his mind over and over. Yet, as hard as he thought about it, no answers appeared.

* * * *

The Devils finished up their morning skate and started to file off the ice. Ranger watched them go with interest, recognizing a few of the guys from previous teams or from having played against them now and again. A few of the younger players he didn't recognize at all, just the names on the backs of their jerseys.

"Darius!"

Out of the corner of his eye, Ranger saw Piper fly across the ice, sans her goalie gear, slowing down just enough before nearly throwing herself into the arms of a dark-haired man. As it was, he wobbled and slid a little on the ice, but quickly regained his balance enough to enfold her in his arms.

"Who's that?" Keith asked.

Ranger answered without taking his eyes off Piper. "Her brother."

"That's Darius Darrow?" Keith persisted. "The phenom that hit the big leagues right out of college?"

"Yep."

Piper talked a mile a minute, grinning like a kid at Christmas the whole time. Darius had the same wide smile on his face. Obviously they were close. Not always the case with siblings, from what Ranger understood.

Ranger lazily skated out onto the ice, heading for the pair. He slid to a halt beside Piper and studied Darius with a keen eye. "You must be Darius. Good to meet you." He held out his hand.

Darius shook it with a firm grip. "Ranger Deacon. I'd know you anywhere." He glanced down at his sister then back up again. "I hear you've been keeping an eye on her for us."

Ranger grinned ruefully. "Well, it's taking a whole hockey team to do that and keep her out of trouble. Too big of a job for one man to do."

"Don't I know it? *Oomph.*" Darius let out a breath as Piper elbowed him in the belly.

"I'm perfectly capable of flying on the straight and narrow. Heck, I've been doing an extraordinary job of it, too. The last thing I need is for some overgrown boys thinking they have to watch over my every move. No thanks."

Ranger chuckled at her haughty tone. "She's a handful all right."

"That's Piper for you."

"Darrow. Come on. Ice time is over. You can socialize after the game."

Piper pouted over at the coach.

The coach shook his head. "Not working, Piper."

"Well, drat." She turned back to her brother. "Sam's being cranky again."

"What else is new?" Darius waved at the coach. "Looks like I'm not supposed to be fraternizing with the enemy."

Piper sighed heavily. "I was hoping to hang out with you for a while. It's been months and I'm sure we have some catching up to do."

Darius pulled her in for a tight hug. "After the game, Piper." He released her. "Mom and Dad are coming, by the way."

Piper beamed. "They didn't tell me that."

"Well, they told me." Darius honked her nose. "Don't have a clue who they'll root for, but I think they mentioned going out to eat after the game."

"I'll double-check my schedule, but I believe we're here for two nights in the same hotel before catching a ride back home again."

"I guess I'll see you soon, then." Darius stared at her for another moment before fluidly spinning around and skating off.

Piper watched him go.

She missed her brother. Big time. Her face told the whole story. Ranger almost felt like a third wheel around them. Yet the fact that they shared such a tight bond offered hope. In this day and time, so much negativity existed. To see absolute love between people made for a sweet change.

The fact she knew Sam Stanton and probably the rest of the Devils' team came as no surprise. Most likely, she hung around after the women's league finished up for the season. Probably played in a few pick-up games with the guys as well. He could see why they'd like her. The same reason he did.

Well, hopefully not exactly the same. She needed more brothers than potential dates.

"I guess we should get this short workout under our belts so we can go back to the hotel and rest before the big game." Ranger nudged Piper when she didn't budge.

"Okay. Okay." Piper turned to face him.

He appraised her carefully. "You going to be good to play against them?"

Her lips thinned as fire flashed in her eyes. "Of course. Why would you think differently?"

He raised one hand at her snappish tone. "Just asking.

Sometimes players have a tough time focusing when they're distracted."

"I'm a professional, believe it or not. When I get out on the ice, I know my job and I do it." She got right into his face. Or would have if she'd been tall enough to do so. "Never question my loyalties, my willingness to take the ice, or my ability to focus." With a heated glare, she skated back to the bench area.

"Whoa." Rocky moved out of her way.

Ranger watched her go, noting the tension in each jerky body movement.

"That one has a temper," Sven said.

"Fiery. Those are the best kind." Axel grinned, his gaze locked on a retreating Piper.

Ranger bumped him in the back. "Hey. She's our teammate, not some puck bunny begging to be fucked. Respect her as such."

Axel shot him a look before heading to the other end of the rink.

"Thanks, Clint. You've done an excellent job. I'll have to tell Frank that you're giving him a run for his money."

"You do that." Clint chuckled.

Hearing Piper's voice, Ranger glanced her direction. Sure enough, she sat on the bench, strapping on her skates. Clint perched next to her, obviously checking on how the blades felt once sharpened.

As angry as Piper had been before, she now smiled sweetly at Clint, praising him for all his hard work.

Not every guy paid attention to the equipment manager. Some only said something when things weren't as perfect as they wanted. Piper, on the other hand, took the time to compliment Clint and make him laugh.

Her talent in life, it seemed.

Before she'd appeared, the men had growled, grouched and snapped at one another. An occasional fight had broken out in the locker room between teammates — something no one wanted to see. As the tension had ratcheted up, morale had plummeted. Then Gunderson had gone out, ending all hope for their season.

With the chips down and no one remotely near happiness, enter Piper.

She treated everyone the same, no matter their status in life. From the waitress to the ton of staff surrounding the Wolfpack, to the upper echelon in coaching and management. Always a smile, pleasant and full of warmth. In the short time he'd known her, she'd never overlooked anyone. Probably one of the reasons the guys gravitated toward her and the coaches treated her like their own daughter. He'd both seen and heard how she'd helped a couple of the men out. A gentle touch, a nudge here and there, solid words of advice and comic relief. Piper provided something they'd been lacking the entire season—the glue that held them together as a unit.

He watched her chat with Clint, noting her beauty, knowing it extended deep inside as well. Something rare. Extremely rare. And damn desirable.

Absently, he considered asking her out. Then wondered if his teammates would pummel him for doing so.

With a bemused shake of his head, Ranger started gliding across the ice, warming up his legs for the practice ahead.

Tommy blew the whistle in order to get the short workout started.

Chapter Eight

Ranger returned to the bench, sat down and took a long drink of water. He was breathing hard after a double shift on the ice. He'd give credit where credit was due. The Devils were big, tough and fast. He'd had his hands full trying to keep the puck on his stick and entering the zone for a shot. More than once he'd found himself checked hard into the boards. Most of the hits, he placed blame on Darius Darrow. The guy knew how to blast a player into the wall. A skill most likely learned from his father.

Rolling his shoulders, Ranger watched as the Devils pushed the puck down to the Wolfpack zone and constructed a play. They passed a couple of times before setting up a screen in front of the net. The shot came from a sharp angle on Piper's glove side. She slid over, caught it on her way down and held on, ensuring the game remained tied late in the period.

The ref blew the whistle to stop play.

"Damn, she's good."

Ranger turned his head to see Rayovic staring with a semblance of awe on his face. "I guess once a goalie, always a goalie, no matter the league."

Rayovic shook his head. "It's different, from what Stanza has said. The men are bigger. The hits more aggressive. There's no stoppage of play when a player steps an inch in the blue paint. She has to learn the tendencies and preferences of a new team almost daily. Stanza gives us a huge printout, complete with pictures, every night. Not as big of a deal if you've faced these guys before. Going in cold, though. That's tough." Marek rubbed at his chin.

"She's small but quick. Shooters are challenging her in every hole. Despite the lack of bulk, she's stopping them. It's pretty damn impressive if you ask me."

"But can she hold up?"

Rayovic shrugged. "She's fierce. Got pounded in that first game more than most. She came back for more."

Ranger nodded in acknowledgment. Fierce. The word fit Piper to a T. 'Driven' came to mind as well.

He slugged some more water and watched as she fended off yet another puck, this one a laser to her stick side. She slapped it down, then prepared for a possible rebound.

Cool as a cucumber, too.

As much as the Devils hammered her with shots on goal, she didn't appear flustered. Instead she went about her job, sliding from side to side, hanging deep in the net while keeping her head up to see around men setting up shop just in front of her.

Tommy tapped Ranger on the shoulder. "Next shift is yours. First line goes out. Axel. Ivan. Go with them. We need to attack their end. If you get a shot, take it."

Ranger set the water bottle aside, stood up and waited until Keith stepped into the bench area. Climbing over the short wall, Ranger picked up the puck mid-stride. The line change had happened on both sides, giving him plenty of open space.

Glimpsing Rocky on his right, Ranger sped toward the net, waiting until the last second before passing the puck over. The motion drew the goalie to the side, opening up the net. Rocky slapped a bullet into the top corner.

"Yes!" Rocky skated by on one foot, fist pumping.

Ranger patted Rocky's helmet. "Nice shot."

"Great assist."

After a short celebration, they returned to the bench and took seats.

Tommy stood behind the bench, watching both the clock and the game at the same time. "They're going to pull their goalie. Penalty kill line will be up. As soon as you see the goalie leave the net, get out there."

Another two minutes passed before the goalie darted to the bench. A sixth player for the Devils darted out.

Ranger stood up as the penalty kill line hit the ice. With a one-man disadvantage, they were defensive specialists who knew how to protect the net.

The Devils sent the puck into the corner. Two players went after it. The walls shook with a hard check thrown by Ivan. He seized the puck, tried to send it down the boards, but the Devils intercepted it near mid-ice. They passed it, only for Axel to get a stick in on the play, breaking it up. The puck bounced over in front of the net.

Piper moved forward, cradling the puck on the tip of her stick. She shifted to her left, outside of the crease, progressed another few feet, lined herself up, then smacked a solid forehand right down the center of the ice. With no one in the center position, the puck skirted the full length of the rink before gliding into the net at the other end.

Mouths fell open.

Ranger couldn't believe what he'd just witnessed. Goalies rarely scored. Hell, they weren't allowed to cross the red center line. The chances of getting a puck through a traffic jam and into an empty net at the other end were astronomical. Yet she'd done just that.

The bench exploded in celebration.

Piper pumped her stick a couple of times, met the other guys presently on the ice, then calmly returned to her area.

Even the opposing crowd applauded her success. Unheard of.

"Way to go, Piper!"

Ranger turned to spy her parents in nearby seats, on their feet and clapping enthusiastically. Gunther Darrow sported a proud grin. Ranger could almost hear him saying, "That's my daughter."

"Did you see that?" The voice came from the stands just above the bench.

"She just scored. I can't fucking believe it," one of the

guys on the bench said.

Men all around Ranger shook their heads in thrilled amazement and marked disbelief.

Ranger couldn't wipe the smile off his face. The final buzzer blew and still he grinned like a kid at the candy store.

He followed the other players back onto the ice, joining the long line to congratulate the goalie, as was traditional in any win. However, this one was special.

Piper had removed her mask and placed it next to her water bottle. She grinned as one Devil after another came over to congratulate her on such a rare achievement. Classy, since it had been scored against them.

Darius pulled her into a hug. He ruffled her hair, said some words, then headed toward his bench.

Finally, the Wolfpack had their turn. Normally the guys would bump fists with Piper or even pat her on the shoulder. Today, hugs were the name of the game. Not something one saw much of in the professional men's league. Just another change since Piper had appeared on the scene.

Ranger pulled her against his chest. "Hell of a shot."

She squeezed him for a moment before easing back to peer up at him. "Thanks. Nice assist earlier. Rocky owes you dinner. "

Ranger grinned, seeing the joy reflected in her eyes. "I think you about gave Tommy heart failure with that shot on goal."

Piper snickered. "Yeah, I expect a stern lecture from him and Stanza both on the proper way to handle a puck in such a situation."

"No guts, no glory," he replied.

"Yep." She collected her water bottle from the top of the net and tucked her mask under her arm. Only then did she head toward the bench, applause greeting her every inch of the way.

* * * *

94

"You've lost weight." Darla sighed as she tugged at Piper's slacks, which were looser than normal.

"It's a tough schedule. Longer and harder than in the women's league," Piper answered. "I'm eating, trust me. The team keeps snacks around all the time for us."

"Well, I'll send some homemade fudge with you just the same. Dessert now and again is good for you." Darla smiled.

Piper didn't bother to argue. "You know your fudge is the best. I'll have to fight the guys over it if they get a single whiff."

"Speaking of, how's the team treating you?" Gunther asked after forking a piece of chicken.

"Really good, actually." Piper took a sip of her water. "They were hesitant at first, but they're coming around to the idea."

Gunther stared at her as if trying to read the truth in her expression.

"I'd say she has a few protectors. Namely, Ranger Deacon." Darius dropped a bite of food into his mouth and chewed.

Piper cut her brother a look.

"Ranger Deacon? That big power forward?" Gunther asked.

"He's the captain of the team, Dad. He watches over everyone as well as keeps us in line."

"Uh-huh."

Piper implored her mother for help. Darla grinned and tossed out another question. "Found one that might make the grade for boyfriend material?"

Piper choked on her water. "Mom!" She patted her mouth with her napkin, cleared her throat and took another long drink.

Gunther looked at Darius. "Deacon, you say?"

"Yeah. He was right on her heels at the morning skate when she came over to give me a hug. All guard dog-like the way he stood there beside her." Darius took a bite and swallowed. "Maybe he was just curious, but I sensed if I'd have gotten out of line, he'd have had no problem punching me in the face."

Piper's cheeks grew hot. She drank more water in an effort to cool off. No such luck. As long as her family stuck to this particular topic, she'd be burning up with embarrassment.

"Hmm. Protective. That's a nice start." Darla grinned at Piper.

Piper rolled her eyes. "Stop it. All of you. There's no budding romance. We're just teammates. For another few weeks. That's it. Period."

Her shoulders slumped at the knowledge that sooner rather than later this whole journey would end. Despite the endless schedule, the practices, the traveling thousands of miles, she was having the time of her life. Surrounded by men, no less. *Go figure.*

Months ago, if someone had told her that she'd be on one very long trip with forty-plus men in tow, she would have recommended they check themselves into the nearest psych ward. Now she rode the crest of her opportunity. She stumbled now and again, but could honestly say the overabundance of men made her feel sheltered, guarded and important. They fell into the role of brothers quite easily.

All except for Ranger. She didn't see him as a brother. *Uh-uh.* He was too sexy, sensual and wicked for that label.

She glanced up to find everyone staring at her. Again. *Just great.* Piper cleared her throat. "Let's go back to talking about my goal. I like that topic better." They'd all congratulated her, praised her and wowed over the rarity of the event. Then, in politeness to Darius, let the matter slip away. Piper hadn't minded. Until now.

Both her parents frowned at the suggestion. Darius leaned over to her. "Personally, I'd rather stick with your impending love life."

She sighed. Some days she couldn't win. "There's no 'impending' about it. I'm not looking for a boyfriend. I'm looking to help the team's overall record." *I'm lying through my teeth. If Deacon asked me out, I'd stumble over my own feet in an attempt to hurry up and say yes.*

He'd been there for her. Supported her even in the beginning. Always kept an eye out for her. While he might do that for others, she knew he did more so for her. And not just because she was a woman. There was more to his looks than just the casual curiosity of a teammate. His eyes burned at times, drawing her in like a moth to a flame.

For the life of her, she didn't have the desire to pull away.

"Keep telling yourself that. It didn't work for me when I met your father. I doubt it will work for you now." Darla pinned Piper with her gaze. From what Piper recalled about her parents' courtship, Darla had played against him growing up as kids. They had gone their separate ways in college, only to reunite when playing professionally in the same city. Since the women's league was still in its infancy, Darla had been one of the founding players. Darla always said Gunther had pursued her, worn her down and finally convinced her to give them a try. Personally, Piper thought the whole event was more an equal balance of one chasing after the other, then switching roles for a short time. That seemed much more likely than her father stuck with love at first sight and pining away for years.

Her father didn't know the meaning of pine. If he wanted something, from a woman to a puck, he went out and got it. Stubborn determination and romantic gestures had won her mother's heart. Not endless sonnets, flowers and mushiness.

"But Daddy is different." Piper argued the same thing she and her mother had waged over the past few years. Darla wanted her to jump in the ocean otherwise known as dating, find a nice boy and take a chance on love. Piper preferred to stay safely on the banks, well away from any sharks that might be patrolling.

"How will you ever know if you don't try?"

Her mother's safe advice left Piper mute. She had no

rational facts to counter with. Unfortunately. "I know. Let's hear about Darius' latest conquests."

Gunther eyed Darius. "Deacon, huh?"

Darius grinned like the cat that caught the canary. "Yep."

Piper kicked at her brother under the table, only able to land a glancing blow. "Stop helping."

He snickered. "Why? It's so much fun."

"Payback, brother. Just remember that." Piper slumped in her seat and started eating as if starved. She couldn't be expected to talk with her mouth full, after all.

Chapter Nine

Piper left her hotel room and made her way down to the lobby. She'd had breakfast, attended the morning skate and now trolled around trying to decide what to have for lunch before hopping on the bus. Two hours away they'd unload and get ready for another night game. Back-to-back game nights. *Ugh.* Luckily, that didn't happen too often.

After the game, they'd board the private jet and head back home for a couple of days off before the next series. As much as she liked the idea of home, she'd almost rather hang out with Darius for another day or so. Normally at this time of year she did. Since both of them had team obligations, plans had changed. They'd just have to aim for the off season instead.

That is, if she ever forgave him for tossing Ranger's name out in front of their parents.

She stepped outside into the warm winter sunshine, glanced up and down the street and tried to decide whether she wanted to eat at the hotel restaurant or take her chances elsewhere.

"Thinking about lunch?"

The familiar voice had her spinning around. Ranger ambled over to her, dressed in jeans and a sweatshirt. With the warm temperatures in southern California, no one had to wear a heavy winter coat. Returning to Denver would be soon enough to bundle up like an Eskimo.

She smiled up at him. "Yeah. Kind of. Any recommendations?" Since he'd been in the league a few years and been traded a couple of times, presumably he'd found some quality eating places during his travels.

"Depends on what you're looking for." He pulled out his phone and scanned through some lists.

"I'm not picky. Just something that will get me thought tonight's game." She edged closer, curious to see what information he was quickly reading through.

"A buddy of mine owns an Italian restaurant."

"Sounds good."

He grinned down at her. "My treat."

Piper frowned. "Nope. I can pay my own way. Besides, it's not like this is a date or anything."

He stared at her for a long moment as if trying to figure something out. "What if it was?"

Off balance with his unexpected question, Piper blinked at him. "You're asking me out on a date?"

"If so, would you say yes?"

She tried to keep up with the volley of questions. Biting her lip, she debated how to respond. As much as she wanted the hunky captain to take her out, she didn't dare appear too eager. Still, opportunities often didn't present themselves twice. "Yes." She peered up at him through her eyelashes.

His smile widened. "Then, date, let's get a move on." He held out his arm.

Piper took it, letting him lead her to a waiting taxi. After she scooted in, he followed suit, telling the driver the address in the process.

A few minutes later, they entered a quaint establishment with tasteful Old World décor. Booths and tables lined the walls while a few filled in the empty spaces in the center. Up front, the kitchen area bustled with activity. The delicious aroma alone made her stomach growl.

"This is great."

Ranger peered down at her. "Wait until you try the food. It's the best."

A hostess greeted them, grabbed a couple of menus and led them to a table in the back corner. She settled them in before walking off to get their drinks.

"Ranger Deacon. How the hell are you?"

A tall man with sandy blond hair, dressed in business casual, approached the table, a wide smile on his face. He stuck out a hand, which Ranger shook immediately.

"I'm good, Terry. How's business?"

"Not bad. Not bad at all." Terry spared Piper a glance then turned back to Ranger. "I hear you have a woman goalie taking Gunderson's place. How's that working out?"

Ranger shared a look with Piper. "Very well. She's great."

Terry eyed Piper with curiosity. "Where are my manners? Terry Masters. I own this establishment." He held out his hand once again.

Piper shook it. "Piper Darrow. That woman goalie you mentioned."

"Uh-oh. Stuck my foot in my mouth again, I see. No offense intended."

Piper grinned at the guy's sheepish expression. "None taken."

"Terry and I played college hockey together," Ranger explained.

"We always knew he'd make it to the big leagues one day."

"We?" Piper asked.

"Yep. All the college guys had bets going on which round he'd be taken." Terry beamed. "I won, by the way."

"Terry. Can I borrow you for a minute?" A woman's voice called him back.

"Be right there." Terry patted Ranger on the back. "I need to get back to work. It's good seeing you again."

"You too."

Terry focused on Piper once more. "From everything I've seen, you're holding your own out there. Pretty damn impressive."

Piper's face warmed as if standing in front of an open oven. "Thank you."

Terry dipped his chin, turned, then sauntered away.

Their waitress returned in his wake. "Have you decided

yet?"

Piper glanced at the options once again. "Spaghetti with meat sauce, please."

"I'll have the same."

"Very well." The waitress collected their menus and hurried off to turn in their order.

Piper took a long drink of her water. "I'm confused. Does Terry think I'm doing well or does he think you're saddled with a one gigantic publicity stunt of a mess?"

Ranger met her eyes. "The majority of the guys were skeptical at first. Now I think you're making a believer out of them. The more you show what you can do, the more the rest of them will fall into line. The same with our team."

She knew he answered with the truth. Their actions spoke loudly to her. Most were civil now, if not somewhat friendly. Still, they had a ways to go before she'd say they were close. Ranger had been the exception. He'd supported her from the start. Which brought up that all-important question. "Why have you been so welcoming? I know the men feel like I've invaded their prestigious man cave. But you've never treated me like an outsider."

He took a sip and set his glass back down. "I've been the outsider. It sucks. People eye you like they can't decide if you're worth the money. Or even worse, wondering if you'll turn on them at the first face-off." He paused. "How and why people are placed on the roster is out of our control. We have no real choice in where they're traded. Neither do we on who else gets added to the team. So the way I see it, we might as well make the best of things for the duration."

Piper nodded. "Thank you for doing that. It would get awfully cold and lonely out on that branch by myself at times."

"Sure." He tilted his head and studied her. "What made you accept the offer to play for us?"

"The challenge, mostly. To be the first woman to break down some barriers. I thought maybe I could help earn women's hockey more respect from the guys and the fans alike." She shrugged. "It was a once in a lifetime opportunity. I just want to hold up my end of the bargain and not let anyone down."

"You're doing just fine. Not everyone could have stepped into that role." Appreciation lit up his eyes.

"Thanks."

Their food arrived. Piper dug in, not starved, but knowing she needed the carb load in order to have enough energy to get through the game. Especially after playing last night. "This is wonderful." She closed her eyes and savored the rich, spicy taste.

"Told you so."

She opened them again to find Ranger looking at her with a hefty dose of amusement mixed with longing. "Yes, you did. Remind me to never doubt you."

His expression reflected pride and determination. Along with something else she couldn't quite identify. "I'll make sure you have no reason to." The softy spoken words surrounded her in warmth.

Unsure what to say, she worked on eating her meal. The silence proved more companionable than uncomfortable, making for a nice, peaceful outing for a change. Before she knew it, her plate had been nearly cleaned. Same for Ranger, who ate like he expected a lengthy, hard-fought game tonight. Such seemed to be the story every game night.

Piper finished eating first, leaving part of her meal untouched. Stuffed, she decided she'd have to nap on the way to their next location in order to digest. "I'm full."

"It'll get you through tonight." Ranger finished his drink. "What was it like growing up with Gunther Darrow as a father?"

Piper grinned. "Amazing. Fun. Lots of lectures." She thought back to all the times her father had scolded her, but had always made a point to explain why. In detail. "He and my mother are like newlyweds, I swear. They still play, chase one another around the house and snuggle on the couch. It's wonderful to see their happiness." She wiped her hands on the napkin. "One of the things I can say is there's no shortage of love with them."

"Your mother was a goalie, too, right?"

"Yep. Initially I wanted to be a forward, like Dad. Mom convinced me otherwise. I still had plenty of lessons on puck control and shooting. I can still take my brother on, either as a forward or a goalie." She grinned.

"Who wins?" Ranger asked.

"It's a draw most of the time. He's bigger, but I'm faster. As a goalie, I have his number, though."

"I see where you get your competitive nature from. With both parents playing professionally, you and your brother were set up as prodigies from the start."

Piper sipped her water. "Yeah. It's really all I ever wanted to do. My parents made hockey look like the best life ever."

Ranger tilted his head. "You don't think it is?"

"Nothing is perfect, but it's pretty close." She offered up a small smile. "What would you be doing if you weren't playing hockey?"

Ranger tapped his chin with steepled fingers. "Good question. I was a health and wellness major in college. I guess I'd be doing something along those lines."

"Such as teaching classes or getting people to go out and exercise?" The idea fit with what she knew of Ranger. Laid-back, quick to smile, competitive and supportive. He'd do well motivating others.

"Maybe. I'm not sure. Haven't thought about it much since hitting the pros. Down the road, when I retire, I might look at it again."

"How about coaching hockey?" She could see him in that role, easily. Just like her father.

"I'm not sure. They take a lot of guff from upper management. Dealing with the team isn't bad. Dealing with the powers that pull puppet strings could be."

"Yeah. I think that might be one of the reasons my father hasn't accepted any coaching offers. He likes to do things his way. That might not gel well with what the guys writing the paychecks would like to see."

"Always a possibility."

The waitress dropped off their bill. Ranger opened up the small booklet and grinned.

Intrigued, Piper tried to peer at the paper from across the table. "What is it?"

He held it up and showed her. "For old time's sake," she read out loud.

"Terry must be in a generous mood today."

Ranger grinned. "Probably." He pulled money out of his wallet and placed it in the holder anyway. "Got a pen?"

"Yep." She dug one out of her purse and handed it over.

After scribbling on the ticket, he handed it back.

"What did you write?"

"Nothing much. It's just an inside joke." He scooted out of the booth and stood up.

"Uh-huh." Piper dropped the pen back in her purse, stood up and placed the strap over her shoulder.

Ranger started toward the exit.

"Come back again. And bring the big gorilla with you," Terry hollered from the back.

Piper laughed. "I'll see what I can do."

Ranger snorted, then placed a hand at her back to guide her out.

She stepped into the fresh air and warmth of the afternoon sun. California had it easy this time of year.

"Where to now?"

She checked her watch. "Not much time. Probably back to the hotel, double-checking the bags, then catching the bus." She focused back on him. "What did you have in mind?"

"This." He closed the distance between them, turned her back to the brick wall of the restaurant, and wrapped his arms around her. For a second, he stared down at her before lowering his head to seal his lips over hers.

Gentle. Seductive. Delicious. Piper felt their lips connect and cling. She placed her hands on his shoulders, adjusted the angle and waited for his lips to return. They did so, providing lazy sensuality which made her stomach flip delightfully. Heat rushed through her veins as Ranger opened his mouth, licked at her lips, then languidly thrust forward to plunder.

Piper gave back in return, albeit a bit shyly. She tapped his tongue and took advantage of the opportunity to slip in and get a taste of him. Pasta sauce and all man. The combination sped her pulse.

All too soon, Ranger eased back to look down at her.

Piper licked her lips and missed the contact already. "Wow."

A proud smile creased Ranger's face. "You can say that again."

She grappled for words. "Spaghetti makes you horny, huh? I'll have to remember that."

He chuckled. "I'm pretty sure it's not the spaghetti." Hailing a cab, he opened the door for her and climbed in next to her. After telling the driver to take them to the hotel, he turned back to Piper.

The brilliant color of his green eyes lit up and the grin on his face that flashed dimples all made her melt.

I have to be careful or he'll steal my heart.

And would that be such a bad thing?

She had no answer.

Chapter Ten

The goon in front of her threw an elbow, hitting her square in the face and sending her tumbling to the ground. *Shit.*

Piper adjusted her mask and stood back up. The ref had blown the whistle and led the offender away. Finally. They'd laid off on calling penalties from the start, setting up the game as a nearly out of control beating—for her as well as the opposing goalie. Retaliation was in full swing.

Not the first time one of the Rattlers had knocked her around. Probably not the last.

At least they live up to their namesake. Lower than snakes, if she were to be truly honest. Every cheap shot had been used. She'd taken the brunt, although the rest of the team had plenty of their own. Personally, she'd been poked at with sticks, brushed by wide shoulders and had had her crease invaded time and time again. Heaven forbid a rebound occur. Then the whole nest of vipers stormed her area in an attempt to knock something in. As much as her team tried to surround her and protect her, they couldn't be everywhere at once.

She watched as one of the Rattlers smashed Rocky hard into the boards, knocking him down, then dashed off with the puck. Piper winced at the violent hit while keeping her eyes on the biscuit. Ranger zipped in, disrupted the pass and returned the favor by sending one of the opponents crashing to the ice.

Piper blew out a breath, stood up and waited for the battle to enter her area once again.

A period and a half yet to go. I'll make it somehow. I always do. She'd been in some rough and tumble games, especially the Olympics. Bruises and soreness were as much a part of the game as the ice under their feet. Her toughness had helped the US team secure a silver medal. A treasure in her collection.

Boy, did that seem like ages ago right now.

She took advantage of the short time out to get a much-needed drink of water. Taking a few gulps, she returned the bottle to the holder on top of the crossbar.

Keith skated up to her. "Hanging in?"

"Yeah." She sucked in some air. "No one told me they played dirty."

Keith grinned. "I thought everyone in the league knew that."

"Obviously not." She settled into position as the guys found their places for the face-off.

The Rattlers won, smacking the puck to a buddy, who sent a laser in her direction.

Piper slammed her skate against the left bar, blocking the puck from entering. It bounced off and back into the zone. She followed it as the opponent caught it on the tip of his stick, guided it around the back of the net and to the other side. Piper glided over to block her flank.

A powerful force slammed into her back, sending her hurtling toward the ice face first. Another player slid down feet first on his belly. She reached out with both arms to break her fall. Too late. She could do little more than put out an arm before she made contact. Right on top of the guy's skate.

She felt a strong fist hit her hard in the gut. No. Not a fist. The blade of a skate.

Breathing became nearly impossible. Even coughing plummeted off the list of her abilities at the moment. She could only stare down at the frozen rink and beat back the panic. The razor-sharp blades of skates had cut more than one player over the years. Some seriously. She recalled a couple who had been unlucky enough to have a skate tear open an artery in the neck and another guy who'd had his

Achilles tendon nearly severed. She struggled to remain calm and just focus on sucking in oxygen.

"Piper? Piper?"

A second later, someone flipped her over. She stared up into the worried eyes of Ranger and Rocky. One of them unsnapped her mask and set it aside.

Rocky waved his arm. Ranger kneeled down next to her. "You okay?"

She managed a squeak and cringed in pain as her lungs tried to expand once more.

"Let me through." The trainer dropped down next to her. "Where does it hurt?"

She gestured toward her stomach.

"She fell on a skate," Rocky replied.

The whole arena went quiet. Piper glanced around to find a circle of men surrounding her, all with concern written on their faces.

"Can you breathe?"

She snorted at that question.

Chester, the head trainer, pressed on her abdomen, then frowned. He lifted up her jersey where the material had been split in two. "Shit." He tunneled deeper through the lining of her protective gear, the gash allowing him to easily part the layers. Until he found the final one intact. "No blood that I can see."

She closed her eyes and sucked in air. A shallow breath, but a start. "Air…knocked…"

He nodded. "Let's get you inside and check you over."

Normally, Piper would protest. Today, she gladly accepted his decree.

He stood up and offered a hand.

"I've got her." Ranger shouldered him aside, bent over, slid his arms under hers and hefted her back on her feet. When she wobbled, he steadied her with an arm around the waist. "Still okay?"

"Yes." She leaned into his large body, needing the support right now. Her legs didn't want to cooperate and sucking in small amounts of air wasn't enough to take care of her needs. She tried for a deep breath and nearly doubled over from the pain. Pulling on her fortitude, she forced herself to remain upright, to keep skating forward. Never had she been carted off the ice and she refused to do so now.

Ranger half carried her, half escorted her to the bench. Players held the door open. When Piper tried to step up, she found herself cradled against Ranger's chest.

Piper peered up at him. "I can...do it."

Ranger met her eyes and shook his head. "I'm not putting you down until we're in the training room. The guys will be just fine without me for a couple of minutes."

Warmth flooded her heart. She felt like a princess being carried. Not necessarily gold stars in the toughness department, but at the moment, she didn't care. Ranger held her securely. Tenderly. Protectively. She found the combination compelling, touching and addictive.

From almost the first day, Ranger had impressed her as a force to be reckoned with on the ice. Big, strong, dominant. As the days passed, she had glimpsed the inner man and had liked what she saw. Now, in front of the world, he'd stepped up to the plate, caring for her as no one had before. Her heart melted.

Chester gestured toward the large padded table. "Set her down here."

Ranger did so, gently and effortlessly. "You okay?"

Piper wanted to tell him she could fly if he'd only cradle her once more. Instead, she smiled slightly. "I'll be fine...in a minute."

Ranger dipped his head once, studied her face, then swooped down to brush his lips over hers. He cupped her cheek and deepened the kiss for a brief moment before pulling back with a wicked grin on his face.

"Just call me Sleeping Beauty." She couldn't have picked a better time for Ranger to make a move. His affections infused her with energy and happiness.

He laughed.

The sound pepped Piper up and allowed her to push through the pain.

"Don't tell me that my kiss cured you."

She sat up a bit gingerly. "Okay. I won't tell you," she replied playfully. "But it's a lot better now."

Ranger glanced over at Chester then pinned her again. "You're one tough cookie, I'll give you that." He bumped her chin and treated her to a final peck. "I'll see you back out there." He strode away.

Piper watched him go with a longing, want and a hefty sense of rightness.

"Lay back so I can check to see if his kiss really did the trick." Chester's put-upon tone hit her as funny.

Piper laughed, then flinched as the movement caused discomfort. "Who knew that power forwards had such healing talents?"

Chester shook his head. "Yeah, who knew?"

Several minutes and one X-ray later, she no longer smiled. "I'm going back out there."

Tommy's gaze flicked from her back to the trainer.

"She's bruised those ribs, certainly. No fractures. Damn lucky that blade didn't cut through to her skin. As it is, one less layer and it would have."

Piper heard the frustration in Chester's voice. The gray-headed physician hadn't been thrilled with her joining the team. Old school. Probably raised where girls didn't play hockey. Still, that belief shouldn't affect his medical diagnosis.

Tommy sighed and eyed her skeptically. "Every time you get hit, it's going to hurt like the devil."

She lifted her chin. "Been there, done that. I survived then and I'll survive now."

His eyes narrowed.

Piper pulled out all the stops. "When I was six, my mother's boyfriend went on a rampage. He beat her to death then turned on me. I managed to call nine-one-one with a broken arm, a broken jaw and with the blows still coming."

Chester's mouth fell open. Tommy's face pinched.

"I've been playing hockey with boys my whole life. All of them wanted to knock me out of the game. No one has done so yet. And they're not starting now." She added firm determination into her voice.

Tommy blew out a breath. "Get her a flak jacket. Wrap her up. Do whatever you need to do in order to protect those ribs. I want her ready to go out in the third period." He turned to leave.

"Are you sure?"

Tommy paused, turned, and looked straight at Piper, still sitting in her T-shirt and game pants. "Yeah. I'm sure."

"Okay." Chester went to the door and hollered, "Clint. I need you pronto." While he waited, Chester hurried over to a trunk and started gathering up supplies.

"Thanks, Coach," Piper said sincerely.

He lifted a hand, then walked out of the room.

* * * *

Ranger jerked his head up as he heard Piper's voice increase in decibels. As the training room was adjacent to the locker room, that was no surprise. With the normal chatting and banging around of the players, the sounds would be covered. Muffled at the least. But the team had come in and sat down, busy drinking and taking in a quick snack as they awaited word about Piper's condition.

"When I was six, my mother's boyfriend went on a rampage. He beat her to death then turned on me. I managed to call nine-one-one with a broken arm, a broken jaw, and with the blows still coming."

Ranger froze. His raked the room, finding the other guys still. Their expressions ranged from sadness to anger, shock to pity. Adam, who'd guessed right on the plane, stared at the floor. Keith met Ranger's eyes, sorrow filling his gaze.

Pieces fell into place. The clouding up of her features when she'd mentioned being adopted. Her panicked reaction on the plane. Everything stemmed from horrible abuse as a child.

His stomach turned at the idea of what she'd experienced.

"I've been playing hockey with boys my whole life. All of them wanted to knock me out of the game. No one has done so yet. And they're not starting now."

He heard the strength in her voice. The power. The warrior-like mentality.

She'd taken one for the team. He'd be damned if he and the rest of the men let her down now.

Ranger checked off each player with a stern look.

Each one nodded in turn. They would battle. Just like Piper had and insisted on continuing to do.

The door to the locker room slammed shut. He saw Tommy round the corner, tried to read his stoic face, and failed. Worried, he sat down next to Axel and waited for what Tommy had to say.

"How is she?" Keith asked.

"Bruised ribs. She had the air knocked out of her and was roughed up a bit, but Chester is getting her padded up to play."

Relief washed over Ranger. He noticed the rest of the guys appeared to relax a degree or two at the news.

"We need to pick up the pace. A tied game doesn't help us in the least. We've got to be aggressive. Take shots. Don't second-guess yourselves and pass the puck along. We're too tight and conservative."

Tommy rattled on.

The door squealed open and shut again, with much less force than before. Piper, dressed in a new, pristine-clean, white jersey, stepped into the room.

All eyes turned to her, including Tommy's. He gave her a slight nod. "As I was saying, we have to take the pressure off our goalie."

Piper sat down on the end of the bench next to Ranger. She leaned over to whisper. "Did I miss anything?"

"Nope." He raked her over. If she hurt, he couldn't tell. He'd meant what he'd told her earlier about toughness. Some men Ranger had played with wouldn't have held up as well as she had or demanded to go back in. He'd already respected her. Now she simply amazed him.

* * * *

Adam took a shot, the puck banging off the goalpost and going wide. One of the Rattlers swiped at it, sending it skipping down her direction in order to clear the zone. She left her crease to collect it, and set it aside for one of the forwards to take.

"Look out!"

A split second later, something big and strong hit her square in the back, slamming her into the wall face first. "Umph." The force shook the boards and stole her breath. Again.

"Welcome to real hockey," the man snarled in her ear before someone else yanked him off.

The guys dressed in white surrounded her, keeping all others at bay. Shoving and pushing broke out. Cussing and insults were a given. A man's steadying hand grabbed one of her arms, helping to remain upright while tugging her away from the scuffle. She glimpsed a couple of men wearing black-and-white stripes stepping into the middle of the melee and blowing whistles to stop the ruckus before it got way out of hand. Several ticks went by before they were able to separate the teams and send the Rattlers back toward their own zone.

Damn. She straightened up and immediately felt the protest of injured muscles. *And I dreamed of being a forward in this league. How stupid was that*? Growing up, she'd so wanted to follow in her father's footsteps. Until she'd learned that women had their own league, where checking was a no-no and goalies ruled. After that, she'd soaked up everything her mother could teach her about the sport and the position. Her father had still contributed, quite a bit, actually. From him she'd learned about shooting the puck, angles and all the details that helped her read other players on the prowl around the net.

"You okay?" one of the refs asked as he stopped at her side.

"Did you get the license of the truck that ran over my ass?" She managed to get the words out despite the throb in her entire body.

The official grinned and shook his head. "You've got guts, lady." He skated off, presumably to tell everyone the ruling and speak to the coaches.

Checking in the back was outlawed, even if she happened to be a goalie outside the crease. He'd get a major penalty for the action. Although since there were less than two minutes left in the game, she didn't think that meant much. A possible fine coming down from the league might do the trick, however.

"Now, tell the truth. Are you really all right?" Adam asked.

She gave a slight nod. "It'll leave a mark. That's for sure. But I'm okay."

His frown didn't project belief.

Stretching, she made sure her arms and legs were still attached. Thankfully, that seemed to be the case. She might hurt, but everything seemed to be in working order.

"If it makes you feel any better, I think Tommy's about to blow a gasket."

Piper peeked over at the bench to find Tommy yelling at the ref. She winced. Yeah, the guy held partial responsibility for this debacle called a game, but still. Tommy didn't hold back when someone got his rancor up.

Play began once more. Piper shoved the discomfort to the back of her mind and focused on the goons crashing the net in an effort to score a cheap goal. After everything they'd put her through, she'd do just about anything to deny them.

Thankfully, she only had to deflect one shot. The other

went wide. After that, her teammates took the fight to the opponent, living in their end of the rink for the remainder of regulation. Axel managed to knock one in on a redirect, ensuring the lead for the last few seconds of the game.

The buzzer sounded, ending the game. It couldn't have come soon enough.

She didn't waste time hanging out. Instead, she met the guys halfway from the bench and allowed them to escort her the rest of the way.

Ranger appeared at her side. "You're hurt."

She shook her head, managing to juggle her glove, stick and bottle of water with the front of her mask flipped up to allow fresh air to help cool her down. "I'm fine. I just need to pee."

His mouth fell open before a slow grin followed. "You're the damnedest woman. I swear."

In a hurry, she handed over some of her gear. "Would you please take these for me? There's not room in the stalls of the staff restrooms for all my stuff."

He took the items before hanging a left back to the locker rooms. She paused to slip off her skates, knowing that walking on the cement wasn't a good idea. Clint worked hard enough on her blades without her damaging them on the unforgiving surface. With her skate guards back in the locker room, she had no choice but to run around in her socks. As soon as she stepped out of the footwear, she grabbed them up and jogged in the opposite direction from the one Ranger had taken, making a beeline for the lower-level restrooms.

One glance in the mirror had her grimacing. She'd carry some colors the next day, for sure.

After taking care of her business, she started to make her way back to the locker room. Turning a corner, she stopped, surprised to find Ivan leaning against the wall. She blinked at him. "What are you doing out here?"

"Making sure no fucking Rattler wants to finish what he started." Ivan's gaze raked the area.

His protective gesture warmed her heart. He hadn't always been a fan of hers, she knew that. Yet here he stood, ensuring she returned to the group without further issues.

Impulsively, she brushed her lips across his cheek. "Thank you."

Shock filled his gaze for a split second before the corners of his mouth curled up. "We look after our own." He pushed off the wall, took her skates from her hands and fell into step beside her.

He held the door open for her. She walked in to find the whole room go silent and all sets of eyes lock on her.

She squirmed under the scrutiny. "Sorry I'm late, but I had to pee. And, well, you know how it is." She waved her hand in the air. "Better late than never, right?"

A couple of men grinned at her.

"Hey, at least I arrived before you guys started stripping for your showers. That would have been…awkward."

Chuckles carried over the area.

Tommy cleared his throat. "You, young lady, have an appointment with the trainer. Now."

"Good grief. Again?"

"Yes, again."

She sighed dramatically. "That man has seen way too much of me already. The least he could do is give me a lollipop or something." She managed her best haughty tone.

Tommy smirked and pointed to the door. "Go."

"Yeah, yeah. I'm going. Before anyone decides to get naked."

She stuck her chin in the air and retraced her steps. A queen couldn't have done it any better.

The sound of laughter followed her out.

Chapter Eleven

"Did you see the knockers on that woman? Holy shit. I could get lost in those." Anthony, one of the forwards, pointed out the obvious to pretty much everyone within earshot.

Adam shook his head. "Biggest set of tits I've ever seen."

Ranger ignored them. After all, he'd heard it all before. He'd been guilty of saying the same thing not too long ago.

Piper walked up to the loading terminal, pausing to stop and listen.

Keith smacked Anthony on the arm and tilted his head toward Piper.

Anthony shut his mouth immediately.

She adjusted the strap on her carry-on. "Just ignore me and go ahead with your conversation. I find what men have to say about women fascinating."

Anthony's cheeks turned rosy. He gathered up his belongings and hurried down the loading ramp.

Ranger grinned. Without even trying, Piper had put the youngster in his place. Good for her. He made his way toward the plane, eager to get going.

He stopped at his usual seat, stored his bag above his head and sat down. Others boarded, pretty much filing in as usual. They'd done this drill so many times, Ranger knew they could load the plane in their sleep, probably had more than once.

Piper stepped on board and headed his direction. She glanced around, then stopped next to the seats opposite him. She gathered her bag and lifted to place it in the storage area, cringing in the process.

Ranger shot to his feet, stepped over and used one hand to shove the bag into the compartment.

"Thanks." Piper smiled gratefully up at him.

"No problem." He returned to his seat.

Piper plopped down in one of the oversized reclining chairs on the plane with a weary sigh. After a second, she shed her coat, tossing it over the back of the seat.

Ranger watched her with a critical eye. She moved well, but he knew soreness and stiffness had already begun to set in, as evidenced by her difficulty with the bag. Tough games left their mark. Literally. Again, he wondered how much more she could take.

Most goalies in the league were big, stout men capable of taking up much of the net just by their mere presence. Piper wasn't big or stout. In fact, she'd be small even for a forward. Presumably, she'd get knocked around much less as a goalie, but that hadn't been the case tonight. *Damn the Rattlers.*

Her phone rang. She dug through her purse and answered. "Hi, Dad."

Oh, boy. Ranger knew that had to be an interesting conversation. Gunther Darrow had a temper, though he doubted Piper ever saw it. However, if Gunther had been at the game, Ranger wouldn't have been the least surprised if Gunther had cornered the guilty parties for roughing up his baby girl and taken them to task. Just because the guy was retired didn't mean he'd let bygones be bygones.

Rocky ambled by, glancing at Piper before sitting down next to Ranger. "Playing guard dog?"

Ranger turned to see the cheesy grin on Rocky's face. "Someone needs to."

"I'm fine, Dad. Really. Look, the plane will be taking off shortly and I need to be off here." Piper continued to talk on the phone.

"Think old Gunther is fuming?" Rocky asked.

Ranger snorted. "I bet he's ready to throw punches. Deservedly so. You know those hits were intentional and not just because she's on our team."

"Yeah. Bastards. Some pricks just can't move past the Dark Ages."

"Bye, Dad." Piper hung up, lowered her phone just as it rang again. "Well, crap." She checked it, then answered. "Hey, Darius. Before you get started, yes, I'm fine." She rambled on.

Ranger shook his head. She needed time to decompress and just rest. Not deal with overprotective and angry men. At least that would stop soon. She'd have to power down her phone before the plane took off.

"At least we don't have games for a couple of days. Maybe she'll have a chance to work the kinks out before hitting the next one," Rocky said.

"Maybe. Something tells me that after tonight Tommy will be benching her for a game or two and letting Rayovic take a turn."

"Yeah, probably." Rocky snapped his seat belt on. "She's not going to like it."

Ranger recalled her insistence to return to the game. She'd wanted to so badly, she'd opened up and blurted out about her past. Something that every guy had unintentionally overheard. Piper had fortitude and more guts than half the guys playing in the league. Good on one hand, a detriment on the other. Even if she were truly hurt, he knew she'd play to the last buzzer. That stubbornness could end up making an injury much worse.

Yet all anyone could do was keep an eye on her, and pressure the opposing defense in order to keep the puck out of their own zone. By doing so, they could shield her from some of the hits. For one thing stood true—Piper was their key to turning the season around. If she went down, they'd be up a creek.

"We'll be taking off soon. Phones and electronics off now, please. Fasten your seat belts," Clara instructed over the intercom.

Ranger clicked his restraint together, absently noting that

Piper stored her phone in the pocket of her hoodie before fastening the straps.

A few minutes later, they were at cruising altitude and Clara announced they could roam, once again, at will.

Rocky headed toward a wide table surrounded by chairs, presumably to play poker with some of the other guys. Most of the others remained where they were, either listening to music or settling in for a long nap.

Ranger scooted over to the other plush seat right next to Piper. "Your family ready to declare war?"

Piper twisted to face him. "You have no idea."

"I'm sorry."

"It's okay." She rolled her shoulders. "It's a sign that they care."

"True." Ranger watched her try to limber up. "Want me to rub some of those kinks out? Those body slams will sure tighten a person up like a purse string."

She paused and stared at him for a long moment as if deciding. "That's asking too much."

He read the hesitation in her face and gave her a nudge of encouragement. "Nah. I don't mind at all. Just spin around and I'll see what I can do."

"Thank you." Piper did so, folding one leg under her and twisting around to present her back.

"Just let me know if I get too rough." He brushed her hair aside, placed his hands on her shoulders and started rubbing gently and slowly. The scent of vanilla wafted to him, reminding him of sugar cookies fresh out of the oven. "Nice perfume."

"It's my shampoo."

He took a deep breath. "It's a keeper."

Her initial tension receded quickly under his touch.

She bowed her head, allowing him to work on the tautness of her neck. "You have wonderful hands."

He smiled, enjoying the feel of her body under his fingers. Muscles began to ease with persistent caressing. He absently realized he hadn't given a massage to a woman in a very long time. Never something he truly enjoyed, this time proved different. Just as Piper's athletic body felt different from some of the thinner ladies he'd seen in the past, so did the whole experience, in general.

Lowering his hands, he worked up and down her spine, then bridged out over her shoulder blades. She winced as he rubbed over the left side.

"Sorry." He immediately abandoned the area. Without thinking, he reached for the bottom of her sweatshirt and lifted.

Piper fussed and squirmed, but not before he glimpsed a large, ugly, purple spot over that one side. *Bruised ribs my ass. More like the entire side of her body.* He returned to her shoulders. "That's one hell of a mark."

"It'll heal," she whispered.

He wanted to kick himself for being so bold and obviously making her uncomfortable in the process. For a long time he focused on the back rub, needing to give, to feel her relax under his care. Gradually she did, leaning toward him as she turned to mush. He resisted the great urge to brush his lips over her nape. With around thirty-plus other men on the same plane, chaperones were thick. Too thick to risk it. For now. As it was, a couple of the guys glanced over at him with expressions of curiosity and shit-eating grins. He'd hear about it sooner rather than later.

"You're putting me to sleep."

"That's okay. We have a couple more hours to go before landing. So you have plenty of time for a nap."

She turned back around in her seat and smiled softly. "Your turn first."

As much as he wanted her hands on him, he knew the resulting hard-on could make things a bit difficult for the rest of the trip. "Thanks for offering, but I'm good."

Her face fell.

He listed to whisper in her ear. "One day when we're alone, with no chance of interruption, I'll let you massage me for as long as you like."

Her lips parted as her pretty blue eyes darkened a shade. Understanding coated her face. "Umm…okay." The quiet words told him he'd caught her by surprise.

Always a good thing to keep a woman on her toes.

"I'm ready for that nap. How about you?" He reclined his chair.

"Yeah." She fumbled, finally found the latch, then lowered the angle of the seat back until she was almost flat.

After turning on her side to face him, she trailed her fingers down his arm. The light caress sent a small zing of electricity through him. "Thank you."

"You're welcome." He stared at her for a long moment before wiggling, getting comfortable and shutting his eyes. The scent of vanilla helped lull him into sleep.

* * * *

A couple of hours later, Ranger led the procession through the airport and out of the front exit.

Ranger held the door open, allowing Piper and several of the guys to exit the warmth of the airport and step into the blustery chill of Denver in February.

"Holy shit, it's cold." Alex set his suitcase down long enough to zip up his coat.

Another gust of wind sent a shiver through Ranger, despite his heavy winter attire. Spending the last few days in the warm desert and southern California had ruined him for this type of weather.

"Brrrr." Piper yanked on mittens she'd dug out of her pockets. "I should have worn my long johns instead of my silk panties. Frostbitten lady parts aren't sexy no matter what a girl is wearing."

Ranger grinned. The guys around him chucked and shook their heads.

Piper blinked up at them. "What? It's true."

"Uh-huh," Alex answered with a grin.

"Don't tell me you guys have insulated boxers?"

"Okay, we won't tell you." Ivan started forward to meet the team bus pulling up to deliver them from the airport back to their home arena, where they'd left their cars. They could have parked with everyone else at the airport, but the team offered the perk of allowing them to leave their vehicles in the parking garage at the facility under security and watchful eyes for the duration of the time they were gone. Thus, they didn't have to worry about arriving back from a game at two a.m., like tonight, and having to dig their cars out of a foot of snow. Something Ranger was personally thankful for.

"Why isn't he a walking snowman?" Piper gestured to Ivan.

Ivan paused. "Ever hear of Siberia?" His Russian accent carried through.

She nodded.

"That's home for me."

Piper's mouth fell open. "You intentionally live there?"

He laughed. "How does one unintentionally live there?"

"I don't know. Maybe the plane was going down, so people had to parachute out? With the blizzard outside, they had no choice but to set up house?" She bit her lip.

Ivan grinned. "Nope."

Piper turned to Ranger. "He's tougher than the rest of us put together."

"Yep," Ivan agreed.

She snorted. "You weren't supposed to hear that. I don't want to be responsible for making your head any bigger."

"Too late." Ivan stepped on the bus.

The rest of the team followed. Ranger brought up the rear. He headed toward the back, found an empty seat and took a load off. At least someone had had the foresight to crank the heater before arriving. He soaked up the wonderful warmth.

The short trip proved uneventful, especially with the streets near empty at that time of night. As soon as the bus parked in the garage near their vehicles, Ranger stepped off. He paused long enough to collect his belongings from the storage area, patiently waiting for others to do the same.

Piper picked up her duffel bag and suitcase, spun, and started to walk down the long line of cars. Ranger quickly moved abreast. "It's late. I'll be glad to drive you home."

She shook her head, sparing him a glance. "Thanks, but no thanks. This isn't the first late-night return from a game I've had to deal with."

He opened his mouth then quickly shut it back before he said something he'd regret, like accidentally stomping on her independence nerve. They'd grown closer this trip, he knew it, and wasn't prepared to chance that feeling fading due to distance. He ran the schedule through his mind. "We have a team meeting and workout in the afternoon. Nothing before. So you want to have an early lunch with me?"

Piper's strides slowed a bit. He decreased his to compensate.

She peered up at him, a slow grin appearing on her full lips. "Okay."

He smiled. "How about I call you? Around late morning?"

"Works for me." She looked at him a beat longer, then closed the distance to her SUV. He watched her out of the corner of his eye as she loaded her stuff into the back before hopping into the driver's seat. While the vehicle wasn't ritzy, it fit her — tough and prepared for just about anything came to mind.

She started the engine, backed out, then waved as she drove off.

Until tomorrow. He tossed his stuff into the back of his SUV, climbed in, cranked the engine and set a course for home, happier than he'd been in a while.

Chapter Twelve

"So what do you think of this place?" Ranger asked as he cut up another piece of sausage.

He'd picked her up from her apartment shortly before and driven them to his favorite restaurant that served breakfast all day long. Despite the clock showing nearly noon, they had loaded up on all the morning favorites.

"It's delicious." She forked another piece of pancake. "I've lived here for years but never been here before. Obviously I've been missing something." She took the piece off her fork and chewed.

"Yeah. One of the former Wolfpack introduced me to it when I first arrived. I've been coming here ever since."

She took a sip of her juice, studying him over the rim of her glass. "You've never mentioned your family."

"Not much to mention. I'm an only child. My parents still live in Minnesota, where I was raised."

"The land of hockey." Piper smiled as she placed her glass back on the table.

He grinned. Memories of skating on frozen lakes ran through his head. "Pretty much. Everyone in my area played. Even the smaller cities managed to have rinks. Peewee games through high school. The colleges had their own as well. Then you step up to the minors and pros. Hockey is an obsession up there."

"I bet you have several friends from there that came into the pros."

"A few." He shrugged. Some of the guys from his region had made it to the big league along with him.

He finished his eggs before taking a large drink of milk.

She ate for a couple of minutes in silence. "About half the team is married. Why aren't you? I know you have lots of women to choose from."

The personal question only mildly surprised him. Since they were on another casual date, he'd figured they'd come eventually. And rightly so. He found admitting his past a bit difficult, but forced himself to tell the whole story. "I used to be one of the playboys. A new girl every night. Took advantage of what opportunities were given me with a dozen beautiful puck bunnies hovering around all the time."

She stared at him with curiosity. No censure. He only hoped her opinion of him wouldn't plummet.

"A while back, I received a court summons. Some woman that I didn't really remember claimed I was the father of her kid."

Piper's eyes widened.

"I wasn't. I knew I wasn't. Still, I had to demand a DNA test, go to the lab and let them take a sample from me." He wiped his fingers on his napkin. "The tests cleared me. Just another case of some woman trying to trap a guy because he has money."

"I'm sorry. I've heard of that happening way too much. A nightmare for some of the pro athletes in particular." Her quiet voice helped restore calmness to his unsettled emotions.

"After that experience, I've been turned off by those women. They're annoying and infuriating. I'd rather they go hound someone else."

"Totally understandable." She lifted her gaze from her plate back to him. "If women are off your to-do list, then how do you explain me…us?"

He grinned slightly. "Because you're the exception in so many ways. Complete opposite of those women. To be honest, you're a breath of fresh air. One that I find interesting and compelling."

She smiled ruefully. "You just haven't seen me on a bad

day, yet."

"I have a feeling you on a bad day will still outshine every other woman out there."

"Just remember I have a large stick and know how to use it."

Ranger laughed then lowered his voice to a whisper. "So do I." He waggled his eyebrows for effect.

Bright pink splashed across Piper's cheeks. The flushing only added to her beauty.

"It's been a long time since I've been around a woman who still blushes."

She patted her mouth with the napkin and peeked up at him from under her eyelashes.

"I like it," he added truthfully.

"Do you ever blush?"

He shook his head. "Nope. Hanging around with the team for a while will take that out of a guy. If he even had it to begin with."

"So they do get raunchy. I never doubted it. Hopefully not too much worse than I've already heard, though."

"Yeah. At times they can." He finished his drink. "Don't the women get like that, too?"

Piper shrugged. "Now and again. Mainly it's telling of their favorite position in bed or their latest sexcapades."

Unable to resist, Ranger went with the flow. "So tell me, what's your favorite position?"

She squirmed in her seat. The heightened coloring returned in force. "I don't have one."

"You don't?"

"Nope."

He studied her for a long moment. Instinct told him her experience had to be limited. The innocent aura she put off. The occasional blushes. The slow pace they were moving in this new relationship. Recalling her past, he revisited his thoughts. "If this is out of line, tell me."

"Okay."

"Have you ever had sex?" He waited with bated breath

for her answer.

"No." She lowered her chin.

He barely heard the whisper. No matter. He easily read her lips on the single word.

A sense of rightness clicked into place along with a fierce protective and possessive streak he'd never known he carried. Patience followed. Given the chance, he'd gladly lead her into sensuality with a gentle hand.

"You're one of a kind, Piper."

She lifted her head and met his gaze. "You don't think I'm some kind of recluse or prude or worse?"

"Absolutely not." He reached across the table and interlaced his fingers with hers. "You're an incredibly smart woman who refuses to give in to society's pressure. You know what you want and won't settle for less. That's to be admired, not criticized."

"Not everyone shares your view."

"Probably not. But I'm smarter than the average bear."

A small smile formed on her lips.

That's better. He hated that she seemed ashamed of her virginity. That would change. He'd ensure it.

"Don't men want seasoned pros in the sack for bedmates?"

"Some might. However, me and a hell of a lot of other men would beg to differ."

"Really?"

"Really." He squeezed her hand. "You don't see it, do you?"

Her eyebrows furrowed in confusion. "See what?"

"The thought of teaching a virgin is the stuff of dreams and hot. Damn hot."

"Oh." Her eyes widened for a second.

"Yeah. Don't believe for an instant that men would turn you away. It's not true. They'd be thanking their lucky stars you chose them."

The tightness in her face softened. "You make me want to believe."

"It's true. Ask around if you want." He paused. "On

second thought, don't. I'd have to carry a broom around to beat the men away."

She giggled. "A broom, huh? Just like the wicked witch?"

"I didn't say a flying broom. Any old sweeping variety would work." He grinned.

Her eyes lit up, making her that much prettier.

Unable to resist, he cupped her cheek and tugged her toward him while leaning in. He brushed his lips over hers then kissed her sweetly. "Let me know if I need to swing by the hardware store."

She grinned against his lips. "Not right now. I think I only have eyes for you."

The words went straight to his heart. After all the turmoil and meaningless nights with women, he'd given them up for good. Piper had changed that. Because a diamond had been placed right under his nose and he was smart enough to take the hint.

* * * *

Ranger dropped his team duffel bag off in the corner of the weight room next to a line of others before lifting his gaze in search of Piper. They'd had a nice lunch, driven to the facility for the mandatory team meeting, then parted ways to change clothes in preparation for the workout session.

"Hey, Ranger. About time you showed up." Rocky slapped him on the back. He turned his head this way and that, obviously searching the room. "Where's your shadow?"

And the ribbing starts now. Ranger rolled his eyes. "Not here yet."

"Uh-huh." Rocky scratched his chin. "Just don't lose her. The guys might start to miss her."

"Yeah." Keith walked by. "Play nice with the pretty goalie."

"Who's playing with Piper?" Riley asked.

"Ranger. He was giving her a back rub on the plane. Thinks himself her guard dog," Rocky answered.

"I thought there was something between those two. As much as they stared at one another with those goofy expressions on their faces," Axel replied.

"Love is in the air." Adam waltzed around the room, humming to himself.

Laughter followed.

Ranger shook his head at their antics.

Piper entered the room, wearing a T-shirt and shorts. Nothing fancy, just loose and comfortable. Her long blonde locks had been captured in a ponytail, the pink scrunchie bright under the lights. He barely noticed as his focus drifted downward to her long, toned legs and an ass that would fit perfectly in his hands. Sexy didn't begin to describe her firm, curvy body in such attire.

All eyes followed her as she carried her bag over and placed it next to the others. She bent over, unzipped it, then screamed and jumped back as one of the other bags came to life.

Roars of laugher filled the room as Sven stuck his head out of the other bag and grinned like a Cheshire cat. "Gotcha."

Ranger got down with the rest of the team. Pranks were a part of the business. He chalked it up to too many hours together and too little entertainment. It also showed comradery, in a warped sense.

Piper huffed, growled and finally grinned good-naturedly. Then her smile turned evil. "Payback is hell, boys. Remember that." She gathered her towel from her bag, slung it around her neck and sauntered toward the far corner as if she owned the whole building.

Ranger made a mental note to lock up his clothes and keep a leery eye out for retribution. Though he hadn't had a part in this one, he wasn't sure that mattered to Piper.

He watched as she went through a series of stretches. When she bent over to touch the ground, her shirt rode up, showing off a white sports bra underneath. That didn't catch his eye nearly as much as the bruise he'd spotted yesterday. It traveled from her waist up and under the stretchy material. "Damn."

A couple of the other guys turned to discover what had drawn his attention. They stared soberly at the sight.

Piper stood back up, looked their direction and blinked. "What?" She turned this way and that.

"Nothing." Ranger headed toward the weight bench. "We're just not used to seeing a woman in here."

"Uh-huh. Anyone ever tell you that your left eye twitches when you lie?"

Some of the guys snickered. Ranger snorted. "Does not." He resisted the urge to check.

"Does so." Piper spun, her ponytail flying as she made a beeline for the free weights. Since the men's and women's team shared the same workout room at the facilities, he figured she had her own routine and regimen. Certainly, she knew her way around the place.

Ranger threw himself into his workout, pausing now and again to hydrate. Occasionally he glimpsed Piper as she made her way around the equipment. First weights, then cardio on the treadmill.

She might not equal the men in the amount of weight lifted, but she didn't slack, either. Not in the least. In fact, she could have kicked most of their butts in the cardio category. She didn't just run, she hit the stair stepper and the elliptical as well. Her shirt was soon soaked with sweat, showing off the outline of her sports bra underneath with ease. The material cupped her small breasts like a loving hand.

Ranger tried not to stare, but found himself checking her out often. Great for scenery, bad for his body, which began to heat as she went through the motions of her workout. More than once, he chided himself for the small torture, knowing a cold shower or ice down his pants would be coming right up if he didn't rein in his thoughts and growing arousal.

Most of the guys had finished by the time Piper turned off

the machine, stepped off, wiped her face with the towel and took a long drink of water.

Ranger, finished just before her, stood against the wall and watched.

Her eyes found his.

He approached her with confidence. "The guys are planning to go out to a club tonight. You want to come along?"

She tilted her head. "After the meeting?"

"Yeah. Probably get to the place around seven or eight."

She glanced around the room. "I won't be a third wheel or crimp your style?"

"No way." He grinned when she lifted her head. "We'll be the envy of all the guys there."

"Delusional." She nodded. "You might want to get that checked out." Piper started toward the exit.

Ranger chuckled and called after her. "So which is it, sassy? Going or not?"

She paused, turned, and offered up a grin. "Going. I'll be sure to wear my go-go boots."

His mouth fell open. "Your what?"

Laughter was his only answer as she left.

* * * *

Piper followed the handful of guys into the door of the establishment. Loud music greeted her, as well as flashing lights and the unmistakable aromas of alcohol, sweat and colognes. The nearly full dance floor held several young couples as they moved to the beat of the music. The men tended toward slacks while the women had pretty much corned the market on short dresses and miniskirts.

She'd chosen a bit more wisely — a longer dress that hung past her knees, and flats. No way would she halfway lame herself trying to pull off high heels for any length of time. Unlike many of the women already there who'd strapped on four-inch stilettos. A couple went even further and basically appeared to be walking on their toes.

Meat market central. She glanced at the upper level and at the fancy bar and tables. *Make that classy meat market central.* A definite step above most of the places she'd been to. Obviously the guys enjoyed life in the fast lane with some luxury tossed in.

She ventured farther, noting the lustful looks many of the woman aimed at the guys. A couple of the bolder ones licked their lips before hopping off bar stools and making a beeline for them.

Piper shook her head. She could see how this kind of attention could spoil a guy, give him a big head and make him think he was the next best thing to a sex god. Axel and Rocky seemed to soak it up as they greeted the ladies and led them deeper into the room. Anthony, obviously the lucky one, ended up with a woman on each arm.

Out of the corner of her eye, she watched Ranger. He approached the bar, asked for a drink, then sat down on a nearby bar stool. A woman approached him, said some words, then left with a frown. Piper recalled his frustration and disgust at the puck bunnies following him around and hounding him even in hotels. That philosophy seemed to carry over to clubs as well.

The fact intrigued her.

Nice to know Ranger followed through with his own rules.

"Would you like to dance?"

Piper spun around to find a blond-haired man dressed in khaki pants and a button-down brown shirt. He smiled encouragingly at her.

"Sure."

He reached for her hand. She intentionally withheld it, not really wanting to touch a guy, especially one that she didn't even know his name. He took the small rejection in stride, found an empty spot on the floor, and started to groove.

Piper sidled up in front of him and started moving to

the beat. She didn't dance much, although her mother had insisted on lessons as a kid. They'd helped with her flexibility and grace on the ice, so Piper had never complained.

Now they paid off. Marginally. She didn't feel like a fat penguin trying to keep up with some of the better groovers at least.

"You're good at this, beautiful."

"Thanks." She had to basically shout to make herself heard above the racket.

Out of the corner of her eye, she glimpsed Rocky sitting at a far table with a pretty redhead perched on his lap. *Looks like he won't be sleeping alone tonight.*

For the life of her, she never could understand a man's attitude toward loose sex. To take a stranger home of all places, strip down, have decadent sex then shoo her away the next day. Not knowing how many other people the girl had been with. The risk of diseases, although she figured the guys always kept condoms handy and used them. What about the basic attitude of another person lying in the bed linens? Right after being out. Whatever happened to cleanliness and hygiene?

The whole idea boggled her mind.

The song ended and a slow one began.

Her present partner reached an arm around her and tugged her close.

Piper pulled out of his hold. She hissed air through her lips and tamped down the urge to hit him in the nose for grabbing her like that.

"My turn to cut in."

Ranger tapped the guy on the shoulder. The smaller man took one look at Ranger, turned around and left.

"Thank you." Piper breathed a sigh of relief.

"My pleasure." Ranger opened his arms, inviting her in.

She didn't hesitate. As soon as she wrapped her arms around his neck, he enfolded her in his embrace. A feeling of security, warmth and caring washed over her. She couldn't miss how well they fit together, either. With a happy sigh, she rested her head on his chest and rocked gently, following his lead.

He lowered his head and rubbed his cheek against hers. "This is nice."

"Uh-huh. Much better than Mr. Handsy."

"You looked ready to clobber him."

"I thought about it. Then you came along like a knight in shining armor."

Ranger hugged her. "I'll be your knight any day."

She peeked up at him before lifting up to brazenly mesh her lips with his.

He cupped the back of her head, tilted his head and guided her motions in the same way he led her on the dance floor.

Piper savored his soft lips, the teasing brushes, the sweet caresses. Ranger kissed better than any man she'd ever given a try. With his size and experience, he could easily overtake and dominate her. Instead, he offered up samples. Coaxed her to respond. Nibbled and teased as if he had all the time in the world and she was a delicious treat to be savored.

He petted her hair before lifting his head. For a long time, he stared down at her as if trying to read something in her expression.

I'm an open book. She smiled. "Did anyone ever tell you that you could make a fortune at a kissing booth?"

"No." He chuckled. "Like my kisses, huh?"

"Yep." She glanced around and stage whispered loudly. "But you didn't hear that from me. I don't want to be responsible for inflating your ego too much."

Ranger grinned. "Think I'm arrogant?"

She shook her head. "Nah. Just self-confident. And not really any more than the rest of the team."

He turned her in a gradual circle. "Not afraid for one of the guys to see us together?"

Piper stuck her chin in the air. "For tonight, I'd just like to kick back and enjoy. We can worry about the quandary of public shows of affection later."

Ranger's eyes darkened. "Works for me." He kissed her once more, briefly.

"Hey, guys." Axel bumped into Piper.

She turned to see his gaze flicking from Ranger to her and back again. A wide smile formed on his face.

"Hooking up for the night?" Ranger inclined his head toward the woman clinging to Axel's side.

"We'll see." He winked, took the woman in his arms and twirled her. They made their way through the masses and toward the bar.

Piper frowned. "I still don't get it."

"Get what?"

"Why people are so giddy about one-night stands."

"It's sex. That's first and foremost. And it's exciting. You can feel free to try all kinds of things with someone who really doesn't matter. No strings attached can be intoxicating as well."

Piper rolled her eyes. "Pretty shallow."

"Yep. That doesn't matter at the time." He scanned the room. "I've grown up. It's not about quantity anymore."

"I'm glad." She grinned mischievously. "I'd hate to have to snatch the hair off a woman's head for trying to move in on you right now."

Ranger laughed. "A man's fantasy come true."

Piper snorted.

He nuzzled her temple before placing a quick kiss. "No worries. No other woman interests me."

The words solidified Piper's feelings. She'd nailed it on the head earlier. Her knight in shining armor. Who just happened to be sweet, bright and downright sexy.

Maybe Ranger is my Prince Charming after all. If only fairy tales could come true.

Too bad she knew better.

She rested her cheek against his chest and let the world's problems fade away, content in Ranger's arms.

Chapter Thirteen

Piper yawned and crossed her ankles. After a late-night home game where she'd ridden the bench so Rayovic could play, she'd climbed out of bed early to go skate before attending the mandatory team meeting. Sleepy, she could easily have nodded off as first one support person then another droned on about schedules, plans and, finally, opponents.

Ranger bumped her foot and whispered. "Wake up."

She sat up straighter. "I'm awake."

"Uh-huh."

His teasing grin sent a cascade of warmth through her body.

Whatever possessed me to admit my lack of sexual experience to him? She still couldn't believe the turn of events that had had her making such a confession. However, his reaction and response made it all worthwhile. She'd gone from embarrassed to feeling treasured in seconds, boosting her self-confidence enormously.

All because of Ranger.

He'd stuck by her side, looking after her, making sure the other guys didn't rattle her cage too much. A big, sweet, bodyguard. Who just happened to have the best ass and dimples in the league.

For the first time ever, she found herself falling for a guy. This one just happened to be tall, strong and one of the best power forwards around. For a girl who'd vowed never to date a hockey player, she'd fallen off her high horse pretty dang quick.

It's his smile. Or those amazing green eyes. Maybe both. Either way, he'd managed to slip under her shields and leave quite an impression.

The squeak of the door opening drew her attention. She twisted around to find a woman entering, dressed in a long coat and escorted by one of the security detail.

The lady marched right in like she owned the place, then raked the group with her gaze. "Sven. I'm looking for Sven."

"Right here." Riley pointed him out.

Sven frowned at his teammate before turning back to the woman. "What do you want with me?"

She smiled widely and removed her coat, revealing a bright red bustier that barely covered her ample bosom and panties scant enough to be less than the size of the marker board eraser. High heels, stockings and a garter belt finished the outfit.

Piper glimpsed shock in all the men's faces. Especially Sven's.

Music started.

The lady approached Sven, shoved the table out of the way and straddled his lap. "I hear it's your birthday. Someone thought you could use a little strip-o-gram to make it more spectacular." She started moving to the beat, giving Sven one heck of a lap dance.

His mouth finally closed, only for a smile to appear. Rosy cheeks told of either embarrassment or perhaps enjoying the feminine attention a bit too much. Piper couldn't tell.

Whistles, whoops and cheers egged her on. Even the head coach sat back and grinned like a kid in a candy store.

Ranger nudged her with his elbow. "Did you have anything to do with this?"

Piper blinked innocently. "Who, me?"

Ranger chuckled. "Thought so." He watched the show for a little longer. "Remind me to stay on your good side." His eyes were riveted to the display. "On second thought, your bad side isn't too horrible either."

She smacked him in the chest.

"*Oomph.*" He rubbed the area. "Can't I tease you just a

little?" He grinned wickedly.

Piper rolled her eyes. All men were the same. Parade big boobs in front of them and they drooled like a baby.

The stripper added some pelvic thrusts, shook her booty in his face then settled in for some up close and personal dancing.

As soon as the music ended, she regained her feet, collected her coat and leaned over to whisper something in Sven's ear. After that, she left the way she came. Appreciative applause carried through the room.

"Damn. I want her for my birthday." Rocky broke the silence. "It's tomorrow."

Tommy shook his head. "Your birthday isn't until June."

"Well, shit."

The group laughed, Sven included. Though he seemed to be a bit distracted at the moment. Probably still replaying the lap dance through his mind. And dealing with the after-effects.

"Now that the entertainment is over we need to get back down to business. Afternoon practice will end early. There's a big snowstorm headed for New York. We have to leave this evening to beat it. We'll arrive at the hotel tonight, have practice as normal tomorrow, then play the next day. The basic schedule will remain unchanged, but we'll be there instead of here."

Piper's shoulders slumped. All this time on the road sucked. Initially, she didn't mind the travel. Now, she longed for days off to rest and relax. To have a few days without having to strap on skates and enter a rink except at her own leisure. With the limited number of women's teams and half the games that the men played, she'd enjoyed a lot more time at home during the season. Now she'd entered the men's realm of being gone all the time.

"Unless there's questions, meeting is over. Get in gear and hit the ice." Tommy gathered up some papers and left the room.

Piper dug through her purse, latched onto a check and

hurried over to Hagan, who still remained in his seat. "Hagan?"

He glanced up at her.

She plopped down in the unoccupied chair next to him. "I wanted to give you this." She handed over the check.

He looked at the amount then turned to her with his mouth open and bafflement apparent on his face. "Why?"

"It's for the charity you run. The underprivileged kids back in Norway. Providing them with winter clothes, shoes and food."

He continued to stare at her.

"I received my first check for playing with the Wolfpack. This is bonus for me since I have my job and my Bobcats pay as well. I decided there were people who needed it more than I did. So I wanted to donate the amount to a worthy cause. Yours."

For a split second, she thought she detected mist in his eyes. He cleared his throat. "Thank you."

She offered up a smile. They hadn't started out on the right foot. She hoped maybe now they could mend the bridges. "You're more than welcome." She started to stand and turn only to be enfolded in his arms.

She hugged him back with a squeeze. Impulsively, she pecked his cheek, then stepped away. Returning to her seat, she gathered up her purse and started to file out with the rest of the team.

"That's a nice thing that you did." Rayovic patted her on the back.

Piper smiled. "It was the right thing to do."

"Come on. We have a session with Stanza."

Piper groaned dramatically.

"Exactly." Rayovic laughed and ushered her in front of him.

She exited the room to find Ranger waiting for her. His gaze landed on her and held. "You've been busy this morning."

Together they started walking toward the locker room.

"Idle hands and all that."

He chuckled. "Speaking of idle hands, just wait to see what happens at the hotel."

"What's going to happen?" She blinked, at a complete loss as to what he was talking about.

"Get twenty plus grown guys together with nothing to do for a couple of days outside of practice and they pull out all the pranks. A hotel is like a pranking playground for us."

"Oh." Piper shook her head. "I'm afraid to ask."

"Don't worry. I imagine you'll be excluded from the worst of them."

"I feel sooo much better. Thank you." She broke into a smile. "Boys will be boys?"

"Exactly." Ranger paused at the entrance to the men's locker room. "See ya on the ice."

"You can count on it."

She watched him go, noticed the gliding steps, the snap and tug of muscles under his jeans and long-sleeved T-shirt, and sighed.

Face it, Piper. You've got it bad.

On that note, she headed to the women's locker room in order to get dressed for another workout.

* * * *

Piper stepped out of the shower in the home team's locker room. They'd arrived a couple hours ago in New York, and strapped on their skates for some ice time before cleaning up to go out to dinner. Tommy had told them it was five-star, thus to dress up for the occasion. She'd brought along a pretty short-sleeved black dress with a skirt that stopped just above her knees. More of a summer cocktail dress. With limited options in her closet since she rarely spruced up so much, she'd gone with the old standby. A pair of flats completed the ensemble.

She towel-dried her hair after patting the rest of herself dry, then made her way to the lockers, where her dress waited on a hanger.

The dress was there. As were the shoes. Her bra and panties were not. She dug through her duffel bag, knowing she'd packed them especially for this evening. Nothing. Irritation shot through her as she realized someone must have snuck in and stolen her undies during practice or while she was in the shower. "Just great. Now what am I to do?" She glanced at the set she'd worn for practice and shook her head. They were soaked in sweat. No way would she shoehorn herself back into them when she'd just peeled them off. The stench of perspiration would permeate everything else.

Well, crap.

Seeing no other option, she pulled on her dress, followed by her shoes. At least they'd left her the important parts. She'd heard her father laughing over pranks where the men lost their suit pants and had nothing else to wear.

Men. I swear. So much for being exempt from the pranks.

Instead of dwelling on something she couldn't fix, she worked on her hair instead, blowing it out for a couple of minutes before adding in curls for a nice touch. She stared at herself in the mirror, judging the results.

"It'll do." She fluffed her hair one last time and tried to ignore the bareness she felt between her legs. Having never gone commando before, the sensation proved a bit unnerving. Especially when she considered at least one of the guys knew she'd be without bra and panties during dinner. *The jerk.*

A plan began to form. Why should he be the only one who knew? Might as well make a public announcement and make the guys squirm a bit. And hope the cold night air didn't make her nipples stand out too much at the same time.

With a new goal and a bounce in her step, she packed up her stuff, zipped the bag, placed the strap over her shoulder then marched out to meet the rest of the team.

Several members stood around, wearing expensive suits and leather shoes, all name brand and shouting wealth.

Cleaned up, they made for some great eye candy. However, given her druthers, she found them more handsome in their hockey gear, dressed up and ready for a game. Even afterward, when sweat coated their faces and dripped down on their shirts. Those images stuck in the mind. Not the *GQ* ones before her.

She started to make her announcement, but decided to wait. Not all the guys were there and she needed that to be the case. So she leaned against a nearby wall and waited.

"You look nice." Adam smiled at her. He'd chosen a brown suit for the evening with a white shirt underneath. No tie. Business casual. Rich business casual.

"Thank you." She tilted her head. "You clean up pretty nice yourself."

"I'm nothing if not fashionable." He snorted at himself.

She chuckled. "I know what you mean. I'm afraid I don't have a collection of shoes long enough to pave the road to the rink and I'm fresh out of runway model winter fads. So I went with the basics—a little black dress."

"It works. Well."

Ranger approached, dressed in a black suit that brought out his eyes. The pristine shirt underneath the coat added contrast and classiness. Even his shoes reflected the light.

Boy howdy, the man knows how to wow. She couldn't take her eyes off him. "Nice. Very nice." She reconsidered her earlier preference for a man in an old jersey and skates. If they all looked like him, maybe she'd take the professional attire over sweat. Maybe.

"And she totally forgets that I'm here," Adam commented blandly.

Piper grinned at Ranger and turned back to Adam. "What were you saying?"

The young forward rolled his eyes. "You might want to close your mouth before you start to drool." He winked at her, spun on his heel and walked toward another small group of team members.

She did a quick head count, then strode over to the larger

of the groups. "Okay, heathens, I'm pretty certain that stealing women's underwear qualifies as a perversion. A particularly kinky one, at that. Or crossdresser-hood. I'm not sure which."

A couple of guys fought to keep a serious expression on their faces. A handful more grinned like banshees. Hard to tell guilt from just scanning the lot of them.

Ranger stared back at her with a spark in his eye. She wasn't sure if that related to his part in the prank or to the fact that he was picturing her without panties and happened to enjoy the thought. Randiness on display, for sure.

"Really? That's all you have? Because I can say from experience, these guys have always been perverts," Rocky tossed out.

She snorted.

Rocky fell under the kinky heading. No doubt about it.

Rocky glanced over at Ivan with a definite wicked smirk.

"Don't look at me." Ivan scowled.

"Why not? I bet you've thought about trying that bra on for size, though I doubt it'll fit," Rocky answered.

"Bastard." He looked around at all the guys staring at him. "Bastards. All of you."

More chuckles followed.

"Uh- huh," Hagan replied. "Takes one to know one."

"Yeah, yeah." Keith rolled his eyes. "It's panties. Not like we're going to wear them on our heads and parade around the hotel."

"*We* wouldn't. *You* might," Ranger fired back.

"Pink *is* your color," Hagan added.

Keith flipped them off. More laughter followed.

Piper waited until they settled down before finishing her stern lecture. "Well, enjoy them. I can't say as they would do anything for your sexiness, but hey, to each their own." She stuck her chin in the air and strode off, making sure to put an extra wiggle in her step.

Chuckles followed her.

Ranger fell into line beside her.

She eyed him warily. "Are you the guilty one?"

He blinked at her innocently. Maybe too innocently. "Guilty for what?"

"Hmmm." She didn't think he'd told a fib, but wasn't sure she knew him well enough to be positive.

She handed her gear to the driver, who busily loaded up their stuff in the storage area, then quickly ascended the steps, lest one of the guys on the ground get a free peek under her dress. After finding a seat, she sat down and stared out of the window, waiting patiently for the short trip to get underway.

Twenty minutes later the bus pulled into the parking lot of a large restaurant and stopped. The driver opened the door and the occupants began to file out and make a beeline for the entrance in order to quickly get out of the chilly temperatures outside.

They ended up waiting as a large group as the hostess ensured the back room was cleared.

Piper stood near the front, fussing with her skirt. "Going five-star in a short skirt and no panties makes me feel a little naughty." She hadn't meant to speak loud enough for the entire crew to hear.

A couple of guys choked. Another groaned. More than one mouth gaped open.

Ranger's eyes heated to molten emeralds. She could almost feel the warmth coming off his body, though a couple of feet separated them. He appeared to be stripping her down with his eyes.

Not a bad thing. Except we're in a busy restaurant surrounded by people. Most notably the rest of the team.

Her breath caught as her heart sped. The rapt attention threatened to turn her into a puddle of mush.

"Allow me." Ranger offered his arm. "Shall we find a place to sit?"

Automatically, she rested her hand on his arm, noticing the electricity flowing between them at the slight touch.

They started forward.

"No panties, huh?"

"Nope. Someone stole them."

"Damn."

She peered up at him. "You're upset someone stole my undies?"

He shook his head. "Nah. I just figure that it's going to be really hard to focus on the food knowing that you're wearing nothing under that little dress."

Her ego bolstered. "That little tidbit is going to drive you to distraction?"

He met her gaze for a moment. His eyes flickered with longing and hunger. She'd wager it wasn't for the expensive food, either. "Absolutely."

"Good." She grinned, found a seat, and let him gently push her chair in.

Ranger took the place next to her. "How did I know you'd be a vixen?"

She shrugged. "I'm just me."

"Uh-huh. 'Just me' has a sassy, devilish streak, too."

Piper didn't bother to argue. After all, it was the truth.

Chapter Fourteen

Ranger swatted a backhand shot toward the net, catching the crossbar and sending the puck flying into the stands. He pulled up and waited for someone to either collect the puck or toss them a new one.

All morning he'd kept checking Piper out, trying to mesh the heavenly vision from the night before with today. She's donned her layers of protective gear, reminding him of a fluffy Eskimo dressed all in white. Much different than the vision in a form-fitting dress. Regardless of the choice of shoes, she'd exuded sexiness in spades. The image, burned into his mind, had invaded his sleep last night in his hotel room, to the tune of some pretty risqué dreams.

When she'd announced she didn't have any panties on, he'd bitten back a groan at the mere thought. His cock had hardened and he hadn't been able to quite stop focusing on her. Then the little minx had made the shocking declaration that she felt naughty. He'd just about come in his pants. The sultry tone, the off-the-cuff quip, had about brought him to his knees. Hell, as it was, he'd spent an extra-long time in the shower in his hotel room, jacking off to the thoughts of her in that little dress without the benefit of panties to shield her folds from the world.

He'd noted that several of the guys had kept sneaking glances at Piper, even grinned at her. He'd read their faces easily enough. Her statement had affected them as well. The only difference was he'd check them hard into the wall if they tried to muscle in on Piper. Sure, she could choose who she wanted. He had no issue with that. But right now he and Piper were at the starting gate of a relationship. No way would he blow it and let an ambitious guy step into his shoes.

What would it have been like to drag his fingers up her thigh and slip under the material? Would he have found her wet?

The thought alone made him groan. His randy dick started to sit up and take notice. Not something he needed right now. *And if I don't get my mind off it and back on the practice, I'll end up with a puck to the head.*

Tommy called for a break. Several of the guys headed toward the bench, obviously searching for something to drink.

"Want to hear a grown man scream like a girl?" Piper asked as Ranger skated by.

He slid to a halt next to her. "Do I want to know?"

"Oh, yeah. This is a good one." She gestured toward their bench.

Sure enough, a few of the guys were asking about something to drink. Clint pointed to a nearby cooler.

Axel opened the lid and jumped back. Another one screamed. The others either cursed or about fell over one another trying to get away. A huge plastic cobra dangled from the cooler's lid, the lower part of its body presumably still coiled inside.

Only Ivan seemed unaffected. "Kids' stuff." He skated off.

Ranger laughed hard. "The look on their faces."

"Yep." Piper giggled some more. "Payback is hell, they say."

Ranger shook his head. "I guess so." He skated by Axel and slapped him on the shoulder. "About to get bit?"

Axel cursed and flashed him the middle finger. As well as anyone could do wearing a hockey glove, anyway.

Ranger chuckled some more. Their little goalie had a knack for pranks. Who would have guessed?

An hour later, Ranger had forgotten all about pranks as he struggled to catch his breath from all the drills Coach had forced them to do. Sprints, in particular, sucked. Sure, they helped with stamina for the fast-paced games, especially in overtime. That didn't mean any of the guys enjoyed them.

It being a day off with nothing more to do, Tommy obviously felt a bit of conditioning before another game tomorrow wouldn't hurt them in the least.

Damn him.

Ranger finished and wiped his face under the clear guard on his helmet. A shower called, as did lunch. After chugging some water, he passed the bottle along to the other guys.

"Hey, you promised to show me the spin-o-rama into a slap shot that you do so well." Piper skated over to him, having shucked her heavy goaltender gear before the drills began. The absence of all the layers made her appear that much smaller compared to the guys, including him.

He offered up a smile. "Think you can keep up after that workout?"

Piper lifted her chin a hair and snorted. "Try me."

"Come on." He grabbed a puck from a nearby bag, clutched his stick and headed toward center ice. Out of the corner of his eye, he noticed Piper following and several of the guys hanging around the edge of the ice to watch. Even Tommy stuck around, though he'd called practice officially over.

Ranger dropped the puck and waited for Piper to draw near. "Just keep your momentum up, don't let the puck stray and keep everything in tight. Players will do all kinds of things to separate you from the puck. You have to be quick, strong and ready." He circled around, kicked the puck to get it going, then cranked on the speed. As he approached the net, he turned in first one circle then another, keeping his stick on the puck and his motion under precise control. He came out of the last spin and fired a slapshot, hitting the empty net easily.

"Very nice." Appreciation flared in Piper's eyes. Her face conveyed interest and respect. She skated over to the bench area and swiped a hockey stick used by one of the forwards.

Not a bad start. Only now he had visions of her eyeing him with longing, lust and sultry desire.

Hockey. Ice. Puck, he reminded himself sternly. Running around with a hard-on wasn't on the agenda now or ever. *Way too uncomfortable. Especially with a cup.* He shuddered at the idea.

"Want to give it a try?" He retrieved the puck and sent it her direction.

She caught it on her stick easily, sped toward the right side, turned and fired. She hit a bar down shot.

"Damn," Ranger whispered under his breath.

More than one of the guys gaped in amazement.

Impressed, Ranger corralled the puck and sent it back to her. "Remind me again why you aren't a forward."

"Too small." She slapped the pass without stopping it first and scored again. Standing up straight, she leaned on her borrowed stick.

"That doesn't seem to matter when you're goaltending."

She shrugged. "I can make up for my size there with quickness. Besides, goalies tend to keep their chicklets better than other players." Chicklets were teeth in hockey lingo.

Ranger grinned. "There's that."

Her attention turned to the guys standing around. "Want to play? I bet we can kick Ranger's ass."

Chuckles echoed across the rink. Several of the guys came forward.

Ranger grinned widely. "You can try. After you put on your pads."

Piper sighed wearily, but hurried over to her small pile of gear. She removed her practice jersey, revealing a light blue T-shirt, before pulling on the white protective layers. Not the full set of pads she wore as a goalie, but the basics, which gave her some coverage but much less bulk. Finished, she yanked her jersey back on and returned to stand near Ranger. "Better?"

"Yep." He cut a look to the other players. "No checking."

They glanced over at Piper then nodded.

She pouted. "Well, hell. Here I thought I could knock someone into the boards for once."

Rocky snorted. "You'd barely knock them off their line, let alone into the wall, sweetheart."

"Gee, thanks." Piper backed up to center ice. "Let's go already."

With no goalies, they had to defend their own nets, just like schoolyard hockey way back in his youth. Since hitting was out, they had to rely on skill, speed and talent. A different kind of game, but a challenging one.

Ranger entered the circle, facing Sven. They hit sticks three times in a bully, as was the traditional start without the benefit of referees to drop the puck. Ranger won the face-off, smacked the puck toward Keith, and quickly moved into Piper's zone.

Anthony pestered Keith, then intercepted a pass meant for Ranger. Ivan took it from there, slapping the puck into the upper left-hand corner of the net.

"Yes." Ivan grinned and pumped his fist. Defensive men weren't normally prolific scorers.

"Way to go." Piper bumped him in congratulations.

"Yeah, yeah. That's just the beginning." Ranger returned to the circle. "Let's see if you guys can keep up."

They kept up, all right. Twenty minutes later Ranger nailed a shot, though too little too late. His made-up team finished down by three goals.

He couldn't recall having so much fun and still being on the losing end.

Piper skated by, her blonde braid flying behind in the breeze created by her speed. He glimpsed a wide smile on her face and knew she was having a ball. Most likely pickup games were as scarce to her as they were to him. With such packed schedules, little down time existed. Even then, many of the players sought other activities for entertainment. This was a special day, one that he wouldn't forget any time soon. Not only because of the enjoyment of just letting loose and enjoying a game he loved without the pressure of performing, but also because the other guys seemed to have had just as much enjoyment. They were quickly gaining cohesiveness and grins. Piper bore responsibility for so much of that.

The team even surrounded her and stuck together in their protective attitudes when faced with opposing teams determined to make a point about women invading their territory. The 'us versus them' mentality didn't hurt, either.

He'd questioned Rob's decision to bring her into the league. Now he found the idea smart. Extremely smart.

The Wolfpack might have been desperate for a goalie after Gunderson's injury, but they'd needed so much more. A spark. A bonding agent. A reason to keep fighting during a particularly bad losing season besides just pride.

Ranger couldn't help but think they'd been presented with the only person who could have filled all those voids — Piper.

The question became how long could she hold up under such pressure and physical play.

His gaze found her once more.

She'd make it. *Because she doesn't know the meaning of the word quit.*

Which left a couple more queries. Could she see him as more than a teammate? And could she be the woman who outshone all the others in his life?

His gut told him yes on both counts.

* * * *

Ranger stared out of the window at the flying snow. The weatherman had called for a snowstorm. He appeared to have been right. New York received its fair share, as he recalled, from spending a couple of years in the city when he'd made his way up through the minors. He'd never paid much attention as a young hotshot in the league. After all, he'd had other things on his mind. Namely fast women and a big paycheck, as well as working his way through the ranks to the big league.

Now he'd arrived at his destination, a more mature man, with different goals and interests. New York, with the prominent night life, didn't fit in. Denver had become his home. Hopefully for the rest of his career, anyway.

Pulling himself away from the sight, he checked his watch, then ambled toward the hotel's dining room. Normally, he'd rather go out to eat at one of his favorite restaurants in the city. Today, with the sloppy streets and inches of snow piling up, he passed. Better to stay in and avoid the headache.

He entered the dining room and found about a dozen people already there, a couple of them his teammates. Ivan and Axel, two of the defensemen who were best friends on and off the ice. They raised their hands in greeting, then returned to their meals.

Finding an empty table by a window, he greeted the waitress, who hurried right over, took his drink order then scurried off, leaving him with a menu. Ranger read the list, immediately settling on grilled chicken with vegetables as a side item. The pictures of pies caught his attention. Dessert might just happen today. He grinned to himself, closed the menu and glanced out the window.

"Have you decided what you want?" the waitress asked.

"Yep." He rattled off his order, then opened the straw she'd placed beside his soda.

"Great. We'll have this out to you shortly." She strode off toward the kitchen.

He sipped his drink, then went back to watching nature's fury.

Bright pink snared his focus. He turned to find Piper entering the room, wearing a hot pink T-shirt with the Denver Bobcats logo on the front and long white sleeves underneath. Her less bright blush-colored sweats didn't manage to tone down the ensemble in the least.

He shook his head. The girl could pull off just about

anything with her blonde hair and trim build.

She turned to the side as if judging one table's pros versus another's cons, giving Ranger a peek at the writing on her butt. 'Bobcats' was spelled out in white letters.

While she might train in that get up, he didn't imagine she wore it in public without attracting plenty of male attention to her derriere. Certainly *he* noticed. "Piper."

She spun at the sound of her name. A small smile appeared on her face.

He gestured to the seat across for him. "Join me."

"Well, okay. If you insist." She sat down gracefully. "I debated bugging Ivan and Axel, but they seem deep in conversation."

Ranger peeked over at the guys leaning toward each other, obviously intent on the subject at hand. "Their loss is my gain."

"Awww." She glanced around the room. "How's the food here?"

He shrugged. "Pretty good from what I remember from last time. There's better restaurants not too far from here, but too much work to get there in this storm."

She nodded.

The waitress returned with water and a menu. Piper waved her hand. "I'll just have what he's having."

The lady blinked. "Are you sure?"

Piper's gaze flicked to Ranger. "You didn't order lamb, did you?"

He smiled. "Nope. Grilled chicken and veggies."

"Smart man." She turned back to the waitress. "Yep, I'm sure. I'll take what he's having."

"Okay." The woman walked off.

"Brave." Amused, Ranger studied his impromptu dinner companion.

"Ehh. I've seen what you eat. Fairly normal and healthy. A man after my own heart." She thanked the woman who brought her a soda to drink, dropped her straw into the glass, then sipped.

He placed his forearms on the table. "Checking out my dietary habits, huh?"

"Uh-huh. What can I say? I'm learning all kinds of things being around you guys." She glanced out of the window.

He wasn't sure what all her comment encompassed, or whether he really wanted to ask.

"You said there are nice restaurants nearby. Besides where we ate last night?"

"Yep. Four or five within a couple of miles."

"Been to many places in New York?" she asked.

"Yeah. I spent some time here in the minors. Since I wasn't really into cooking, I pretty much ate out every day. Found some great places and some that needed to be avoided at all costs."

"I bet you liked the nightlife. Lots to see and do."

"There was. Boredom wasn't an issue." Not with an abundance of nightlife available.

Her eyes met his in amusement. "Did you ever learn to cook?"

"Oh, yeah. I had to get serious in the pros. Pizza no longer did the trick. Especially with nutrition coaches harping on us about what we ate." He matched her smile. "Cooking isn't hard. It's just time-consuming and takes a bit of creativity."

"Yep. All kinds of things to make as long as you have motivation and a cookbook. Or a mother on the other end of your phone call."

He chuckled. "Call for backup often?"

"Now and again." Piper took another drink. "I grew up in the kitchen with my mother. The basics I can do. The bigger stuff is still a challenge."

"I bet your cooking is delicious."

She tilted her head and grinned. "Maybe one day you can sample it and see."

"I'd like that." He spoke truthfully. The thought of her fixing him a meal felt right. Just like taking her out to eat and watching out for her on the ice.

All part of the package when it came to Piper.

Chapter Fifteen

Ranger stepped out of his hotel room and shut the door behind him. Game day. In New York. After a full day of goofing off, another physical battle loomed just hours ahead. The story of his life during the hockey season.

He turned to find Sven approaching with a quirky grin on his face. "You're up early after the night you had."

Ranger, totally bumfuzzled, frowned at Sven. "What do you mean 'the night I had'?"

Sven's smiled faded. "Didn't you and Piper mess around last night?"

"No." Ranger looked at him in confusion. "I haven't seen her since lunchtime yesterday. As far as I know, she planted roots in her room and stayed."

"Oh."

Ranger's internal radar pinged. "Why would you think that?"

"I tried prank calling Piper with a six a.m. wake-up call. She never answered her cell or the room phone."

Ranger checked his watch. Barely seven. Most of the players wouldn't be up and around for a couple more hours. "Maybe she went to the rink for an early morning skate."

"In the blizzard?"

Well, hell. He'd forgotten the heavy snow that had started before they made it back to the hotel last night.

"She wouldn't break curfew, would she?" Sven ran a hand through his blond hair.

"Like you said, in the blizzard? She was with us last night. Sneaking back out wouldn't be like her and downright

stupid to boot. No, she has to be around here somewhere."
Mild worry began to creep into Ranger.

"Maybe she hooked up with one of the other guys. Or someone she met last night?" Sven shifted weight from one foot to the next.

Ranger ran the idea through his head and immediately dismissed it. "Not her style." He considered where she might go and came up with a couple of answers. "Let me check the workout room. She might have gone there this morning."

"Okay. I'll run by the hotel restaurant, although I doubt anyone is in there yet, even the coaching staff." Coaches and support staff normally hit the buffet early. The players came later, as they enjoyed sleeping in when they could.

Sven hurried off.

Ranger took the elevator down to the ground floor, stepped out, and followed the signs to the exercise room. There, he found Piper. The clear glass walls offered a perfect view of her at the back of the room, presently beating the shit out of a punching bag.

After pulling his cell out of his pocket, he sent a quick text to Sven.

I found her. She's in the gym.

Sven sent a message right back.

Does that girl ever sleep?

Good question.

Ranger stowed his phone and focused on Piper. Her charcoal-gray tights outlined every inch of her form, leaving little to the imagination. The crop top cut off below her breasts and showed off her defined abs while displaying the ugly green bruise in the stages of healing on her left side. As he watched, she alternated between punching the bag and throwing hard kicks that sent it swinging wildly.

Gloves covered her hands, protecting them from the hard leather.

Her motions seemed effortless, yet powerful. Fluidity and grace combined with accuracy and strength. Sweat glistened on her forehead and the back of her neck. However long she'd been at it, she now breathed hard as she danced around, aiming at her chosen opponent.

As impressed as he was, he couldn't shake the feeling that something was bugging her. Not just an excess of energy or lack of an ice rink to zip around, either.

He opened the door and walked in.

Piper glanced his direction, then immediately returned to her workout.

Ranger closed the distance between them, stopping nearby. "You're up early."

"Yeah." She punched the bag a couple more times.

"Any particular reason you're not snug and warm in bed like the rest of the team?"

She turned to him. "You mean like you are?"

He heard the bite to her tone and read the tension in her entire body. Something was bothering her. Immensely. He just had to get to the heart of the matter to find out. Difficult, but not impossible.

He changed tactics. "You're pretty good at that. Kick-boxing, right?"

"Yeah." Piper paused and grabbed the bag before it could bump into her. "I've been doing this and karate since I was six years old. I wanted to be able to protect myself."

Ranger treaded carefully. "Odd for a six-year-old to think about having to protect herself."

She lifted her chin and met his gaze as her eyes welled up. "My mother always seemed to have to have a man around. I remember one right after another. Then she chose this one loser. He slapped her a couple of times. I was scared and told her. She tried to reassure me that she'd made him mad and that it was no big deal. I knew it was wrong, but didn't know what else to do. Then, one night, they argued.

He started beating on her. I hid, hearing her screams as he yelled and continued to knock her around. I didn't know what to do. Too scared to do more than hide under the stairs, I waited for it to end. Once it went silent, I decided to run and made it almost to the front door before he grabbed me. One look at his face and I knew he'd kill me. Somehow I made it to my mother's cell phone and called nine-one-one. It was too little too late for my mother." She sniffed and raised one shaky hand to wipe her forehead.

The story tore at him. He wanted to break the guy's neck for daring to lay a hand on Piper and for stealing her mother from her. Just as powerful an urge, he wanted to shelter Piper, to reassure her that not all men were such brutal bastards, to hold her, protect her and show her how a real man treated a woman. As angry as he'd been in the past, he'd never once considered hitting a lady. He might punch it out with a rival team player now and again, but that was sissy stuff compared to what Piper had witnessed and experienced. Only a lowlife bastard could do such a thing.

He studied her face and saw how much pain that event still caused her. He'd gladly take that agony away from her if he could. "It's nothing to be ashamed of, Piper. You survived. You did what you had to do and survived. That's commendable. Heroic, even."

She shook her head and wiped as a tear overflowed. "You don't understand."

Exasperated and hurting for her, he grappled for words of wisdom that might make an impact on her. "Try me."

"How can I be a hero when I was too frightened to move? Too scared to do anything more than hide? That cost my mother her life."

"You were six. There wasn't much you could do."

"I know." Her gaze fell to the floor.

"You made it. That's what counts."

She looked down. "I still carry issues. Back on the plane—"

"Was a knee-jerk reaction. We didn't understand then,

but we do now and don't think badly of you for it."

Piper froze on a gasp. "We?"

Shit. He shut his mouth and scrambled to find words to explain the slippage of his tongue.

He debated for another few seconds. Lying had never been his strong suit. Besides, it just didn't feel right to do that to Piper. He blew out a breath and went with his gut. "We overheard you telling Tommy what happened when you were just a kid. About your mother and her boyfriend, when you were trying to convince him to let you back into the game."

Piper nodded slowly, her gaze falling to the floor. "How many know?"

"All the guys were in the locker room at the time. We all heard," he answered quietly.

"I see." She turned and started for the door. Her shoulders slumped and she moved like she'd just aged fifty years. As if the life had been sucked out of her.

"Piper. Wait." He hurried to catch up, stepping in front of her to stop her progress. "It's not a big deal. Hell, to be honest, the guys respect you all the more for it."

Her eyes grew watery. He read the sadness and shame in their depths. His heart broke for her. "Oh, sweetheart."

"Excuse me."

Piper pushed past Ranger and darted out of the room.

At a total loss, Ranger stood and watched her go. He saw her pain, felt it as his own. Yet, for the life of him, he had no clue what to do or say to make things better.

* * * *

Piper emerged from the shower, squeaky clean yet less than energetic. She went about drying off, then combed out her hair. The familiar actions soothed her only marginally.

What a hell of a day. Too bad it isn't even noon yet.

She'd woken up around four with a nightmare. The same one she had now and again about that horrific night. Rattled and knowing she'd never return to sleep, she'd opted to get dressed and go for a workout. Since the rink was a distance away through white-out conditions, she'd settled for the hotel's gym. The punching bag had served her needs well enough.

Until Ranger had popped in and delivered the bomb that the entire team know about her past. Her failures. Her issues.

They must think I'm one messed-up woman. She'd freaked out on the plane, and now this. As hard as she worked to earn their respect, she feared she'd lost that in one fell swoop. They'd either try to forget it happened and move on or they'd pity her. She'd been through this before. With her adoptive parents. Her brother. Her friends. Their perception of her had changed when they'd learned about that fateful night. No one ever put her down. They just treated her with kid gloves. She both appreciated it and hated it at the same time.

Her stomach rumbled with hunger. She dug out a pair of yoga pants and her favorite jersey which had once belonged to her father. The old shirt might be way too big, but it provided comfort in more ways than one. Settling for tying her hair up in a ponytail, she fluffed the ends, brushed her teeth and added a smidgen of makeup to cover the dark circles under her eyes. She put on the clothes, along with a light sweatshirt under the jersey to ensure warmth. After one more glance in the mirror, she slipped her feet into a pair of tennis shoes and headed out of the door.

And nearly ran over Ranger in the process.

He sat on the floor outside her door. Not bothering to get up, he simply swung around to face her. "Hi."

"Hi."

Guilt rode her hard. He'd tried to be helpful earlier. And honest. Still, his words had sent her on overload, giving her reason to bolt before she cried in earnest.

Gracefully, he stood. "I was hoping you might go to breakfast with me." He pinned her with his concerned gaze.

She sighed. Ranger had been there from day one of this journey. He'd always been supportive and encouraging. If he saw her as lacking, he'd never showed it for a moment. Considering he'd known about her past for over a week, that said something. The other guys, too. "I'm sorry."

He tugged her to him and held her tight. "You have nothing to be sorry for. I'm the one who's sorry. The words just slipped out."

She wrapped her arms around him in return. "No, you were right to tell me. I don't like secrets. They always come back to bite you in the ass." She rested her head against his chest and listened to his heart beat steadily. "I just overreacted."

"Shhh." He nuzzled her cheek before leaning back to look at her. "It's okay. We're okay."

Her stomach chose that moment to make its demands known with another loud growl.

Ranger grinned. "We're also hungry. So, will you have breakfast with me?"

She didn't even hesitate. "Yes."

He took her hand in his, shortening his strides to keep pace with her. "You don't have to hide from me, Piper. There's nothing you can't tell me."

"You trust me." She peered up at him to read his features as she uttered the words.

"Yes, I do." He squeezed her hand. "Like I said before, you're different. You make me smile, laugh and want to step up and be a better person, like you." He pushed the button on the elevator. "I saw what you did for Hagan. That was a very good deed. One he's still talking about."

She shrugged, not entirely comfortable with all the praise. "I meant what I told him. What I make playing with you guys is bonus. There's people out there who need it worse than I do."

He shook his head. "Some of the guys are out buying huge houses, fancy cars and the most expensive luxuries money can buy. You make far less in the women's league.

Finally get a chance to get paid what you're worth and you donate it to charity." He stepped into the elevator, pulling her with him. Once there, he hit the button with his free hand. "You're one special lady." He brushed his knuckles over her cheek, then leaned in to seal his lips over hers.

She accepted the tender inquiry and responded in kind. Soft, sweet kisses entailed. Ones she savored and knew she'd dream of the coming night.

The elevator dinged as it hit the bottom floor.

Reluctantly, she moved back. So far she and Ranger had shown little affection in public, especially where the other guys could see them. Maybe because they wanted to keep their relationship under wraps for a bit longer. Maybe because they didn't want the media to latch on and start a storm. Maybe because they had business to attend to for a few more weeks, preferably without distractions.

Whatever the reason, she expected Ranger to release her hand as they entered the restaurant.

He held snug.

She blinked up at him. He smiled back. "It's not like it's a huge secret. The guys already accuse me of making goo-goo eyes at you."

She grinned. "Goo-goo eyes? How exactly does that work?"

He shrugged. "I have no idea. That's just what they say."

"Uh-huh." She noticed Axel, Ivan and Riley sitting at a table near the back. They glanced up as she and Ranger neared the buffet. Each one appraised them before going back to their breakfast.

"See. Not one of them fell out of their chairs in shock." Ranger released her in order to grab a plate.

"I'm not sure if that's good or bad."

"It's all good, vixen." He smiled ruefully then started loading up his choices for the meal.

The way he looked at her soothed the last of her doubts. They had a full day off at the hotel, no practice, no meetings. She needed to buck up and enjoy it. With Ranger.

Scooting in next to him, she took the top plate from the stack and started collecting food.

* * * *

Piper clicked the Send button then stretched her arms over her head. After breakfast she'd returned to her hotel room, determined to tackle some work and get it knocked out. Three hours later, she'd successfully caught up. For another week or so, that was. Even though she made an extremely nice salary right now compared to her usual amount, she knew that would end soon enough. Thus, she needed to keep her year-round job in order to help pay the bills down the road. It all fell into the category of 'no rest for the weary' in her book.

At least she'd worked through most of her volatile emotions this morning. Between the earlier match with the punching bag and, more recently, Ranger's attentiveness during breakfast, she'd managed to put the incident behind her. While she wasn't thrilled the guys knew about her past, she had no one to blame besides herself. They'd obviously not let the information change anything in how they viewed her. So she could do the same. *Buck up and move on already.*

She stood and ambled over to the window. Large snowflakes still fell from the sky, but the wind had died down and a sea of white lay across the ground. Obviously the storm had weakened and mostly traveled to other parts.

A flash of color caught her eye. Sure enough, a couple of the guys, bundled up in coats, gloves and stocking caps, were chasing each other. Or at least tried to through the thick snow. Snowballs flew in both directions, only lagging when they stopped to create more.

That looks like fun. Piper laughed at their antics. She glanced over at her coat and made a hasty decision. Pulling it on, she found mittens in her pocket, along with a fuzzy headband to protect her ears from the frigid temperatures. After slipping those on, she took a second to turn off her laptop, then hurried downstairs to join in the game.

No sooner had she left the hotel than a snowball caught her in the stomach. "Hey!" She blinked, trying to adjust to the brightness outside compared to in. A couple of seconds later, burly men came into focus. Ivan, Rocky and even Hagan. They all grinned at her mischievously.

She strode over to the nearest snow bank, created when the employees had shoveled the front entryway clear, quickly made a snowball and tossed it at Ivan. It smacked him on the arm, leaving a white mark behind.

He retaliated.

Piper jumped into the heaps of snow and darted away, forming another ball as she went. He bombarded her, only for the rest of the guys to cover him in snow. She added to the volleys with one nicely aimed throw that hit Ivan square in the rump.

The lot of them turned on her, sending a wall of snow in her direction. She squealed and ducked, all to no avail. Snow coated her from head to toe. That didn't deter her a bit. She fired back, intent on holding her own.

She laughed as Rocky took one in the chest.

"You're asking for it." He uttered the threat while holding up an already made snowball.

Piper squeaked and ran once again, ending up with a wet tush in the process.

She returned the favor, smacking Hagan in the shoulder.

How long the game continued, she didn't know. Just that time flew as she played in the new snow like she hadn't done since she was a kid. For a moment in time all responsibilities, worries and pressure fell away, leaving her with simple joy in an age-old sport.

Ranger stepped outside.

Piper spun around and nailed him in the breadbasket with a precise shot.

He arched an eyebrow, then darted after her.

Her boots and the mountains of snow slowed her down. She barely made three strides before he tackled her, twisting around so he took the brunt of the fall.

Piper landed on top of him. "*Omph.*"

He grunted as he tightened his hold on her.

She wiggled. "No fair. Tackling is outlawed in snowball fights." She pouted at him.

"I don't remember snowball fights having rules." Ranger grinned wickedly.

"They do. I'm pretty sure. Somewhere." She stared down at his sparkling eyes and ceased protesting. Instead, she rubbed her nose against his. "Eskimo kiss."

"Mmm. I'd rather have a real one."

"Would you now?" she teased.

"Oh, yeah."

Unable to deny him, she lowered her head and kissed him softly.

Wolf whistles and catcalls came from nearby.

Piper sat up and narrowed her eyes at the guys. "Don't make me fill your pants with snow."

"Gotta catch us first," Rocky hollered as he, Hagan, and Ivan bounded to the other side of the entryway.

Piper shook her head before turning her attention back to Ranger. "I guess we should get up before you frostbite that perfect rear of yours."

He laughed. "Might be a good idea."

She climbed off, offered him a hand, then helped pull him to his feet. "Ever build a fort in the snow?"

"Yep. All the time."

"I suggest we do that then declare war on the opposing team." She tilted her head toward the other three guys still tossing snow.

Ranger's eyes lit up. His excitement and happiness reminded her of an overgrown boy. After all, that was pretty much what men tended to be. "You're on."

Together they started digging and building. Within a few minutes they were lobbing snowballs at a fast clip, hitting their marks as the other guys scrambled to make their own shelter.

Piper watched a snowball careen off Ivan's shoulder then ducked behind the barrier once again.

Ranger did the same, pausing to simply look at her.

His smile did the trick. Her breath caught at the expression on his face. Happiness. Amusement. And something more.

She kissed him again, this time longer, deeper and filled with passion. Just as she got into it, a bucket filled with snow rained down over her head.

"I'd say we won," Rocky announced proudly.

Ivan, Rocky and Axel just about died laughing as she tried to brush the cold stuff off her.

Ranger shook his clothes and stood up, tugging her along with him. "On the contrary, I'm pretty sure I won."

Piper committed the moment to memory. Her time with the guys would be coming to an end soon. She could only hope that at the season's finale, when everyone parted ways, she and Ranger would be the exception.

Chapter Sixteen

Piper entered the visiting team's locker room, where her guys were preparing for the upcoming game, scanned over the faces, found the men all dressed and quietly giggling like kids. *Something is up*. Being loose was one thing. This was another.

Not noticing anything out of the ordinary, she was ready to chalk up their behavior to some devious plan destined to play out later.

Then Ranger turned around, placing his back to her. Piper bit back a laugh seeing a large pair of lipstick-red lips painted on the left butt cheek of Ranger's game pants. Since they were white and the red so big and bright, it stuck out like an elephant dancing through Times Square. "Why does it look like a giant girly gorilla kissed you on the ass?"

Ranger scowled. "Because someone had way too much time on their hands and decided to pull pranks."

The guys snickered. Piper glanced over the group. She'd bet nearly all of them were in on it.

"Cute." Piper shot him a mischievous grin. "Do I want to know how it got there?"

He snorted. "Like I could tell you?"

She giggled. "Good point." She started for the ice only to stop and turn back to Ranger. "You do know the announcers, media and fans are going to have a heyday with this."

Ranger sighed heavily. "Yeah. Bastards." He eyed his teammates once more.

They tried to keep straight faces but failed miserably.

Piper did as well. She left the locker room still chuckling.

A little over two hours later, she was no longer laughing.

The Tide team had her scrambling to protect her net. Not only that, they'd scored the tying goal a few minutes earlier on a diverted pass that had switched directions so fast she hadn't been able to keep up. Now the final seconds of overtime ticked down.

She slammed her leg down on the ice, blocking a puck around that one of the guys tried to jam in on the very edge. Her skate stopped it, but she couldn't bend down quick enough to cover up. Instead they took the puck around the net once more, then tried a sharp-angled shot from the corner.

She blocked it with her stick, then focused on the scramble in front of the crease.

The buzzer sounded loudly.

Piper sighed in relief, taking the opportunity to guzzle some much-needed water. Both teams had fought hard despite the few spectators in the stands. Eighteen inches of snow the night before evidently kept most at home, still digging out.

Fans or no fans, the men still had their pride and competitive natures. Thus the back and forth battle all the way to the end.

The ref skated up to her. "Shoot-out. Five skaters. Your team shoots first."

She nodded that she understood, took one final drink, then replaced her water bottle in the holder on top of the net.

Rocky took the ice. He took the puck down the rink, faked right, lunged left, and slapped the puck hard with his stick. It sailed in.

Piper didn't have time to celebrate as the Tide player was already preparing for his turn. She watched his every movement, saw the puck leave the stick, and dropped down in the splits, cutting off the unguarded area, and managed to block the shot just in time.

She stood back up and watched the scene repeat. Unfortunately, after that first try the Tide grew fancier, trickier and more powerful with their tries. She missed the next by a hair. Slid across on the third, narrowly missing once more. The fourth she flat out guessed wrong. Finally, with the score still tied, she faced the final skater. If he scored, the Tide won.

Crouching, she readied herself as he kicked the puck with his skate to get it moving. He used his stick, moving it from side to side, listed to the left, then sent a flaming backhand to the right upper corner. She couldn't catch up.

The small crowd cheered.

"Nice shot." She tossed out the compliment then grinned at the stunned look on the guy's face. He bobbed his head once in acknowledgement.

Reality sank in. She'd lost the game due to her miss. Piper lowered her head in defeat.

It's not like you haven't lost before, Piper. She tried to bolster her spirit. *Besides, even the best goalies in the world lose. No one has a perfect record.* She'd wanted to have just that. For the guys. To prove her worth and show the world that women could play as well as men, at least in her position.

Worn out, she flipped her mask up in order to get some cool air blowing on her heated face, collected her bottle, then headed for the bench.

She stopped at the door in the wall. "I'm sorry."

Tommy patted her shoulder. "It's okay. You put in a good game."

"I should have done more."

He shook his head. "You're in the big leagues now. Name the best goalies of all time. They all lost. Pucks get by. That's reality. You played your heart out, so shake it off." He opened the door to let her in.

Adam ruffled her hair, not really doing much damage since she kept it in a single braid for games. "We can't win them all." He smiled at her. "You did great. So don't worry about it."

Their comments eased her guilt. Somewhat.

"It's nice to know you're human." Rayovic walked by her

on the mat laid out that led to the locker room.

She snorted good-naturedly. "Gee, thanks."

"Welcome." He held up a hand as he passed her by.

She made her way back to the locker room in order to listen to any words of wisdom Tommy had to impart. Afterward she'd hightail it to the women's facilities, thankful they had them in this arena.

Ranger appeared at her side. "You did a good job out there."

"Thanks, but I feel like I could have done better."

He flashed a grin. "That's your competitive nature coming out." He opened the door and ushered her in.

The rest of the team filed in. Tommy stood at the front of the room already. Odd, since he normally stepped in later.

"Listen up. We've got to get a move on. There's a huge snowstorm heading toward Denver. Like we didn't have enough of it in New York already. Anyway, if we skip dinner and hit the plane directly from here, we can make it home for the two days off. If not, we'll have to stay another day here then move on to Toronto after that, a day early."

The guys grumbled in unison.

"I figured you'd rather spend the two days at home if possible."

"Yeah," several of the guys affirmed.

In this instance, Piper didn't care either way, but understood those with families would like to see them as much as they could rather than sitting around a hotel for another day.

"Then let's get going. The sooner we get out of here, the sooner we get back home." Tommy clapped his hands.

Piper grabbed her bag and headed for the women's locker room. She hurriedly stripped down, took a very quick shower and pulled on casual slacks and a sweater to wear home. As much as she preferred to go comfortable, the team's management preferred a much more professional look coming and going from games.

By the time she finished getting cleaned up, packed her

bag and made her way back, many of the guys stood in the hallway ready to go.

Ben, the team organizer, ushered them to the bus, assuring them they'd already picked up the suitcases from the hotel. The equipment bags and duffels went into the same storage bin.

Something hard and painful struck her in the back. Piper yelped and spun around.

"Go back to the pussy league, cunt!" A man on the other side of the rope waved his arm, showed the rock he had in his hand, and threw.

The rock struck her in the shoulder, leaving a sting behind.

"Son of a bitch." Ranger grabbed her, shoved her in front of him and half-carried her to the bus steps. The other guys formed a barrier around their backs.

"Where in the fuck is security?" Ben hollered.

She caught a glimpse out of the window of a couple of men tackling the heckler to the ground.

"Sit down." Ranger nudged her into a nearby seat. "How bad is it?"

She read the concern on his face, the barely leashed anger, and knew he'd love to go a couple of rounds with the idiot who liked to throw rocks.

"I'm fine."

Chester appeared. He started asking questions, then motioned for her to swivel around. When she did, he lifted her shirt to look at the injury.

He tugged the material back down and shook his head. "Bastard. Just a small red mark or two, didn't break the skin. Might bruise, but that's all. You got lucky." He wandered off.

Odd, she didn't feel lucky. "I guess I haven't won over everyone to the idea of women playing with men yet." Her sarcasm fell flat.

Several pairs of eyes focused on her, all flashing with worry and apology.

"You can't teach new tricks to moronic assholes," Ivan

gritted out before heading toward the front of the bus.

"True." Piper repressed a shiver, not wanting to appear shaken or weak. However, deep down, she was rattled.

Ranger took the seat next to hers. "Tommy is going to make heads roll." He pointed out the window at Tommy yelling at one of the security guards.

"They can only do so much." She drew in a steadying breath. "Besides, everyone who has broken boundaries in the past has suffered at the hands and lips of hate."

"That doesn't mean it's right," Adam pointed out.

"I agree, but don't have the power to change the world."

Ranger brushed his knuckles over her cheek. "It won't happen again. Promise."

Piper smiled softly at his sweet gesture. "You can't promise such a thing. The acts of others are out of your control."

"I'll do my damnedest to make sure it doesn't happen again. Better?"

She grinned. "Yes, better. With you and the rest of the guys as guard dogs, I'm sure I'll be in the best of hands."

Tommy stepped onto the bus and pinned Piper with his fiery gaze. "Are you okay?"

"Yes, sir. Just call me Teflon." She saluted him.

He shook his head, took the front seat and spoke to the bus driver. A few seconds later, they were on their way.

Piper checked her cell phone. No messages, but the weather alerts were blowing up her phone. Winter weather warnings. Blizzard warnings. None of them looked promising.

"What's with the long face?"

She passed the phone over to Ranger. "It's gonna get bad."

He shook his head. "Eighteen to twenty-four inches. That'll shut down the city for sure."

"Think we can make it home in time?" She bit her lip. Even though she had an SUV, that didn't mean she could navigate through that much powder to make it to her apartment in the suburbs. Her parents' house, to the south of the city, would also be nearly impossible to get to. If roads and interstates started shutting down, she'd be in a pickle.

He handed her phone back. "Worried about getting home?"

She sighed. "Yeah."

"You can always crash at my place. I don't live too far."

The offer didn't surprise Piper, nor did it turn her away. Instead, a refreshing surge of hope flared. Along with a healthy dose of desire. She studied his face for a long moment. "You wouldn't mind?"

He smiled. "Not at all. I've got three bedrooms and three bathrooms. Plenty of space for one little goalie."

She couldn't help but grin at his statement. "We'll see what it's like when we get to Denver, but I'll keep it in mind."

"Good."

* * * *

Three hours later, she stepped off the bus that had taken them from the airport to the parking garage at the rink facilities. They'd made it home in time. Sort of. From what she could see, probably four or five inches of snow blanketed the ground. The wind whipped, blowing so badly seeing became difficult. Even with snowplows already out in force, she knew they couldn't keep up.

Tommy, Ranger and a couple of the other guys offered an open door policy to any of the team who wanted to camp out at their houses, which were in the city and much closer than the suburbs. Since they had practice in just over twenty-four hours, a few of the guys took them up on their invitations. Piper held her tongue for the moment.

She went to the baggage area, collected her suitcase and duffel, then picked Ranger out of the crowd. On the way to him, she checked out her small SUV, finding it safe, sound and free of snow in the protected lot. Once she drew in close, she quietly asked, "Can you fit one more into your vehicle?"

He glanced up from checking the tag on his luggage. "Yep." After picking up the bag and juggling his carry-on, he gestured with his head. "Come on."

Piper fell into step.

He loaded their belongings into the back of the SUV then motioned for her to climb into the passenger's seat. She didn't hesitate, eager to get started on the trek to his house before the conditions worsened.

"Is there anyone else coming with us?" She fastened her belt.

Ranger slid into the driver's seat, shut the door, shoved his key in the ignition and clicked his seat belt. "No. Axel lives close by as well. I think Keith, Rocky and maybe Sven were going to hang out with him."

"Think anyone is going home with Tommy?" Piper grinned at the thought. More than likely, breakfast at Tommy's house would consist of hockey plays and critiques.

"Probably not." Ranger chuckled. "The guys want to kick back and relax, not attend a college-level instruction seminar on the ins and outs of hockey."

He pulled out of the shelter and into the storm. His car didn't appear to have much issue with the depth of the snow. Visibility was the main concern with the darkness and heavy flakes peppering the windshield.

She took a moment to text her mother, reassuring Darla that she'd returned home safe and sound. Piper didn't bother to elaborate at whose home she would happen to be staying. No sense in opening that can of worms just yet. She also mentioned that she had a couple of days off, so they didn't have to worry about her trying to drive through the mess to the rink until roads were in much better shape.

Task complete, she turned her attention back to Ranger. "Thank you for letting me stay. I'm not sure I could get home to Westminster."

"No problem. I'm in the Polo Club Neighborhood. So, really close." He drove with ease, his hands light on the steering wheel.

Damn impressive. Not just where he lived, but also the way he handled the car.

She would have been gripping the wheel tightly and have had her nose plastered almost to the windshield in order to be able to see. Ranger did just the opposite — sat back in his seat, let the wiper blades do their job, and watched the road with lazy interest.

Piper shook her head. "Why do I get the feeling that nothing fazes you?"

He spared her a curious glance. "Where did that come from?"

"Because you play hard and tough, but never seem to get frustrated or agitated. Same with driving in a blizzard. No nerves. No tension. Just a typical late-night Tuesday drive through the scenic flatlands at the base of the mountains. Granted, I've only been around you for a few weeks, but nothing rattles you."

The corners of his mouth turned up. "I guess I'm pretty laid-back. I have it good and know it." He cut her a glance that sent her stomach into a slow somersault.

A few minutes later he pulled into the driveway of a gray brick ranch house on what appeared to be probably a couple of acres or more, based on the old wooden railing that presumably outlined the property. The single-level home spoke of affluence without being over the top. Neat, tidy and inviting.

"This is beautiful."

"Thanks. It's not a huge mansion like some of the guys favor. I'm pretty simple and rational. No sense in having a monstrosity of a house if I'm the only one living in it."

"True." She began to see the real Ranger coming through. Practical. Kind. Caring. All the traits she enjoyed in others that resonated through her as well.

He clicked a button and one of the three garage doors

opened. He drove in, hit the remote again, then shut down the engine. "Let's get unloaded and inside where it's bound to be warmer."

Piper hurried to the back and started loading up both of their stuff. With straps over her shoulders, she bent down to get the suitcases, only for him to beat her to them.

"I've got it. You're weighed down enough already." He took a piece of luggage in each hand, then led the way to the door. Opening it, he stepped inside before holding it open for Piper.

She entered the house, immediately noting the comfortable temperature, significantly better than outside. A large kitchen loomed ahead, the walls holding all the typical amenities in shiny metallic colors. A brown speckled countertop ran the whole length, most likely granite judging by the appearance. In a corner sat a table with a chair located on either side. The tile floor reflected the colors of the countertop, earthy tones that added to the overall feeling of comfort and home.

"Gorgeous."

"Drop off the stuff and come on in. I'll give you the tour."

Piper set the bags on the floor before slipping her shoes off.

He did the same, turned, and gave a quick nod when he noticed she had removed her shoes. "Habit?"

"Yeah. I just hate the thought of wearing shoes in the house. After everything we walk through. Yuck."

"I agree." He smiled and reached out his hand.

She took it, letting him guide her from one room to another. Deeply rich hardwood floors with a glossy coating continued as far as she could see. Painted walls in lighter hues complemented as well as added a bit of brightness. The combination worked perfectly, in Piper's opinion.

The living room came next. Large. Open. With a giant television that even a blind man could see. Leather-covered furniture sat here and there, adding an Old West feel. The hallway sported a nice-sized bathroom. Two bedrooms were at one end of the house, the master opposite. 'Airy' and 'spacious' came to mind as she checked out each area. Ranger's decorations tended toward 'less is more', but seemed entirely fitting to the whole theme of the house. No clutter took away from the place. Nor did a thick layer of dust. "Do you clean this yourself?"

"Nope. I have a housekeeper come in once a week. With me being gone all the time, it only makes sense." He winked down at her. "Besides, I hate cleaning."

She chuckled. "Not my favorite part either, but it has to be done or the dust bunnies would get so large, they'd take over the world."

He grinned. "There's that." Opening a door, he stepped aside so she could enter.

Piper found herself standing in the middle of a hockey fan's dream world. Plaques, pictures and even a signed framed jersey hung from the wall. Two curio cabinets contained more memorabilia. Not just current stuff, but old-time skates, pictures and Hall of Famer-autographed pictures sat under glass.

"Wow." She couldn't believe the collection Ranger had on display. "Just amazing." Every which way she turned, new delights caught her eye.

Ranger leaned on the doorframe with a proud smile on his face. "I kind of like it myself."

She peered over at him. "You've got some great stuff here."

"Yeah."

"Anything of my father's?" Curiosity prodded her to ask.

"Just a couple of pictures is all."

Piper nodded. Her father had spent nearly twenty years in the league and held a prominent position in the Hall of Fame and in many players' esteem. He was a legend in his day and still carried sway and earned respect wherever he went despite being retired.

She made a mental note to ask her father to sign something good for Ranger. After all, he went out of his way to make her comfortable and safe. Not only tonight but since she'd appeared on the ice as a brand new member of the Denver Wolfpack.

"I could spend hours in here looking at all this stuff."

"I do now and again." He stood up straight. "However, right now, I think food is in order, then perhaps some rest. It's been a long day and I know we're both tired."

"Good idea." They'd been given snacks on the plane ride home. That had curbed her appetite for only a short while.

She fell into step with him as he made his way back to the kitchen.

"I have some frozen dinners we can nuke. Not a five-star meal, but quick and easy."

"Works for me." She started toward the cabinets. "If you'll tell me where everything is, I'll gladly help."

He pointed to a nearby one then opened the freezer door and gathered up a couple of boxes. "Glasses are up there. Utensils are the drawer right under it."

She plucked out the necessary items and carried them over to the table. He followed with a large bottle of soda.

The microwave beeped, declaring one of the meals finished. Ranger plucked it out and set it on the table before placing the other inside.

Piper filled their glasses with ice and poured the drinks. "Do you miss Minnesota?"

Ranger turned to look at her. "Yes and no. My parents still live there, so I visit fairly often. Not to mention we play a few games in that part of the country. But I'm pretty happy here. Sure, the season started out pretty damn bad. It happens. We're clicking now and I think the guys are loose, happy and having fun once more." He studied her for a moment. "I bet you moved around as a kid with your father being traded a few times."

"Yeah. It was always a pain. Having to pack, find a new house, new friends. When he came here, I felt like this was home. I think my parents believed the same thing. That's why they stayed. So, when the opportunity came to play for the Denver Bobcats, I jumped on it. Playing for the home town crowd, so to speak."

"What about your brother out in southern California?"

Piper shrugged. "He seems content there. Of course, he's living it up as a playboy. What's not to love when you have sun, beaches and women in skimpy bikinis for scenery?" She grinned.

Ranger chuckled. "There's that." He moved closer. "Personally, I'd much rather be snowed in here with you." He brushed his lips over hers.

Before she could respond, the microwave sounded again. Ranger collected the last meal and placed it on the nearby table. "Let's eat."

She sat down, enjoying the steam coming off the food as it warmed her hands. "Question?"

"Answer." He shoveled some mashed potatoes into his mouth then quickly took a drink, as if they were still a bit too hot.

"Did any of the guys ask about staying with you? Or was I the only one?"

He grinned mischievously. "Think I masterminded having you all to myself, huh?"

She arched an eyebrow. "Maybe."

For a moment she thought he wouldn't answer so she dug into her peas.

"I wouldn't have turned any of them away. Personally, I think they heard you ask and deliberately avoided being the third leg."

"Oh." She let that sink in. "Ohhhh."

He smile widened. "Wanna bet which one of the three that saw us holding hands in the restaurant blabbed to the rest of the team?"

"Axel, Riley and Ivan. Hmmm." She considered what she knew about them. "I'd say all of them."

"Safe bet. They all can be pranksters and love juicy gossip."

She rolled her eyes. "And they call women busybodies."

Ranger ate in silence, quickly finishing his meal. Piper wasn't far behind. The snacks on the plane had tided her over marginally. The food, though a frozen dinner, hit the spot. She probably would have done the same thing or even simply fixed a sandwich if she were at home.

With both of them helping, they had the kitchen cleaned up in only a couple of minutes. She emptied her glass of soda then placed it in the sink beside his.

Anticipation surged as she wondered what they would do now. She glanced at her watch, finding the time just past eleven at night. Not horribly late for a hockey player. Though it had been one really long day.

"Ready to crash?" He nudged her toward the large sofa in the living room, then took a seat.

"Getting there." She sat down next to him.

He pulled her against him, holding her snug. She rested her head against his shoulder. "Thank you again for taking me in."

"My pleasure." He pressed his lips to her temple. "I'm glad you decided to come. Otherwise I'd have been worried about you getting home safely."

"Me too." She peeked up at him. "I'm pretty darn happy right now. It might be a blizzard outside, but I'm here. With you."

Ranger smiled. "I never thought I'd be thankful for a snowstorm."

She considered her present situation and realized she'd been missing something important in her life. Ranger filled the void she hadn't known existed and had stolen a piece of her heart along the way. "You know. I vowed to never date a hockey player. Too cocky. Too rough. Too arrogant."

"Uh-huh." He rubbed his chin on the top of her crown. "And now?"

She sighed. "I think I've fallen for one."

He stilled for a second. "Anyone I know?"

"Maybe," she teased. "He's big as a bear. Dark-haired too. Strong, yet gentle. He can flatten a guy against the boards with one swipe, but kiss me with such tender reverence." She lifted his hand and placed her palm against his, noting the size difference between them. "Big hands. Big feet. Big guy."

He grinned.

"Smart and dang talented at hockey, too."

"That helps."

"Laid-back. Not one of those hotheads with a hair trigger, either."

"Hmm." Ranger squeezed her a little. "What else do you like about him?"

"He's caring and considerate. Got the best booty in the league," she added tongue-in-cheek.

Ranger chuckled. "Aha. Now we're getting to the important stuff."

She couldn't hold back the grin. "Did I mention he's sinfully sexy?"

"Sinfully sexy, huh?" Ranger arched an eyebrow.

"Oh, yeah." She pulled her legs up and cuddled into him. "Yummy and definitely lickable."

He sucked in air. "Lickable?"

"Yep." Piper nodded. "Lickable."

A slow smile grew on his face. "So, tell me, where exactly do you want to lick this guy?"

She feigned innocence. "I'll have to think about that."

Ranger groaned dramatically. "Don't take too long."

"I'll try not to." She brushed her lips across his and barely suppressed a yawn. "How about I take tonight and I'll get back with you in the morning?"

His eyes met hers. "Works for me."

"Good."

For a long time, he simply held her tucked against his side. They didn't speak, just listened to the wind outside and enjoyed each other's company.

Piper saw the writing on the wall. She'd come home. In the arms of the man she'd fallen in love with on the first day she joined the team, although she hadn't known it at the time. Now she had two days alone with him. She planned on enjoying every minute. After she got some much-needed sleep.

Closing her eyes, she drifted off, dreaming of a great knight who fell in love with a princess.

Chapter Seventeen

Piper awoke early, her typical time, then glanced around at the unfamiliar surroundings. A second later, she recalled that she'd spent the night in one of Ranger's spare bedrooms. Safe and warm, well away from the blizzard raging outside. Or that had been. With any luck it had wound down.

She climbed out of bed, took a couple of minutes to make it again, stretched, then checked out the window. Sure enough, whiteness enveloped just about everything in sight. She shivered at the view.

Wearing an old pair of silk pajamas, she quietly left her room and made her way to the nearest bathroom, glancing at a nearby clock on her way. She had plenty of time to get cleaned up then fix breakfast—the least she could do to partially repay Ranger's hospitality. With plan in hand, she stepped into the kitchen, investigated the fridge and started pulling out items.

Twenty minutes later, she had bacon cooking in the microwave, pancakes in a skillet on the stove and a large pan of poached eggs just about ready to be taken up. Sausage, almost an afterthought, had a few more minutes in the oven before it could come out.

She twirled around the kitchen, spatula in hand, humming as she gathered up milk, juice and butter for the bread just waiting to be toasted.

Last night had been magical. Ranger had held her on the couch until after midnight. She'd fallen asleep and stayed there until he carried her to bed, tucked her in and kissed her goodnight. A gentlemanly thing to do. A fact that resounded with her.

Always before, she'd size a man up and invariably find him lacking. Too gruff. Too conceited. Too much of a loose cannon. Trust came hard and only when earned. A throwback from her childhood. Only one other man had earned her complete trust besides her father and her brother — Ranger.

He'd given her something to think about. A big something.

She'd confessed her feelings. Well, mostly. The 'L' word hadn't been mentioned. He'd seemed receptive in their subtle conversation, giving her plenty of time to think things over. She had. By the time sleep had claimed her the second time, she'd made up her mind.

Ranger had her heart. For now and hopefully for always. She couldn't find a better man and didn't want to leave his house without making headway in their previously slow-moving relationship.

"Something smells delicious."

She spun around, saw Ranger walking toward her wearing only a pair of sweatpants, and grinned. *Nothing like a generous helping of delectable eye candy to brighten up the day.* "Good morning, captain. Ready for breakfast?"

"Ugh. Don't tell me you're one of those peppy morning people that resemble that damn pink bunny."

"Okay, I won't." She didn't take offense to his slightly rough tone. Many people were that way. Give them food and coffee and they changed their tune.

He sat down at the table.

"Don't tell me you're one of those non-morning people that wake up like a hibernating bear, hungry and grumpy." She tweaked his words and fed them back to him.

He leveled her a look. "Just remember bears eat little bunnies for breakfast."

She blinked at him, getting the impression he wasn't just talking about the survival of the fittest in the wild.

Intrigued with the line of conversation, she considered her next move while passing out plates, glasses and utensils.

The timer went off, indicating the sausages could come

out of the oven. After grabbing them, she placed them and the plate of pancakes on the table. She plucked the bacon from the microwave and collected the eggs on the next trip. Next, she slapped the lever down on the toaster, then flipped the last of the pancakes and took the opportunity to check Ranger out.

Without the shirt, she had a bird's-eye view of his wide chest, the six-pack abs and everything in between. Only a few dark hairs sprinkled between his pecs, then a few more leading downward from his belly button. Toned, powerful shoulders drew her eye. Something about a man with chiseled muscles in his arms made her sit up and take notice. Ranger was no exception.

"You look particularly feral this morning." His tousled hair and wrinkled clothes took the edge off his otherwise serious presentation.

"Thanks." He grabbed a piece of bacon and bit down. "You're bright-eyed already. Do you ever sleep?"

She poured herself a glass of milk, then hurried back to collect the toast, which had popped up. Dropping a couple pieces on Ranger's plate, she placed the other two on her own. Finally, she sat down and added a pancake and link of sausage to her plate. "I do, actually. Problem is I'm an early riser. My inner alarm clock goes off and I can't go back to sleep."

"Bummer." He poured some orange juice before taking a long drink.

"It's not so bad. I get the ice to myself most mornings that way."

He shook his head. "I don't know how you do it. Our hockey schedule is relentless, yet you're still perky after a short night of sleep. Beats me how you keep up."

Piper grinned. "Because I'm just like that damn pink bunny you seem to dislike."

He snorted before taking another bite. "This is good. Really good. Thanks."

"You're welcome. I figured food might be in order this

morning." She forked some pancake, placed it in her mouth, chewed and swallowed. "I actually like cooking. Well, most things. I'm far from a gourmet chef, but I can make a mean breakfast ensemble and bake up a decent cake for dessert."

The sleepiness seemed to be receding from his face as he ate. She almost missed it. "I never knew men liked to cook much. But, I've learned a few of the hockey guys are downright gourmet chefs."

"I'm not in their league, but I do okay. It's not my favorite hobby, but I get by. Better than eating out every night."

"True. Cheaper too." She took a sip of her drink.

He glanced up at her. "Are you keeping up with your other job? The bookkeeping? With all the traveling, games and practices we're doing?"

She nodded. "Yeah. It's been tougher than I initially thought. I make time when I have to. Luckily, I can knock out a week's worth of spreadsheets in a couple of hours uninterrupted. As you know, I make use of bus time and also down time in the hotel. We don't have that much longer to go, so I'll be able to direct my full attention to it at that time." As soon as she said the words, she wished them back. The reminder of the mere few weeks left in the season made her stomach sink with sadness. "Do you miss the guys during the off season?"

Ranger took a few more mouthfuls before answering. "We get together fairly often. Run into one another at the facilities working out. Pick-up games on the ice. Charity events. All kinds of things. Heck, some of them end up underfoot looking for a buddy to just hang with."

"I guess I figured they'd all go back home." Piper considered the guys on the team. While most lived locally, she thought some had houses elsewhere. Not to mention the ones from other countries.

"They do. For a visit. The international players tend to return to their own country for a longer time. However, hockey is a year-round sport. While no games are happening, training never stops."

"Tell me about it." Piper finished her toast and wiped her hands on a napkin she'd placed on the table earlier. "Even though the women's league has a much shorter season, we're all expected to stay in tip-top condition. No one dares return in the fall out of shape. That would earn a coach's wrath. Big time."

Ranger cleaned his plate, then stole the last piece of bacon off the platter. "Since we don't have to worry about hitting the ice today, what do you want to do?"

"Oh, I don't know." Piper peeked up at him from under her eyelashes. "We could venture outside and make snow angels."

Ranger chuckled. "Yeah. Fall in and never be found again until spring."

"Okay. Maybe not." She caught his amusement and grinned in return. "What are your suggestions?"

His eyes softened as he rubbed his chin, which sported a five o'clock shadow.

Piper's breath caught at the expression on his face.

"I vote we jump in the shower then decide." The quiet timbre of his voice rolled over her nerves like warmth from the sun after a long winter's blast.

"We?"

He arched an eyebrow. "How do you feel about water conservation?"

Piper squirmed under his intense gaze. "Ummm. I'll think about it while I'm in the hallway shower getting cleaned up." She stood up and carried the dirty dishes to the sink.

Ranger did likewise. He returned for the leftovers and drinks, placing everything in the fridge while Piper stacked dishes in the dishwasher.

She'd just added detergent and pushed the Start button when he finished clearing the table. Needing something to do, she spun around in search of a rag to wipe the counters down.

He stepped in front of her to halt her nervous movements. One hand lightly latched onto her forearm. "Hey. I'm just teasing you. No pressure. Promise."

"Thanks." Piper's heart sped from his touch alone.

"It's your call, Piper." He studied her for a long moment, released her, then headed back toward the bedroom.

Wow. Piper could finally breathe when Ranger pushed past her. She took the opportunity to check out his butt until he disappeared from sight.

What am I going to do with him?

Take a chance, that's what.

With the decision made, she hurried to the bathroom to get cleaned up for the day.

* * * *

After leaving the shower, she returned to her borrowed bedroom, dug through her suitcase and debated what to wear. For this trip, she'd packed extremes. Dress up and dress down. Nothing really casual. Since she intended to spend the snow day lounging around, she opted for an oversized white sweatshirt and light blue sweatpants. Comfortable, warm and something less than sexy. Unfortunately.

Truthfully, she didn't think Ranger would expect a little black dress and heels today. She couldn't be herself dressed like that anyway. Always a tomboy, she rarely ventured into the world of fashion and the latest fads. None of that interested her. Clothes that fit well and were everyday useful made their way into her closet. There were few exceptions.

She sighed as she wandered into the hallway and made her way to the living area. Drawn to the large picture window overlooking the back yard, she stood in front of it and peered outside. White snow lay as far as the eye could see, deep and still coming down at a fairly good clip. A covered patio allowed her to estimate the amounts from where a little managed to blow onto the cement to that first doozy of a step. A person would likely sink down to their knees in the frozen fluff.

Footfalls announced Ranger returning from the restroom. She glimpsed him heading her way, felt and heard him stop right behind her. He drew up close before sliding his arms around her from behind. His bare chest brushed against her back. At least he'd changed sweats to a pair that didn't have nearly as many wrinkles. The light gray color suited him better as well.

Piper smiled softly and leaned back against him while resting her hands on top of his.

He brushed her hair aside before pressing his lips to her nape first, followed by right behind her ear.

She sighed in contentment and rising pleasure. "It's so beautiful. Brutal, but beautiful."

"Yeah. But not as beautiful as you." He sniffed her hair. "Sugar cookies."

"It's my shampoo. I swear."

"Don't stop using it." He nuzzled her cheek, leaving tiny flares in his path.

She tiled her head, allowing him to pepper kisses over her shoulder, revealed by the oversized sweatshirt. A few more of those lit up her libido, sending hot waves of need rolling through her. Her stomach flip-flopped in the most delightful way.

Turning in his arms, she rested her hands on his shoulders. He lowered his head and she met him halfway, sealing her lips over his and immediately opening when he licked at the seam. Piper welcomed the sweet invasion by tapping his tongue and returning the favor, slipping in for a taste of the man who'd turned her world upside down.

He roamed his hands up and down her back, tugging her closer, before one cupped her head, holding her still for his plundering.

She gasped as the sultry heat intensified.

Ranger drew slightly away, brushed her hair aside so he could trail his fingertips along her cheek. The entire time, he stared at her as if she was a priceless treasure he'd searched for all his life.

"Tell me what you want."

She nearly melted at his soft, gentle tone combined with the mix of want and appreciation in his expressive green eyes. "You."

His breath caught. "Are you sure?"

"Yes." She ran her fingers down the center of his chest, enjoying the silkiness of his skin along with the definition of thick muscles. Curious and emboldened, she explored his entire nude trunk, from shoulders to waist, finding all the dips and valleys along the way.

He brushed his lips over hers. Once. Twice. Then meshed them with a kiss that could only be called an eruption of passion mixed with equal parts tenderness. He slipped his tongue past her lips and explored, leaving no area untouched.

Piper welcomed him with gusto. She took cues from him then gave back by mirroring his moves.

Ranger dropped his hands to her waist, dipped them under her shirt and traveled upward until he cupped her bare breasts in his hands.

She shivered at the novel touch and gasped as he first weighed her breasts then rolled the tips between his fingers.

He pulled back and peered down at her. "Tell me if I'm going too fast. Or if I'm doing something wrong." He continued to mold the sensitive area, sending decadent surges of pleasure through her. "In a way, this is as new to me as it is to you."

She kicked her muddled brain into gear and blinked up at him in puzzlement. "What do you mean?"

"I've never initiated a virgin before," he whispered.

His quiet confession drove last of her concerns away. She grinned and placed her hand on his cheek. "We'll learn together."

He turned his head and kissed her palm. "I like the sound of that."

"Me, too."

Ranger bent over, scooped her up and carried her to

his bedroom. After laying her in the center of his bed, he sidestepped to a nearby table, opened the drawer and pulled out a condom.

This is really going to happen.

Butterflies took flight in Piper's stomach.

He stood motionless for a long moment. Piper took advantage of the opportunity to feast on the sight of his primed body. Including the tenting of his sweatpants. That, in particular, intrigued her the most.

Ranger placed his knee on the bed then crawled over to her. With a hand behind her back, he pulled her into a sitting position before grabbing the bottom of her sweatshirt and lifting it over her head.

Piper barely noticed the temperature difference as her entire body heated under Ranger's intense gaze. The second his hands came into play once again, she forgot all about modesty. All that mattered was that Ranger touch her. Kiss her. Continue to draw her under his delectable spell. For she'd never craved anything more.

His lips found hers. Coaxed. Teased. Then settled in for a show of gentle domination. He seized control, thrust his tongue inside and explored in a sizzling foray. All the while, his hands produced magic across her body. He explored every inch as if trying to learn her by feel alone.

Leaning away, he showered her with kisses as he slowly pressed her back down to the mattress. He loomed over her, dipping in frequently to treat her to more fiery lip locks.

Piper trailed her hands over the muscles of his shoulders and down across his chest. Impishly, she found his nipple and rubbed.

He groaned and glanced up to meet her eyes.

Bedroom eyes. She'd heard the term before but hadn't really been able to say she'd seen such an expression. Now she knew, with certainty. Hooded and molten, Ranger's eyes pinned her with the sheer need she saw in them.

"Am I going to scare you being on top like this?" The words came out hoarse and husky.

Piper smiled at his sensitivity. "No way. I like you close. Touching. It makes me feel…" *Loved.* She bit her lip and wracked her brain for a replacement. "Hungry. Protected. Safe in your arms." All those were also true.

He nuzzled her cheek then scooted back to place kisses on the remnants of the large bruise along her left side. "I've been wanting to do this since I first saw the mark on the trip home."

The admission touched her where it counted most—her heart.

He took a second to climb out of bed, slide off his pants, and toss them to the floor.

Piper gawked at his nude body, unable to tear her focus from his jutting shaft. Large. Exceptionally so. Full. Thick. "You're big all over."

He chuckled, returned to the bed and stretched out over her, careful to keep his weight on his hands and knees. "Yep." He settled on his side next to her, took her hand and placed it on his erection. "Touch me."

She lightly explored by forming a circle with her thumb and fingers. First she tested with a tentative squeeze, then ran the length of his cock and back up to the tip. Ever so lightly, she caressed that area with her fingertips, amazed when a drop of moisture emerged from the small opening. Smearing it with her thumb, she trailed her hand down to the base, and lower.

A shiver ran through Ranger.

Piper peered up into his face. He watched her hand with rapt attention, his teeth clenched, lips pulled back in a grimace.

Carefully, she cupped his sac and rolled the balls inside. "Does that hurt?"

He shook his head. "Feels good. Too damn good." He sucked in air and removed her hand from his body. "Enough of that. Any more and I'll be coming before we really get started."

The knowledge that her touch alone carried the power

to bring him to the breaking point buoyed her confidence. "We can't have that."

"Nope. Not when we have so much else to see and do." He smiled as he sat back up, hooked his fingers in her sweats and gradually tugged them down, catching her panties along the way.

Piper lifted her rear in an effort to help, then her feet, for him to remove them completely. He gave them a toss as she planted her heels on the bed, her thighs slightly open.

Ranger wasted no time in running his hand up the insides of her thighs and pressing lightly. "Open for me."

A bit hesitantly, Piper obeyed.

He scooched into the space created, cupped her mound and glided a finger through her folds.

Piper startled at the unfamiliar experience and tried to bring her legs together again. Not possible with Ranger in the way and his hand smack dab on her delta.

"Shh. I'm just touching." He eased her thighs apart, tunneled through to her slit, then pressed inside.

Piper's breath caught at the feel of his entry.

"You're wet. Really wet. I can't wait to make you cream." He delved a bit deeper. "Tight." And a little farther.

Piper jumped as he hit a tender spot, sending a jolt of discomfort through the maze of pleasure.

"Okay. I get it." He retreated only to return, though not as deep. After a couple of times, he added another digit.

The fullness increased, as did Piper's arousal. She squirmed against his hand in search of anything to take her higher.

He twisted his wrist.

The unexpected brush of a finger over her ultra-sensitive bundle of nerves drew a ragged cry from her throat. She tilted her pelvis in an attempt to bring it back.

"Right there?"

"Yes. Whatever you did, do it again."

He repeated the motion.

Piper clutched the comforter in her fists and began to

pant. The brief sensations rocked her, burned her with sensual heat and made her desperate for more.

He plied her with tender caresses, driving her crazy. She forgot everything but Ranger and his ability to strum the pleasure centers of her body with perfection. Between the fingers stretching her core and his thumb rubbing her clit, she scaled up a ladder of erotic bliss. "Ranger…"

"That's what I want to hear," he gritted out.

Piper heard the pride in his voice as well as the sultry undertones. He was just as turned on as she was, but put her needs above his own. Her feelings for him solidified with the realization.

"I need you." Her words broke on a gasp as he circled her nub again.

Ranger's eyes darkened a shade. He removed his touch, hurriedly opened the condom and rolled it on. Afterward he lowered his body to cover hers, his weight supported on long arms planted on either side of her head. He edged closer until his erection pressed against her folds.

A last-second bout of nerves struck with his initial penetration. She braced herself by holding onto his shoulders, digging in with her nails as the pressure intensified.

Ranger swooped down and kissed her. "Relax."

Peering up into his eyes, she found solid truth, encouragement and a gentle expression that told her all she needed to know. Gradually, she released her death grip.

"That's better." He rubbed his nose against hers. "Stay with me. Just hold on. It'll be a bit rough for a second. Then I'm going to teach you to fly."

How he knew, she didn't have the brain power to ask. Instead, she went with his wisdom and prepared for a crucial moment in her life. One she wouldn't share with anyone but Ranger. "Okay." She lifted her chin so he could trail a line of kisses along her throat and over to her ear. He nibbled then nipped sharply at the same time as he thrust.

Piper inhaled sharply at the prick of discomfort, flinching

and jerking in an instinctive reaction to withdraw.

Ranger slid deep then stopped. For a long moment he did nothing more than pepper sweet kisses over her face and lips.

She soaked up the affection, noting the sting had already started to fade. Pain had been part of her world as a child and now as an athlete. Something she could handle. Including this.

He lifted his head and stared down at her. "You okay?"

She nodded, still trying to adjust to his invasion. Full didn't begin to describe how she felt. More like stretched and stuffed.

His lips parted as she wiggled in an attempt to ease the burden. Concern mixed with hot arousal flashed across his face. "Bear with me, sweetheart. It's going to get better soon. So much better." He arched his back and lifted just enough to find her breast and pull the pebbled tip into his mouth. He sucked and licked, working the nipple with precision.

Fire zinged through her blood. She forgot the discomfort, the little pinch. Passion erupted, causing a great need to establish itself and demand fulfillment. She lifted against him, wanting to be closer, unable to hold still under the burning sensations driving her. "Please, Ranger."

He released her breast and glanced at her. "Please what?"

She shook her head in frustration and a lack of words. "Move. Do something."

He eased back before reversing course. At the speed of an aged turtle. "Still okay?" His hands, braced next to her head, held his weight off her.

She bent her knees and lifted them to serve as a vise on his hips. "Yes. Oh, yes." The adjustment allowed him to slide deeper on his next stroke. He pinged a hot spot along the way, setting off another cherry bomb in her rapidly rising arousal. Peeking down, she watched as he worked in and out. The sight added that much more to her escalating heat. The overwhelming urge to touch took over. She trailed her fingers over his chest and shoulders, then around to lightly scratch her nails along his flanks.

He growled and picked up the pace. Marginally. "You're so fucking tight. Hot and tight."

The words stirred her a little bit more. Experimenting, she arched her pelvis, meeting Ranger's downward thrusts. She rolled her hips, then gasped as she ratcheted higher.

He set an easy rhythm, one that she could follow without difficulty.

Piper couldn't hold still. She didn't have a clue how to reach the pinnacle, to ramp up her desire to that all-important climax. All she knew was that Ranger held the keys and she couldn't get enough of him. She met his downstrokes, circled her hips and watched as his cock disappeared inside her body over and over again.

The sight, so stimulating, pushed her that much closer.

Unable to resist, Piper caressed every part of his body she could reach. She plucked at his nipples, made her way around his flanks, even squeezed his butt cheeks as she tried to yank him closer. When he maintained the steady pace, she whimpered.

"Patience, sweetheart. You're getting close. Really close." He dropped his head and bent his elbows to mesh his lips with hers.

Piper moaned as his kiss mimicked the action down below, where their bodies joined. She splayed her legs and rounded her back. The result was a thrust that went so deep she didn't know where her body stopped and his began. "Yes. Oh, yes."

Ranger grunted as he alternated between long, slow thrusts and short jabs.

She loved them all, yet nothing struck the right chord. "I need…" She turned her head this way and that while raking her nails softly down Ranger's side.

"Just let go. I'll catch you." Ranger licked at her nipple.

Her whole body tightened and her breath came out in pants. She arched her back. Still she couldn't find what she sought. On a rack of sizzling desire, she held tight to

Ranger. She cried out as he moved forward, then lowered his body over hers.

Each breath rubbed her breasts against his chest. Every penetration wedged in deeper, harder, tickling hot spots with each movement.

"I've got you, Piper. Come for me." He whispered the words, tilted his head then kissed her as if the world was ending.

The tautness intensified tenfold. Then she shattered.

Piper released a high-pitched sound as powerful contractions took hold, sending waves of rapture rolling through her.

He groaned next to her ear, surged in strongly then shuddered.

She could only ride the high crests and pray she didn't return to earth any time soon.

For a long while Ranger rested on top of Piper, trying valiantly to catch his breath after such an amazing orgasm. He couldn't recall one nearly as powerful or earthmoving as the one he'd just experienced.

He glanced down, noting Piper's flushed face and chest. She also breathed hard. Where they connected, her core still milked his cock, although not as hard or often. The snugness of her body remained, however, adding stimulation to his quickly fading erection. As he watched, she opened her eyes and met his gaze.

"Hi."

He grinned. "Hi."

She pushed a strand of hair out of his face with a smile. "You, sir, definitely don't disappoint."

The praise bolstered his ego and strummed his pride. The relaxation on her face, the happiness, told him all he needed to know. She'd enjoyed his lovemaking.

Lovemaking. Not sex. Never before had he considered any difference in the terms. Today, he saw them. Felt them. Understood them. Piper indeed made it all different.

She lowered her legs to the bed. "When can we do that again?"

Satisfaction flared at her question. He kissed her sweetly on the lips. "Later. First things first."

Confusion flashed across her face.

He quickly explained. "We both need to clean up. Then, if you're up to it, we'll see about answering your question."

Ranger rotated and levered back until his spent cock slipped from her, then climbed out of bed. After shucking the used condom, he headed to the bathroom. Task complete, he stepped from the small room and nearly bowled her over. He scanned her face as he steadied her.

"My turn." Her pinkened cheeks amused him as well as turned him on.

She entered the bathroom and closed the door behind her. He heard the water running in the sink before being shut off.

Not wanting to be caught eavesdropping at the door, he made his way back to the bed, sat on the edge, and waited for her to reappear. He didn't have to wait long.

A couple of minutes later Piper stepped from the bathroom, one of his dark-colored terry cloth towels wrapped around her. It covered the area from her breasts to her upper thighs. All the good parts were kept out of view. Shyness. He had anticipated such from her. Still, the sight snared his attention and refused to let go. Modest breasts bobbed under the cover as she made her way toward him. The sway in her walk accentuated the flare of her hips, while the toned and defined muscles in her legs reminded him of her unleashed power. Softness over granite. "You're so beautiful."

She smiled coyly. "I'm glad you think so." Standing between his legs, she ran her fingers through his hair.

He kissed her stomach and squeezed her rounded rear before giving the towel a yank. It came loose easily. He tossed it aside just in time to glimpse the assets Piper had covered before she got feisty.

Piper squealed and giggled. She jerked out of his hold, dove on the bed, then started tickling him from behind.

Not to be outdone, he flipped over and tried to do the same, but found her agile and slinky. After missing a couple of times, he finally wrapped her in his embrace, twisted so her back was to the mattress, then lowered his weight on top of her to hold her still. His chuckles faded, as did hers. Other matters drew his focus. Namely how his dick rested between her legs, kissing her folds. How she linked her hands behind his neck and arched her pelvis to encourage the caress. Her breasts pressed into his chest, tickling the skin and adding to the list of nice sensations that all merged into one.

He tried to sit up. She held on tight and tugged him back down until he covered her completely. Most of his weight was dispersed between his knees and bent elbows, keeping him from squishing her as he gave her what she craved. Closeness. Skin to skin contact. Cuddling in the aftermath of bliss. He knew because he wanted the same thing.

"Please don't leave me. Not yet."

"I'm not going anywhere, Piper," he breathed against her ear. "But I'm going to get damn heavy real quick."

She lapped at his nearby earlobe. "That's okay. I don't mind at all."

He chuckled, wrapped his arms around her and rolled until she rested on top of him. "That's better."

She grinned down at him. "Uh-huh." Impishly, she wiggled her rear, brushing up against his quickly recovering erection in the process.

His grip on her tightened as a surge of arousal coursed through him at the speed of light. His shaft responded instantly, filling to capacity. Enough to cause a dull throb. "Keep that up and you're going to be too sore to walk, let alone take the ice."

Intrigued, she blinked down at him. "Is that how it works?"

"I have no idea." He groaned as she repeated the actions.

"But I do know you're playing with fire." He grew serious. As much as he enjoyed the foreplay, he would rather have walked out of the bedroom than cause her a moment's more pain.

"It's only fair. You make my body burn with need and pleasure." The admission slipped from her lips.

His breath caught as rampant hunger leaped to the fore.

The vixen didn't know what she did to him. First with the generous gift of her virginity, then wanting him to pancake her into the mattress because she didn't want the moment to end. Now she told him he cranked up her lust to a fevered pitch while showering her with ecstasy.

A guy could only take so much. And she'd just pushed him to the breaking point.

He yanked back on the reins of his control even as his cock started to ache demandingly. If it were anyone else, he'd pound into her until they both cried out in orgasm. Hard. Fast. Furious and hardcore.

If it were anyone else, he'd be bored and wishing they'd leave.

The realization added another dimension. A protective streak along with the understanding that Piper fit perfectly with him. Physically and emotionally. He knew he'd never get enough of her.

Suddenly his needs took second place to hers. Even if he didn't do anything else today, he'd please her in bed. Totally. Fully. In all ways possible that she deserved. "God, I need you Piper. Bad. But I don't want to hurt you." He laid it on the line.

She grinned ruefully. "Then you better make love to me again and soon. I ache for you."

Hearing that, nothing short of Armageddon could have stopped him. Probably not even that.

Still, he recalled she was literally one step from virginity. Gentleness ruled the day.

"Can you grab a condom out of the nightstand, please?"

She briefly left the bed to follow his order, then tossed it to him.

He used his teeth to open the foil before rolling the condom on with practiced ease. "Now, climb back on."

He glimpsed her pink slit hidden under short blonde curls as she moved to straddle his hips. A single touch confirmed what he saw. "You're so wet. At this rate, you'll soak my balls."

Arousal flared hotly in Piper's eyes.

He grinned at the telling reaction. *So she likes dirty talk. I can deal with that.*

"Scooch back." When she did, he grabbed his cock and placed the tip against her folds. He rested his other hand on her hip. "Now lower yourself. Nice and slow."

She did so, then grunted when the wide head of his cock slipped inside.

"Hurt?"

"No." Piper bit her bottom lip.

Ranger watched her face carefully. She might not admit to any discomfort, her pride and excitement shoving such details to the bottom of the priority list. No matter. He'd gladly call a halt if he thought she was in pain.

She took another couple of inches before pausing. "I didn't realize how big you really are. Until now."

He delved his fingers between her spread thighs, found her clit and skimmed, earning a gasp for his endeavors. "Looks a little different when you're on top?"

"You can say that." She grinned, gyrated her hips, then took the rest of him in one single motion.

"Damn." He jerked under her. The sensation of her tight, damp channel welcoming him back was nearly enough to make him come. As it was, he held her still with a firm grasp on her hip and worked on a bit of distraction. Anything to pull him back from the edge. When he had iron-clad control back, he focused on her sensitive bundle of nerves, working it with exquisite precision.

Her mouth fell open as she began to struggle against his hold. He released her then moaned as she ground against him, back and forth, before lifting and dropping back down.

He struggled to keep up with her near frantic movements, then stepped it up a notch when she placed her hands on his chest and settled into long, sure strokes that gripped his cock like a snug velvet glove.

The expression on her face told it all. Mouth open. Eyes closed. Head thrown back. She rode him like an expert breaking a wild stallion. He knew he'd never forget the sight of her in that moment.

At least this position made for easy access to her body. He took advantage, cupping a breast now and again while focusing his attentions on her clit.

She whimpered and mewled. The sexy sounds made a beeline for his balls, tightening them as well as causing his cock to throb impatiently.

Still he held back, not about to blow his load until she found release once again. "That's it. Take what you need from me." He bent his knees, placed his feet on the bed and met her on the next drop.

"Oh, oh, oh." She gyrated wildly. "Oh, God. Ranger."

Knowing she was a hair away from toppling over the edge, he delicately strummed her clit, rubbed then gently plucked. Her entire body went rigid. She sucked in air, arched her back, then ground her pelvis against his.

Once more he fluttered his fingers over her nub.

She yelped, stiffened and jerked. A split second later, her core compressed his cock so hard he couldn't have moved if he'd wanted to. Ripples followed, each one squeezing and massaging his shaft until he rocketed to the summit and over.

"Fuck. Oh, damn." He grasped her hips, slammed into her, then rode out the storm filled with towering crests and rhythmic pulses.

Piper draped herself over him with a deep sigh. She rested her head on his chest and struggled to catch her breath.

He wrapped her in his embrace and held tight.

One way or another, he'd make this work. He'd been

around the block a few times and knew perfection when he saw it.

What they had was simply too good to give up.

Chapter Eighteen

Ranger quietly leaned against the doorjamb, crossed his arms, and watched as Piper slept on the couch in the den. She sighed in her sleep and his heart tugged.

After rousing from bed, they had worked together to cook lunch. With the kitchen cleaned and full stomachs, he'd suggested a movie on the big screen TV in the den. She'd picked out a comedy, lain down and rested her head on his lap, and was asleep halfway through. For the longest time, he'd stroked her hair, then he'd turned the station to play soft music, replaced his leg with a throw pillow, stood up, covered her with a blanket and left the room. He would have stayed longer, but his bladder had begun to give a pressing warning, forcing him to move.

Now he couldn't stay away. He checked on her fairly often and smiled at the small bundle she made on the couch.

Alone he would have probably screwed around until boredom set in. Those were the days before Piper. Starting last night, he found contentment in being home, finally understanding why the married guys were so keen on getting back to be with their families. Playing hockey might be a sport they all loved and excelled at, but their hearts were with their wives and kids.

Piper had turned his house into a home just by being there.

He'd never brought a woman to his house before. Piper was the first. And the last. Just as he couldn't imagine her not being in his life, he also couldn't see ever considering another woman for a date. Piper had ruined him for all the others. Thankfully.

He turned from the sight and retraced his steps to the living room, keeping quiet in order not to disturb her. She needed sleep. The road trips, the many games, the physical hits and demands put on her during those same games, it all added up. Factor in her juggling another job and the early times she woke each day no matter the late hour getting home. That alone would exhaust even the strongest person. Top it off with this unbelievable morning in bed together and she had to be completely worn out. No way would he wake her from the well-earned afternoon nap.

Heading to the large window, he stared out over the snow-covered land. Nothing more fell from the sky and the wind had ceased howling. At least the storm had passed, allowing road workers to scrape the streets and clear the way. He had no doubt tomorrow's drive back to the facilities would prove much easier and less hazardous than the journey home last night.

A pink cell phone caught his eye. Piper's. She'd texted this morning, presumably her parents or brother, maybe a friend or two.

He glanced back toward the den, then back to the phone. For a minute, he hesitated.

Piper lit up his life, bringing with her amusement, caring and the best sex he'd ever had. She kept him on his toes and made him eager for team activities so he could see her again. Now that she'd settled in for a couple of days with him, he realized he didn't want to spend another night without her next to him.

Which meant he had to step up to the plate. In a major way. Starting with retrieving a phone number to use at a later date, when privacy would be guaranteed.

After grabbing a piece of paper and a pen, he scrolled through her contact list, found the number he wanted and jotted it down. He tucked the paper between his own cell phone and its cover. That way he wouldn't worry about losing or forgetting it. Afterward he cleared the screen of her phone back to the main one and started to walk away.

A chiming sound caught his attention. He returned to the kitchen cabinet and picked up his phone, finding a text from Rocky.

How's the sleepover going?

Ranger snorted. Of course some of the guys would notice Piper had climbed into his vehicle to come home with him. His luck wouldn't go any other way. Not in this situation.

He started to reply then changed his mind. Let Rocky sit and wonder along with the rest of the crew.

With a smirk, he carried the phone to the living room sofa and plopped down. First he sent a message to his mother, letting her know he had a day off while snowed in at home. She tended to check her phone more often than his father and passed things along readily, thus cutting down on the need to fire off duplicate texts.

The music in the other room stopped suddenly. A couple of moments later, Piper appeared, a little tousled from her rest, but damn sexy all the same.

"Hi."

"Hi." He smiled at her. "Have a good nap?"

"Yeah. I think I must have needed it."

"I think so." He patted the couch. "Have a seat."

She arched an eyebrow, closed the distance, then sat down. "This sounds serious."

He blinked, taking a second to understand the meaning behind her comment before immediately picking her up and placing her across his lap. "Not at all. I just wanted an excuse to touch you again." He nuzzled her temple and nibbled on her earlobe.

She tilted her head to give him easier access. "Who knew earlobes were so yummy?"

He chuckled. "Yours are. I can vouch for that." He wrapped an arm around her middle, keeping her securely on his lap.

She sighed and leaned into him.

He nuzzled her cheek. "How are you feeling?" Whether or not she admitted soreness, he knew it had to exist.

"Wonderful. Happy." She kissed his chin. "Cherished."

"I'm glad to hear that, although I was aiming for more of a physical nature."

"I'm fine. Really." She skimmed her fingertips over his bottom lip.

He kissed them. "No aches or pains?"

A totally feminine smile appeared on her face. Sated. Content. With a bit of mischief thrown in. "Nothing worth worrying about or preventing me from doing whatever I'd like."

His libido jumped. "What would you like to do?"

She peeked at him coyly from under her eyelashes. "So many things. Too many to count, probably."

Curious, he kissed her ear and held tight when she giggled. "At least give me a hint or three."

"Hmmm." She rested her head on his shoulder then licked his ear in retaliation. "After a long, hot bath, I think I'd like…"

"Yes?"

"For you to teach me how to play poker." She sat up and met his eyes. "Strip poker."

He groaned as his body responded to her sultry tone and the spark of longing in her eyes. Piper didn't come close to a shrinking violet. She told it like it was. Thank goodness. "Maybe you should get started on that bath before I spontaneously combust."

She chuckled, pecked his cheek, then stood up. "I won't be too long." With that said, she strode down the hall and disappeared into the bathroom.

He rested his head on the back of the couch and blew out a long breath. *She might be the death of me, but I'll go happy.*

An hour later, he burst out in laughter as he saw her emerge from the spare bedroom she'd claimed the night before. Bundled up with multiple layers, she appeared more like a woman intent on a long hike through the snowdrifts and harsh elements than one preparing to sit down for a card game. "Are you hot?"

The corners of her mouth hitched upward. "Getting there. But it's worth it."

He shook his head. She had silliness down to an art. He found the trait endearing and entertaining. "I've got the cards. If you're ready?"

"Yep." She followed him to the kitchen table and sat down. Her long coat hung over the sides of the chair.

"How many pairs of socks do you have on?" He scooted his chair closer to the table before shuffling the deck.

"Ummm. A couple."

Ranger rolled his eyes. "It's going to be a bit odd when you're dressed for making snowmen and I'm in my birthday suit."

Her eyes sparked. "Awkward isn't the word I'd use." Her husky voice told of her arousal and intent.

Hell, he'd lose on purpose just to watch her eye him with appreciation, awe and hunger. He'd have to be sneaky about it, though. If she had an inkling, she'd kick his ass for sure. "Five card draw. Do you know how to play?"

"Yeah. I've watched enough to pick up the basics." She took her cards in hand and stared at them.

He scanned his, then discarded a couple. "How many do you want?"

She pursed her lips. "One." She rejected a card and picked up the new one. "I call."

He blinked. "Already?"

"Yep." She grinned. "No use betting since only the winner of the hand receives a reward."

"True." He placed his motley mix of cards on the table.

She did as well, showing a full house.

"Damn."

Piper grinned wickedly. "Start stripping."

Ranger dutifully tugged his shirt over his head, leaving his torso bare.

She licked her lips and he bit back another groan. At this

rate he'd have a boner for the ages by the time the game finished.

Several hands later, he sat in his tented boxers, trying desperately to pay attention to the game instead of fantasizing about what he'd like to do to Piper if he could ever get all those layers of clothes off her pretty body. He couldn't remember the last time he was this turned on. His cock throbbed, his heart pounded, and all he wanted to do was yank her garments off, lay her across the table and surge balls-deep into her searing heat.

"Pair of kings." He slitted his eyes as she pulled off her sweatshirt, leaving a white, lacy bra to cover her perfect breasts.

"I seem to have hit a streak of bad luck." She smiled at him.

His stomach clenched in delicious torment as his dick jerked in reaction to that teasing grin. "I say we call it a tie."

"A tie?" She scanned his body with her heated gaze. "Do I still get a prize?"

He stood up, walked to her side and pulled her to her feet. "You get me. All of me. For as long as you want me." He rapidly undressed her, doing what he'd wanted to do a long time ago. Clothes were tossed here and there. He didn't care. The only thing that mattered right now was getting her naked and in his arms.

Piper slipped her fingers into his underwear and cupped his erection.

His heart skipped a beat as he sucked in air. "Too many clothes." He unsnapped her bra, easily pulled it off, and gave it a toss, all the while barely having the control to avoid ripping her panties away. As soon as the final garment dropped from her body, he pulled her into his arms, meshed their lips and kissed her with all the passion and need he felt. Aggressively, he delved inside, sharing his immense desire in the best way he knew.

She gasped, clung to his shoulders and trembled as he fastened his mouth over one perky breast. "Yes. Ranger.

Yes."

Her breathless words spurred him further.

He dipped his hand to the junction of her thighs, delved into her slit and found her damp. Juicy. More than ready. Twisting his wrist, he slipped a finger into her core, noting the snug heat that had seared him earlier in the day. Heaven on earth and he couldn't wait to experience it again.

Yet his gut warned him to remember her innocence and past. He couldn't just flip her over and thrust away. Piper's special situation called for tact among the intense burning desires. "How do you feel about me taking you from behind?" He leaned back enough to read her face. "Will it be too much? Maybe a little frightening?"

She closed her eyes briefly as a sweet little whimper escaped her throat. A moment later she met his gaze steadily, an impish grin appearing on her lips. "I think you should mount up, cowboy."

He blinked at her choice of words, then smiled like a Cheshire cat. She might be inexperienced, but she was a vixen after his own heart.

"Turn around. Bend over the table." He assisted with a firm grip on her hips. The moment she stretched out before him with her ass in the air, he nearly lost his mind as a recent fantasy came into play. "Spread your legs." He ran his hand over her rear, testing the hard muscles underneath the silky smooth skin.

She jumped then settled back down, her head resting on folded arms.

Ranger made a quick side trip to his wallet on the living room table, dug out a condom, and sheathed himself before making the short trek back. He stopped right behind her and found her with his fingers once more before slipping a couple in.

She gasped. He pumped.

Unable to wait a second longer, he removed his hand, grasped his cock and used the tip to spread her folds. "I can go really deep like this. Tell me if it hurts." He languidly pressed forward.

Her body welcomed him with tight heat and ample slickness. Inch after inch disappeared as he joined their bodies slowly and carefully. Only when he hit bottom did he pause. "Still all right?"

"Yes." She wiggled her rear as if trying to make fine adjustments for comfort.

He bent over and kissed her back. "You don't know what you do to me. I'm so hard right now. So damn hard."

She moaned and rocked.

He easily absorbed her movements, merging them with his own. Her next cry sent fire rushing through his blood. Cinching her with one arm around her stomach, he plunged the other between her legs, found her clit and caressed.

Piper yelped and bowed her back, presenting her upturned rear all the more.

"That's it, baby. Tell me that you like it."

He picked up the pace, working long strokes before switching to short, powerful jabs. All the while he worried her nub. "So. Fucking. Good." He punctuated each word with a deep, strong thrust.

She squirmed and writhed. A grunt left her throat as she surged back to meet his next penetration.

Knowing he wouldn't last much longer, Ranger draped his body over hers, careful not to lower his weight as well. He tucked his head near her ear and whispered, "I can't get enough of fucking you. Hearing those sexy cries. Feeling you fall apart when you come with my big cock buried balls-deep."

She looked straight ahead, quickly inhaled, and gyrated in his tight hold before going wild under him. She bucked, jerked and trembled.

"You're going to come, aren't you?" He strummed her clit a bit harder, then ever so lightly plucked.

Piper arched her back and stiffened.

He easily read the signs and intensified his touches at the same time as he sprinted for home with near frantic thrusts meant to send her racing to orgasm. Kissing her shoulder, he breathed harshly in her ear, "Work that cock, Piper. Cream all over it."

A muted squeal escaped just as she shoved back against him with strength. He stroked her clit, thrust for all he was worth, then yelled as all the tension in his body exploded in his groin. He shot over the edge as Piper's core clamped down in a perfectly timed vise.

Ranger widened his stance and rode out the waves. However long he stood there, he didn't have a clue. Wouldn't have budged except Piper's legs started to buckle. He scooped her into his arms, carried her over to the couch and rested her on his lap.

Over and over he kissed her temple, her cheek, the crown of her head as she struggled to catch her breath.

An overwhelming urge to protect and care for her took him by storm. "You okay?"

She nodded before resting her head on his shoulder.

Concerned, he inclined her forward until she met his eyes. He detected no pain, thankfully. Just tiredness and contentment in her bright gaze. Something else, too—the keys to her heart. Tears formed and overflowed.

"What's this?" He wiped at the telltale drops.

She remained silent.

"Did I hurt you?"

"No," she whispered. "It's just that...you came along and turned my world upside down. Then you rocked it." She sniffed and shivered. "I never knew it could be as wonderful as this."

"Neither did I." He snagged a nearby throw, draped it over her, then eased her back to her previous position, uncaring that he sat on his own couch buck naked and still wearing a condom. Her need to be held trumped everything else at that moment.

"I've got you. Never going to let you go." He whispered the words against her hair, knowing them for the truth.

Chapter Nineteen

Piper woke warm, comfortable and with a large heater against her back. She opened her eyes, fixated on the wall, and recalled where she was. Ranger's bedroom. At his house. Naked in his bed.

The last part heated her cheeks. A new experience, definitely, and one without a single regret.

She carefully turned over to find Ranger sprawled out on his back. One arm rested on her pillow above her head. The other lay against his side. With the covers pushed away, she had the luxury of checking out his nude body while he still slept.

His tousled short black hair added a softness to his features. The long eyelashes as well. In rest, tension dissipated, leaving him relaxed and quite handsome in a gentler sense. She glanced lower, noting again the powerful shoulders and wide chest that poured down into a narrower waist and six-pack abs. His strong thighs were spread, drawing attention to his morning erection, thick, full and potent.

She peered up at his face, decided he wasn't playing possum, and opted to do a bit more exploring now that she finally had a chance. Starting at his chest, she lightly brushed her fingertips over his sternum, followed by the dips and valleys of his stomach. Finally, she grew bold enough to wrap her fingers around his cock. She ran her hand up and down his shaft, marveling at his size and feel. Velvet over steel. Impressive and a teeny bit intimidating as well. How she fit him inside still baffled her. *Goes to show what love and arousal can do for a girl.*

Love. She had no doubt the emotion ran strong between

them. At least from her to him. All these years and a few bad dates had given her experience to know the difference. Ranger drew her like no other, then kept her with his generous ways, sense of humor, gorgeous body and kindness. He made her feel beautiful. Special.

No one else had ever done that for her before. Which was probably why she'd never seriously considered bedding any of the men she'd met. They just didn't have the qualities she insisted on. Then came Ranger. Her knight in shining armor turned prince.

"Find something to play with this morning?" His sleepy voice broke through her thoughts.

"Uh-huh." She met his gaze, finding him all the sexier with his rumpled hair, lazy expression and bedroom eyes, freshly awake from a good night's sleep.

A small bead of moisture appeared at the tip of his erection, snaring her attention. She caught it on her finger, then lifted that same finger to her mouth. Tasting him had become a temptation she could no longer ignore.

Ranger's eyes darkened and turned smoky as he watched her sample his essence. "Damn, Piper. You sure know how to torment a guy."

She grinned saucily and returned to petting his cock. "You like?"

"Hell, yes."

Her confidence grew. "Then I'm doing something right."

"Honey, you're doing everything right." He followed with a low moan as she tightened her grip slightly, bent over and flicked her tongue over the broad mushroom head.

His hips thrust upward as his breath hitched.

Piper decided she loved making him squirm in pleasure. Needing better access, she rose to her knees next to his side, giving her free rein to use both hands as well as making for a more comfortable position to taste him thoroughly. She repeated the caress before taking the tip in her mouth and laving.

He brushed her hair aside and groaned as she added vacuum and lowered farther.

"That feels so good." His softly spoken words encouraged her to experiment more.

Bobbing a little, she kept everything light and shallow while trying to figure out what he liked best. She'd never done anything like this before, but Ranger gave her the confidence to let go of her inhibitions and try something new—like giving him a blow job as a wake-up call.

He ran his hand through her hair.

She swirled her tongue all over the tip then right under.

His lower body lurched once more. "Damn. You're going to make me come."

Piper took that as a challenge. She poured on the vacuum, took more into her mouth then moaned low in her throat.

Glancing up, she found Ranger tossing his head on the pillow and clenching the linens in a death grip. Tension radiated from his face—his lips parted, eyes closed—and muscles were locking in his arms.

Each jerk, every cry pushed her to do more. To send Ranger toppling over the edge.

She gave him a tongue bath, as she'd imagined since waking. Dropping her free hand, she tenderly cupped his sac and rolled the balls within.

He became restless. The incredible sensations only increased as Piper pushed him that much further. "Fuck."

No sooner had the word slipped out than his cock pulsed, sending the first stream of cum into her mouth. She swallowed. And swallowed. And swallowed. Finally, he grew lax, the delicious treat ceased and he blew out a long breath.

She licked the last drop, felt him flinch, then sat up to appraise her results.

Ranger's chest rose and fell in rapid fashion, although his grip on the sheets had eased considerably. He opened his eyes, still smoky, and pinned her with his gaze. "That was amazing."

She smiled warmly. "I wanted to give you a gift. It seemed like a good idea at the time."

He rose to meet her, cupped the back of her head and brushed his lips over hers. "A very good idea." He sought a deeper caress.

Piper eagerly accepted, not about to deny Ranger anything. After all, he had her heart in his hands.

* * * *

Ranger followed Piper into her apartment, automatically scanning the small area. Clean, tidy and unassuming came to mind. The one-bedroom flat had a small living area with an adjoining kitchen. A loveseat and a recliner sat against a far wall, facing a modest-sized television on a wooden stand. Medium-brown carpet covered the floor, except in the kitchen area, where tile took over. A short hallway led to, presumably, the bedroom.

He shut the door behind him. "Nice." While the place fell well short of the square footage of his house, he didn't feel crowded. Not in the least. The soft colors surrounding him made the space appear much larger. Beige walls offered natural brightness, as did a large sliding door that led to a balcony. Sunlight poured in, despite the fresh snow on the ground.

"Thanks." Piper set her suitcase on the couch and started unpacking. Clothes piled up next to her. "It's not much, but it suits me for now. I'm gone a lot during the season, so this works out well."

He removed his shoes in the entryway as she'd done before walking over to the glass and peering out. From the second floor she had a decent view overlooking the swimming pool. He turned back and appraised her once more. Something told him she didn't take advantage of the amenities and don a bathing suit often. Most likely, she strapped on her skates at the rink instead of lounging around getting a tan.

She carried the pile of clothes to the first room past the kitchen.

He heard some dials turn, a door open, then the sound of running water. "Ever thought of buying a house?"

She returned to the area a few seconds later. "Now and again. I'd like to use what I pay in rent on a mortgage payment, but I'm a bit hesitant."

He strode over and sat down on the love seat. "Afraid you'll be traded?" In the professional hockey ranks trading happened all the time, even throughout the season. One day a guy could play for one team, get traded mid-game, then show up in a totally different city the next day to join his new one. Made for a crazy life, especially if he had a family and a house in his old city. Most guys ended up just renting an apartment unless they were certain they'd be at the new place for a long time to come. As many road trips as they had, it made little sense to try to buy a new house, get moved and settle in, when a guy had to be on a plane once or twice a week.

"Kind of. Though Liam, the Bobcats' head coach, tells me not to worry about it." She plopped down in the chair and pivoted to face him. "Money is also an issue. I have to be able to pay the bills. With hockey and my side job, I can afford a small place. Nothing like where my parents live. Which is okay," she hurriedly added. "I don't need much."

Ranger studied her for a long moment. She stared down at her hands folded in her lap. He could almost see the wheels turning in her head and the concerns right below the surface. She gave off the feel that she knew she didn't stack up in the home department and it bothered her. "I think this place is classy. Old town. You've done a great job with decoration." The walls boasted a few pictures— some family, others were paintings. They added to the overall feel of the place. "And the size of the home isn't as important as who lives there." He offered up a reassuring smile. "You should have seen my apartment in college, then the one when I was in the minors. Pretty bare and probably wouldn't pass the white glove test ever."

She grinned at him. "Housecleaning isn't your strong suit?"

"Nope. I can do it, but prefer not to. Right now I'm lucky enough to be able to hire it done. Win-win for me and the maid."

Piper nodded. "I don't have much, so cleaning is a snap."

"Smart." He scratched his leg and pointed toward one of the pictures. "I like that picture of you as a kid with the rest of your family. What were you? Six? Seven?" She stood out from the rest with her blonde hair and blue eyes. Her parents and brother all sported brown locks and matching eyes.

She followed his hand. "Six. They'd adopted me just a few months before the family photo was taken."

He knew the topic of her adoption was a sore spot, but curiosity prompted him to dig a bit deeper. "How did they find you? Were they foster parents at the time and took you in?"

"No." Piper sighed. "I was in the hospital after the attack. Dad…Gunther…and Darla were visiting as part of the team's holiday tradition. Many of the players did it. It just so happened that they stepped into my room to see me." She lowered her gaze as if remembering. "When Gunther walked in, I was scared. He looked huge. A giant. Then Darla appeared, walked right over and started talking to me. I don't remember what she said, just that her voice reminded me of my mother's as she read me stories at night." Piper met his eyes. "From what I understand, they asked the nurse about me, who told them the story. They contacted the social worker immediately and started asking about the adoption process. A couple of weeks later, they took me home from the hospital into foster care. Three months after that, they formally adopted me."

"Were they already fostering children or looking to adopt?"

"No. Mom says once they met me and found out what I'd

been through, they just knew I belonged with them. Even Darius welcomed me." She smiled softly.

His heart tugged. Respect for her parents and brother increased, not that it had much further to go. Gunther possessed a reputation for fair play and generosity across the league, especially when it came to charities. Yet to take on a traumatized child out of the blue took tons of heart and dedication. Even with all the love in the world, not all children could grow up to be normal kids who walked the line.

Piper had. Due in a large part to her family. He saw now, possibly, what they'd seen in a hurt and scared six-year-old girl — fortitude and determination.

"When did you start skating?"

"About the same time as they adopted me. Dad took Darius to the rink one day. I tagged along. Loved it. After that, I begged to keep going back."

Ranger read between the lines. Skating wasn't just fun, it was an outlet for her. Perhaps a place where she could be free and forget her past. Either way, she'd committed herself to the sport and become an elite athlete along the way. "Why not figure skating?"

She cut him a glare.

He laughed and held up his hands. "Just asking."

She snorted. "Both my parents played hockey. Darius played hockey. There wasn't any other sport in my house growing up." Her lips softened into a grin. "Besides, I had big shoes to fill between Mom and Dad. Projections and expectations started early. I saw them as challenges to show them that I could make it in a rough sport despite being one of the smaller players."

"You've done one hell of a job, Piper." He complimented her sincerely. She'd overcome some huge odds to be where she was now. "Not everyone could have succeeded like you have."

"There wasn't much choice." She shrugged and smiled wider. "Besides, I had to keep up with Darius. He didn't know how to give up or back down. Heck, I'm still trying to keep up with him."

Ranger heard the love in her voice when she spoke of her brother. He'd seen it before when they'd greeted each other after Darius' practice had ended on his home rink. Now he understood the bond that much better. Darius bore just as much responsibility for Piper's outlook and skating as her parents.

Must have been a great family to grow up in. Good for her.

She wiggled in her seat to a crossed-leg position. "Did you start thinking about what you'd do after hockey?"

Ranger considered the inquiry for a long moment. "I'm not sure. Like I mentioned before, I was a health and wellness major in college. Perhaps something along those lines. Maybe a personal trainer. Maybe open a gym." He waved his hand. "I hope that's a few years off still."

"Oh, it will be. A guy as big as you isn't going to break down any time soon." She grinned.

Ranger smiled in return. "You sure?"

"Oh, yeah. Definitely."

He turned the tables. "What about you? Have you thought about life after hockey?"

"Yeah. I have. Probably because I have to think about finances during hockey as well." She paused for a second. "I like my bookkeeping job, especially the flexibility of it. Will I do that forever? I don't know. It works for now. If and when I walk away from the game, it would depend on the situation. Maybe I could teach hockey to kids? Be a coach for peewee camps. Maybe retire to become a librarian and motor around on inline skates among the long aisles."

"What about a family?" He asked the question that had been sitting on the tip of his tongue.

She lowered her gaze. "For sure I'm not having kids without a husband. So I guess that depends on whether some guy will like me enough to want to spend the rest of his life with me." Piper exhaled. "I've got baggage. I'm far from perfect. Some guys don't like that I play hockey, let alone invaded their league."

Ranger moved over to kneel in front of her. Gently, he cupped her chin and lifted until she met his eyes. "Don't sell yourself short, Piper. You've got so much more to offer than you give yourself credit for."

A wave of happiness and relief crossed her face. "Thank you for saying that."

"It's the truth." He leaned in to press his lips against hers briefly. "What do you say when we're done here, you come home with me?"

She ran her finger down the slope of his nose. "Not tired of me already?"

"No way." He kissed her fingertip. "I've gotten accustomed to having you in my bed at night, keeping me warm."

She rolled her eyes. "I'm just a bed warmer?"

He chuckled at her huffy tone. "You're more. So much more." He kissed her again, not breaking contact until the need for air forced him to. "Please come home with me?"

She didn't even hesitate. "I'd like that."

His spirit soared as warmth flooded his system. While her staying another night wasn't in itself a commitment, it was a start. A damn good one at that.

Chapter Twenty

Ranger watched Piper dive across the ice to deflect a sailing puck. It bounced to the side of the net, where Sven sent it flying to him. Ranger snagged the puck with his glove, dropped it to the ice then took off for the opposing net. He faked left, went right, found a clear space as he crossed the face-off circle. A quick backhand and the puck lasered into the back of the net, having slid between the goalie's legs. The buzzer sounded just after, ending the first period.

"Yes." He pumped his fist. The rest of the first line surrounded him, patting him on the back and head in congratulations.

"Nice buzzer beater," Rocky said as he skated beside Ranger toward the bench.

"Thanks. I get lucky now and again." Ranger stepped off the ice and headed straight for the locker room, eager to get some drinks and snacks down in order to replenish the copious amounts of energy he was losing each time he took his turn playing.

As usual, he found a basket of snack bars. Plastic bottles filled with various kinds of juices sat on a short table. He snagged one of the fruit-flavored granola snacks and two drinks. With food in hand, he sat down at the end of the bench and dug in.

The other guys filed by. Piper pulled up the rear. She rifled through the basket and frowned. "Where's the chocolate? There has to be some in here."

Ben, the guy who organized their entire lives during the season, shook his head. "Chocolate is just a quick sugar fix.

You'd do better with something else. That's what Jeremy always says."

Piper narrowed her eyes and glared at the man. "I. Need. Chocolate." She bit out the words, seemingly uncaring that the entire team blinked at her in shock. "If I don't get chocolate, I'm trading in my hockey stick for a baseball bat and commencing whoop ass." She glanced down at the weapon in hand. "Although this could work just as well in a pinch."

"Okkkaaaayyy." Ben dragged the word out and started for the door. "I'll just go see if the vending machines might have something for that craving of yours." He ducked out fast.

Ranger bit back a grin. He'd seen Piper in many moods, but this was a new one. He also had a good idea what caused it. No way would he stand between her and the treat she demanded. *I'm not that dumb.*

He scanned the room, discovering a mixture of expressions. Understandably enough, they varied based on age and marital status. The young, single guys tended toward curious horror. The married ones simply stared in dreaded resignation as if they were saying 'Shit, not again'. Obviously, they recognized the impact of hormones and kept their mouths shut.

Ranger had newfound respect for the men who chose to coach women's hockey.

"What in the hell did you do to her?" Rocky nudged Ranger in the side with his elbow. "She was sweet and funny. Now, after two days hanging around with you, she's on the warpath." He finished his juice. "I'm not even sure if she's kidding about beating people with her stick."

"It wasn't me."

"Uh-huh."

She hadn't eaten well this morning for breakfast or for the pregame lunch with the team. Combining hunger with PMS and a Piper on edge made complete sense.

Ben returned, marched over to Piper and held out a

handful of candy bars. She looked them over before picking one, ripping it open and taking a bite. Her eyes closed as she chewed.

"Damn," Ranger whispered to himself. The expression resembled the one she had right after she came—the sign of sated bliss. Only related to a sweet treat instead of his lovemaking. His body couldn't tell the difference, as his cock responded instantly. Just what he needed at the moment. *Not.*

"Thank you, Ben. I really appreciate you going above and beyond for me." She smiled sweetly.

"No problem." Ben tossed the other candy bars into the basket and moved across the room, well away from Piper, who ate as if starving.

Ranger barely contained his laughter at Ben's apparent uneasiness around Piper. Smart man to stay out of the line of fire.

"Whatever you did, you should apologize," Rocky nodded.

Ranger rolled his eyes. "This isn't my fault."

"Still don't believe you. Even if you're innocent, you should do something."

"Like what?" Ranger leveled his gaze at his teammate. The kid should sit down and have a long conversation with a couple of the married guys. Educate himself a little.

"Get her more chocolate."

Ranger tilted his head as his attention turned back to Piper. She licked the remaining candy off her fingers as if unable to resist every drop. "You might be smarter than you look after all."

Rocky snorted. "I grew up with three sisters. Trust me, the answer is always more chocolate."

"My condolences." Ranger smirked at his friend. "A house filled with estrogen." He shuddered dramatically.

"Yeah, yeah. Why do you think I spent so much time at the rink?"

Ranger might have done the same thing if he'd been in

Rocky's shoes. Since he had no siblings, he really couldn't say.

Tommy stepped to the front of the room and started talking. He pointed out weaknesses and missed opportunities, potential plays and defensive strategies. After drawing on the dry erase board a couple of times, he checked his watch, then motioned for the team to head back to the ice.

Ranger stood up and waited for Piper to draw abreast of him. "Did you finally find something you wanted to eat?"

She blinked up at him. "Finally. I swear. What's a granola bar without chocolate?"

He shrugged. "I don't know."

"Cardboard, that's what." She smiled impishly. "Ben fixed it though, so I'm good."

"Uh-huh. Should the rest of us be afraid?"

Her expression could only be called wicked. "Oh, yeah."

The quick banter brought amusement into what otherwise was a serious game. Only Piper could twist things around to make him shake his head in wonder. "How did I know you'd say that?" He allowed her to go first, then followed onto the ice for a quick warm-up.

Ten minutes later, he wasn't amused or laughing. Not when one of the Toronto players had made it his job to harass Piper.

Ranger clearly saw Jones head toward the crease and cause havoc. Not the good kind either, as he slapped at her legs with his stick, then flew across, presumably after a loose puck, kneeing her in the head as he passed by.

Piper went down. Hard. She clutched her head on impact.

Ranger surged to his feet, yelling at the bastard. Anger and frustration nearly overwhelmed his self-control. It took all his willpower not to vault over the wall, track the fucking idiot down and tear into him.

The Wolfpack members on the ice surrounded her, with Ivan offering a hand to help her back to her feet. She took her mask off, shook her head, then replaced the mask with a small nod while the referee escorted Jones to the penalty box.

Payback. Ranger couldn't wait for his turn. He'd make an impression. Hopefully of Jones' body into the thick wooden walls.

Thankfully he didn't have to wait too long. First line surged onto the ice. Ranger darted toward the puck, glimpsed Jones out of the corner of his eye in one of the corners trying to dig the puck out, and lined him up in the crosshairs. Jones went down, then jumped right back to his feet. Ranger went about his way, chasing the puck, then trying to steal it back when a Toronto player intercepted it at center ice.

Jones took the puck to the right side, setting up a play.

Ranger didn't even hesitate. He sped toward Jones and crashed him into the boards. Again. The loud *thud* only marginally made a dent in Ranger's fury.

"Son of a bitch." Jones threw down his gloves and stick, facing off with Ranger.

Not about to back down, Ranger did the same, then started pummeling the guy who had sent Piper tumbling to the ice earlier in a purposeful hit that had most likely left her bell ringing for a second or two.

The teams both banged their sticks on the wall, but Ranger didn't pay them much attention. He was too busy trying to beat the shit out of the guy who had dared mess with his girl.

The refs let them go at it for about half a minute, undisturbed.

"What the fuck is your problem, Deacon?" Jones boxed back, landing a glancing blow to Ranger's jaw.

"You are. You and those cheap shots on my goalie. Bastard." He smacked Jones hard enough in the nose to draw blood.

The refs blew their whistles and separated them. Jones retreated to the bench with spots of blood on the front of his jersey. Ranger headed to the penalty bench willingly. He'd earned his two minutes, as had Jones. Though he'd came out ahead in the short pounding session, leaving Jones with a few bumps and bruises to nurse. A busted nose would have been the cherry on top, but the guy had a damn hard face.

Not since high school had he let his temper get the better of him. In all his years as a pro, he'd never scuffled. Until now. Seeing Piper go down had snapped his control and set him on the path of revenge.

He'd get ribbed about his actions. That didn't matter. All that did was he stood up for his team and Piper suffered no retribution for his actions.

In the end, he didn't need to worry about Piper. She came off scot-free. Unlike him.

After his run-in with Jones, Ranger carried a target on his back. How many times he'd been checked hard, he couldn't recall. Just that he saw the ice up close and personal way too often. All part of a physical game and well worth the bumps and bruises he'd have, as long as Piper didn't get banged around anymore.

Chivalry was tough sometimes, but he wouldn't want it any other way.

* * * *

"A Gordie Howe hat trick. Who knew you had it in you?" Adam slapped him on the shoulder, referring to Ranger's accomplishments of a goal, an assist and getting into a fight in the same game.

Ranger grinned. "Thanks." He'd rather have had a traditional hat trick with three consecutive goals scored in one game, but he'd take what he could get.

At least the slugfest had ignited the team.

They'd scored four unanswered points afterward, cruising to a decisive win.

"Great game. Still going to be able to move tomorrow?" Piper asked as she walked by with a suitcase in one hand and her duffel strapped over her other shoulder.

"Yeah. After I soak for a bit."

She stared up at him. "After dinner I'll give you a rubdown. It'll help."

His excitement level jumped up. "You don't have to." The thought of her hands on his bare skin opened the door on his libido. Though it had only been a couple of days since they'd been together, he craved her more than he ever imagined. Not just the sex. Her peppiness. Her sassiness. The way she offered both comfort and sizzle at the same time.

"I want to. Besides, I owe you one." She grinned and strode down the hall, pausing at her allocated room.

Ranger stopped at his door and shoved the key card into the lock. Other teammates did the same all up and down the hall, most likely eager to shower after a tough game, then start thinking about dinner. As the team wasn't eating together tonight, they were on their own when it came to a meal.

After stepping into the room, he shut and locked the door behind him, then set his bag and suitcase down in the center of the large living area. One check of his watch told him he needed to get a move on in order to accomplish all his plans for the evening. Starting with a shower. Ending with a backrub from Piper. Some really important stuff in between.

He stripped down and headed for the bathroom, not willing to waste any time.

No sooner had he stepped from the shower than he heard a knock at the door. He tied the towel around his waist, peered through the peephole, saw Piper standing there and immediately opened it. "What's up?"

She raked him from head to toe and back again, appreciation reflecting in her blue eyes. Dressed in a pair of loose sweats, she appeared ready to call it a night and stay in. She held up a box and a drink carrier. "Dinner." After ducking under his arm, she headed for the loveseat and coffee table. She set the box down then unloaded the second item filled with drinks and napkins.

The delicious scent of freshly baked pizza made his stomach rumble. He shut the door and locked it. "To what do I owe this?"

"We have to eat. Besides, the sooner we take care of the basics, the sooner we get to your backrub." She waved him over and patted the seat beside her. "I brought napkins, but no plates. We'll have to make do."

Not the least embarrassed with being caught wearing a wrap of terry cloth, he sat down next to her.

"I went with pepperoni. Hope you don't mind." She opened the lid.

"Not at all. It's my favorite." He dipped in and picked up a slice.

"That's what I read in an article a while back. Your favorite junk food, I do believe." She smirked before lifting and biting into a piece.

He chewed and swallowed. "Been checking up on me, huh?" Hungry, he took another mouthful, quickly working his way through the first slice like a man starving.

"Yep." Her eyes twinkled with mischief. "Can't know too much about a guy, after all."

"Uh-huh." He took a drink to wash everything down, then dove in for another piece.

They ate quickly. Ranger finished first, gathered up the empty containers and tossed them into a nearby trashcan.

"I need to get my bags from the other room." She started toward the door.

"You do?" He immediately wanted to kick his own ass at the question. "Sorry. That didn't come out right."

Piper stopped with her hand on the doorknob, lowered her head and bit her lip. "I thought…after your backrub I might stay the night." She paused before taking a couple of strides toward him. "No big deal. I'll just do that massage then go back to my room." Her pasted-on smile didn't convey warmth.

He felt lower than a worm. "Yes, it is a big deal." He met

her halfway, placed his finger under her chin and lifted until she met his eyes. "I was trying to figure out a way to sneak to your room later on without the rest of the guys giving us all kinds of grief and harassing us endlessly."

"You think they would do that?" Her voice strengthened a bit.

"Oh, yeah."

Piper grinned evilly. "Let them try."

Ranger picked up on her spicy mood and chuckled. "You're a spitfire. I love it." Leaning down, he brushed his lips over hers. "I was going to try to find you some chocolate, as well. But you arrived too soon."

Her face lit up. "Make it tomorrow and I'll still act surprised."

He grinned at her excitement. "You've got a deal."

Chapter Twenty-One

Piper took a seat in the empty ice rink and patiently waited. One of the hockey national sportscasters had contacted team management and asked for an exclusive interview with her. They'd agreed. Thus, she'd hurriedly cleaned up after a practice skate and hung around while the rest of the team had a bit of free time before loading up on the bus and heading farther east in Canada.

Not the first time she'd been interviewed, but this time was different. A national top-line reporter and Hall of Famer would sit down and chat with her. The big leagues in the television world. A bit nervous, she picked a piece of lint off her sweater and tried not to dwell too much on what they might ask. She needed a distraction and the events of the night before suited well.

Giving Ranger a backrub had been a new experience, though quite satisfying, too. She'd familiarized herself with his body, the hills and valleys created by thick muscles and a large frame. Gorgeous. Powerful. Yet so gentle. Each bruise he sported had received a kiss. Something he'd grinned at, but hadn't deterred.

For how long she had worked on him, she didn't know. Just that he had fallen asleep under her ministrations. She'd thought to quietly leave the room so he would remain undisturbed. Yet the second she'd tried to leave the bed, she had found a band of steel around her waist.

Ranger had tucked her against his side, spooned up behind her, thrown the covers over them and held her throughout the night.

A sweet, restful, glorious night. One that she hoped to

repeat over and over again.

This morning had been another surprise. Chocolate. Lots of it. Not just from Ranger, but from other team members as they'd loaded the bus this morning. Obviously they'd decided that if a little was good, a lot was better. Whether they were driven by the need to keep her happy or to prevent her from harping on them in irritation, she didn't know. Instead, she'd thanked them mightily and sincerely, praising each one for their thoughtfulness.

"Miss Darrow?"

She twisted around to find a middle-aged, dark-haired man staring at her. He smiled warmly. "I'm glad you could make it."

She stood up and moved closer to the reporter and his cameraman, who presently stood in the aisle. "No problem. Where did you want to go?"

He gestured to the front row of seats. "How about just where you were?"

"And make your cameraman stand on the ice?" She arched an eyebrow.

The guy pursed his lips and threw a glance back to his helper. "Good point. We can take it up a section."

"Works for me."

"I'm Hatch, by the way." He held out a hand.

She shook it with a firm grip. "Piper, as you already know."

"The hockey prodigy."

"That would be my brother." She found another seat and sat down.

Hatch followed suit, leaving one empty chair between them. "I understand it can describe you as well."

Piper ignored the camera and focused on the man asking questions. She sat quietly and waited for him to come up with the next topic.

"What was it like growing up with Gunther and Darla Darrow?"

She smiled genuinely. "Wonderful. As busy as they were,

they always made time for Darius and me. We didn't lack for love, attention or anything else. At the same time, we had responsibilities and hard work was an expectation. No freebies in life just because of their status." She brushed a stray lock of hair away from her face. "If anything, we were raised to understand that we had to make our own way. We supported one another, always will, but everything we attained had to be earned."

"Just like on the ice? You're earning respect out there." He shuffled his papers and stared at her.

She shrugged. "I'm doing my job. Respect comes with it."

His lips thinned a hair, telling her he hadn't gotten what he wanted out of her. "Let's talk about some of the hits you've received. More than most goalies would face in a whole year, you've taken in just a few weeks."

"I have to prove myself to them. No, I don't like getting roughed up, but standing in and taking what comes is part of the process." She offered up a sly grin. "Besides, the more penalties on the opposing team, the more power plays we get. That helps in the win column."

"Yes, it does." He nodded. "What do you think about the future of women playing hockey in the men's league?"

"I hope it's a fact, but have some doubts, especially as long as the women's league exists."

"Why is that?"

"Because of the differences in the game. The teeth-rattling checks in men's hockey are hard on a body. Even the guys'. A woman would presumably take the brunt of many of those hits. After a while, her body will wear down."

"So perhaps women can play as a goalie, but not other positions?"

Piper frowned. "Women who play hockey are tough. Really tough. Playing hurt is all part of the game. A goalie gets hit much less, so presumably that lends toward longevity. It's the other players who will get slammed into the boards. Some of the men are big. Really big. They can cause some damage. I support women one hundred percent.

I'm just not sure that any of them can go a full men's hockey season without injury, especially as they'd be skating with targets on their back."

He paused to glance down at his notebook. "Speaking of the men, how are they accepting a woman among them?"

Piper smiled. "My team is great. They've taken me under their wing and turned into protective brothers. Fun and full of pranks, yes, but a band of brothers, definitely." That was how she thought of them, after all.

"And the other teams?" he persisted.

"Most have been wonderful, even taken the time to congratulate me or offer a few words of wisdom. A few still live in the Dark Ages. It's all about respect. The more I show that I belong and can play at this level, the more come around."

Hatch nodded, his eyes lighting up as if he thought she'd said something spot-on. "Speaking of play at this level, what about next year? Will you be back with the Bobcats? Or stay with the Wolfpack?"

"I really don't know right now. That's up to management and the coaches. I'd love to keep playing, but understand that this is probably a once-in-a-lifetime shot in the men's league."

"The Wolfpack's season has turned around sharply since you joined. The team has won twenty of the last twenty-two games. Even Tommy Smith is citing you as the reason. To what do you credit the fast turnaround?"

Piper wiggled a bit in her seat for comfort. "The guys have loads of talent. All smart, able and the top athletes in their sport. They hit a rough patch is all. Too many injuries, some tough games and bad luck put them into a slump. It happens. I'm not the person who's responsible for the turnaround. It was them. I just sit in front of the net and block shots." She tilted her head. "I like to think that I arrived at the right time to enjoy this outstanding run."

"A humble goalie." Hatch grinned. "Imagine that."

She beamed. "I'm having the time of my life. Enjoying

every minute. The guys are absolutely great. I wouldn't trade this for the world." *It's the truth after all.*

"If there's anything you could change, what would it be?"

She considered the question for a second. "Stronger air fresheners in the locker room."

He laughed heartily. "I've heard you keep the team loose and entertained. I can see why they say that now."

Piper shrugged. "I'm just me."

"It's been a pleasure." He reached out to shake her hand.

She reciprocated. "Thank you for taking the time to talk to me."

He studied her for a second. "I'll be honest. At first I didn't agree with the idea of letting a woman play in the man's league. Thought it was a publicity stunt. You've changed my mind. You hold your own on the ice. You've taken some tough hits and got right back up. Your save percentage is in the mid-nineties. To boot, you've rallied this team into a group of guys that are having fun again. Amazing."

A bit embarrassed, she lowered her gaze. When she looked up, she found an expression of appreciation on his face.

"You've made me into a believer, Piper."

The softly spoken words from a Hall of Famer touched her heart. He didn't toss out compliments willy-nilly. That gave his statement even more credence. "Then I'm doing something right."

"You're doing a lot of things right."

* * * *

"I'm sorry, sir. Your reservations are for tomorrow night. We're completely full tonight."

Ranger noticed the distress on the man's face as he turned back to a woman holding a small baby. Several other families stood behind him, all having just left the hockey game, judging by their attire. Granted, they wore the other team's shirts, but he wouldn't hold it against them.

He grinned to himself for a brief moment, then worked his way to the front of the unmoving line at the hotel desk. Checking in normally went smoothly, considering all their rooms were pre-booked. He stopped beside Ben, who as organizer had set up all the travel accommodations. "What's going on?"

"From what I gather, they thought they had rooms reserved for tonight. The hotel has them for tomorrow night instead."

Ranger peered out of the glass doors, noting the snow continually falling, so thick a person could hardly see. At least half a foot coated the ground as their bus had carried them from the rink to the hotel a half block away. Between the limited ability to see and the fast-accumulating snow, people were sure to be stuck for the night. The frigid temps promised frostbitten parts in a matter of only a few minutes.

He turned his attention back to the baby and several kids in the group. Decision made, he addressed the hotel host. "How many rooms are you short?"

The man met his gaze. "Five."

Ranger nodded. "Give them mine. I'll share with one of the team." He strode over and handed the key to the man who had worry written clearly on his face. "Here. Take my room."

"I can't. It's—"

"The only right thing to do," Ranger finished. He turned back to the employee. "Since the rooms are already paid for, I expect you to not charge them, either."

"Yes, sir." The guy nodded.

Hagan came over next, followed by Axel and Keith. Even Tommy turned over his key.

Pride grew as Ranger watched disbelief turn to amazement and joy on the faces of the fans.

"There's sure to be more coming in from the game that can't make it out of the parking lot," Ben commented. "We'll just all double up. That'll give you several more rooms to fit those people in as well."

Relief covered the host's face. "Thank you."

"It's the least we can do. No sense in being stingy when there's a real need." Ben turned and stepped away.

Piper walked up to the desk, holding her key in the air. "Who wants to camp out with me?"

Since they had an even number of players and ancillary staff, they all had to double up or two of them would still have their own rooms.

He figured Piper would get angry if she couldn't help out, in addition to feeling guilty for having a room to herself when everyone else didn't. What he'd learned about her thus far was that she wanted to be one of the guys and hated special treatment. Except when it came to chocolate treats, of course.

Ranger bit back a smile as the rest of the guys either blinked at her or found the floor enthralling. A few stared in his direction, as if begging him to step up and take one for the team.

It wasn't them that motivated him to show his hand. It was the moment Piper's happy expression started to fall. His gut clenched, demanding he intervene. "I will."

Piper's grin returned, then turned a bit wicked. "I was kind of hoping you'd say that."

Her loud whisper set loose butterflies in his stomach as well as cranked his libido.

"Chocolate tamed the little beast. You were right." Rocky nudged Ranger in the back.

Ranger chuckled.

Piper snorted. "Oh, it's not just the chocolate."

All eyes turned to him. He stared back, his mouth firmly shut. *Let them wonder. Hell, most of them probably have figured it out already.* Which offered up one explanation to their lack of willingness to share a room with her. They refused to poach, especially when they figured he'd stomp them if they dared try.

"Thank you again," the woman holding the baby said.

Ranger dipped his head. "My pleasure." A sudden

thought struck. "Have you guys had dinner yet?" The early game had allowed them to get to the hotel at a reasonable time and still hit the dining room before closing.

She shook her head.

Ranger smiled warmly. "Drop your stuff off then meet us in the hotel restaurant. Dinner's on me tonight."

Her eyes widened and her mouth fell open. "That's too much."

"It's the least I can do," Ranger assured her.

Her presumed husband grinned from ear to ear. "We appreciate this. So much."

"Anything for a hockey fan." Ranger gestured to one of the kids. "Even if you happen to root for the other team."

The man laughed. "I have a feeling after tonight our allegiance might change a little."

Ranger nodded. "I'll set the meals up with the host here. Just tell them to put it on my tab. Ranger Deacon, if you didn't know."

"Oh, I'd recognize you anywhere." He held out his hand.

Ranger shook it without hesitation.

"Thank you. Really."

"Welcome." Ranger turned back to find Piper and the rest of the guys watching him. "What?"

Piper linked her arm in his. "You did a good deed. We're proud of you."

He shrugged. "It's not like they had anywhere else to go."

"Still, you went out of your way," Piper persisted.

The guys filed past, most pausing to slap Ranger on the upper arm. "Nice move," Axel said.

"Class act." Tommy squeezed Ranger's shoulder. "I'm proud of you."

"Thanks, Coach." Ranger scanned the room, finding himself pretty much alone with Piper as everyone else headed to the elevators.

She adjusted the strap on her duffel and picked up her suitcase. "Ready to spend the night with me?" She waggled her eyebrows. "The guys think you're pretty brave. Or suicidal. One of the two."

He shook his head at her playful antics. "Nah. They just think I'm certifiably nuts."

"For wanting to shack up with me for one night?" She huffed. "What do they think? That I turn into a fierce dragon at night and eat unsuspecting men?"

He opened his mouth but she pushed past him, rambling away. "I swear. Why would they think I'd eat someone like you? You're gorgeous, sexy and kind. I'd spare you. Now a couple of the others, though. They might end up on the dinner plate."

He followed along, thoroughly amused at her jabbering. "Good to know you'd spare me."

She paused at the elevator, allowing him to draw abreast. "I'd not eat you. Well, not in that way. Of course, you are good enough to eat…in other ways."

His arousal jumped to attention. Uncaring of who saw, he leaned in and sealed his lips over hers for a chaste but lingering kiss. When he once again stood up straight, he smiled down at the perplexed happiness planted on her face. "Talking like that gives me a hard-on, making it a bit uncomfortable to walk around a public hotel."

"Oh." A slow, seductive smile replaced the moment of surprise. "I do have a sudden craving for…meat. Good thing I know how to fix that."

He groaned to himself. Piper was turning out to be one hot tamale who kept his motor running.

The elevator door opened. He stepped inside and pushed the button to their floor. Piper stood next to him.

Since they were alone, he decided to clarify something. "I thought this was a bad time?"

"A bad time for me doesn't mean it's a bad time for you." She licked her lips. "I wonder…"

He knew he shouldn't ask, but couldn't seem to help himself. "Wonder what?"

"How late we'll be to dinner if you drop trou when we get to the room, I commence a thorough taste test, and you get a pre-meal happily ever after."

His breath caught as fire zinged through his veins, converging in his cock. Unable to form words, he grabbed her arm and led her quickly down the hall. After two tries, he managed to get the key card to work. He had no more stepped inside the room, dropped his belongings and shut the door behind Piper when she reached for his pants, unzipping them at a snail's pace. He took over, slipped the button through the hole and shoved his slacks and boxers down in one motion.

She dropped to her knees, wrapped one hand around the base of his dick and flicked her tongue over the tip.

He steadied himself by grasping her shoulder with one hand while pushing the hair away from her face with the other. In all his experiences, he'd never felt or seen anything as hot as watching Piper suck his cock. Her enthusiasm complemented her growing skill, lashing him with burning pleasure so intense he could barely do more than breathe. "Yeah. So damn good." Another moan slipped past his lips. The urge to thrust became almost unbearable.

She opened her mouth and took the head inside, immediately adding vacuum to the myriad sensations she lavished on him.

His arousal ratcheted up tenfold. Words left him as he could only manage to stay upright and revel in her attentions.

She found his slit with her tongue, boldly licked, then swirled to hit all the hot spots surrounding the head.

Bright sparks fired in his mind as his dick began to throb. His balls drew up tightly and a tingling at his lower spine told him that he wouldn't last much longer.

She stroked with her hand, laved and sucked. The second she cupped his tender nuts, he rocketed over the edge, coming in near record time.

He grunted and rode the waves, noting how Piper stayed the course, not backing off despite the seemingly endless streams of cum.

By the time he collected himself, Piper had stood back up and was grinning at him like a Cheshire cat. "All better?"

He drew in much-needed air, tucked his rapidly diminishing shaft into his pants and zipped back up. "Oh, yeah."

For a long minute he studied her.

She blinked back. "What?"

"You're one surprise after another." Never before had he met a woman who seemed to enjoy giving as much as Piper did. She didn't have a selfish bone in her body.

"Always good to keep a guy guessing. Or so I hear." She brushed at the knees of her slacks.

He shook his head, marveling at his great fortune. Emotions welled up. He pulled her against his chest and kissed the top of her head.

She snuggled in for a second before squirming.

Reluctantly, he released her.

"If we don't get to the food, there won't be anything left."

He grinned at her practicality. "There's that."

"Granted, I have plenty of chocolate, but Peter would have a fit if we skipped a healthy dinner and lived on junk food."

"Uh-huh." He turned the knob and opened the door. "After you."

She lifted up and brushed her lips over his chin. Her mouth opened but no words emerged. Instead, she met his eyes, held them, then turned to step into the hallway, the moment broken.

They arrived in the restaurant in the midst of the rush. No one seemed to notice their tardiness.

Chapter Twenty-Two

"Get much sleep last night?" Rocky started stripping down, exchanging casual business wear for a T-shirt and pads.

Ranger accepted the ribbing with ease. He'd heard similar comments off and on all day, thankfully well out of earshot of Piper. The guys at least possessed some tact. "Actually, we both crashed right after dinner. Slept in, too." He spoke the simple truth. No reason to lie. Still, he wasn't about to disclose that they'd shared one of the double beds instead of each taking a separate one. *I'm not that dumb.*

He'd gauged Piper's fatigue accurately yesterday. The ruthless schedule was wearing her down. While still peppy, she napped when she could during travel and appeared to fall asleep quickly snuggled up next to him at night. Sure signs of growing exhaustion. He'd been there himself, still was, but had grown accustomed to the constant moving around over the years.

Rocky shook his head. "That's all you two did? Just sleep?"

"Yep." Ranger pulled his jersey on.

"I would have been tempted to do a bit more than sleep," Adam tossed out.

Ranger glared at him. "You really don't want to go there, Lancaster."

Adam held up his hands. "Right. I don't. Shutting up now." He returned to the task of getting dressed for the game.

"A bit testy today," Riley said.

Ranger shrugged.

"Seems you and Piper are an item," Keith commented from the other line of lockers. "Holding hands. Hanging out. Roommates."

Ranger felt like he was on trial. Or worse, the same way he had as a kid when his parents had bumbled their way through trying to explain the birds and the bees to him. Considering he'd already known the basics, the whole conversation had proved awkward and way uncomfortable. "And you guys have an issue with that?" He raked the room, finding a few smirks, a couple of smiles and several blank expressions.

"Nope. Not at all. Just wanted to make sure we were reading the writing on the wall accurately." Riley grinned ruefully.

Ranger flipped him off. "What's between me and Piper is personal. I'm not blabbing."

"Kiss and tell already," Axel added.

"Yeah," a couple more of the guys agreed in unison.

Ivan clasped him on the shoulder. "Ignore the nosy ones. They're just jealous."

"We want to make sure she's getting a good deal." Rocky slipped on his jersey. "That's what brothers are for."

Ranger held his annoyance in check. "You know me better than that, Tremblay." He rarely used Rocky's last name, and only when it was serious. Like now. "I'm past the puck bunny stage, believe it or not." He bit out the words. Granted, in their boots he'd have done the same thing in questioning Ranger's intentions. That realization kept him from truly becoming angry.

"Just looking out for Piper's interests is all." Keith held up one hand when Ranger leveled him with a look. "Honest."

"Who's looking out for my interest?" Piper stepped into the room, silencing the discussion.

Ranger glanced her direction and found her suited up, her blonde locks corralled into a thick braid. "All of us. Seems you've found a legion of guard dogs."

Piper blew at her bangs, barely getting them to budge. "A

legion, huh? Is this like my legion of men after the women's games?"

"Even better," Anthony replied. "You get the eye candy without the one-liners."

Piper's mouth fell open before she shook her head. "And that's better?"

"Absolutely," Adam insisted.

She tilted her head this way and that. "Perhaps you're right. I don't have to feed you or cuddle with you. I can just play with you now and again then put you out for the night." She bobbed her head. "Yep. Guard dog sounds much better."

Ranger grinned at her sassiness.

"Bet you don't put Ranger out for the night," Rayovic quipped.

Ranger swung toward the backup goalie and scowled.

Rayovic, to his credit, stared right back.

Piper sighed. "I guess it's no longer a secret."

Ranger turned back to her, studying her face in order to read her emotions on this subject. He came up empty.

"Want to hear the story?"

"Yeah," several of the guys answered.

"Okay." She cleared her throat. "A while back, I was hurt and scared after some evil person sneakily blindsided me. Knocked me down. Tried to get me to call it quits. I didn't know where to look or what to do."

Not sure where she was going, Ranger listened in, noticing the rest of the team was doing the same.

"Lost and alone, I looked for someone to step up to the plate, to pull me from the hellish rabbit hole I found myself in." She scanned the room, checking off each guy with her gaze, drawing them in with then inflections in her voice. "I found men, several of them, who would take up arms to defend me."

"Then what?" Adam asked.

She moved her hands, adding motion to her words. "Still, the evil battered at me, demanding I buckle at once. To throw in the towel for good. The men fought. Hard. Yet they still couldn't protect me from the all-powerful evil that had targeted me."

A long pause followed. "Then, through the haze, Ranger appeared. Big. Strong. With a long, hard…stick."

Chuckles followed.

"His kiss healed me. Good as new, I watched him ride off to battle. He fought bravely, finally destroying the evil witch that fed me the poisoned apple in the first place. Kingdom saved. I became the lucky princess." She waggled her eyebrows for emphasis.

Men laughed. Several rolled their eyes.

Ranger grinned at Piper's version of the old Snow White tale.

"You had to turn us into the seven dwarfs?" Riley snorted.

"Better than the goose that laid golden eggs, right?" she replied.

"Okay, gentlemen and lady. Story time is over. We have a game to play." Tommy clapped his hands.

A chorus of "aww" ensued.

Ranger waited for Piper to amble over before whispering in her ear. "Nice decoy maneuver."

She grinned mischievously. "I was only telling the truth. Your kiss healed me. Just like a modern day Prince Charming." With a quick wink, she headed toward the ice.

She took a piece of his heart along with her.

* * * *

Ranger hit the bench and slugged some water after a fast-paced double shift on the ice. The opponents were quick and efficient, zipping from one end of the ice to the other, snatching up loose pucks and sending flames toward the net. Piper had managed to stop all but two of them. Those goals had come early in the game. Since then, she'd been perfect.

Unfortunately, the Wolfpack's scoring had leveled off

after a single goal. Ranger himself had made several shots, all denied by the other goalie.

"Our offense is struggling," Tommy said. "We need to pick it up."

No shit. Ranger took another large gulp and tried to catch his breath. What they really needed were some lucky breaks. Unfortunately, the Stars weren't making many mistakes to capitalize on.

Ranger watched as the Stars' forwards took the puck to the Wolfpack end, set up a play and start hammering away.

Piper slid from side to side, blocked a couple more attempts before finally covering up the puck and stopping play.

At least they aren't trying to pummel her into the ice like some of the teams we've faced. A nice change, although she'd be worn out after such a relentless effort.

Glancing up at the clock, Ranger noted the time winding down on the second period. Not much time to even the score before another break.

Tommy hit him on the shoulder. "First line up."

Ranger jumped to his feet and hurried out the open door as the previous line filed back in. He saw his chance, intercepted the puck and flew toward the opponent's end.

"Man on!"

The yelled warning told him he had a defender closing in fast on his back. Ranger angled to the left, waited for the right moment, then hit a sharp-angled slap shot flying toward the net. The goalie swatted at it, although too late. The red light flashed, signifying a goal.

Ranger raised his stick in celebration. The rest of the guys skated over and congratulated him. He patted them on the helmets and took his position near center ice for the face-off. Hagan won the battle, but was unable to do much as the buzzer sounded two seconds later, ending the middle period.

Without pause, Ranger headed back toward the bench, stepped onto the skate-guard flooring surface, and made his way toward the locker room.

"Hey, hotshot. Wait up."

He paused and turned, seeing Piper hurrying to catch up.

"Nice goal." She smiled at him, her mask perched on the top of her head.

"Thanks." He grinned in return. "I got lucky."

She snorted. "That wasn't luck. That was sheer skill."

Her praise added another element of excitement to the game. Not only did he want to do well for the team, he also wanted to please her. Keeping her happy and healthy had moved to the top of his priority list at some point in these last few weeks of the season. "Maybe you're biased." He bantered with her as they continued on their way.

"Maybe. But I happen to know talent when I see it." She peered up at him. "A hunk with a big heart, too." She stepped in front of him, lifted up and brushed her lips over his.

Ranger responded instantly, taking control of the kiss, moving his lips over hers in a soft exploration that spoke of affection and care.

"Good grief. This isn't the kiss cam, you two." Riley strode by with a huff.

"Even better. Get a room. Later. Much later." Sven chuckled.

Ranger lifted away from Piper's lips and at the same time flipped off his teammates.

"Guess the cat is really out of the bag, now." Piper licked her lips.

The action sent a bolt of arousal through Ranger. He ignored it. "Is that so bad?"

She shook her head. "Nope. In fact, it's a welcome relief. We don't have to worry about sneaking into one another's hotel room."

He grinned. "That's a good thing. I wasn't doing well with the sneaking part, anyway."

"Neither was I." She lowered her chin. "Besides, I've kind of gotten used to you hanging around all the time."

His heart buoyed at her words. "Does that mean you're going to keep me?"

Her eyes met his and sparked.

"Come on, you two. We haven't got all day to figure out a plan of action to win this damn game." Tommy held open the door and leveled a stern look their direction.

Ranger sighed, nudged Piper ahead of him and took his seat at the end of the wooden bench next to her.

Soon. Very soon. We'll get some things ironed out. Because there's no way I'm letting her go.

Ben strode over, offering a basket of snacks along with bottles of juice. Piper dug through first, found a candy bar and beamed up at him. "You remembered."

Ranger bit back a grin. Like anyone could forget her demand for the specific treat at the last game.

"I did." Ben pushed the container toward Ranger.

"Well, thank you," she mumbled around a bite.

He picked a fruit-flavored granola bar and unscrewed the lid on his apple juice.

"Did Piper get chocolate?" Adam asked as he craned his neck then nodded. "Thank God. Talk about a woman on the warpath if she was denied. Again." He shuddered dramatically.

Piper rolled her eyes then blew him a kiss. "Nice to know you're thinking about me and my ability to kick your ass."

Ranger smirked and bit into his bar.

"Yeah, yeah." Adam finished his drink. "You can try."

Piper grinned confidently. "Anytime, Adam. Anytime."

The expression on her face portrayed the warrior Ranger knew her to be. Fierce. Competitive. Unbending. The confidence she exuded flowed through the room, lending itself to every player and their individual game. He knew because she did the same for him. He played harder and looser knowing Piper had their backs.

"Enough of the posturing. We've got a tie game and twenty minutes to go. Time to focus on what's important." Tommy stepped to the front of the room and started talking.

Ranger turned his attention to the coach, but kept an eye on Piper. When it came to importance, she outranked pretty much everything and everyone. At least in his eyes.

Chapter Twenty-Three

The next few days flew by. Games, practices, meetings, workouts. They all became a blur. Add in another two stops inside Canada and Piper decided they were always on the go. Bus. Plane. A combination thereof. The pace intensified to where she wasn't sure when one day ended or the next began. Keeping up with nearly a different city each night became too complicated to worry about. One thing was for certain—the guys endured a brutal schedule, especially at the end of the season. The good news was they won all the games except one. Not bad for a seemingly endless road trip.

She found herself napping more, trying to combat the lingering fatigue of three and sometimes four games per week, thousands of miles traveled and hours upon hours of ice time. Between that and trying to keep up with her bookkeeping job online, she was scrambling more than she ever had before.

At least I have a couple of days off to rest before the mad dash to the end of the season.

Piper stowed her gear in the back of her SUV, noting the dreary day filled with drizzle mixed with light rain along with chilly temperatures of early spring. Late March in Denver could be unpredictable, from blizzards to gorgeous temperatures to rival Florida. They'd had the blizzard not long ago. Thankfully, today seemed to lean toward blah instead of the bone-chilling cold she'd experienced over the last week traveling through the frozen tundra otherwise known as Canada on a way-too-long road trip.

Just two more weeks.

The thought brought both relief and sadness. She hated the reality of her dream ending so quickly. Yet it would. No matter how many times she did the math, the Wolfpack simply couldn't earn a trip to the playoffs. Too many losses earlier in the season to overcome, even if they were perfect in the home stretch. Too bad. She'd have loved to have played in at least one series, comparing how it rated with the women's league version.

She and Ranger hooked up when they could, spending more time together than apart. Although, most of that time they weren't alone. Amazing how thirty-plus chaperones could dampen the most romantic of intentions.

"You're coming over, right?" Ranger asked as he opened the back door of his SUV and placed his belongings inside.

"Not tired of me yet?" she asked, knowing the answer, but needing to hear the words.

"Not even close." His grin reassured her as much as her words. Possession. Need. Even pride flashed across his face. The spark of desire didn't go unnoticed, either.

While they spent nearly every day at hotels, they still cozied up at night. The one night she'd snuck back to her own room, she'd tossed and turned, missing the giant teddy bear she'd grown accustomed to in such a short period of time.

"Let me swing by my apartment first to get a change of clothes."

He nodded. "If you need to wash some, just bring them with you."

She blinked at him.

"What?" His face scrunched in confusion.

"Sharing a washing machine just seems like an important step." A small thrill zinged through her at the thought. To her, when she'd started leaving clothes at his house, that had meant they were pert near living together. A big step indeed.

He closed the distance between them, pulled her into his arms and kissed her with enough zest and passion to silence all her doubts in one fell swoop.

When he leaned back, she offered up a small grin. "Okay. Joint laundry tonight. Got it."

"Go grab what you need then come on over." He released her to stare for a long moment.

She nodded. "If you're sure…"

"Either you come to me or I'll come to you." His firm expression solidified the statement. One way or another, he intended to camp out with her.

She'd rather hang out at his house than her small apartment. "I'll pack an extra bag and head your way."

"Good." He flashed a grin, climbed into his vehicle and cranked the engine.

"You look happy," Stanza said in his accented English.

Piper startled and turned to see her goalie coach ambling over. "You could say that."

He watched Ranger pull away then turned his attention back to her. "He's a good man."

"Yes. Yes, he is." Oddly enough, talking to Stanza about Ranger seemed like a precursor to telling her father.

"Don't let happiness slip through your fingers," he advised.

She studied him for a moment before searching inside herself. It only took a couple of seconds to find the answer. "I don't intend to."

He gave a quick nod. "Be back day after tomorrow, ready to skate."

"Yes, sir." She saluted him, climbed into her vehicle and set a course for home. One day off wasn't much, but she'd take it. Especially if that meant staying with Ranger. Alone. At his house.

Butterflies took flight inside her stomach. She couldn't dismiss the feeling of rightness at the thought of spending all her free time with Ranger. The man who meant so much. The same guy who'd awakened her desires and dominated her dreams.

He'd captured her heart along the way and refused to let

go.

She pushed the key in the ignition, started the engine and pulled out of the garage. After a short visit to her apartment, she had a meeting with destiny.

* * * *

The washing machine hummed softly in the background as Piper took a seat. She'd tossed a load of her stuff in along with Ranger's as soon as she'd arrived. Considering she had other plans, she didn't want to waste time on laundry when multitasking was an option. They'd picked up dinner on the way home, eaten and cleaned up the kitchen before Piper wandered into the living room to take a load off and rest for a bit.

Ranger had stayed behind in the kitchen in order to make up a couple of glasses of hot chocolate to conquer the evening chill from the damp day, promising to bring them out as soon as they were ready.

Piper glanced around, noting how everything reflected Ranger as she knew him. Hockey player extraordinaire. Athlete. Laid-back good guy with a softness he showed to those he cared for. Warmth. In such a short time, she'd grown comfortable here. With Ranger.

She reflected on her past and how Ranger had pushed the nightmares aside and replaced them with brightness and love, gentleness and humor. His touches turned her to a puddle of molten fire while, at the same time, his quirkiness made her laugh. Never before had she met anyone who could set her aflame with a smile, a glance. Nor had she imagined losing all her inhibitions in bed like she'd done with Ranger. He made her ache deliciously while showering her with affection and comfort. The unique combination set her heart to pitter-pattering as well as rocketed up her libido to record heights.

He made her feel like the princess in a fairy tale. One that would hopefully continue on, happily ever after, as promised in those same stories. For she'd fallen for her modern day Prince Charming, no glass slipper needed.

Ranger returned with two steaming mugs in hand. She raked him from head to toe, finding nothing but perfection in every graceful step. His jeans, though loose, hinted at power while the form-fitting, long-sleeved shirt left no question about the strength of his muscles or the superior conditioning of his body. The view stole her breath, but not nearly as much as the way he watched her, as if she collected the stars in her hands and tossed them into the night sky each evening.

Never had anyone looked at her in such a way.

Ranger hung the sun every day and froze the water to ice every night. She recalled Stanza's words and found them to be wise. For her, Ranger was the only one who'd do.

He stopped right in front of her and handed one of the mugs to her, as she retained her seat.

She reached up, accepted the glass, and met his eyes. The softness and possession there spurred her to utter the words she'd been holding back. "You know I love you, right?"

He blinked at her. "Because I brought you hot chocolate?"

She shook her head and smiled softly. "Only partly. I love you because of everything you are. Smart. Kind. Sweet. Sexy. Everything I ever wanted in a man rolled into one."

A slow grin formed on his face. His emotions rolled through his pretty green eyes, everything from protectiveness to happiness to hunger. He sat down beside her, angling so he could face her, his long legs stretching out in the process. "That's a relief, since I love you too."

"Really?"

He sipped his drink then set it aside on a nearby end table. "Absolutely." He took her cup, placed it next to his, then hauled her onto his lap. "I'd given up on women. Thought I'd never find one that could care for me more than for her own wishes and wants. Then you appeared. Fierce and ready to take on the world. You battle on the ice, but your sweetness and good heart shine through otherwise. Not only to me, but to the other guys as well."

"They're like brothers to me," she whispered. "You're the only one that gets my motor going."

"As it should be, because I'm not sharing you with anyone." He nuzzled her temple, sending a cozy warmth through her. She'd never known such closeness could exist between two people. Sure, her family loved her and they got along fabulously, yet this was different. More like the love she saw between her parents. The way her mother lit up when her father entered the room. The tenderness, the way they held hands and still snuggled on the couch.

For nearly as long as she could remember, she'd wanted such a relationship with a man. Complete comfort. Respect. Unquestionable love.

Now, she'd found it.

This is the way I want to spend the rest of my life.

As much as she enjoyed simply being held, hunger demanded more. Too many days had passed since she'd lost herself in his lovemaking. *Time to make up for lost time.*

She turned to meet his questing lips with a rising passion long denied and emboldened by the certainty of love. Bracing her hands on his wide chest, she leaned into him, smiling when he wrapped his arms around her and pulled her snug.

He sampled her lips before dipping in, seeking a deeper taste.

Piper instinctively allowed the invasion, then went on the offense, mirroring his actions in detail.

He cupped her breast through the material, molding before skimming his thumb over her nipple.

She gasped at the electric current caused by his touch.

"Do you want me?" The low rumble of his voice could be heard as well as felt from where she sat.

"Yes." There was no hesitation or question in her mind. She'd always crave Ranger. His loving. His wicked smile. His path to paradise. "I want you more than chocolate." She grinned wickedly.

He chuckled. "Now, that's saying something." After running his hands through her hair, he pushed the long locks aside and rested his palm against her cheek. "I love you, Piper. With all that I have and all that I am."

Tears pooled in her eyes as his words struck a chord. She wiped them away. "I love you more."

"Not possible." He kissed the next tear away while grabbing the hem of her shirt and lifting it over her head.

"Going to show me?" The question escaped her lips while she dropped her top carelessly behind her.

His eyes darkened a shade. "Oh, yeah." He pinched the clamp on her bra, pushed the material aside and drew her bare breast to his mouth. He lapped before gently sucking, drawing the nipple into a tight bead. "Definitely. I'm not stopping until you scream my name." Heat enveloped her as he tugged her bra off and tossed it to the floor. A second later, his lips worried her other breast.

She bit back a moan. "Is that a challenge?"

He lifted his head and stared into her eyes. "It's a promise."

No words followed. They didn't need to because he returned to his sweet torment, kissing first one breast then the other. After a couple of minutes, he hooked his thumbs in the waistband of her jeans and tugged. "Off."

Piper stood and quickly undressed. As she stepped out of the denim shackles, she watched his face. The intensity in his gaze made her chew her bottom lip in a moment of nervousness.

"You're beautiful."

The appreciation in his eyes along with the tightening of his jaw told the story. He wanted her. Badly.

The realization gave her the courage to bend over and start pulling the clothes from his body. First his shirt joined hers. Then she took her time exploring his torso before dipping lower, unfastening the button of his jeans then taking down the zipper at an impatient pace. He sucked in air then lifted in order to assist in removing his pants. The moment his clothes slid down, his erection jumped free, thick, full and impressive.

She pressed her lips to his chest while letting her hands roam over the contours of his shoulders, trunk and abdomen. The hardness covered by silky skin intrigued her almost as much as his large shaft, presently resting against his stomach.

He patted the couch, found her hand and encouraged her to sit. As soon as she did, he turned her to face him and rose up, pressing her back against the cool leather of the couch.

"I've been thinking of doing this since you gave me that blow job in Toronto."

A shiver of anticipation quaked through her body. Piper leaned up to watch as Ranger lowered to the space between her thighs.

"Open for me, love. I need a taste."

Her heart sped as he slid his hand from her inner knee upward, stopping when he cupped her mound. He parted her with his fingers.

Uncertain, she held her breath, then jerked at the decadent sensation of Ranger licking across her most sensitive areas.

"Delicious. Just as I knew you'd be." He dipped a finger into her channel and at the same time returned to lapping at her slit.

Hot pleasure speared through her. She writhed and squirmed under his ministrations, an occasional moan escaping when he hit a particularly sensitive spot. He drove her crazy with his questing tongue, the licking, the touches on her heated body. The, he used his finger to set a slow rhythm, pressing inward each time he strummed across her sensitive bundle of nerves.

"Ranger. Please." She tossed her head back and forth, quickly closing in on climax. Yet she couldn't quite make it to the top. Instead she stalled near the peak, strung out on a burning bed filled with passion and searing pleasure. Unable to verbalize more, she knew he'd carry her on over. In time.

Ranger guided her left leg to the side until her foot rested on the floor. The other he lifted to hook over his shoulder, leaving her spread and vulnerable.

She trembled at the new level of intimacy.

His mouth returned to her folds while he added another finger to her depths. "So sweet. So beautiful. I'm going to watch you come apart." He punctuated the promise by swirling his tongue over her clit.

Piper bucked and cried out. She panted for breath as he covered the area with his lips and began to suck.

Bright stars danced in front of her eyes as she shot straight into orbit. A sharp cry tore from her throat as her channel spasmed in one of the most intense orgasms she'd had to date. She rode the waves until they faded. The second they diminished, Ranger pulled her into his arms, sat down on the couch and settled her so she was straddling his lap. He produced a condom, presumably out of his wallet, and slipped it on.

He smiled wolfishly at her. "Ride me, baby." He used one hand to position the tip of his cock against her opening. The other rested on her hip with a sure hold that nudged her downward.

Renewed and all the more aroused, she lowered gradually, feeling the stretch of her body to accommodate his thick width. Taking her sweet time, she welcomed him inside, thrilled to have him back after several days' absence. She hit bottom and paused.

"Okay?" He breathed against her lips.

She nodded. "You fill me up. And then some." She smiled and met his hungry lips with a kiss full of promise and fire.

Instinctively, she began to move. Up and down at first, just enough to massage a couple of hot spots, then in more of a circular pattern. Unable to decide which she liked better, she settled for a combination of both.

"So tight, Piper. It's so fucking good." Ranger grasped her hips, keeping her strokes measured and slow at the same time as he supped on her breasts, bringing forth a sweet burn in his wake.

A moan escaped her at the tender assault he plied on her body.

He lifted his head. "Look at me, Piper."

She complied, fascinated by the molten heat flaring in his eyes.

"Yeah. Just like that. Now stay with me."

The closeness astounded her as she gyrated on his lap, never once closing her eyes or turning away. The partaking ratcheted up her arousal enormously and proved to be the most intimate thing she'd ever done. As if she could see clear through to his soul and share in his pleasure. Amazing and so erotic she knew she couldn't last.

He found her clit with his thumb and pressed lightly.

Her breath hitched as a wave of searching heat washed through her.

He slid his other hand around to cup her bottom, assisting with every motion.

The caress intensified the bright passion, mixing with the other brilliant sensations to create a boiling cauldron about to explode. "Oh, God. Ranger." She whimpered and swiveled her hips before grinding against him.

"Right there, baby. You're so damn hot and wet. I'm not going to last much longer." His thighs tightened under her, thrusting his granite-hard shaft higher.

She eagerly accepted the small change, her muscles closing in tightly.

He circled her clit then brushed over it with exquisite precision.

Piper cried out, rocked harder and nearly slammed into him in her eagerness to take him completely, leaving no area of her core untouched.

He groaned, low and deep, rumbling from his chest.

The sound compelled her to focus on his face. The way it screwed up in bliss, the parting of his lips, the dilating of his eyes. She saw the cords of his neck stand out as his grip tightened significantly on her butt. His light skimming over her nub remained tender, though it became more frantic.

Needing to watch him come, she trailed her hands over his chest, found his nipples and lightly pinched.

Ranger gave a muted shout, wrapped his arms around her and thrust hard. Once. Twice. A third time.

She shot over the edge and into pulsating rapture. All the time, she watched his face, though it blurred now and again. No doubt existed in her mind that they shared the overwhelming pleasure cascading over her in high crests. She stayed the course, shivering as the final contractions faded, leaving her breathless, sated and tired.

Piper slumped against his chest. His strong arms were a band of steel holding her in place. She nuzzled the warm flesh under her cheek and sighed happily.

"Damn, Piper." His slightly out of breath voice puffed air that tickled her ear. "Better each time."

She smiled at his compliment. "For me, too." Sitting up, she stared at him. "I never dreamed of finding a man like you."

He kissed her soundly, showing, rather than telling, her how much he cared.

She didn't budge for the longest time.

Chapter Twenty-Four

Ranger woke with bright sunlight pouring in the window and coating his body with additional warmth along with the blankets and a certain lady tucked against his side. He took a moment to stare down at her, barely noting the tousled hair. Instead, he felt the soft skin of her arm under his. Saw the quiet rise and fall of her chest as she breathed. The aura of contentment and beauty she exuded without the benefit of makeup, high fashion or even being awake.

His heart pounded against his ribs as emotions surged to the fore.

I can't imagine a day without her.

Love had snuck up and bitten him in the butt. Thankfully so. He'd been jaded toward all the women he'd seen until Piper had landed in his path. From the start, he'd found her different — compelling, brave and silly. She'd become the glue that held the team together as well as a source of much-needed comic relief in difficult circumstances. The tides had changed the moment she'd joined them. From rough and turbulent, filled with anger, gradually to a tranquil sea. She'd never take credit for the difference, but he knew the truth. Piper had turned their hockey season around, touched all the guys and made the game worth playing once again.

For him, she had become more. So much more. And now, with the season winding down, he needed to take some steps to solidify his future.

Carefully, he lifted the covers, slid out of bed and rearranged the blankets over her, ensuring her comfort with him gone. He wouldn't wake her for the world. They'd been up late making love. Between that and the past few weeks of nonstop travel and hockey thrown into the mix, Piper needed all the sleep she could get. Especially now, when he had a plan come to fruition requiring a bit of privacy.

He quietly left the room, shutting the door behind him. Chilly, he headed to the living area, found his discarded clothes from last night and tugged them on. Wrinkles didn't matter at that point. Only covering his bare skin did.

With that task accomplished, he palmed his cell phone and glanced around, listening for sounds that Piper might be getting up. Hearing nothing, he strode away from the bedroom, into the den of his collectibles, and shut the door behind him. He sat down in the old recliner, pulled out the number hidden between his phone and the cover, then paused for a beat.

First things first.

He dialed his mother.

She picked up on the third ring. "Ranger!"

He smiled at her enthusiasm. She always greeted him in the same way. As if she missed him greatly and couldn't wait to hear from him. Something that always made him grin. "Hi, Mom. Just wanted to make sure you and Dad are coming in for the final game like planned." Every season they flew down to watch the last game, then stayed with him for a few days afterward. A vacation for them. A nice visit for him.

"Absolutely. I have the tickets on the counter, waiting to go."

"Coming in Friday afternoon still?"

"Yes."

"Good." He ran one hand through his hair.

"What aren't you telling me?" Her voice grew suspicious.

He shook his head. She could always tell when he had something on his mind. "I want you and Dad to meet someone."

A short pause followed.

"You mean that woman goalie?"

His mouth fell open. "How did you know?"

She laughed. "Ranger, I know you. Been watching your games. You're like a shadow to that girl."

He couldn't argue the truth. "Well, she's more than just a teammate."

"Do tell."

He could envision his mother plopping down on the couch, leaning back and waiting for him to spill the beans. Drove him nuts as a teen. Now he didn't mind nearly as much. "I love her, Mom. She's the whole package and I'm going to ask her to marry me."

"She must be something special, then."

"She is."

"I can't wait to meet her. I'm sure your father will be just as excited."

He heard her enthusiasm. "She doesn't know about the proposal yet. I'd like to keep it under wraps for a while longer."

"We can keep a secret." She blew out a breath. "Do you have a ring yet?'

"No. I thought maybe I could go look for one when you guys arrive."

"That would be splendid. I'm sure your father will even get excited this one time about shopping."

Ranger smiled. His father avoided the mall like a moat filled with crocodiles. However, this once he might jump in with both feet. "Sounds great, Mom." He checked the clock and winced. "Listen, I've got to go. I have another call to make and time is running short."

"No problem. I'm so happy for you, son. We'll see you Friday."

"Okay. Love you, Mom."

"Love you, too."

Ranger hung up knowing his mother had probably started punching buttons right away to call his father with the news. He missed them and couldn't wait for them to share in the moment.

Speaking of…

He glanced down at the number written on the paper. Perhaps a bit old-fashioned, but Ranger knew he needed to toe the line when it came to Piper and her family. Talking to her father was a sign of respect — something Ranger knew about from his time on and off the ice.

He took a deep breath and made the call.

"Hello?"

"Gunther? Gunther Darrow?"

"Yes?"

Ranger drew in a steadying breath. "This is Ranger Deacon. If you have a minute, I'd like to chat with you. It's about your daughter."

"What about her?" The deep voice came across as a mixture of curiosity and command.

"Well, you see…"

* * * *

Piper woke to discover Ranger gone. She lifted her head and scanned the room, finding herself alone. A quick check of the clock clued her in even as she cringed. Almost noon. No wonder Ranger had risen and disappeared. He'd probably been starved after all their activity the night before.

She rolled to her back and smiled at the memories. He'd cherished her. That was the only way she could explain the way he made love. Completely. Thoroughly. Attentive to details. No roughness. No rushing. Just a perfect blend that sent tingles through her even at the memories.

He loves me.

The realization still thrilled her. She saw the signs in everything Ranger did. He made her feel like the luckiest woman in the world. Beautiful. Smart. And more than that. 'Special' came to mind.

And if I don't get moving, he might change his mind.

She grinned and shook her head. Not likely. But she still

needed to get up. They had afternoon practice, then a flight to catch.

The scent of hot food wafted to her. Her stomach growled in appreciative hunger.

Piper climbed out of the bed, quickly making it from years of habit, then searched for her clothes. Belatedly she remembered that her bag with all her items remained in the living room. The only things with her were her toothbrush and toothpaste in the bathroom. Clothing, even what she'd worn last night, was in other parts of the house.

Not brave enough to wander around naked, she eyed his closet. A second later she opened the door and peeked inside. A long-sleeved old jersey caught her eye. Tugging it from the hanger, she dropped it over her head, smiling as it covered her to mid-thigh. *Good thing Ranger's big. Really big. In all senses of the word.* She bit back the clamor of passion as it returned with power.

Food first. Playtime later.

She stuck with the sensible choice, took a couple of minutes in the bathroom to brush her hair and teeth before quietly leaving the bedroom, and followed her nose to the kitchen.

Ranger stood at the kitchen table, placing silverware on each plate. He glanced up, raked her from head to toe, and grinned. "I was just about to come wake you."

"I hope you don't mind." She tugged at the shirt. "I didn't have anything else handy to wear."

He approached her with a mischievous grin and molten eyes. "Not at all. Feel free to put on anything of mine you want." He pulled her snug, lowered his lips to hers, then palmed her bare rear. "No panties?"

She jumped and blinked up at him. "Same problem with the rest of my clothes."

His smile turned wolfish. "Remind me to hide your bag more often."

She snorted.

He found her earlobe and nibbled. "The thought of you

nude under my shirt turns me on."

Piper chuckled as her stomach somersaulted in blissful decadence. "I don't think it takes much to turn you on."

"Not with you, anyway." He brushed his lips over hers, stepped back then made his way to the stove. "Breakfast is ready."

The mention of clothes rang a bell. "The laundry. I should—"

"Already done." He cut her off. "The last load of both your stuff and mine is in the dryer right now."

Piper sat down as Ranger carried the pancakes over to join the scrambled eggs and sausage already on the table as well as milk, juice, butter and syrup. She looked at him apologetically. "I'm a lazy bum. I should have been up earlier and working on the laundry. Or at least helped with breakfast." She had never been one to sit idle and let others take care of her. Heck, her mother had taught her better.

"It's okay." Ranger took the chair beside her.

"I'm sorry. Thank you for doing all this." She sighed heavily.

"Hey." He waited until she met his gaze before saying more. "As far as I'm concerned this is a two-way street. There's going to be times when one person shoulders more of the load than the other. That's the way it works. You're exhausted and need some rest."

"But—"

He shook his head. "Piper. You've been living on a rocket ship the past couple of months. Playing double the games you did with the Bobcats, traveling twice as much and practicing about the same. Not only have you been roughed up and playing your ass off, you're trying to balance all that with your bookkeeping job. Add in an introduction to sex and anyone in the world can clearly see why you're fatigued." He took her hand in his. "Give yourself a break, okay? Let me pick up some of the slack now and again."

Ranger's light tone and simple explanation bolstered her spirit. "Thank you." She offered up a small smile.

"Welcome. Now dig in before the food gets cold."

She didn't argue. Instead she started loading up her plate, suddenly hungry. Vowing to return the favor, she poured syrup on her pancakes and took a bite. "Wonderful."

He smiled as he chewed.

For a while they simply ate in silence. Piper had demolished two pancakes, a sausage and most of her eggs when he spoke.

"My parents are coming in for the final game. They'll be staying with me."

"Is that a tradition?"

"Pretty much, yeah. They normally take vacation time around then so they can visit for a few days before going back to Minnesota."

"Do you go stay with them during the off season?" She'd always been close to her family. The thought of being a few states away saddened her. Granted, people were different and men probably didn't like their parents swinging by when they might have a bedmate over for the night.

She shook her head. That had never been a problem for her. Until possibly now.

"Sometimes. I stay around here most of the time. As do some of the other guys. We play pick-up games, go to the facilities to work out. Hang out a lot." He took a long drink of juice.

She did the same, but rarely ran into the Wolfpack players. Probably because she preferred to be up at the crack of dawn and hitting the ice as the sun peeked over the horizon. The women had their own lockers, so there wasn't much mingling at the facilities anyway, even if they shared the weight room.

"Don't the women hang around during the off season?"

"For the most part. Some go home. Those that live around here tend to show up at the gym or the rink now and again. Remember, most have jobs or a family to take care of, or both. So they're much less free to just play."

He nodded.

She voiced one of her concerns. "Do you think your parents will like me?"

He grinned wide. "They're going to love you."

Understanding the importance of first impressions, Piper ran some ideas through her head. "Do I need to dress up? Dress casual? Stay quiet until spoken to?"

"None of the above. Just be you, Piper. Really." He pinned her gaze.

"Really?"

"Really." He finished off his drink. "They're going to love you just like you are. Because I do."

Her libido sat up and took notice of the spark in his eyes. She stood and started clearing the table. The sooner they finished the task, the sooner they could move on to other activities. Her stomach flip-flopped at the thought. "I'm glad. Although, I think I need a demonstration of your love."

His eyebrow arched. "What kind of demonstration?"

She placed the dirty dishes in the dishwasher, added detergent and pushed the Start button. That done, she collected the other items and stored them back in the fridge. Chore complete, she stopped next to Ranger, bent over and nibbled his earlobe. "Oh, I don't know. Perhaps another example of your excellent lovemaking?"

He groaned and turned.

She noted his eyes darkened a shade as his jaw tightened.

"You like the way I make love to you?"

She smiled warmly at him. "Like isn't the right word. Try love. Try crave. Maybe even revel in." She ran her hands over his shoulders and down his chest. "You show me the heavens and make the world fall away when I'm in your arms. I'll never get enough of you."

He stood in a rush, swept her up in a cradle hold and carried her to his bedroom.

Piper watched his face as she held on. Emotions carried in his expressions and his gaze. One she read loud and clear — he loved her. Fully. Totally. And without exception.

"I love you, Ranger."

He brushed his lips over hers. "I love you too." He placed her gently on the bed and started stripping down.

Piper enjoyed the show. Immensely.

As he moved to cover her, she forgot everything but the man who turned her world upside down and showed her what love could be.

She didn't rouse again for a while, too sated and comfortable, wrapped in Ranger's arms.

Chapter Twenty-Five

Ranger watched Piper settle into a nest in the recliner next to him. They'd boarded the private plane a few minutes ago and had just hit cruising altitude on their way to the southwest part of the country for the next game.

Against the Rattlers. Again.

He cringed as he recalled the last time they'd taken the ice against the lowlife bastards. They'd nearly knocked Piper out of the game with their hard hits and constant pressure. Once more he recalled her small frame compared to some of the bigger guys playing for the opponent. No way could she handle a beating like last time.

"Piper?"

"Huh?"

"Have you thought about sitting this one out?"

She froze and pinned him with her gaze. Her lips flattened into a line. "Why would I do that?"

He exhaled slowly and toed the line between protectiveness and tactfulness carefully. "You know what assholes they are and what they did last time."

"Yes. Even more reason for me to play." She bit off the words and spoke a couple of decibels higher.

Rocky, Marek and Ivan closed in.

"What's going on?" Rocky asked.

Ranger peered up at them then back to Piper. "I'm trying to get her to reconsider playing against the Rattlers."

Riley sauntered over, shaking his head. "I have a feeling all you're doing is pissing her off."

Piper eyed the guys and gave a quick nod. She turned her focus to Ranger. "Do you think that I can't hold up under the pressure?"

"That's not it at all." He ran one hand through his hair. "It's just that I don't want to see you clobbered and taking a beating because they can't accept that you're a woman playing in the big leagues."

"Bet you wouldn't say that to Gunderson," Marek quipped.

Ranger glared at him. "I wouldn't have to. The Rattlers wouldn't go after him any more than the other goalies in the league. Piper is the exception here."

"Time to step back, guard dog," Rocky said. "I think the lady can handle herself."

Rocky's comment didn't settle well with Ranger. "It's not that she can't. I just know how those hosers think. They'll be ripe for revenge and have Piper on target."

"Ranger. I know you're worried about me, and I really appreciate it, but don't be. I can take it." Her firm resolve came through in her tone. "Besides, this is about pride. If I don't play then not only do I appear the coward, so do the rest of you. It would reflect badly on both me and the team. Copping out isn't an option."

Ranger understood her sentiment, but didn't like the situation any better. "What if they hurt you? Badly? What if they really do knock you out of the game this time?"

Piper leveled him a predatory look. "Then I'll take the hand I'm dealt. But nothing short of Armageddon will keep me from a rematch with those jerks." Determination filled her voice as well as a hint of anger.

Ivan grinned wide. "You can't keep a warrior down or on the sidelines, bro." He smacked Ranger in the upper arm lightly.

Riley agreed with a nod. "She's got a score to settle with them. Personally, I feel almost sorry for those fucking Rattlers. Almost."

Piper smiled at them in obvious appreciation as they took her side. "Thank you for the votes of confidence." She turned back to Ranger. "I have to do this, Ranger. For myself. For the team. For the future of women in the sport."

He hated that she shouldered so much, but couldn't do a damn thing about it. Her fierceness was one of the things he loved about her. Mental toughness she had. Too bad she wasn't built bigger to handle the hits sure to come.

"I get it." He checked off each of the men. "We just have to find a way to take the pressure off her and play in the Rattlers' end."

"You worry about playing your own game. I'll worry about mine. They're hard hitters, aggressive and fast," Piper reminded them.

"Yeah," Ivan agreed.

Ranger turned back to her, noting the furrowed brow and slightly hurt expression. *Shit.* "I'm sorry, Piper. I just don't want you banged up."

"Then you've picked the wrong sport and the wrong girl. Excuse me." She stood up and walked past them toward the front of the plane.

Ranger watched her go with a long, frustrated sigh.

"Don't baby her," Rayovic warned. "She's one of the best goalies around. Wanting to bench her in order to protect her won't earn you any brownie points in her mind."

"I'd say you just stepped in it, bro," Rocky said.

Ranger nodded, unable to take his eyes off Piper, who sat next to Stanza and snacked on a granola bar. "I hate the thought of what those bastards did last time. They'll for sure be bent on revenge."

"Could be. That's why we hit them where it counts the most. On the scoreboard." Rocky scratched at his chest.

"Give Piper credit. She knows what she's doing." Marek spun around and wandered back the way he came.

Ivan bumped Ranger on the shoulder. "Be watchful, but don't leash her. We'll find a way."

"Yeah." Ranger blew out a breath. "We'll find a way to keep her on her feet and in one piece."

As the others moved away, Ranger wracked his brain, falling short in the idea department. He couldn't play his position and watch over her at the same time. No matter how hard he tried, Piper would be on her own.

The thought stirred his concern all the more.

* * * *

Warm-ups finished, Ranger stood at the bench with the rest of the team, waiting for the signal to take the ice. His gaze landed on Piper, dressed in her gear, near the back of the line. With her mask resting on the top of her head, he could easily read the determination on her face as well as the knowledge of the upcoming battle.

He had to let her free, but couldn't prevent himself from giving her one more bit of warning. Walking over, he cupped her chin and tilted until she met his gaze. "Stay in the crease, Piper. Promise me. Any stray pucks, let them go. We can get them ourselves. No need to risk yourself going after them just to put them behind the net for us."

She shook her head. "Ranger. I only know one way to play hockey. That's all or nothing."

He blew out a breath in frustration. "You're not invincible or bulletproof. Those bastards are going to pick up where they left off last time."

"And we beat them." She grinned wolfishly. "We're going to do so again." Her smile faded. "Don't try to change me. Please."

Protectiveness warred with the need to make her happy by giving her free rein to play her game. *What am I saying? She's going to do it anyway.* "Just be careful out there. They nearly broke you last time," he warned.

"I know what I'm getting into, Ranger. Trust me. But giving up and running isn't an option. If I don't stand up and fight, I'll lose respect for myself and from everyone else." Her eyes implored him to understand.

Unable to resist, he caved. After a quick peck to her cheek, he brushed his glove over her nose. "Keep your head up."

She beamed up at him. "I will." She kissed him back for

an all too brief second before walking toward the ice, her back straight and chin held high.

He'd never been more proud of her than in that moment.

A hard hand on his shoulder snared his attention. He swung around to see Stanza standing next to him.

"She will be fine. No need to worry."

If only it were that simple. "They're headhunters." Ranger watched Piper settle into her crease and begin stretching.

"She can handle them." Stanza cleared his throat. "I would not say this about any other woman, but Piper is different. She's special."

Ranger nodded. "That she is." He spoke from the heart.

"Don't cage her, son. Let her shine." Stanza released his hold.

Ranger absorbed his advice and blew out a breath.

Piper would hold her own. It was up to him and the rest of the guys to put them ahead on the scoreboard and keep it that way.

Rocky nudged him in the side. "We've got this."

"Yeah."

Rocky swung around in front of Ranger, cutting off his view of Piper. "Listen, bro. We all know how you feel about her. It's written on your face."

Ranger scratched at his shoulder, wondering where Rocky was going with this. "So?"

"So, it's obvious she's damn smitten with you. Who knows why?" He chuckled when Ranger playfully smacked at him. "Maybe you need to step up and do something about it."

Ranger smirked. "I already have."

"You have?" Rocky's mouth fell open.

"Yep. I just need a bit more time for things to fall into place."

"Well, hell, Ranger. Looks like you're ahead of the game after all."

"As usual." Ranger shoved Rocky toward the ice. "I might need a favor, though."

"Anything for Piper." Rocky started skating in a slow, large circle on the Wolfpack end of the ice.

The admiration and affection for Piper didn't go unnoticed. Ranger respected the guys for including her in their fold and making her the sister they'd really never bargained for. "Get through this game and I'll tell you all about it in the locker room afterward. *If* you can keep your mouth shut around Piper."

"Deal."

Fifteen minutes later, Ranger had forgotten all about swearing Rocky to secrecy as he focused on staying upright, keeping his head on a swivel and avoiding being pancaked into the boards more than his fair share.

Shit. They brought out the Gong Show tonight. A Gong Show included lots of heavy checks, several penalties and tons of scoring. The rapid pace and physical nature of the game set it up for a perfect representation of the term.

The hits had started right up front, along with a fight within the first minute of the game. Rocky had managed to score a goal, which the Rattlers quickly evened up on a puck deflected off a stick that had skirted the crease and blocked Piper's skate from moving. As much as she and Tommy had argued, the referees had let it stand.

He'd been too busy trying to keep his head attached to his neck to watch over Piper. Deep down, he believed in her. That didn't keep him from worrying. He'd gladly take the beating for her if he could. Since that wasn't an option, he took the fight to the upfront guys and worked his ass off to keep the puck in Rattler territory. The plan had worked somewhat.

Shift change came. He skated to the bench and plopped down, eagerly taking the bottle of water passed around. After taking a long drink, he handed it to the next guy and watched the game unfold before him.

The Rattlers controlled the puck, streaming down center ice only to set up in the periphery of the Wolfpack zone. They passed back and forth until one took a shot. Piper rejected it only to be swallowed up in the scramble for the rebound. Wolfpack players swooped in to form a protective ring.

The referee blew his whistle, unpiled everyone, and took the puck from Piper's glove.

The face-off in the Wolfpack zone allowed the Rattlers to seize the puck and send a laser toward the net. Piper dropped down into the splits, closing the gap and allowing the puck to bounce off her lower pads. One of the guys grabbed the rebound with his stick and swung.

Piper dove to the side, snared the puck and ended up taking the stick to the mask at the same time.

Ranger jumped to his feet, cussing a blue streak. Keith shoved the player away, then found himself in the middle of a swarm of red jerseys. The other Wolfpack players joined in, mouthing and muscling right back.

Piper regained her feet, took off her mask and got a drink as the refs took back control of the game. He noted the sweat pouring down her face. The heavy breathing. She was already working her ass off. And it was only the first period.

By the end of the third period, Ranger had started feeling the numerous hits he'd taken. He could only imagine how Piper felt, as she'd been knocked down a couple of times and fought off numerous hits on goal. He'd assessed her at each intermission, found her holding up, but wearing down. Still, she'd skated out and taken her place for the final period. The one-point lead wouldn't last long if she couldn't stay the course for a while longer.

Ranger took the pass from Hagan and started toward the Rattlers' end. He glimpsed Rocky to his right and Sven on his left. Splitting the defense, Ranger headed toward Rocky, then sent a quick pass back to Sven, who slapped it immediately toward the goal. The red light flashed.

"Yes." He raised his hands in a short celebration. "Nice shot." He patted Sven on the back.

Sven grinned. "Nice assist."

Rocky came over to join the party. Together they skated to the bench, allowing the next line to take the ice.

As if in desperation, the Rattlers picked up the pace, hovered around the Wolfpack zone and crashed the net more than once. Ranger hollered encouragement for their defense, though he knew the guys were playing their hearts out.

Piper skated from side to side, continued to turn each scoring attempt away, and remained steady under the intense pressure.

Pride filled him as she didn't back down, no matter the odds. He finally understood. She played the game like she looked at life. Hiding or running wasn't an option. She'd done just that as a child and had still received the brutal beating. Now she faced everything head-on, stood on her own two feet and refused to break. Fortitude, gumption and inner strength kept her going. She certainly had those traits in plenty. Thankfully. Otherwise she might not have turned into the woman she was today.

While he couldn't quell the protective instinct, he could enjoy the beauty of watching Piper play at top level. Fluidly. Effortlessly. Quickly. Precisely. Electrically.

The clock ticked down to two minutes. The Rattlers pulled their goalie, allowing for another forward to take to the ice. Sure enough, the new guy entered just as the goalie stepped off the rink. He seized the puck and drove straight for the net.

Piper shifted her feet and dropped farther back.

The guy took a sharp angle, then hit a flaming backhand.

Piper blocked it with her stick.

The Rattlers gained the rebound and pounded it in for a score.

"It's okay, Piper," Ranger yelled. The rest of the team responded in kind.

She took a drink, slapped her mask back down and took her position once again.

The result of the face-off landed them back in Wolfpack

zone, the extra player giving the opponent a decided advantage. Tommy put his best defensive guys out on the ice in hopes of staving off any more goals until the end of regulation.

Ranger wiped the sweat off his forehead as he saw the Rattlers swarm. They passed the puck back and forth on the outskirts, waiting for an opportunity. One shot bounced off Ivan's stick, another banged into the side bar and flew out of play.

"Hang in there, guys. Thirty more seconds," Ranger mumbled to himself, on edge with the closeness of the fierce game. He longed to join the melee, but knew their best chance lay with the penalty-killing unit.

The Rattlers' power forward took up position directly in front of Piper. Ivan went with him. Another forward came in hot with the puck from the right. Piper shoved her skate against the bar just as the guy tried to poke it in. Two more men flocked to the area, one slamming his shoulder into Piper, sending her toppling into the other bar, which rocked the net off its bearings.

The red light flashed on, earning a huge cheer from the crowd.

Ranger held onto the wall in front of him, willing Piper to get back up. She did. Slowly.

Ivan and Adam spoke to her. While Ranger couldn't hear, he could easily imagine what they asked. Piper nodded then went for her water bottle.

He released a long sigh as she seemed to be moving okay. For now. Later, he knew, the aches and pains would appear.

The referees checked the video and waved off the score due to the opponent being in the crease at the time.

To the "boo" of the crowd, they restarted the game for the final few seconds.

Piper blocked one more shot before the buzzer sounded. Right afterward, one of the Rattlers' players skated by and shoved her in the back, sending her sprawling hard on the ice.

Ranger leaped over the wall and flew to her side, the rest of the team beside him. He made a beeline for the bastard and threw a right hook. His fist met flesh with a satisfying crack. The referee forced himself between them, stopping Ranger from pummeling the idiot, finally managing to shove the guilty player away before Ranger could take another powerful swipe. Rocky, Ivan and Axel were close by, ready to punch the guy's lights out.

"You lowlife piece of shit!" Ranger spat at the guy's back. With the game over, no penalty could be assessed. He could only hope the league slapped a huge fine on the motherfucker's head.

Turning, Ranger found Piper already on her feet, surrounded by the team, Rocky, Ivan and Axel pulling up to group. Adam steadied her with one arm while the others stared at her with worry in their eyes.

Ranger moved closer. "You okay?"

"Yeah." She sounded out of breath, but lifted her gaze to meet his eyes. "I hope someone locks him in detention. For life."

Ranger swiveled to glance at the opponent's bench, which was clearing fast. "I'd like to do more than stick him in detention." Anger still rode him hard.

Her hand on his arm drew his attention back to her.

"Let it go. Life's too short to sweat the small stuff." She offered up a small smile.

"That's not small stuff."

"Trust me. It is." She looked at the rest of the team. "Guess this means you like me after all?"

Riley shook his head. "Was that ever in question?"

"Yep. That day when you all joined me for suicide sprints. I had a feeling not everyone was on board with that idea."

Adam chuckled. "You could be right. Good thing we've kept an open mind and reconsidered."

She tilted her head. "Reconsidered?"

"There was some talk about a one-way ticket to Siberia if those suicide sprints became a daily thing."

She arched an eyebrow at Ivan. "Siberia?"

He shrugged. "You wouldn't be dropped out of an airplane and left to fend for yourself. I'd have made arrangements with my family to take you in." A wicked smile grew across his face.

Her blue eyes landed on Ranger. "You were in on this?"

He squirmed a bit. "Well…"

Piper rolled her eyes. "Remind me to tell Santa on all of you." She tsked and headed toward their bench.

Ranger followed on her heels with a small grin. Piper might be sore as hell and completely exhausted, but she hadn't lost her sense of humor in the process.

Just another reason she'd stolen his heart.

The moment they entered the locker room, Tommy stopped them. "Piper, the trainer wants to see you."

She sighed wearily. "Again? Oh, good grief. At this rate I'm going to have to claim him as a BFF and send him Christmas cards even though he still hasn't produced a single lollipop."

Ranger chuckled.

Tommy's lips twitched. "Go, Piper."

"Yeah, yeah. I'm going." She shuffled off toward the second door.

"She's got more balls than a lot of goalies that I've coached."

Ranger turned back to Tommy. "That she does. That…she does." He watched the door close behind her then found his temporary locker, sat down on the bench in front of it and started peeling off equipment.

She might as well hang out with Chester for a bit. Since she avoided the locker room after games due to the chance of seeing the guys naked, she needed a place to change in private. The training room would work just as well.

As for a shower, he'd make sure the guys cleared out in ample time to give her the opportunity to use the facilities. After that, she wasn't getting out of their sight until they packed up and flew out of town. The sooner the better.

Chapter Twenty-Six

"You sure you're up to this?" Ranger asked for the third time in the past ten minutes.

"Positive." Piper offered up a reassuring smile. Her whole body ached, but the nap on the ride home from the game had infused her with enough energy to be playful. At least with Ranger. He'd been fussing over her since before the game. While a bit irritating at the time, she'd come to enjoy his devoted attention and care.

Now, back at his house, she couldn't wait for this next adventure to begin, especially since she craved his touch. In a major way. The whole ride home from the airport had been a torment. She hadn't been able to resist the urge to explore, focusing most of her attention on the intriguing bulge under his slacks. Good thing there wasn't much traffic in the wee hours of the morning or they might have been pulled over and declared risky drivers.

Face it, Piper. You're downright horny.

Never before had she been so wanton, so aggressive. With Ranger, she couldn't seem to help herself. Especially tonight.

As she'd removed her clothes earlier, she'd watched his eyes flare with anger as each bruise and abrasion came to light. Now she wanted nothing more to see another emotion in his beautiful green eyes. Hunger. Lust. Love. Any and all.

"I need you. All of you." She glanced down at his thick erection, now sporting a condom. Reaching out, she ran her hand over him with familiarity. "I think you want me too."

"I'll always want you. I just don't want to hurt you." He

nuzzled her ear and weighed her breast with one large hand. "You've had a hard night already."

"Uh-huh." She lifted her chin to allow him to lap at her throat. "And I want something else hard, too." The hills and valleys of his six-pack drew her attention. She flicked her fingertips over the area then dipped lower to cradle his sac before gently rolling his balls.

Ranger's groan added fuel to her already nearly out of control blaze of passion. He scooped her up, carried her to the bedroom and deposited her in the middle of the bed. "You're killing me."

Piper smiled wickedly. "It's only fair. I'm on fire for you and you're dragging your feet." She reached out to him, sighing happily when he crawled on the bed and over her. Immediately she wrapped her arms around his neck and kissed him with everything she had. Lifting her hips, she encouraged him to join their bodies.

Unfortunately, Ranger didn't appear to be in any hurry. He pressed his lips to the large bruise on her shoulder, then meandered down her side and finally to her breast. She'd seen how colorful she'd become after the game. While the purple splotches slowed Ranger's advances, they did nothing to deter her from her goal. The sensations grew, adding more heat to the already blistering fire in her blood. "Please, Ranger."

"Patience, love."

Unable to wait a second longer, Piper sat up and grasped Ranger's cock, working in a fast rhythm to stoke his arousal to a fevered pitch nearing what she felt. "I. Can't. Wait."

He smiled wolfishly at her demanding words and tone while flicking his finger over her pebbled nipple. "Don't you know waiting makes it better?"

"Uh-huh." She bent over and lapped at the tip of his cock, frustrated by the condom already in place. Not to be deterred, she lowered to her stomach and bathed his balls.

Ranger's powerful thighs spread and the muscles tightened to hold his weight. He pulled her hair out of the way and moaned low in his throat. "Oh, shit. Piper."

After a few more licks, she sat back up, still caressing his cock. "I need you. Inside me. Now." The breathless statement seemed to ring a bell with Ranger.

He sat down and crossed his legs. "Come here."

She started to stand up, only for Ranger to grab her around the waist, lift, then ease her down on his lap.

"Wrap your legs around me." He breathed the order against her ear.

She did so, along with her arms. Shocked at the closeness and skin contact, Piper took a second to kick her mind into gear. Especially when Ranger dabbled between her folds, discovered her clit and ever so lightly brushed over it.

Her breath caught.

"You're so wet. So fucking wet and tight. I can't get enough of you. Of this."

He plucked gently before moving his hand altogether. Piper whimpered at the loss.

"Shhh. I'm not going anywhere." He cupped her rear, lifted, then impaled her on his shaft with controlled strength and exquisite finesse.

The fullness returned in force, along with the slight burn of her body stretching to accommodate him. She eagerly embraced both, needing him deep inside. Steadily, she lowered, her muscles alternating between clenching and relaxing in welcome.

She found his earlobe with her teeth and nipped.

He jerked and growled. The motion shoved him the rest of the way and locked him inside her.

She grunted, then sighed as she finally had what she'd needed for the past few hours. Ranger. Buried deep. With his lips leaving a trail over her chest and neck. She couldn't believe the intimacy of this position. As if they shared each breath. Every movement transmitted directly to the other as well as the additional stimulation of skin rubbing on skin. She felt protected. Cherished. Loved. "Oh, Ranger." She rocked her hips in counterpoint to him.

"Damn, vixen." His breath began to pick up.

She recognized the immense strength in him, but not an ounce of fear entered her mind. Always gentle and cognizant of his size, he treated her with great care. The fact, along with the incredible power he wielded, only added to her hunger, her need. Her love.

A small cry left her throat as he splayed one hand over her rear, the other a snug band around her waist. She'd ridden him before, but knew each time was better. Hotter. More intimate. The slow motions caressed both her clit and a hot spot deep inside, sending her shooting up the cliff toward completion. Ranger's grunts and harsh gasps lashed her all the more.

She held snug and pressed needy kisses to his cheek and mouth.

Together they found a rhythm, the pace lazy and mellow.

Flares shot through her body, a precursor to the big event. She tightened her grip on him and rode with as much skill and energy as she could muster.

He used his strength and hold to direct her movements, driving her closer to the climax just out of her reach.

Dangling on the edge, she jerked against him, rubbing her throbbing clit in the process.

She soared. Heat overtook her as her channel clamped down in sultry delight. The nearly overwhelming tension shattered, setting her free on the wings of a massive, fiery orgasm.

Ranger groaned in her ear then thrust as if seeking the very depths of her body. She locked down on his invasion and reveled in the moment as crest after heightened crest cascaded through her.

A grunt and a shudder from Ranger announced he'd fallen over the precipice along with her. The knowledge satisfied her, adding to the intimacy of the moment.

Her world narrowed down to Ranger. Nothing else mattered as she struggled to draw in enough oxygen and to slow her galloping heart. The world and time fell away as she rested her head on his shoulder, safe in his arms.

Still dazed, she felt Ranger lower her to the mattress then slip off the bed. Trying to catch her breath, she noticed the dip in the mattress, opened her eyes, and saw Ranger scooting between her legs with a washcloth in hand. Embarrassed, she turned away.

"Piper. Look at me."

She complied, finding his steely gaze too compelling and demanding to break.

"You're mine to take care of." He ran the warm cloth between her legs, cleansing her of stickiness. "Besides, you'll sleep better this way." Again, he wiped the area before leaving the bed once more. When he returned, he settled next to her, pulled the covers up, then tugged her into a spoon position flush against his chest.

Piper wiggled for comfort, found a pillow under her head and relaxed into him. With his body draped around her and his arms holding her tight, she knew contentment. "I love you, Ranger," she murmured as she began to doze off.

He kissed her ear. "I love you too."

Piper slid into sleep. Protected, warm and totally in love with her overgrown guard dog.

* * * *

Ranger glanced over at Piper and grinned to himself. Since she'd hopped into the passenger seat and strapped herself in for the relatively short ride to the airport, she'd been antsy. Her leg bounced as she stared out of the front windshield, her full lips thin with concentration. As he watched, she lifted her index finger to her mouth and started to chew on the nail.

Oh, yeah. She's nervous. He'd never seen her this way before. The thought of getting planted into the ice by a goon didn't faze her but the notion of meeting his parents did. *Go figure.*

He took her hand in his and gave it a squeeze. "They're

going to love you. Just like I do."

She gave a brief nod. "I'm going to miss staying with you."

"Me too. You know you can stay."

"Thanks, but you need time alone with your parents." She turned to stare out of the side window.

Piper had insisted she be dropped off at her apartment once he picked up his parents. She didn't want to tarnish their impression of her. He'd accepted that, along with the fact that she was still a bit shy when it came to their sex life. The idea of curling up in his bed with his parents next door made Piper self-conscious and uncomfortable.

She'll change her tune soon enough. I'll see to it.

He walked a careful tightrope in wanting Piper to be with him all the time and pushing her too far, too fast. To date, they'd found an easy middle road. He hoped that remained the case as his plans revolved around Piper not renewing the lease on her apartment, packing up and moving in. After his parents left.

He pulled their joined hands up and placed a kiss on the back of hers.

She focused on him with a soft smile. "How do I rate getting you?"

"I'm the lucky one." He faced straight ahead in order to watch the road. "I wanted what some of the other guys had. Like wishing under a lucky star, you appeared."

"A lucky star, huh?"

"Yep." He pulled into the airport lot, found an empty spot, parked and cut the engine. "Don't underestimate yourself, Piper. I've seen what other women have to offer. They don't hold a candle to you."

"I have issues… Things set me off, still."

He trailed his knuckles over her cheek. "You've moved past them. Sure, they might appear now and again, but we'll handle it. Together."

Her eyes met his as if seeking the truth of his statement.

"Your past doesn't define you. You define you." He

released her hand. "You're the woman I love. So get over it." He waggled his eyebrows and grinned playfully.

She snorted. "Get over it, huh?" Her lips curled up in a reluctant grin.

"Yep." Happy she'd responded to his banter, he gestured toward the airport looming in front of them. "You coming?"

She nodded, unclicked her seat belt then opened the passenger door.

He did the same, exiting through the driver's side, shutting the door behind him then clicking the locks with the key fob once Piper joined him. He reclaimed her hand and led her through the front door.

"Which gate?"

He scanned the direction signs hanging from the ceiling. "Seven." Finding what he sought, he headed to the left, automatically shortening his strides to accommodate Piper.

By the time they arrived, the plane had started unloading. He waited patiently for his parents to appear. The moment they did, he stepped forward. "Mom. Dad."

They looked up in unison, locked their gazes on him, and grinned happily.

"Ranger." His mother hurried over to hug him.

His father followed at a more sedate pace, but his embrace was no less welcoming. "Good to see you again, son."

"You too." He stepped back and nudged Piper forward. "Mom. Dad. This is Piper. Piper, these are my parents, Leigh and Preston Deacon."

She held out her hand. "Nice to meet you."

They shook it warmly while appraising her.

"So polite. I knew you'd be beautiful under all those pads you wear for the game," his mother remarked.

Ranger caught the flare of appreciation in his father's eye. He might not have expected Piper to be such a compact package, but he knew a pretty girl when he saw one.

Piper blushed. "Thank you, ma'am."

"Oh, please. Call me Leigh. Nothing formal about us."

"Okay, Leigh."

"If you're ready, we'll go get your luggage, then swing by Piper's apartment to drop her off." Ranger rounded up everyone and herded them toward the exit. Piper tried to hang back, but his mother tugged her along, still chatting away.

Ranger grinned at the reception. He'd known his parents would like Piper. They would only grow to like her more as time went on.

Thirty minutes later, he drove the SUV away from Piper's apartment and back onto the highway. His father sat in the passenger seat while his mother occupied the next row.

"She's a doll," his mother announced.

"She's got guts playing with the men. I saw a few of those hits she took. Would have knocked more than one guy out of the game. She bounced back up and carried on," his father noted.

Ranger cringed at the reminder of her latest beating. He'd seen the resulting marks still splotched across her body this morning. Days would pass before they'd heal enough to fade. "She's fierce. Stubborn, too. Won't sit the bench to avoid the worst teams, either."

"Brave. I like that in a woman." His father grinned.

"She's so sweet. Easy to talk to. I can see why you love her, Ranger."

He caught his mother's smile in the rear-view mirror.

"We were beginning to think those women had ruined you," Leigh remarked.

"Mom!" While the abundance of sex wasn't a big secret in the professional ranks with the masses of puck bunnies hanging out, that didn't mean he really wanted to discuss his past encounters with his parents.

She waved her hand. "We're just happy you found a nice lady to settle down with."

"You're really thinking of marrying her?" Preston asked.

"Yes. She makes my life complete." He didn't know how to sum it up any better than that.

"Got a ring yet?" Leigh scooted forward to stick her head

between Ranger and his father.

"No."

"Well, I'm sure there's plenty of time for a little side trip. Right, Preston?"

Preston nodded. "I imagine so."

"Great. Take us to a nice jeweler, Ranger."

Ranger shook his head, but didn't bother to argue. He'd hoped they'd be agreeable to tagging along for the big decision. Just in case, he'd searched the Internet for a couple of high-end stores with flawless reputations. "If you really want to."

"We really do," Leigh answered.

He knew matchmakers when he saw them. Neither parent would stop pestering him until he fell into line. Not that he'd expected any different. They always had his best interests at heart. Even if they stepped into the nosy and pushy categories at times.

"Better get a ring on that girl before someone else snatches her up." Preston rubbed his chin.

Not going to happen. She's mine and I don't share.

Ranger grinned confidently, clicked his blinker and made for a nearby exit.

Chapter Twenty-Seven

Piper stood against the door to the rink, looked out over the vast amount of ice and sighed. The final game of the Wolfpack's season wouldn't start for over three hours, but she'd wanted to arrive early. To be there before everyone else and simply take a moment for everything to sink in. The rink served both the Wolfpack and Bobcats, yet today it radiated with a different energy — it was the final game for several months to come, until next season.

A sense of sadness creeped into her as she realized this was probably the very last time she'd play professional hockey with the guys. Her heart hung heavy at the thought. *No sense in sugar-coating the truth, Piper.* Gunderson should return in the fall. Rayovic had grown and matured, enough to take over several games if needed. In essence, she no longer had a place on the team.

Her Cinderella ball was quickly coming to an end.

Memories played through her mind. From the first day of practice on this very ice, standing up to a team filled with doubts about whether she could handle the rigors of the men's game. The many venues they saw. Endless travel all over North America. The games. *All* the games. From relatively effortless to an all-out beating, both physical and on the scoreboard, too. Hard knocks had been a given as she strove to win people over. The fans. The team. The opponents. While only marginally successful, she counted it as a victory. Being the first person to break through barriers was never easy. Maybe she'd made enough of a trail that others could follow.

She sighed as she considered how much she'd miss

the guys. The same ones who had been a hard sell in the beginning had soon surrounded her with caring, respect and appreciation. They were truly a band of brothers who looked out for their sister. She'd never felt more protected than when they were in warrior mode, ready to deal out punishment for daring to bump into her. Especially Ranger. He'd taken her under his wing from the start. Watched over her. And stolen her heart along the way.

Footfalls snared her attention. She turned to find her father approaching. He closed the distance between them, then stopped next to her and faced the ice. She watched him out of the corner of her eye, not quite sure why he was here. "Hi, Dad."

"Piper." He bent over and rested his forearms on the wood. "Looks a bit lonely out there."

She tilted her head and appraised the ice. "I guess." Most days she preferred to have the ice all to herself. Lately, though, her attitude had changed.

"Still, it calls to a person." He spoke softly, profoundly.

"Yeah, it does." She raked the area with her gaze once again. "You miss it."

"Parts of it, sure. But there's more to life than hockey."

Piper knew where he was coming from, yet couldn't prevent the heart-wrenching words from slipping out. "It feels like the end."

He glanced over at her with a wise smile. "Or the beginning."

Befuddled, she turned her focus to him. "Of what?"

He went back to staring at the ice.

A door clicked. Piper found the source of the sound as Ranger stepped onto the rink and began skating with leisurely movements. Unable to take her eyes off him, she watched poetry in motion. Despite his size, he glided effortlessly, smoothly, and with a hint of the strength he carried.

She noted her father was watching Ranger as well, studying the power forward like a scout or potential head coach.

"Life is a series of journeys, sweetheart. When you finish one then it's time to start another."

She deciphered his words. "So this will be my last game with the men. No owner or coach will take a chance on me." The realization stung.

He shrugged. "Time will tell. You've done a kick-ass job. But some people aren't ready for change. They might never be."

Piper nodded. That she could understand.

He stood up and peered down at her. "You have to decide what you want to do. Sure, you might get picked up by a team, but would you want the role of a backup goalie? Playing only now and again?"

"I don't know, Dad. It'd be tough to sit the bench all the time." She blew out a breath, her gaze automatically locking on Ranger. "I want what I have now."

He stood silent for a long while. "Seems to me it's yours for the taking."

"Are we still talking hockey?" She blinked at him.

A small grin appeared on his lips. "We're talking life."

She rubbed her forehead. "Sorry, Dad. You're going to have to spell this one out for me. I'm not keeping up."

He pulled her into a hug, then kissed her crown. "If you want something, then go out and get it." Stepping back, he met her eyes and smiled.

She caught another glimpse of Ranger.

"Go on." Her father gave her a nudge. "Your next journey awaits."

The wheels in her mind finally started spinning. She gave her father a huge hug and a kiss on the cheek. "Thank you, Dad." With that said, she took to the ice, her skates gliding easily as she set a direct course for Ranger.

He stopped, looked up, and opened his arms to catch her as she hurried over. The grin on his face said it all.

"I missed you." She leaned back enough to kiss his chin. Since he wore regular clothes, no thick pads or helmet obstructed her. The same for her, since she'd worn her tights and her father's lucky jersey in preparation for the upcoming game.

He smiled warmly and brushed his lips over hers. Once. Twice. A third time. "I missed you more."

The issues weighing her down evaporated in Ranger's embrace. Everything would work itself out. She just knew it.

"Come over and meet my dad." She latched onto his hand and tugged him to the bench.

Ranger stuck his arm out. "Pleasure, sir."

Her father shook it immediately. "Call me Gunther. It's good to finally meet you."

Piper picked up on the mutual respect between the two men. And something else. Her father didn't grumble or scowl like he had with her former boyfriends. Instead, he smiled as if Ranger made the grade. Considering what he'd told her earlier, before sending her onto the ice, she wasn't surprised. The two guys had bonded. She'd bet her fat paycheck on it.

Gunther turned to her. "I've got to run an errand and get back to pick up your mother in time for the game."

Piper bobbed her head. "I'm glad you're coming."

"I wouldn't miss it for the world." He grinned at her, pulled her into a hug and kissed her forehead. "Have fun out there." With one more glance at Ranger, Gunther turned and strode away.

Piper watched him go.

Ranger wrapped his arms around her middle, pulling her to lean her back against his solid body. He nuzzled her cheek. "You okay?"

Her father disappeared from sight. "Yeah." After turning, she looped her arms around his neck. "I'm always better when you're here."

He stared down at her as a flicker of concern flashed through his eyes. "You sound sad."

"No. Just thoughtful."

He rubbed his nose against hers. "Care to share those thoughts with me?"

She smiled. "I was fretting because one part of my life seems to be coming to a close. My father reminded me that another journey would begin. It always does."

"What kind of journey?"

She pursed her lips. "I think…a wonderful one filled with surprises and happiness."

He grinned. "Am I included?"

"Of course." She peered coyly through her eyelashes at him. "You've got the lead role, after all."

He laughed, then sealed his lips over hers.

Piper's heart took flight.

* * * *

Ranger sped down the ice, puck on his stick. He found a spot, split the defense, did a quick spin-o-rama, then shot. The red light flashed with the goal.

"Nice." Sven skated over and bumped fists.

"Pretty goal," Rocky added.

"Thanks." Ranger couldn't wipe the grin off his face as they made their way back to the bench.

The last game of the season against the Tide had played well to their strengths. With a few hard checks and some quick turnovers, the Wolfpack had secured a two-point lead toward the end of the game.

Of course, Piper had ensured their lead remained by rejecting every shot with the exception of one. In her element, she showed she belonged just like she had since day one.

Ranger took a seat, drank some water and found her with his gaze. She stood in front of her net, moving from side to side in order to meet the next attempt. As he watched, a Tide player tried a wraparound. Piper managed to block it with her leg pads. Another guy slapped at the stopped puck only to find it quickly covered by Piper's glove.

The play stopped momentarily as the ref took the puck to the face-off zone.

Clint, the equipment manager, strode over. "Still going through with it?"

Ranger nodded. "Absolutely."

"That's what I wanted to hear." Clint slapped him on the back. "Remind me to hand over the box when you're done with the last line change." He walked off.

Ranger smiled at the guy he'd picked as the perfect one to hold the precious item throughout the game. After all, Clint specialized in equipment. Organizing, sharpening. Keeping them all in running order. Overseeing one small box would be an easy task.

"A breakaway," the announcer called.

Ranger turned to find a Tide player moving fast toward the net. Piper skated forward slightly to meet him.

The Howitzer, a hard-hit shot, rocketed in her direction. Piper threw her body in front of it, then quickly regained her feet as the Tide swarmed for a rebound attempt.

"Damn, she's good," Rayovic muttered next to Ranger.

"Yes, she is." Ranger watched history in the making. At the top of her game, Piper could hold her own against any team and any other goalie. She'd made a believer of him as well as many others in the sport.

Another shot went wide. Keith charged to the corner, checking the Tide player trying to get a handle on the puck.

Ranger glanced at the clock. Less than five minutes to go in the game. He blew out a breath and took the opportunity to glance around the stands behind the bench. Gunther Darrow caught his eye. Piper's mother sat beside him, Darius next to her. He'd flown in just for the game and had to get back tomorrow since his team had qualified for the playoffs.

The Wolfpack, on the other hand, hadn't. Too little, too late. Ranger regretted the fact, but didn't get too worked up. Nothing to do about it now, anyway.

He scanned further, locking on his parents sitting just

above Piper's family. They seemed to be just as involved in the game as the rest of the crowd. He saw his father lean down and whisper something to Gunther. Gunther nodded and replied.

Looks like they're getting along.

With the reassuring thought, Ranger prepared for his next shift, coming up soon.

"Change it up."

Ranger exploded off the bench, over the wall and onto the ice. Rocky beat him by a second, took the puck as the entire line changed on the fly. He sent the puck into the corner for a dump and chase. Ranger went after it, battling a couple of hard checks in the process. He passed the puck back out to Sven, who put some mustard on his shot down the center. The *ding* announced the puck had hit the bar. Referees blew the whistle since the puck had flown out of play.

Ranger waited for the face-off. The Tide player won, slapping a long shot down center ice to a teammate. The breakout started. With a muffled cuss, Ranger sped after them, knowing he'd be too late. Instead of setting up a diamond, the Tide crashed the net.

Piper managed to block one shot, then dove for the rebound. She couldn't collect the stray puck as players from both teams poked at it.

Ranger heard a yelp as the big power forward on the Tide skidded and fell on top of Piper, knocking the net off the bearings in the process.

His heart thudded against his ribs as he hurried over to help push the goon off Piper.

Frantically, he scanned her as she first sat up, then tried to stand. He grabbed her arm and gave her an assist.

"Thanks."

He pushed the mask to rest on the top of her head. "You okay?"

"Yeah."

He frowned, knowing she'd never admit to being injured. "I heard you cry out."

She blinked at him sheepishly. "I saw that lumbering buffalo falling toward me and knew I'd be squished. Gut reaction and all." She shrugged.

The things she said boggled his mind sometimes. "So you're not hurt?"

"Just a bit smashed is all." She smiled and peered up at him from under her lashes. "He weighs as much as you do, but I like so much better when you cover me..."

The tension changed from fear to halfway aroused in a split second. He shook his head, chuckled, and rested his gloved hand on the top of her head. "You're something else."

"Is that a compliment?"

"Oh, yeah." The ref waved them in. "Square up, sassy. It's time to finish this game."

She slapped her mask back over her face and took her position.

The next face-off went their way. Ranger sent the puck into the Tide's zone, then headed for the bench so the next line could take over.

Keith used up more clock time as he ragged the puck. A few passes back and forth as well as a couple more shots on goal effectively ended the game.

The buzzer sounded.

Clint slapped something into Ranger's hand. "Go get 'em."

Ranger handed over his gloves, his stick and his helmet to Clint in exchange, then grinned as he slipped the small box into the pocket of his playing pants. He opened the door and stepped back out onto the ice, knowing the rest of the team would follow. Not just because of the tradition of congratulating the goalie with a win, but because this was going to be a momentous occasion.

Ranger led the line of men straight to Piper. He stopped next to her. "Take your gear off."

She blinked up at him, her mask already tucked under her arm. "What? Why?"

"There's going to be a presentation and the fans are going to want to see you, not the layers of padding."

"Oh, okay." If she questioned his reasoning, she didn't ask. Instead, she shrugged and started stripping off her leg pads after laying her glove, stick and mask on the ice. Everything came off except her upper pads under her jersey, her pants, and skates.

"The rest of your pads, too."

She tilted her head in question.

"Just do it. Be quick. The announcer won't wait forever." He encouraged her to hurry, his nerves starting to crackle now that the time had arrived.

She removed her team jersey, handing it to Ranger for safekeeping. In a few seconds, she dropped the upper body gear to the ice, leaving a gray T-shirt to cover her trunk.

He gave the jersey back and smiled when she pulled it on, letting the hem fall past her hips.

Sexy didn't begin to describe her. Even in the poorly fitting clothing.

A couple of the guys hurried over, collected her stuff and made their way back toward the bench.

"Hey!" She frowned at them.

"Can't have people tripping over stuff," Ranger offered as an explanation. He palmed the small velvet box in his pocket and lifted it out.

The announcer picked up on the movement and interrupted the murmur of the crowd with his loud voice. "Ladies and gentlemen, if I might point your attention to the ice."

Ranger took in a deep breath, flipped opened the box, and lowered down to one knee. "Piper Darrow, will you share your life with me? Marry me?" He watched her face carefully.

Shock quickly transitioned into joy as a bright smile appeared. Her eyes lit up like fireworks in a summer night sky. She covered her mouth and nodded.

"Is that a yes?" he asked, needing the words, although he

had no doubt of her decision.

"Yes. Absolutely, yes!" She leaped into his arms, nearly knocking him backward and onto the ice. As it was, he managed to keep upright, hold onto the ring and embrace her at the same time.

She kissed him with enthusiasm and excitement.

He shared the happiness. As long as he lived, he knew he'd never forget this moment.

Ranger stepped back, took the ring in hand, and placed it on her finger. The rightness of the act made his heart thump against his ribs.

Tears pooled in her eyes.

All around them, applause echoed in the arena. The crowd rose to their feet in a standing ovation. He glimpsed his parents among them as well as Piper's family. They all seemed to share in the joyous occasion.

He pocketed the box, stepped closer and swung Piper up into a cradle hold.

She beamed at him. "I can't believe you did all this for me."

He brushed his lips over hers. "Believe it, love." Holding her securely, he skated toward the bench, escorted by a double line of Wolfpack players, coaches and staff who made a lane and showed the way. He spared them a look, finding grins on each of their faces.

"Thanks, guys."

"No problem, captain. Anything for you two," Rocky answered.

Ranger carried Piper to the locker room, not about to put her down until he absolutely had to.

He had a lifetime ahead to spend with the woman who'd stolen his heart.

Starting with right now.

Epilogue

"Interference," Piper called out. "You'd be in the box for that."

Ranger smirked. "I couldn't help it. You're just so damn sexy in those tights."

"Uh-huh." She gave him a hard shove in the chest. "Are we playing hockey or not?"

It was the afternoon before their wedding. Piper, a bundle of nerves, had headed to the ice rink to work out some tension. The rehearsal and dinner were to follow that evening before the big day tomorrow. Her house was filled with wedding gifts and craziness, leaving Piper questioning her sanity.

Only one thing kept her on track—the knowledge that Ranger loved her as much as she loved him. Well, almost. She still believed she held the upper hand in that department.

She grinned to herself as she recalled how Ranger had shown up at the rink not long after she had. Someone must have called him or he'd simply read her mind. Either way, he'd skated onto the ice as if he owned the place and challenged her to a game. Obviously one where rules were suspended in favor of groping, teasing and an occasional kiss.

"Well..." He swung her around, wrapped his arms around her waist and swooped in for another potent lip lock.

She parted her lips on a gasp.

He took advantage, slipping his tongue inside for a thorough plundering that left her breathless.

"Hey. Can anyone play?"

Piper squirmed out of Ranger's hold to find her father, Darius, Rocky and Adam standing in front of the bench, gloves and sticks in hand, dressed for some light hockey.

"Sure. Three on three. I like it," she replied.

Ranger groaned dramatically.

Piper laughed at him. "What? You can get all touchy-feely with the others too. Though they might punch you for doing so."

Ranger rolled his eyes. "You're loving this, aren't you?"

"Yep." She spoke the truth.

She'd never considered herself a fairy tale kind of person. Yet the next day she would marry Ranger, her Prince Charming, and start the next journey in her life. With her family all around, the band of brothers from the Wolfpack and most of the Bobcats' players, she felt like a true princess. Loved and adored.

And about to get my butt kicked in a pick-up game.

After a quick rush to the sideline, where she plucked a helmet out of her father's hands and placed it onto her head then quickly put on some pads, she returned to center ice, noting Ranger did the same. With the addition of other players, they needed a bit of safety gear. Thankfully, her family had thought to provide for both her and Ranger.

"Thanks, Dad." She smiled up at him.

He grinned back. "Anything for my baby girl." His gaze raked the Wolfpack players. "I'm pretty sure we can take them."

"Only pretty sure?" she asked.

Darius waved his hand. "Easy-peasy."

"Uh-huh." Piper glanced back at her teammates. Former teammates. A contract offer had come to her a few weeks ago. The offer of a third line, replacement goalie position had left a sour taste in her mouth. She'd declined to sign and gone with the Bobcats once again. After giving Rob an earful on what she thought about the demotion.

He'd simply reminded her that the men's league wasn't

ready for a woman. Maybe in due time, he'd speculated, but not right now.

She didn't believe him. After all, she'd dug him out of a hole and earned the respect of her teammates, other players, and many of the fans. The guys had rallied around her, all to no avail. Management had spoken. She refused to move away from Denver, where Ranger would still play, so offers from other teams fell short.

At least she'd be around her guys, since her soon-to-be husband still played for the team. A small fact that helped ease the pain a bit.

So be it. She might not be in the limelight anymore, but she'd show them she belonged. Starting with right now.

She tapped her forward stick on the ice as her father and Darius lined up at her side. "Bring it on."

Ranger slid up to take the face-off. "Do you know what you're getting into, vixen?"

Piper beamed back. "Oh, yeah. A lifetime with the man of my dreams."

He grinned, pecked her on the lips then slapped his stick on the ground before smacking hers three times to start the game.

Piper kicked the puck toward Darius.

The game was on.

Darius caught the pass and sent it to Gunther, who hustled down the ice toward the opponent's open net.

Piper caught a glimpse of Ranger as he skated to her side. "Remind me to tell you that I love you after this is over."

"You don't love me now?" she asked.

He nudged her gently in the hip. "You threatened to put me in the penalty box."

She grinned wickedly at him. "Like I would have let you go alone?"

His mouth fell open.

"Keep up, moose. Winner takes all." She sped up a little, eager to be in on the action.

"I've already won. I have you."

The words warmed her heart all the more. She stopped, pulled him around and rewarded him with a kiss filled with passion and promise.

"Oh, good grief. Not this again."

"Just skate around them. They'll eventually come up for air."

A group of players zipped by them. Piper barely noticed them as Ranger held her tight in his strong arms.

"There's no getting rid of me now," she warned.

Ranger chuckled. "I'm keeping you. That's for sure. After all, you have my heart."

"As you do mine." She grinned up at him, knowing her true feelings were clearly on display. "Now, about this game…"

He laughed once more.

She'd never tire of the sound. Or the man.

Tiger's Lily

Excerpt

Chapter One

Four forty-five. Fifteen more minutes before their extended Thanksgiving holiday began. Margaret, the receptionist, had dashed off right behind the final client of the day, eager to hit the grocery store and begin cooking for her large brood. The benefits and expectations of being a grandmother, she'd pointed out. That left Lily to clean and stock up after the harried day, while the doctor finished his notes.

Lily pulled the last bag from the trash can, adding it to her increasing pile to be taken out as she left work for the day. Mundane chores didn't care if she was a housekeeper or a nurse like she was—all part of the job. A job she was more than happy to have after her life had toppled like a deck of playing cards.

If there ever was an angel, Carson fit the bill. If he

wasn't married, probably every woman in a fifty-mile radius would be banging on his door for some undivided attention from the handsome, smart, and friendly doctor. He radiated compassion and caring, working long and often late hours in order to see any client with a need – all his dedication along with a smile, kind word, and gentle hand. He'd given her a job when she had needed it most. For that, she'd happily spend the rest of her working life picking up the trash and whatever other task needed doing in his small practice.

Quickly, Lily tied up the final garbage bag, before stuffing a clean replacement in the plastic can near the back door while mentally checking off the closing routine chores.

The back door whined as it opened.

Spinning around, Lily saw a tall, dark-headed man step confidently through the back door, camouflage covering a powerful build. Her attention quickly moved from the man to the weapon he carried in his right hand. A rifle for sure, but not one used for hunting game. More like what she would expect someone in the military or even a SWAT team to use. Her heart raced as she kicked her stunned brain into action.

The newcomer's stark blue gaze quickly raked over the room before landing on her. His grim mouth, with a deep scowl, spoke of his current mood. Black smudges covered his face, sending her fear skyrocketing.

She opened her mouth to scream, only to find the strange man's hand immediately covering her mouth. His other arm wrapped around her middle, keeping her in place, facing away from him, but easily under his control. Instinctively, she began to struggle, kicking and pulling at his arm, anything to try to break free.

"Hold still. I'm not here to hurt you." The deep husky voice penetrated her brain.

That's probably what all the villains told their victims, lured them into a false sense of safety then did their worst. A momentary pause later, she renewed her fight.

He shook her a bit, the strong, tanned hand immobile over her mouth. "Stop it. I don't have time for this."

The sheer frustration and annoyance in his voice stilled her endeavors for release. That and the brute strength she felt in the body holding her told her that this man possessed the ability to do just about anything he wanted to her and there would be little she could do about it.

"Mayberry!" he shouted through the clinic.

Confused, Lily focused on breathing and searching for any opening to escape. Mayberry? What did that mean?

Carson strode quickly into the back room, coming to an abrupt stop when he spied the situation. A frown covered his face as he blinked a couple of times, as if trying to figure out some complex puzzle. His hands clenched into fists before his body stance relaxed. "Tiger?"

If the man acknowledged the name, Lily couldn't tell. Instead, she watched her employer's face, hoping that recognition meant a happy reunion, not a past of hatred. Her fear lessened as she heard her captor's voice once more.

"Sorry to barge in like this, Mayberry, but it's Dillon."

Immediately, Carson stepped forward. "Release my nurse and tell me what you need."

His hand loosened slowly along with the snug hold he had on her body. "No screaming." With that warning he set her free.

Without thought, she slammed her elbow back into the guy's gut, grumbling when he stepped away in the nick of time, only receiving a whisper of the impact.

"Damn she-cat."

She turned to glare up at the man who scared the living daylights out of her, even opened her mouth to give him a piece of her mind, but the doctor quickly interrupted.

"Dillon? What happened? Where is he?"

Both men hurried out the back door.

A minute later, they re-entered the room, supporting a man between them. They both wrapped an arm around him from each side, carrying him in a standing position.

Lily moved into action, clearing the path to the exam table, noting the state of the obviously injured newcomer. Close-cropped hair made the color difference between dark blond and sandy brown too difficult to call. Not quite as tall as the first guy, he still carried muscle and mass enough to impress. Both had scruffy whiskers, hinting at a few days without seeing a razor. Dust and dirt clung to his camouflage clothing just like the other man's with one major distinction. A large tear ran down the left thigh. Blood soaked the area, both fresh and dried.

Dillon, they'd called him.

He groaned as they laid him easily down on the exam table.

Lily raced for the bandage scissors, yanked them from the nearby drawer, and handed them over to Carson. As he cut the clothing, she dashed from cabinet to cabinet, gathering any supplies she thought might be needed. The men spoke softly in the background as she scurried around. Gauze, cleaning solutions, bandages, tape, and a sterile tray soon piled up on a nearby table, all within the reach of the doctor.

"How long ago was he shot?" Carson whispered across the space.

Tiger glanced at his watch. "Approximately fifteen hours ago."

"Damn." Carson continued with his work, cleaning and inspecting the wound. "Should have sought the nearest hospital, Tiger. This could be bad."

"Couldn't." The words rasped out of Dillon.

"Bullshit. Flash any of those high security clearance government passes that I know you both have. The locals wouldn't have batted an eye."

Everyone watched while the doctor worked in silence for a bit longer. He turned Dillon over, asked him a dozen questions, and studied the leg thoroughly before releasing a breath.

More books from
Cheyenne Meadows

When quitting isn't an option, a girl has to cowgirl up.

CHEYENNE
MEADOWS

*Cowgirl
Strong*

A girl has to be cowgirl
strong to make all her
dreams come true

*When life is full of lemons, a girl has to be cowgirl strong
to make all her dreams come true.*

All he needs is a second chance.

Book two in the Wind Warriors series

Loco knows he'll give his life in the line of duty as a Wind Warrior sooner rather than later, but once he meets his new neighbour, Oakley, he has something to live for. Love.

About the Author

Cheyenne Meadows

Growing up in the Midwest, I began reading romance novels in high school, immediately falling in love with the genre, to the point where I decided to write professionally for a career. However, that dream splattered against a brick wall, resulting in a quick death in my first writing class in college when my professor told me bluntly that I wasn't any good at it. I shifted gears quickly, and left my writing dreams behind, eventually settling on becoming a nurse.

A few years back, I stumbled across a fan-fiction writing site on a favorite author's webpage. I began to read stories others wrote, not only making some wonderful close friends from the experience, but also, really learning to write for the very first time. Here I was able to share short stories, practice my writing skills, and truly develop into a writer. More than that, the experience allowed me to revitalize my dream, as I rediscovered joy in writing. Now, I spend my days off with my alpha male characters, quick witted heroines, and see how much trouble everyone can get into.

When I'm not working or writing, I enjoy working in the garden, canning, and seeing my backyard as a living canvas for my whimsical landscaping, and, of course, reading romance novels.

Cheyenne Meadows loves to hear from readers. You can find contact information, website details and an author profile page at https://www.totallybound.com/

Home of Erotic Romance